ASHES TO WATER

—

ASHES TO WATER

IRENE ZIEGLER

FIVE STAR
A part of Gale, Cengage Learning

GALE
CENGAGE Learning™

Detroit • New York • San Francisco • New Haven, Conn • Waterville, Maine • London

GALE
CENGAGE Learning

LIBRARY OF CONGRESS CATALOGING-IN-PUBLICATION DATA

Ziegler, Irene, 1955–
    Ashes to water / Irene Ziegler. — 1st ed.
      p. cm.
    ISBN-13: 978-1-59414-860-6 (alk. paper)
    ISBN-10: 1-59414-860-0 (alk. paper)
    1. Families—Fiction. 2. Pyschological fiction. I. Title.
PS3576.I29325A94 2010
813'.54—dc22   2010007267

First Edition. First Printing: June 2010.
Published in 2010 in conjunction with Tekno Books and Ed Gorman.

For Addison.

ACKNOWLEDGMENTS

My first thanks go to my agent, Jack Ryan, for taking a chance, then sticking with me. Thanks also to Laurie Walker for advice and editorial assistance with the first draft. And thank you to James River Writers in Richmond, Virginia, for sharing collective brilliance and fellowship. A final thank you to my generous husband, Graham, who loves Annie as I do and wanted more from us both.

PROLOGUE

November 29, 1962

Damp and heavy-limbed, nine-year-old Annie Bartlett jerked awake beneath her father's chin. The scent of pine needles and lake mud snaked through jalousie windows. Lying still, Annie breathed her father's expelled air and thought of mermaids.

They lurked in Widow Lake, she was sure of it. She had only to unlock the mystery of breathing underwater and her own transformation would be complete. Her mother, who used to be a professional skier at Cypress Gardens, claimed to know the secret to breathing underwater. She spent time with Annie in the lake, whispering words that awed and excited: "Learning takes time, but if you are truly dedicated, and want to breathe underwater more than anything in the world, you will succeed and become a mermaid."

Annie could hardly wait for her next lesson. Once changed, she would fly unencumbered in that quiet, watery world, free of the restless tensions that permeated the Bartlett household and infiltrated Annie's dreams. Instinctively, she moved her ankles together, as when kicking water behind.

Her father stirred, and Annie froze. If he woke, he would order her from bed. Annie was too big to be crawling into bed with Daddy, but in her own bed, she dream-twisted. Her older sister, Leigh, drove her out as well, ordered Annie to stay on her own side of the room. Only her mother tolerated Annie's knees and elbows, but Helen worked nights, didn't arrive home until first light, now breaking. Annie would scoot when she heard the front door creak.

Her mother had been strange, lately. During the day, she roamed about the house, there-but-not-there, blackout mask pushed to her forehead. When Annie talked, her mother stared as if she didn't know where Annie had come from.

Leigh appeared in the doorway. "Get up," she whispered and gestured to Annie. "He'll be mad."

"Is Mom home?" Annie whispered back.

Leigh shook her head. Annie slipped from bed.

At thirteen, Leigh looked taffy-pulled: arms and legs too long, middle stretched thin. Her musk, both sweet and sour, was new. She was blond and fair skinned, unlike dark Annie, with alert, suspicious eyes constantly surveying their father. Leigh had lately taken to calling him Ed.

"Get ready for school," said Leigh. She stood flamingo-like before the full-sized mirror, one foot resting high on the other leg.

"But where's Mom?" asked Annie.

"Late, I guess."

"She's never late."

"Then I guess she's dead."

Leigh rarely spoke unless in sarcasm. Annie ducked the blow and dressed for school. In the kitchen, she stood before the sliding glass door and looked at the lake, holding the white rabbit coat she got for her birthday. The newly hatched sun, already stoking, stirred the mist atop the water. November, and not even cold. Annie had been waiting weeks to wear her new coat, but it seemed this Indian summer would never move on. Her father complained, too. When it was warm like this, no one used furnaces, and he didn't deliver fuel oil in the truck.

"Where's your mother?"

Annie turned. Her father stood scratching. "I don't know.

She's not dead." Her father looked and, for those few seconds, was hers. She smiled.

"You want cereal?" Annie nodded. "Sit down, then."

Ed looked at the stove clock. "I guess I'll have to drive you to school in the oil truck."

"Leigh hates the oil truck."

"Leigh hates everything," Ed muttered. He dialed while opening a milk carton one-handed. "This is Ed Bartlett. I'm looking for my wife. Is she still there?" Annie crunched corn puffs. "Well, if you hear from her, would you tell her to call home?" He hung up.

Annie put on her rabbit coat.

"You don't need that coat today, Annie. It's going to get real hot."

"But I want to wear it."

"Not today."

Leigh glided into the kitchen and opened the refrigerator door. "It's her coat," she said. "Go ahead and wear it if you want to, Annie."

Ed scowled. "When did you become head of this household?"

A soft light bathed Leigh's face as she peered into the fridge. Ed pointed his chin at Annie. "Take off the coat. I told you, it's too hot. Now, take it off, c'mon."

Leigh slammed the refrigerator door. Annie looked at her.

"Just do it before he has a hissy."

When Annie removed the coat, Ed seemed to implode. With controlled fury, he asked, "Did you take it off because I told you to take it off or because Leigh told you to take it off?"

It was a trap. Annie didn't know in which direction to step.

"Put it back on," Ed commanded.

Annie blinked, confused.

Leigh took her sister's hand. "Come on, Annie."

"I said, put it back on." Annie looked at Leigh. "Don't look at your sister, look at me." Annie looked at Ed. "Put it back on." Annie slid her arms into the coat. Ed looked at Leigh, triumphant.

Stepping outside was like entering a closed-up car, and it wasn't yet eight-thirty. Ed opened the passenger door of the fuel oil truck, urged the girls inside. Annie's white rabbit coat dusted the seat as she slid.

Leigh stepped up, then pointed. "Hey, Ed, there's mom's car."

Sure enough, Helen's green Falcon sat parked in the front driveway. Ed blinked at it. "Get in," he said, already moving toward the car.

Leigh called after him. "I don't want to get in if we're just going to sit here."

Ed, head inside the Falcon, didn't answer. Calling Helen's name, he moved briskly to the house. Annie climbed from the truck, looked inside her mother's car. On the passenger seat, her mother's nurse's uniform lay in a white heap, cushion-soled shoes on top.

Annie went into the house, stopped before the sliding glass door. Outside, Leigh crept into her peripheral vision. Annie followed her point. Lake fog, like velvet curtains, lifted, and suddenly Ed was running.

"Get back!" he called to Annie, who chased behind. "Get back in the house!"

Ed barged into the water, then dove. Six minutes later, he pulled his drowned wife onto mud-soaked grass and collapsed beside her. Leigh howled as if being wrenched into some unholy thing.

Annie looked at her wet, naked mother on the grass. She was not fooled. Her mother knew how to breathe underwater. She had become a mermaid, that was all. Annie shed her coat and draped it so that, when she woke, her mother would not be cold.

In the weeks following the funeral, Helen appeared to Annie in Widow Lake, a luminous cloud in the distance. When Annie swam toward her, Helen retreated. Annie followed until Leigh jumped in with an inner tube and gave her holy hell for working herself into the middle of the lake.

"I was trying to swim to Mom."

"We've been over this, Annie. Mom's dead. She's gone."

"No. She breathed underwater and became a mermaid."

"There's no such things as mermaids. Mom drowned, she did it on purpose, and it's Dad's fault."

"No! She didn't do it on purpose! She loves us!" Annie pushed from the inner tube, flailed toward deep water.

Leigh clamped a wrist and pulled Annie onto the inner tube. "Listen to me!" Leigh's tone forced Annie's eyes open. "I am very sorry Mom died. I'm going to miss her, too. But if you don't stop this craziness, I won't let you sleep in my bed anymore."

Annie could imagine nothing worse than being banished from her sister at night, when she most needed her. She stopped talking, but she didn't stop seeing. There was Helen in her white uniform on the school playground, peeking from behind a distant oak; at the end of a grocery isle holding a box of cereal. The appearances relieved Annie's longing. She trusted her mother too, knew, for instance, she would not jump out and yell "Boo!" or turn into a skeleton hung with bits of rotting flesh. Slowly, Helen came closer. One day, she spoke.

Annie smiled. Of course it would be their little secret. Of course.

Helen told Annie she was spending too much time with Ed. If Annie insisted on being friends with her father, Helen would not come to her again. Annie argued, but her mother was firm. Annie must stop riding in the fuel oil truck, stop kissing Ed goodnight. It would be difficult at first, but Annie must understand, as Leigh did, that Ed had made them unhappy and did not deserve her love. Only her mother deserved such devotion. After all, she had chosen Annie, would talk to no one else. Didn't Annie want her to stay?

That night, Ed put his hand on Annie's head, and she pulled away. He didn't seem to notice, but Leigh did, and made room for Annie in her bed. Each time her father entered a room, spoke, reached for her, another heartstring broke, until, in time, Annie no longer felt the tug.

CHAPTER 1

July 12, 1981
Nineteen years later.

Annie Bartlett, dressed in jeans, black T-shirt and stiff wedding veil, crouched behind a rickety tripod and squinted into a second-hand 35mm camera. Her mother, Helen, in a white nurse's uniform, squirmed before an artfully draped thrift store curtain.

"I don't understand why you have to take your own wedding pictures," said Helen.

"Because I'm good, and I'm cheap. All I have to do is set the timer, and . . ." A muffled pop, and an umbrella light flashed. The tripod's legs splayed, and the camera dipped. "Oops," said Annie. "I bought this stuff used. I haven't beaten it into submission yet."

"Honestly, Annie, just hire someone."

"I did. I hired me. Now please, Mom, stay there. I need to get the hang of this thing."

Annie raised the tripod and peered into the camera's viewfinder. Though it was 1981, Helen appeared as she had nineteen years ago: skin the color of uncooked chicken, dry lips, and dull, uninquisitive eyes. Straight black hair, parted in the middle, was coaxed over her ears and into a low, loose bun, a style long abandoned by mothers-of-the-bride in today's magazines. Still, Annie loved the way her mother looked, drew comfort from its predictable sameness.

"After I press this little button, we have ten seconds. Here we go." Annie pressed the button and high-stepped into place. "Ready?" She brushed the wedding veil over her shoulder. "Ten, nine, eight . . ."

"If your marriage turns out to be anything like mine, then I feel sorry for you," said Helen.

"My marriage won't be like yours."

"How do you know?"

"Because I'm not marrying dad . . . three, two, one!" Annie struck a pose. She hoped the jazz hands and goofy smile would improve her mother's disposition, perhaps—heaven forbid— make her smile.

Click.

Annie gave her mother a playful elbow poke. "I'm getting married! Get with the program!"

When the phone rang, Annie expected Camp, calling to cancel lunch. Since they'd announced their engagement, few arrangements went off as planned because, as Camp explained, "you never know with teenagers." The teenager you never knew about was Camp's fourteen-year-old daughter, Kirsten. In recent weeks, Kirsten had perfected the art of concocting schemes, which forced Camp, at the last second, to call Annie and say, "I'll make it up to you." Kirsten's manipulations stemmed in no small part from Camp's ex-wife, who seemed unwilling to help Kirsten adjust to changes. When she picked up the phone, Annie imagined Camp would say, "Kirsten needs me to drive her to the mall," or "Kirsten wants me to watch her dance class," or "Kirsten says you suck, Annie, and wants you to go to hell." This last hadn't happened, but Annie awaited the day.

"What are you going to do?" Helen whined. "Run back and forth from the camera the whole time?"

"No, I'm going to run back and forth from the camera when

I'm taking pictures."

"You'll trip and get your dress dirty."

"Then I'll wear jeans."

Then again, thought Annie, the caller might be her sister, Leigh, who was, as usual, AWOL. Annie had sent a wedding invitation to Leigh's last known address. With the wedding only three weeks away, the stamped response card had not come back. Maybe Leigh was calling to say she would attend?

"What are you going to do with your hair?" Helen asked, peering critically.

"Down, I guess."

"Annie, you have to get your hair done."

"I like it down, Mom. So does Camp."

Helen sighed. "It's your wedding."

"Atta girl."

Nor had Annie heard from the gallery in a while. Maybe this was the owner, calling to say a rich couple had just paid through the nose for one of Annie's photographs.

"Aren't you going to answer that?"

Annie picked up the phone. It wasn't Camp, or Leigh, or the gallery with news of a big sale. It was Deputy Sheriff Raina Salceda from DeLeon, Florida.

"I'm sorry to have to tell you, Miss Bartlett, but your father has been murdered."

A barrage of conflicting emotions assaulted her, and Annie leaned on the tripod for support. The floor zoomed toward her, and everything crashed.

CHAPTER 2

Annie felt wrenched apart. She cared her father was dead, but the slightest demonstration set off her mother, who had greeted news of Ed's death with predictable scorn: "He never loved you girls. The only thing Ed Bartlett loved was Ed Bartlett." Annie escaped to the darkroom to sort her feelings, knowing her mother would not follow; the red light bulb gave Helen the willies.

Annie heard her fiancé enter the studio. "I'm in the darkroom, Camp," she called. Before her, a sheet of photographic paper swam in chemicals. The converted closet smelled of fix.

Shave and a haircut, two bits.

"Don't come in," said Annie.

"Love you, too," said Camp, cheerful. "You ready?"

"I can't go to lunch, Camp. My father was murdered last night."

A pause, then Camp's voice, low and distinct, issued through a crack in the door. "What did you say?"

"I can't go to lunch."

"No, Annie, the other part."

Annie knew she was being flippant but couldn't help it. When she thought about Ed being dead, guilt flapped in her stomach like a big, black buzzard tearing its way out.

"Sorry, Camp," said Annie. "I'm not myself at the moment. I got a call about an hour ago. My father's girlfriend hit him over the head with an oar. He's dead."

18

"My God, Annie, are you all right?"

Her hands shook. She felt untethered, as if she might drift away. She wanted Leigh.

"I wasn't close to my dad. You know all that."

"Yeah, but murdered," said Camp, reverent. "Let me come in."

"Not yet. I've got something developing."

"Jesus, Annie, I want to hold you."

She heard the longing in his voice and fell in love with him all over again. She had done the right thing, falling for this divorced man eleven years older. They'd met in a gallery in Ann Arbor. Camp was a "barn saver," as he put it, and wanted to buy Annie's only exhibited photo, a portrait of a weathered barn in northern Michigan. She had used a filter, which threw into high contrast the rough texture of the barn siding against the cloudless sky. Camp had placed the tips of his fingers beneath Annie's elbow, an old-fashioned gesture that shot her through with pleasure. I know you, the gesture said. You see what I see. Camp asked Annie to dinner. She resisted, unsure about his marital status or intentions, which he then made clear: "I'm divorced, I have a teenage daughter, and I don't sleep with my ex-wife. I love your work, and I want to know you. Please say yes." When she nodded, Camp looked as if a light inside had switched on. For weeks after their dinner date, he called daily, engaged her in long conversations, made her laugh. Camp admitted guilt for leaving his marriage, for failing his daughter who, after four years, still struggled with the changes divorce had thrust upon her. Annie listened and soon found herself disclosing the raw parts of her past, including bitter feelings toward her father. Over dinners of ribs and beer, Annie studied the gray in Camp's temples, the lines at the corners of his blue eyes, his large hands, made rough with salvaging antique barns. Camp loved the virgin timber in the two-hundred-year-old structures. He explained the austere genius of post and beam construction, how badly he wanted to buy an old barn and move it to the modest acre lot he owned on a lake. It was his dream to convert the barn into a home.

"What's stopping you?"

Camp's smile thinned. "Kirsten doesn't want to live in the country," he said.

"But she's only with you weekends, right?"

"I can wait." His eyes settled on Annie's. "I'm good at waiting for the things I want."

Annie didn't make him wait long. She fell in love with his capableness, his passion for his work and his support of her career. She fell in love as she took pictures of him planing barn planks into wide, smooth floorboards. She fell in love with the way he forgot the pencil behind his ear, how he patted his pockets searching. She fell in love as he scanned a menu, reading glasses perched on the tip of his nose. She loved his penchant for neighborhood bars and locally grown produce, his beautifully imperfect body. Most of all, she fell in love with his eagerness to slay her dragons—at least the ones whose hiding places she revealed.

"Tell me about your mother."

Annie balked. Best not to leave herself entirely vulnerable. She offered only minimum facts: her mother had committed suicide, and both girls blamed their father.

"Suicide! My God. I'm so sorry."

"Thank you," said Annie, fighting back tears. "Do you mind if I tell you about it some other time?"

"No, of course not. I didn't mean to pry."

"You didn't. It's just that . . . it's a story I'm not ready to tell. Will you trust me on this?"

Camp placed his hand over Annie's. "When you're ready to tell, I'm ready to hear."

I doubt it, thought Annie.

Camp did not ask a second time about Helen's suicide, and Annie did not volunteer it. She hated withholding but feared losing the one person she loved more than her sister, this man who now stood outside her darkroom, eager to hold her.

"Have you talked to your sister?" Camp asked at the door.

"Not yet. The only number I have is for a bar where she hangs out. I guess I've been putting it off." She nudged a photo with tongs; a ghostly shape emerged.

"Can I come in yet?"

"Sorry, I'm at a critical point." The image darkened. Annie pulled the photo from the developer and slid it into the fix. She scrutinized the image. Not bad. She'd just been fooling around, of course, testing the timer and so forth, but definitely not too bad. Once she became familiar with the camera, she could adjust for things like the white-white of the veil, which was a bit too hot, and the deep black of her T-shirt, not quite black enough. Annie smiled. What a silly pose. With her jazz hands and overly animated expression, she looked like a second-rate Vaudeville act. She lifted the picture from the fix, clothes-pinned it to a wire above her head. She studied herself, alone in the shot.

"Little Orphan Annie," she whispered.

Annie turned off the red light. Immediately, she sensed movement.

"Mom?"

Silence.

"Annie?" Camp's voice was soft, concerned.

"One more second," Annie said, savoring the darkness. Like breathing underwater, she thought, taking black air into her lungs. Like drowning alive.

"Come out, Annie."

Annie gripped the doorknob, then opened the door, ready to be held.

CHAPTER 3

Leigh hated getting calls at the bar. Always creditors, pushers, or old boyfriends, all wanting sex or money. The bartender, in a Lambda Chi T-shirt, placed the phone in front of her and held out the receiver. "It's your sister. She says it's important."

Miguel leaned in, and cutting through the noise of the band, growled, "Make it quick." A tattooed snake slithered across the cracked landscape of his forehead.

Ever since dragging Leigh back to Atlanta, Mig had ordered her around like he owned her. If he didn't drop the caveman act, she would have to rethink a few things. There were plenty of guys who would love to be with Leigh. These college boys were all over her when Mig wasn't looking, and Leigh was ten years older, not that she broadcast it. With her bed-messy blonde hair, flat stomach and long legs, Leigh had only to crook a finger at any of these guys, and so long Miggy. For a while, anyway. Until he bonked her on the head and dragged her by her hair back to the cave.

From a crumpled pack, Leigh withdrew a cigarette with her lips and scratched off a light. She moved away from Miguel and put the phone to her ear. "Annie?"

"Leigh? I can barely hear you."

"That's because you called me in a bar." Leigh turned to see the bartender take her unfinished beer and signaled she wasn't through with it. Miguel plucked the glass from the bartender and emptied its contents on the floor, all the while looking at

Leigh. His sick smile reminded her of an alligator she'd seen wrestled near Hollywood, Florida.

"Can you hear me okay?" asked Annie.

Leigh moved from the bar, but the snarled phone cord allowed only a step. "I'm sorry I didn't send back that little card. I haven't missed the wedding, have I?"

"I'm not calling about the wedding, Leigh. I have really bad news. Dad is dead."

"Dad is what?"

"Dead."

"Hold on," said Leigh, and pressed the phone to her other ear. "Say again?"

"He's dead, Leigh. Dad was murdered."

Leigh went cold. "Oh my God."

"They arrested his girlfriend. She's supposed to have hit him over the head with an oar."

Leigh turned in small circles, trying to get a fix on what she was hearing. "Jesus. When was this?"

"Last night."

"Christ," breathed Leigh. "Holy shit." Leigh pressed the heel of her hand against an eye. Her father, murdered. Jesus. "Do we get the house, or any insurance money, or anything?" asked Leigh.

"Is that all you can think about?"

"Of course not. But do we?"

"I'm sure he left a will, but I doubt we're in it."

Through a screenless window, the scent of urine wafted from the alley. Leigh's stomach hitched. "This is so fucking weird. Are you all right?"

"No," said Annie. "But Camp will be here soon. What about you? Do you have someone you can talk to? I don't think you should be alone."

Miguel signaled to cut it short. Looking at him, a wave of

24

sadness washed over Leigh. She wished she had someone nice to care for her, comfort, understand. Instead, she had Miguel.

"I'll be okay."

"I'm leaving for DeLeon in the morning. It shouldn't take us long to take care of things. Two, three days at the most. Will you come?"

"I can't promise anything. I don't have any money." Leigh could almost hear Annie rolling her eyes.

"I guess I can loan you some . . ."

"I'll pay you back," said Leigh.

"Sure."

"I'm really sorry to cut this short, but someone wants to use the phone. I'll call you back," said Leigh.

"I need you to come, Leigh. I need my big sister."

"I'll try, Annie." They said their goodbyes, and Leigh hung up.

Murdered. Jesus.

She needed a drink. No, a pill. No, two pills. She located the plastic bottle in her purse, shook a couple into her palm.

"What was that about?" Miguel asked.

"Nothing." Leigh threw back the pills, reached for Miguel's beer.

"Somebody eighty-six your old man?"

Leigh stared, pills thick on her tongue. "How did you know?"

"I know everything," Miguel said. "You remember that the next time you steal from me."

Leigh made a derisive sound, brought Miguel's beer to her lips. "I didn't steal from you."

Miguel's backhand rammed the glass across Leigh's teeth, into her gums before it hit the bar spewing suds. The bartender looked about to say something, then seemed to think better of it. He gave an impotent scowl.

Leigh held two fingers over her bleeding upper lip. Miguel

turned to her, smile gone. "Give me your purse."

Leigh weighed her choices, then gave up her purse. Miguel shoved through the usual detritus and extracted a large baggie of yellow pills.

"This time, I'm not going to hurt you. Next time, I do." He extracted a wad of cash big as his fist. Leigh watched him remove a money clip shaped like a snake. "Now, what's up with the phone call?"

"I have to go to Florida."

On top, one-hundred-dollar bills. On the bottom, twenties.

"You were just there," said Miguel, irritated.

"For chrissakes, my father was just murdered. I have to go."

Miguel narrowed his eyes, his voice playful. "You're not thinking of running away from old Miguel, are you?"

What would it take, she wondered? She thought she had lost him the last time, but Miguel's arm was long. It had snaked around the rehab center's No Visitors policy, yanked her out, shot her up. Without money, how far could she run?

Leigh shivered. "Naw, I wouldn't run from you, Miggy. You're too good to me, baby."

Miguel smiled. "And don't you forget it. Hey, frat boy, give her another beer."

When the drink arrived, Miguel placed two yellow pills in front of Leigh. As Leigh washed them down, she tracked the cash sliding into his pocket. She closed her eyes and tried to think of nothing as beer, bar noise, and painkillers filled the cavities in her heart.

CHAPTER 4

Before boarding the airplane, Annie folded herself into Camp's arms. The scowl on his daughter's face was almost funny, but Annie didn't feel like laughing.

"I'll be back in three days," Annie said to her fiancé. "Try not to miss me too much."

"I miss you already."

"We have to go, Dad," Kirsten said, blank-faced and staring. "She has to get on the plane now."

She? Annie certainly wasn't making much headway in the popularity department. She didn't even have a name anymore.

Kirsten was put out and making no attempt to get over it. She had a dance class later, and not only did she have to get ready early, she was forced to suffer a ride to the airport with her father's girlfriend. The sullen fourteen-year-old sat in the back with her plump arms crossed, staring a hole into the back of Annie's head. Annie gave up trying to engage the girl, difficult enough when Kirsten wasn't being a pill, but what do you say to an angry, overweight teenager who still carried a Winnie the Pooh lunchbox? The usual subjects—boys, fashion, make-up—were poison. The politely interested questions, "who's your dance teacher, how long have you been dancing, can I come to your recital?" were met with sparse, bored answers. "Miss Carlton, two years, I don't care." Never a sparkling conversationalist, Kirsten became decidedly worse after Camp told her he and

Annie were getting married. Until then, at least Annie'd had a name.

"Kirsten's right," said Annie. "I better go."

"You heard her, dad."

"Here, honey, go get an ice cream cone."

Kirsten accepted the five-dollar bill with a huff, then about-faced in the direction of the food court.

Annie asked, "Do you always bribe her with food?"

"As often as possible."

"Have you talked to her any more about us getting married?"

"She doesn't want to discuss it, Annie. She wants to be mad. Once her mother calms down, Kirsten will come around."

"So Dee Dee is fueling this attitude?"

"Big time. I'm the bad guy, remember?"

Oh, yes, she remembered. Dee Dee's alter ego: Super Victim.

Annie swung her carry-on bag over one shoulder. "I'll call you after I get settled in. I love you, you know."

"Daaaad!"

Camp looked at Kirsten, who waved him along. "My daughter, the chaperone from hell."

Annie smiled. "You better go."

Camp kissed Annie, then walked backward, blowing kisses, turning only when he caught up with Kirsten. Annie watched him go, feeling a familiar loneliness, one honed to a fine point at her father's knee. It seemed she'd spent the better part of her childhood watching his retreating back.

"Are you going to Daytona Beach, ma'am?" asked the young ticket agent. Annie nodded, and gave up her boarding pass. Entering the corridor, she glimpsed, in her mind's eye, her father's smile and stumbled.

A hand appeared beside her, and Annie accepted it. She rose and looked into her mother's eyes.

"Careful," said Helen.

"My marriage to your father was a disaster," said Helen. "He cheated on me so often I almost got used to it."

Annie stared out the airplane's window. "I know, mother, I was there."

Annie had spent the better part of her childhood soothing her perpetually distraught mother, who lay atop a disheveled bed, smelling like cotton in an aspirin bottle, tears tracking the folds at either side of her mouth. Annie patted her mother's hand as in Loretta Young movies, said "There, there" and "It will be all right," while her mother's head rocked back and forth on the pillow, refusing consolation. "Your father doesn't love me and he doesn't love you girls," Helen said over and over. "Only your mother loves you. Remember that, Annie."

Annie remembered. So did Leigh.

"You did the right thing, cutting your father out of your life. The only thing Ed Bartlett loved was Ed Bartlett."

The airplane's engine droned. Annie felt a headache coming, and it was going to be a doozie. "I don't want to hear that right now, Mom."

"I was the one who held this family together," Helen continued. "If it wasn't for me, we would have starved to death."

True enough, thought Annie. As a nurse in the university infirmary, Helen's job paid little, but Annie and Leigh would get a free college education. Unfortunately, Helen died before cashing in on her one perk. Annie applied for a student loan and moved to Michigan, pursued a degree in photography. Leigh, during her "actress years," lived in New York, then Los Angeles, Chicago, Boston, Minneapolis, Atlanta. The sisters kept up for a while, but rarely did Annie catch Leigh at home. If she really needed her, she called the local bars.

"Do you know what your father called me when I took that job at the university infirmary?" Helen asked.

"A rug," Annie muttered.

"He called me a rug. He said only Mexicans worked for so little. It may not have been much, but it was more than what he was bringing home, which was nothing."

"He drove that fuel oil truck for a while."

"A while is right. How long did that last, a week?"

"Two winters, I think."

The drink cart clattered up the narrow aisle. *Clack, clack, clack.* Annie's head began to pound.

"That bastard even slept with one of my patients."

Technically, the young woman had been Dr. Boyd's patient, but Annie wouldn't quibble. On weekends, Helen often brought infirmary patients home. The lake cheered them. One Saturday in May, Helen brought home Marsha, and Annie's father offered to take her canoeing. That Annie had been begging her father to take her canoeing for weeks was lost on Ed. Marsha climbed in, and Ed paddled the canoe out of sight. Annie remembered standing at the edge of the lake, waiting for them to return. Leigh joined her, and with one remark, catapulted Annie from the age of innocence.

"If Marsha comes back with her pants on backward, I'm telling mom."

Marsha came back with her pants on frontward, but Annie saw in their smiles that something had happened between them. She heard it in her father's voice, pitched a tad too high. She smelled it when he walked past.

Clack, clack, clack.

"He loved his girlfriends more than he loved you."

Annie pressed her palms against her temples. "Could you be quiet for a minute, Mom? I've got a killer headache."

"Do you want me to get rid of it for you?"

"No, please. Just quiet."

Helen unbuckled her seatbelt. "Turn toward the window."

"You're not supposed to unbuckle until the pilot turns off

the—" Annie shut up. Maybe it would help. She turned, and Helen placed hands on Annie's head.

"Remember we used to do this all the time when you were little?" said Helen. "You used to ask me all the time, 'How do mermaids breathe underwater, mama?' Remember that?"

Annie nodded. She had wanted to be a mermaid more than anything in the world.

"And I told you, 'You have to breathe underwater. Only after you learn that can you become a mermaid.' "

Annie smiled. Yes.

Helen massaged Annie's temples. "First, take a big gulp of air so you can stay under water a good, long time." Helen's voice was smooth, rhythmic. "Then, let the air out and sink to a sitting position on the lake bottom."

Annie expelled air.

"Now, count to three, then inhale through your nose—just enough to feel the water travel up your nostrils."

Yes.

"Now, breathe out."

Annie exhaled.

"Then try it again. One, one-thousand; two, one-thousand; three, one-thousand . . . breathe! You must control the water, keep it where you want, train it. You have to be the one to decide when you are ready to pull the water in, or your lungs will fill up, and you'll drown."

One, one-thousand; two, one-thousand; three, one-thousand, breathe.

"Learning takes time, but if you are truly dedicated and want to breathe underwater more than anything in the world, you will succeed and become a mermaid."

How Annie had loved the mermaids in Weeki Wachee springs. How she had longed to be one!

One, one-thousand; two, one-thousand; three, one-thousand, breathe.

"Something to drink, Miss?"

Annie's eyes flew open. Before her stood the flight attendant, holding a small white napkin. Next to Annie, a large, bald man looked at her, eyebrows raised.

"I'm sorry, what?"

"Would you like a drink?"

"Sure. Diet something."

"Pepsi?"

"That's fine."

"And you, sir?"

"The same." The man smiled at Annie as if they had something in common. The flight attendant took care of them with quick, efficient motions, then moved on.

"You're traveling alone?" asked the man.

"Yes."

The large man stood, and from the luggage compartment brought down a pillow the size of a book. "Have a pillow. I find them pretty good company myself."

Annie smiled. "Thank you."

"Take my magazine, too. I'm done with it." The man resettled himself, then cocked his head toward Annie. "I think you were talking in your sleep there."

"I wasn't really sleeping; I was just . . ."

I was just what? Talking to my dead mother?

"You go ahead and conk out if you want to." The man pointed a thumb at his chest. "I won't let anyone mess with you."

Annie smiled at the man. *Where were you nineteen years ago?* She opened the magazine to the crossword page, but the man had inked in all the wrong answers.

CHAPTER 5

Eugene was born with fire in his brain. The scorched and melted matter inside his head rendered him stupid, a word he heard often at eighteen, and hated. His man's body lashed out. Children who teased ran crying to mothers who phoned, demanding something be done about this retard who shouldn't be allowed to run free. Those days, like today, were bad days. On those days, like today, Eugene went to the woods with matches.

In a small clearing rimmed with scrub, Eugene pulled a matchbook from his pocket and dropped to his knees. He was good at this. The doctors said he would never be good at anything, but they were wrong. Eugene could start a fire.

Smokey Bear would be ashamed of you.

The teenagers who had teased him this afternoon were younger than Eugene and half his size. One had lured him into their circle with a dollar. "You want this?" Pierce taunted. "You want this?"

Eugene did want it. Pierce held the dollar out, and when Eugene reached for it, drew it back. The teenagers laughed. Eugene, who knew this game, laughed too, exposing short white teeth. He reached again.

"I waaaaah," Eugene bawled. "I waaaaah!"

"Aw, just give it to him," one of the boys said to Pierce. "You teased him long enough."

Pierce held out the dollar. Eugene reached. Pierce snatched it away.

"Come on, Pierce, just give it to him," the boy said again. "This isn't funny anymore."

Pierce held out the dollar. Eugene reached. Pierce snatched it away.

Never mind.

Sweating in the Florida sun, which had seared the land to crisp brown tinder, Eugene gathered twigs and pine needles, made a small, loose mound. Even in this partial shade, his neck flushed pink. Eugene drew the matchbook to his face and worked it with short, pudgy fingers.

He hated those teenagers.

Pierce snatched the dollar away yet again. "We could do this all day," he said. "How stupid are you?"

At that, Eugene saw red. He flew toward the boy, caught him under the jaw with a fist, and sent him to the pavement, hard. The laughter stopped. The boys looked at Eugene with fear, stumbled over one another backing away.

"Take it then, you freak," Pierce said. The dollar disappeared inside Pierce's fist, emerged again as a hard paper ball which sailed, surprisingly fast, toward Eugene's forehead, bounced off, causing him to blink.

The match snicked, sparked, bloomed. Soon Eugene would burn the teenagers from memory. He lowered the flaming match to the mound. Pine needles smoked, then glowed brilliant red, and Eugene felt muscles clench with the first wave of excitement. He lowered his face to the smoking mound and gently blew. A tiny flame leapt. Eugene clutched himself, watched as the mound released ringlets of gray smoke. He had seen hair like this once—perfect spiral curls—had wanted to touch this hair, but the girl ducked, eyes darting.

The flame grew, burning the memory.

Eugene's mother told him he mustn't make fires, but he made good fires. This one was catching nicely, going snick, snick, snick. Eugene thrust his pelvis in a jerky dance and accidentally kicked sand into the fire. The twig mound collapsed. Eugene froze, stared. After a moment, flame bloomed again. He threw back his head and howled.

The fire wanted more. Eugene fed twigs, then a brown palmetto frond that crackled as it burned. He held out a fistful of pine needles, then snatched back. He held them out again, snatched back. The fire grew angry. A flame jumped, sunk its heat into his hand, and Eugene fell back, huffing great breaths. Angry now, he kicked the mound, scattering embers that lost their glow when they hit the ground. He would have to begin again.

He heard a twig snap, then another. Eugene scanned shadows beyond the clearing. He wasn't alone.

Smokey Bear!

Eugene spun, grew dizzy, fell down. Disoriented, he crawled a distance before staggering to his feet. He pushed the matchbook deep into his trouser pocket. He would hide it before his mother found it and made him run water over the red tips.

Remember, only you can prevent forest fires.

Eugene looked to make sure the fire was out.

It was.

He ran.

CHAPTER 6

Annie smelled smoke. She scanned the sky outside the Daytona Beach airport, but saw only heat waves rising from pavement. She had forgotten how brutal Florida heat could be. And during a drought like this one, underbrush would dry out rapidly, providing abundant fuel for a firestorm. Growing up, Annie heard about wildfires in other counties, but none had threatened Volusia. She hoped this smell was nothing serious.

"Annie!"

Over a sea of heads, a hand.

"It's me, Pete!"

Annie squinted at a tall, well-dressed man wearing sunglasses. Petey Duncan? Stuttering Petey Duncan who couldn't bait his own fishhook?

"Wait up!" he called.

Annie recognized his lope and felt immediately grounded. Petey wore a Brooks Brothers suit and shiny black shoes. His brown hair was shorter than Annie remembered, but she hadn't seen him in what, ten years?

"Petey Duncan, as I live and breathe," Annie cooed in her best *Gone With the Wind* accent. She extended a limp hand, every bit the stereotyped Southern belle.

Petey approached, long arms outstretched. "Can't spare a hug for your old boyfriend?" As they swayed back and forth in a bear hug, Annie breathed heat and Old Spice. Petey held her at arm's length, his smile wide and perfect.

"God, it's great to see you. You look terrific."

"When did you get so tall?" *And gorgeous,* Annie thought, reflexively glancing at his bare ring finger. "I mean, look at you. You used to be this skinny little kid."

Petey patted his taut middle. "Possum meat," he said, and Annie laughed. "Your flight was early. Lucky I saw you."

"You're here to meet me?"

"I didn't get a chance to talk to you before you left Michigan. I'm real sorry about your dad, Annie."

"Thanks. It's weird. I don't . . . I don't know what I feel."

"I'm sure it must be hard for you. Ed did his best, you know?"

"I know." Bracing for a pinch from her mother, Annie added, "Still, I just want to get it over with."

"There's some things going on I need to tell you about. Can I drive you into town?"

"Sure."

"And, it's Pete, not Petey."

"Excuse me?"

"My name." Pete picked up Annie's luggage. "I'm an attorney now. I go by Pete."

Pete Duncan drove a Mercedes-Benz 380 SL convertible with metallic blue exterior and blue leather seats. Annie whistled.

"Wow. Are you in private practice?"

"I wish. I bought it used with a ton of miles on it."

"Still."

"Don't burn your legs when you sit down. The leather heats up like a skillet." Pete shed his jacket. His short-sleeved shirt exposed tanned, muscled arms.

When she was ten, Annie had challenged Petey to a swimming match. Annie had her eye on Petey's raft, a makeshift platform Petey's father built from four oil barrels and two-by-fours. Annie's competitiveness got the best of her, and knowing she was the better swimmer, named high stakes: "Winner gets the raft."

Petey asked, "What do I get if I win?"

Confident, Annie said, "Anything you want."

It only took a moment for Petey to reply. "If I win, you have to take off your bathing suit." They locked eyes, and sealed the deal.

Annie had won the race easily but wasn't satisfied. It hadn't been the raft she wanted; it was Petey's dad. Annie's father had never built her anything, nothing he actually finished, anyway. It wasn't fair. Jealous-crazy, Annie held Petey's head underwater. When he finally broke from her, sputtering and humiliated, Annie was shocked by her own cruelty. Petey wouldn't look at her, not even after she apologized. So Annie did the only thing she thought fair. She peeled off her bathing suit and showed herself to him.

After that, they were friends.

At eleven, they were fighting again. At twelve, they fished together and traded comic books. At thirteen, Petey lured her behind a pine tree and kissed her. At fourteen, Annie scraped bark off that pine tree and carved their initials inside a heart. At sixteen, they experimented with sex. Seventeen, they found others more interesting, discovered marijuana and alcohol, paired off when convenient for both. They stuck up for each other and cared what the other thought. Then, on her eighteenth birthday, saturated with small-town life and her father's indifference, Annie bade Petey a tearful adieu and left behind all she knew.

"The whole town is pretty shaken by what happened to Ed," said Pete. "People aren't talking about much else."

"I can imagine. You said you had something to tell me."

"Yeah." He paused. "There's no easy way to say this, so I'm just going to say it. I've been appointed by the court to defend Della Shiftlet."

"Who's Della Shiftlet?"

Pete looked away. "The woman accused of killing your father."

Annie went silent. Conflicting emotions, impossible to organize, kicked and rattled. My best childhood friend is defending my father's accused murderer. Pine trees ticked by, straight as rulers. The high, hot sun seared the cloudless sky a brilliant blue. By the time they completed the eighteen-mile ride to De-Leon, her nose would be burnt.

"I'm sorry I upset you."

"Who said I was upset?"

"You look upset."

Annie leaned forward. "Does this thing have a radio?" She punched buttons haphazardly until disco music thumped.

"Annie, I'm only defending Della Shiftlet because I have to. Judge Lanier appointed me."

"Judge Lanier? She's still around?"

"Oh, yeah."

Judge Marguerite Lanier had been the talk of the town when, unmarried, she gave birth in late middle age. Back then, almost twenty years ago, people called babies like Eugene "retarded" and women like Judge Lanier "loose," but in DeLeon, where Judge Lanier was an influential civic leader, nobody dared say either word out loud.

"Why didn't you refuse the appointment?"

"I did. I told her I was close to the family—"

"Oh, please. My father couldn't stand you."

"Okay, close to you, then, or have I got that wrong, too?" Annie was silent. "Anyway, I told Judge Lanier to get someone else, but she wouldn't. She said I was on her court-appointed list, and my number was up. I swear, Annie, if I hadn't been forced—"

Annie concentrated on the tires rolling over the seams on Highway 92. The sound helped counter the sensation she was traveling backward, to a place shifting beneath her feet and pitching her askew.

"The evidence against Della is pretty incriminating. If her case goes to trial and she's convicted, she could get the electric chair. After we set bail tomorrow morning, I'm going to try to make a deal with the State's Attorney."

"What's the evidence against her?"

According to Pete, a neighbor heard Ed and Della arguing and caught Della standing over Ed with a rowboat oar. Ed lay beside his moored boat, bleeding from the head. The neighbor said Della and Ed had been fighting "like cats tied to a clothesline."

"A crime of passion, then," Annie said.

"On the surface, but she may have had another motive. Della stood to inherit your father's property." Pete looked at Annie to see how this was going down. "Did you know you and Leigh were not primary beneficiaries?"

"I suspected." Her voice caught. Even though she had initiated their estrangement, the truth stung; he loved someone else more than he loved his daughters. "You're telling me that Della killed him for the house?"

"That's what it looks like."

"You don't believe she's innocent, then?"

"It doesn't matter what I believe. It only matters that a jury believe her, and with the evidence against her, things don't look so good for Della Shiflet."

"The Widow Lake house can't be worth an awful lot."

"Ten years ago, it wasn't, but things are changing. DeLeon is going through a major development phase, and lake property is leading the way."

"Any proof she killed him for the property?"

"Not really. That's why I think the state's attorney will deal. A jury might believe property was Della's motive, and they might not. I don't plan to let it get that far."

"What were Ed and Della fighting about?"

With his middle finger, Pete pulled his sunglasses to the tip of his nose and peered over them. "We're talking about Ed here, Annie. What do you think they were fighting about?"

Strange women.

Her father was out with strange women. As a child, Annie conjured images of circus freaks and toothless hags. Maybe Ed was out with Mrs. Beagen, bent like a willow from osteoporosis. Or maybe he was with Digger Pugh's mother, who came to the school playground every day, wearing the same shabby lavender hat, and gave Digger his paltry lunch in a full-sized grocery sack.

Leigh, four years older, had set Annie straight. "It means dad's sleeping with them."

Even then, Annie didn't understand the fuss. She herself slept with Pamela Hooks on the occasional Friday night, and Pamela was strange as they came.

Leigh tried again. "It means he's cheating on mom."

Annie remained confused. Were they playing cards?

Leigh leveled her stare. "He has sex with them, Annie. He's only supposed to have sex with mom."

Once Annie figured out sex, she was properly outraged and joined her mother and sister in a realigned assessment of her father's character.

Pete turned down the radio. "How long are you here?"

"I'm just going to bury my father and go home. I'm getting married in three weeks, and I'm not going to stay any longer than I have to."

"I heard you were getting married. Congratulations!"

"Thanks. I got a good one."

"He'd have to be."

"How did you know I was getting married?"

Pete looked off. "I don't know. Grapevine, I guess."

"I didn't think anyone around here knew or cared."

"Well, I care. Can I take you to lunch tomorrow to celebrate?"
Annie felt herself blush. "I better not."

"Oh, come on. Let me buy you lunch. I'll even floss, how about that?" Annie laughed. "Is that a yes?"

"Okay."

Pete nodded. "You look good, Annie. I wish Ed could have seen you so happy."

"Yeah. Me, too."

Annie felt a kick from the back seat, turned around. Helen, dark hair whipping, raised an eyebrow.

"Be quiet," Annie mouthed, then faced front. In the distance, smoke.

CHAPTER 7

The pigeons roosting in the Volusia County Courthouse's copper dome had, in ten years' time, turned its beautiful patina a calcified white. To Annie, everything else looked the same. Gas-guzzling cars in angled parking spaces exposed bumpers to one-way traffic. Old men wore straw hats too small and pants too high. Looking up, Annie felt welcomed by the tower's giant clock face, which still lied about the time.

The sheriff's office, inside the courthouse, was located at the end of a concrete block hallway painted an innocuous off-white. Annie pushed the door. Were it not for a blast of walk-in-refrigerator cold, she would have had no greeting at all. Taking center stage was a talking bear. At least, that's how he first appeared. Huge, dark and dressed in a brown suit, a man with blue-black hair stood growling at Sheriff Dade Newcomb, who was taking it sitting down.

"That's the fifth fire in three months!" The bear pounded a desk, which, surprisingly, neither collapsed nor split in two.

Seminole, Annie thought. *I wonder if he'd let me photograph him.* The sheriff was matter of fact. "If you don't calm down, Kingfisher, I'm going to have to throw a net over you. I already told you the Fire Marshal's on it."

Kingfisher pointed a finger as thick as his cigar. "Somebody is targeting my properties, Dade. I don't care what the newspaper says. I've alerted the FBI."

"What the hell did you do that for?"

43

"Jimmy Lee said we can pin this guy with extortion and interfering with interstate commerce. You should be happy, Sheriff. A federal task force will rake the woods for this guy."

"I don't let lawyers run my office, King, and even if I did, I sure as sweet hell wouldn't listen to Jimmy Lee. We don't need a federal task force in our business."

"Then do something. You got a retard out there playing with matches, and we both know who it is."

The sheriff cleared his throat. "I don't think Judge Lanier would appreciate you referring to her son as a retard."

"If I catch Eugene trespassing, the judge will have a lot more to worry about than name-calling."

The sheriff cocked his head at his deputy, a Hispanic woman in her early thirties. "You hear that, Salceda?"

"Yes, sir, I did."

"You heard Kingfisher Powell threaten Eugene Lanier?"

"Yes, sir, I did."

"Yes, sir, she did." Sheriff Newcomb leaned back and nodded at Annie. "You hear that threat, young lady?"

"Hey, I'm just here about a dead body."

The spotlight shifted, and Annie blinked beneath sudden attention. The sheriff jabbed a finger. "You're Annie Bartlett."

"Guilty."

"Holy moley, I didn't recognize you. You got all pretty on us."

Sheriff Newcomb was never known for tact, but Annie knew what he meant. Leigh was the pretty one. She emanated a light that drew people like moths to a candle. They fluttered, especially the boys, darting in and out of her hot and cold attentions.

Kingfisher Powell turned hypnotic eyes on Annie. She tried to look away, but he held her fast. Finally, Annie broke and took a step back. "I didn't mean to interrupt."

"King was just leaving."

The bear swung his head. "I'm not finished, Sheriff."

The sheriff rose. Not a small man, he nonetheless appeared diminutive opposite Kingfisher. At sixty, Sheriff Dade Newcomb had thickened around the middle. His hair, almost white now, had been recently cut. A patch of untanned skin peeked above his collar. The sheriff placed his knuckles on his desk, distributed his weight over them.

"I'm going to tell you what I'm going to do. I'm going to talk to the Fire Marshal, look at the evidence, and if I think it prudent to have a talk with Eugene Lanier, I will have a talk with Eugene Lanier."

Kingfisher opened his mouth, but Sheriff Newcomb pushed through. "I know your development outfit has lost a lot of money from these fires, King, and I'm not blind to what's going on in my own jurisdiction. But so help me God, if you ever threaten someone in my presence again, or in the presence of my deputy, I'll climb so far up your Miccosukee Indian ass you'll be shitting me for a week. Do I make myself clear?"

Annie looked at her shoes, at the wall, at her shoes, at the wall.

When he spoke, Kingfisher's voice was calm as a lake after a hurricane. "My people have a saying. A man who fights alone is enemy to himself." He paused while his words mixed with the manufactured air. "You tell Judge Lanier hello for me." King turned to Annie. "Ma'am." He tipped the brim of his dove gray Stetson and exited.

The door sucked shut, and Annie found her voice. "Did I come at a bad time?"

"Don't mind Kingfisher. He's on the warpath lately."

"What did he mean about 'a man who fights alone is enemy to himself'?"

"Who the hell knows what King ever means?" The sheriff

extended a hand. "How are ya', Miss Bartlett? Just get in?"

"Yes. Pete Duncan met me at the airport."

"Your sister coming down, too?"

Annie nodded. "I'm supposed to meet her later."

The sheriff swung a hand toward the Hispanic woman. "You meet my chief deputy, Raina Salceda?"

Deputy Salceda was shorter than Annie and solid. Dark hair pulled into a tight bun emphasized her round face and honey-colored eyes. She stepped forward, extended a hand.

"I'm very sorry for your loss."

"Thank you."

The sheriff crossed arms over chest. "We're all sorry as we can be about Ed. I swear, this world gets meaner and meaner. Didn't used to be this way, did it, Salceda?"

"No, sir."

"No, sir. One of these days, I'm just going to turn my back and walk away from all this. Pete Duncan fill you in?"

"As much as I want to know."

"Uh huh. You gonna stick around a while, let all the old timers get a look atcha?"

"I'm just here to bury my father."

Sheriff Newcomb scratched behind an ear. "I'm going to miss old Ed. Hell of a fisherman. He ever tell you about that marlin he caught off a pier in Key West?"

"My father and I didn't speak much."

The sheriff's eyebrows shot up. "Uh huh. Well." Fingers drummed his belt. "I guess there's no chance that's gonna change now."

Deputy Salceda turned quickly to Annie. "Would you like a glass of water or anything?"

Annie appreciated the young deputy's attempt to diffuse the sheriff's remark, but in truth, Salceda looked more embarrassed than Annie had been.

"No, thanks. I'm fine. Can I see my father?"

"I'm not sure you want to do that," the sheriff said. "He's not going to be all pretty like at the funeral parlor, you know."

"Don't I have to identify him or something?"

"No, we figure it's him."

"Oh," said Annie, disappointed. "It's just that . . . I feel I need to say good-bye."

"Really? Huh. Funny time to be feeling that."

Annie's skin tingled as if someone were rubbing it the wrong way. "I can assure you, Sheriff, there's nothing funny about any of this."

"I can take you," Deputy Salceda said.

The sheriff looked at Annie. "You're sure?" Annie nodded. "Okay, then. Salceda, go 'head and take Miss Bartlett to her dearly departed father."

"Excuse me, Sheriff, did I do something wrong? I get the distinct feeling you don't approve of me being here."

"Oh, I don't have a problem with you being here, Miss Bartlett. It just would have been nice if you'd arrived before now, that's all."

"And why is that?"

"Because Ed is dead. And it might have gone a long way to changing that rueful conclusion to his worthless life if you and your sister had been just a little more attentive."

"Are you blaming me and Leigh for my father's death?"

The sheriff sucked his teeth. "Naw, a'course not. It's just that I got a daughter, and when her mother and I split, she wouldn't have nothin' to do with me, either. I gotta tell ya, it 'bout tore me up. And I see you standin' there after all these years, cool as granite and every bit as hard, I got to wonder if it's possible for a man to question the course of his life, much less change it, without having to pay for it with his children."

"With all due respect, you don't know anything about me, Sheriff."

"Maybe not, but I knew a lot about Ed, and I find it a shame you can't say the same."

Annie allowed Salceda to pull her gently. If this were any indication of the welcome she would receive from others, perhaps three days in DeLeon would be two and a half days too long.

"Salceda, I'll need you back here within the hour."

"Yessir."

The courthouse clock struck two, and the sheriff looked at his watch. "All right. Y'all have fun."

CHAPTER 8

Everyone said Ed Bartlett was a handsome man. Annie loved being told she had his good looks, and spent long moments before the mirror, staring at herself. After careful scrutiny, Annie decided Ed's good looks looked better on Ed. On her, proportions were wrong—eyes too far apart, nose too large, jaw too square.

Staring at her father now, Annie sucked breath after breath of chemically tainted air. One side of Ed's head was crushed. A dark crust formed where the skull had opened at the temple. Left eye and cheekbone sagged, giving the impression of a face melting. His skin, always tanned to a brown roux, was now black, blue and gray.

Annie looked at her father's pulped eye. With a mere wink, this eye had pulled her into a world holding just the two of them, if only for a moment, and she had loved that world. This cheek she'd kissed when he gave her money for her camera. She looked at his mouth, which had sung country songs in a voice as gravelly as an unpaved road. To ride on these bruised shoulders was to stick her head through a ceiling of sky no one else got to see. This skin, which had smelled of salt and sweat, encased all the things Ed had been afraid to show the world: vulnerability, insecurity, pain. This man had been her father. Now, he was nothing.

Annie's hand went to her mouth. She willed her stomach to quell. Groping, she appealed to Salceda with a look.

"Down the hall."

Annie bolted.

The bathroom echoed from long ago. It wasn't the cracked tile and stained sinks that cued Annie's memory; it was the smell, a mixture of pest control chemicals and deodorizing spray. She'd come in here one time with her mother and Leigh. Why? Something about her father.

My handsome father.

Annie leaned over the bathroom sink and rinsed her sour mouth, ran a finger over smudged mascara. A small movement coaxed her eyes upward, where a mud nest protruded from one ceiling corner, its carpenter wasp regurgitating clay, fashioning, with front legs like knitting needles, chambers more complicated than the human heart. Deputy Salceda handed Annie a paper towel; she buried her face in the stiff brown paper.

"She battered in his skull for his property?"

"That's what the State's Attorney will argue, yes."

Annie dropped her head, stared at the rust stain ringing the drain. She balled the paper in her fist.

"I want to see Della Shiftlet."

CHAPTER 9

Sheriff Newcomb had been against the nonscheduled visit, but Annie knew he could allow it. There was no such thing as "by the book" in his office. Sheriff Newcomb was the book. Even so, he had made her squirm before giving the nod.

"I thought you just wanted to get in and get out," the sheriff had said.

"I want to see the monster that did that to my father."

"Ah, hell, Della Shiftlet isn't a monster."

Annie wouldn't hear it. "Are you going to let me have that visit or not?"

Sheriff Newcomb studied Annie for a moment. "You mean to tell me you never met Della Shiftlet before?"

"No, why?"

"Never seen a photo, anything?"

"I wasn't interested in my father's life, Sheriff Newcomb, and I sure didn't keep up with his girlfriends."

If the air conditioner was broken, which it wasn't, the sheriff's flat, judgmental "uh huh" could have frosted the room. "My daughter, now," the sheriff said, rolling onto the balls of his feet. "Far as I can figure, she was angry because I ruined the fairy tale, you know?"

Knowing this was about to steer in her direction, Annie braced for impact.

"So how come you never made peace with your daddy? Was it on account of your mother?"

"Yes," said Annie, stone-faced.

Sheriff Newcomb looked expectant, as if Annie would say more, but she was through.

"Fair enough. Salceda, you busy?"

"No, sir."

"Then jump to. The bereaved needs transport to the jail."

The Volusia County Branch jail, baking beneath the brutal sun, emanated waves of heat visible from the cruiser. The memory of Ed's staved-in skull burned. Annie felt a boiling hatred for the person who had done that. She flattened a hand over her stomach, which threatened to turn again.

The visitation room was a cinderblock rectangle, painted an off-white gone dull pink with age. A primitive mural of beach sand and palm trees splashed across the main wall. The state of Florida had definitely spared taxpayers in furnishing this place. The metal conference tables, arranged in a rectangle, were of a type favored by local schools and churches; the gray folding chairs, standard issue.

"Siddown ri' chere," said the corrections officer and pivoted a chair on its rear leg. "The sheriff says you got ten minutes."

A door opened, and Della Shiftlet stepped forward, followed by a wide-shouldered officer holding her upper arm. Della Shiftlet wore a short-sleeved, orange jumper, much too big. It drooped at the crotch, pooled at the ankles. Annie drew a shocked breath, then stared into the woman's face, eyes wide.

Della Shiftlet looked just like her mother.

"Holy Jesus." Annie stood, ready to bolt. Opposite, Della Shiftlet stopped in mid-sit.

The corrections officer moved toward Annie. "You got to siddown, Miss. All visits are conducted while seated at the table."

Annie sat. The prisoner mirrored, wary.

Della's eyes were not as dark as Annie's mother's; the brows

52

more sharply arched. Her hair was different, too—short, dark hair with frazzled blonde tips. Della had Helen's generous mouth and taut jaw, was the same height, and from what Annie could discern beneath the ridiculous orange body bag, same thin frame. Annie put her age at mid-thirties, the age Helen had been when she drowned. The female corrections officer left; the other stayed close by.

"You'll have to excuse my appearance," said Della, then smiled. "I look like death in orange." Annie stared. Della's smile wilted. She pushed her fallen hairdo with fingertips. "You don't happen to have a rat tail comb you could slip me, do you, maybe inside a hollow Bible or something? They took mine."

Annie didn't move.

"Well, never mind. I'd probably stab someone with it, anyway."

Why hadn't the sheriff warned Annie that Della Shiftlet looked exactly like her dead mother?

"That was a joke," said Della.

One, one-thousand; two, one-thousand; three, one-thousand; breathe!

"Look, you're the one who requested this visit," said Della. "So why don't say what you have to say, and let me get back to my knitting?"

She needed a second, just a second, to work this out. Over the last twenty years, her mother's appearances had blended with Annie's reality, but Annie knew Helen wasn't real, had always known. Her mother was dead, drowned in Widow Lake. That Annie still communicated with Helen was, as one medical text had put it, "a grief-engendered coping mechanism, triggered by sudden loss at a young age." Cumbersome babble, but Annie understood, accepted.

But this.

This was no coping mechanism. This was Ed's killer, and the

resemblance to Helen rattled Annie to the bone.

"So, are you going to tell me why you're here, or am I supposed to guess?"

"I wanted to see what a murderer looks like."

Della shifted uneasily under Annie's scrutiny. "Honey, I promise you, I did not kill your father."

"First, don't call me 'honey.' Second, give me one reason why I should believe you."

"Because I loved him."

"What do you do to the people you hate?"

"I'm telling the truth."

"A neighbor heard you fighting."

"People fight all the time. Your daddy and I were no exception. He could be a pain in the ass, but I still loved the son of a bitch."

What had her father been doing with a woman fifteen years younger? Was he pretending she was Helen, reliving his life as it might have been had he not been such a screw up?

"I was glad when they told me you wanted to see me," Della said.

"Why?"

"Because I need your help. I'm being framed. I know that sounds stupid—"

The corrections officer sniggered. Della shot a look, then said in a sharp, shrill voice, "You got something to say, Owen?" Owen moved his head in a lazy circle. "Then mind your own cotton-picking business."

From his look, the corrections officer didn't like Della's mouth, but it didn't appear he would do anything about it. After burning a half-lidded stare into Della, he rested his upper back against the wall and looked straight ahead, mouth twisted.

"Like I was saying—" She glanced quickly at Owen, eyes hard, then back. Her voice dropped to a whisper. "I'm being framed, and I think I know who's doing it. There's this local developer, big Miccosukee, named Kingfisher Powell."

In spite of herself, Annie focused.

"He's been buying all the property around Widow Lake. He wants to develop it. He did the same thing opposite the Bobcat Bay State Forest."

"The property that's been on fire," said Annie.

"That's right. King was after your father to sell. He pressured him hard, offered him lots of money, but Ed wouldn't budge."

Ed turned down lots of money? That didn't sound right. "Why not?" Annie asked.

Della's voice appealed for understanding. "It was our home. Ed loved the place. He loved the lake, even after your mother . . ."

At this mention of her mother, Annie's eyes went hard.

"Anyway. Ed knew Kingfisher would turn the place into something tacky. Ed told King to get lost, but he kept coming back. Last time, Kingfisher threatened him."

"With what?"

"I don't know; King talks in riddles. Something about 'the last man standing,' some Indian bull like that. It sounded like an ultimatum to me."

"So, you're saying Kingfisher Powell killed my father?"

"Or had someone do it."

"You need to tell this to the sheriff. I can't help you, even if I wanted to."

"I did tell him, but he thinks I'm guilty, like everyone else in town."

"Tell your lawyer, then."

"I did. Pete Duncan said a jury wouldn't believe me, that it didn't matter whether I killed your father or not. It all comes down to whether the state can convince a jury beyond a reasonable doubt that I did it."

Annie could see that. With evidence stacked against Della, it seemed unlikely a jury would buy a conspiracy defense.

"It doesn't make sense," said Annie. "Even if Kingfisher killed my father, he still doesn't get the property. It belongs to you."

"Not if I'm convicted. There's this law, see. Convicted felons can't inherit property from their victims. If I'm convicted, the property goes to you and Leigh."

"What's that got to do with King?"

"He'll come after you to sell, and you'll do it."

"How do you know?"

Della came to life. "Okay. There you are, you and your sister, sudden owners of a ramshackle house in Nowheresville, Florida. You have bad memories of the place; you live elsewhere; you aren't interested in moving back. I'm good so far?" Annie gave a shruggy nod. "So now, here comes Kingfisher Powell. He offers you cash, more than the property is worth. What do you do?"

Annie got a sudden picture of Della talking to her father this way, leaning on the kitchen counter, selling him. Della's demeanor was so different than Annie's mother, who had been such a vague presence, invisible in a crowd. Annie couldn't imagine Della invisible anywhere. She was the type of woman Ed loved but hadn't married: dramatic, fiery, in love with life. When animated, like now, Della glowed almost as bright as her prison garb.

"I don't know what I would say," Annie said. "I'd tell him I'd have to think about it."

"Let's say you do that. You think about it. Next day, Kingfisher makes you a bigger offer, but it has strings attached. You have to decide today, or he's going to walk. Now what do you do?"

"I'd call his bluff. Let him walk."

"Why risk it? The money's in front of you. Come on, Annie.

What do you do?"

Annie, annoyed, said, "Cut to the chase."

"You sell!" Della slapped the top of the table. "You and Leigh split the money—probably more money than you've ever had. Kingfisher gets his development. Della goes to prison. Happy ending, right?"

"If you say so."

"No, Annie, it's wrong. I'm as innocent as you are, and that is God's truth." Della's eyes begged to be believed.

"Why should I help you? I don't even know you."

"I don't have a good answer to that. All I know is, Pete Duncan wants me to admit to a murder I didn't do."

"He's trying to save you from the electric chair."

"Maybe pleading to second degree murder will save me from the chair, but it won't save me from prison, and it will surely strip me of the property that your daddy, of sound mind and body, willed to me. My life goes down the toilet, Annie. I got nothin' but an orange jumpsuit and a tin cup. And why? Because I loved your father and wanted to live out the rest of my life with him in a little house on a sleepy lake. For that, my life is ruined. Now you answer me this: Is that all right with you?"

Annie searched her gut for the answer. If Della was making this up, it was a compelling lie. On the other hand, the woman was no cream puff. Judging from Della's interaction with the corrections officer, Annie believed her capable of violence under the right conditions. Could she have bashed in the brains of a man she claimed to love?

"I'm sorry. There's nothing I can do."

Della seemed to deflate, then looked up, eyes hopeful. "What about your sister?"

"Leigh?" Annie sputter-laughed. "Don't count on it."

"Right. Well." She looked away. "There it is."

"What about family? Can't they help you?"

"No. I have second cousins somewhere, but it's been so long since I was in touch. I wouldn't ask them for help, anyway. They're all Bible thumpers."

"Friends? Anybody?"

"Nope." Her head tilted to the right, and she gave a sad smile. "Your daddy was it."

Officer Owen pushed from the wall, shook a leg to wake it. "That's ten, Shiftlet. Wrap it up."

"That can't be ten minutes," Della argued. Owen tapped his watch.

"I guess I should go, then," Annie said.

"Wait." Della leaned forward. "I know you've always blamed your father for your mother's death, Annie—you and Leigh both—but your father did not deserve to die like this. Isn't that what you came in here to tell me? That his life was worth more than that? Find out who killed him, Annie. You owe him that much. You know you do."

A sudden wave of guilt and sorrow knocked Annie underwater. She tumbled, kicking to reach the surface, lungs bursting.

"Just talk to Pete Duncan. That's all I'm asking. Maybe you can get him to defend me instead of writing me off."

"I really don't think anything I say could influence Pete Duncan one way or the other."

"But you will talk to him—?"

Owen closed around Della. "Time's up."

"Annie?"

Unhinging herself from the now, Annie pulled back and took a long, hard look at Della. What unexplainable mysteries had conspired to bring her mother's reincarnation—or doppleganger, pooka, reconstitution, whatever the term du jour—to ask Annie to save her?

"You'll help me?"

What she would give to have heard those words from Helen,

herself, nineteen years ago. Annie was just a nine-year-old girl, but she would have found a way to sharpen the edges of her mother's fading presence, fill her hollow heart. If she had appealed to Annie, Helen would be alive, not a figment that popped in and out of Annie's daydreams.

"You'll talk to Pete Duncan?"

Owen slipped a hand under Della's forearm, lifted.

"I can't promise."

"But you'll think about it, right?"

A few minutes later, Annie retrieved her purse from the locker and returned the key to the woman behind a Dutch door. She walked past Deputy Salceda, through the automatic door, and onto the steps outside. Heat assaulted her. For a moment, she wished she could melt and not have to think about anything.

CHAPTER 10

Leigh drove a pyrotechnic display onto the parking lot of the Sha-D-Land Motel. The 1969 Nova scraped, rumbled, banged its way to the motel entrance where Annie stood, transfixed. Leave it to Leigh to make an entrance that would upstage a brass band. When the engine cut, the ensuing quiet seemed fake.

"Annie!" Leigh kicked open the door, emerged beaming. She was thinner than at Thanksgiving a year and a half ago when she dropped in on Annie unannounced. She'd looked healthy then, but now her slightly skeletal face, with protruding cheekbones and sharp chin, betrayed a diet of whiskey and cigarettes. Still, Leigh was a head turner. Her summer clothes were tight; her tangled mane, loose. The sisters locked themselves together, moved side to side in a stiff-legged waltz, turning slowly as ballerinas in a music box.

"Hey, goon girl," Annie whispered into Leigh's damp neck.

"You're a goon girl," came Leigh's customary response, spoken now with reverence and affection. The small ritual comforted them, made unnecessary the words both were thinking: All we have now is each other. Annie did not want the hug to end. She was still smarting from her earlier encounter with the sheriff. After the jail visit, she had barged into his office and angered a hornet.

"Why didn't you tell me Della Shiftlet looked like my mother?" she demanded.

"Why do you think I owe you anything, Miss Bartlett? You don't talk to your father for ten years, then come in here and expect other people to break rules so you can feel better about yourself. I did you a favor. So I didn't tell you Della Shiftlet looks a little bit like Helen, so what? I'm busy putting out fires of my own, and if you don't mind, I'd like to get back to it. Salceda, you busy?" the sheriff barked.

"No, sir."

"Then give our out-of-town guest a ride to her motel. And that, Miss Bartlett, is the last favor you get out of me."

The sisters pulled apart and smiled. Annie looked into Leigh's eyes, glazed with a strange light. "You look like hell," said Annie.

"Thanks. You, too. You got anything to drink in the room?"

"Bottle of wine."

"Perfect. Break it out while I drive my car around back."

"You're fine where you are. Leave it."

"Nah, I better move it. Security reasons. I don't want to tempt anybody."

Annie stifled a laugh. Who the heck would be tempted by this piece of junk? The Nova was littered with the usual trash, and lots of it: cans, fast food bags, empty cigarette packs, clothing. As far as Annie could see, it had nothing a window-shopping thief would fancy, including hubcaps. "Leigh, it's probably safer in front, where the clerk can keep an eye on it."

"That's okay. I'll meet you in the room. What's the number?"

Number nine was next to the office. Mrs. Voorhis, the gray-haired proprietor behind the desk, had insisted Annie take that one. "I keep the single ladies next to me. Safer that way," she said over the sighing of her afternoon soap opera.

Annie wished now she had argued. Mrs. Voorhis's soap opera leeched through the wall to work out its conflicts in room number nine. Other problems were further up the complaint list, including a carpet that smelled of stale beer, tap water that ran brown ("You gotta let it run fer a minute"), a mildewed shower curtain, peeling paint, and sagging mattresses. Annie believed in patronizing Mom and Pop places, but she also appreciated the adage, "you get what you pay for." She was thankful the linens smelled laundered and the bathroom scrubbed with bleach. So far, she had seen no large insects, but Annie was sure they lurked.

After washing highway grime from her face with a sliver of soap, Leigh plopped down on one of the two double beds. "Did you bring wine glasses?"

"No, but I believe these fine plastic cups are complimentary."

From her purse, Leigh produced a Swiss Army Knife, went to work, and the cork came to mama. "I love that sound," she said.

Annie proposed a toast. "To Dad."

"To Dad," said Leigh. The cups kissed, and Annie sipped. "That son of a bitch."

The laugh traveled down Annie's nose, hit the cup, and caused a wine tsunami. Annie spilled, then Leigh spilled, and the bed was anointed in laughter and death.

Annie scooted to the bottom of the bed, facing Leigh. "It's good to be with you, Leigh."

"You, too. What did you do today?"

Annie held her wine in her lap, stared at the cloud on its surface. "I saw Dad."

From the office, soap opera voices shouted ultimatums.

"Wow, no kidding. What was that like?"

A dozen answers raised their hands, stood on tiptoe, begged to be picked. There was Distant Memory, bubbling up as it had this afternoon. There was Bloody Detail, from which Annie had not been able to avert her eyes, and Delayed Emotional Reaction, which would hit at the most inopportune time. In the end, Annie called on none of them. "Bad," was all she said.

Leigh took Annie's ankle in her warm hand. Had she not, Annie might have floated off to numbness. "I met the girlfriend, too," Annie added.

Leigh was still. "You did? My God, Annie."

"And you'll never guess what."

"What?"

"She looks just like mom." Annie watched Leigh for a reaction. "Isn't that a trip? He shacked up with mom's clone. Pretty sick, huh?"

Frowning at Annie, Leigh sat up.

"Talk about freaky. I almost had a brain hemorrhage. I thought I was in the Bizarro World or something." Annie laughed. "Oh, wow, I haven't thought about that in years. Remember that? Superman's alternate universe where everything had a Bizarro counterpart, even Superman?" Leigh picked up the wine bottle and poured. "I wonder what happened to all those comics me and Petey used to have? We had a gazillion of the things. I'll bet they're worth something now."

"For God's sake, Annie, shut up!"

Annie stared. What had happened? Had she floated off?

"You're babbling like an idiot! Stop it. I don't like you talking like that."

"Leigh, my God, what's the matter?"

Leigh paced as a commercial for toilet bowl cleaner jingled through the wall. "I thought you grew out of that. I thought you were over it."

"Babbling? I didn't know there was an age limit."

"Over mom! Seeing mom!"

Annie's smile melted as meaning dawned. "I'm not crazy, Leigh."

"You're talking crazy."

"Dad's girlfriend really looks like mom."

"Annie—" Leigh sighed, then changed the emotional channel. "This has been such a stressful day for you."

"You don't believe me?"

"I'm concerned about you, that's all."

Holding her wine high, Annie scooted off the bed. "This is hilarious. I can't believe you don't believe me."

"It's not that I don't believe you."

"Her name is Della Shiftlet, and she looks just like mom, and if that makes me a schizophrenic, then so is Sheriff Newcomb because he sees it, too."

"Annie—"

"I know the difference between reality and fantasy, Leigh. I know a real person when I talk to one."

"Good—"

"Just because I sometimes have these . . . these—" Wine sloshed as Annie groped. "—visits, it doesn't mean I'm suddenly seeing my dead mother every time I turn around."

"I'm glad to hear that."

"That said, I have to tell you, Leigh, the woman is a dead ringer, excuse the pun, and if you don't believe me, you can go to hell." Annie finished her wine, cracked the plastic cup in one hand, and threw it in the trashcan. "What's on TV?" She punched a square button on the television's panel.

Leigh punched it off. "I'm sorry."

"Which bed do you want?" Annie buzzed about the room, looking for something to rearrange.

"I didn't mean to upset you."

"I'll take the one by the bathroom. You can have the one with the wine spot." Annie swung her bag onto the bed, unzipped it, plunged in search of nothing.

"Come on, Annie. We just lost our father. We shouldn't fight."

"I don't like being talked to like I'm defective."

"Did you hear me say I was sorry?"

"Yes."

"So?"

Annie sighed. "I'm hungry. Let's get out of here."

Mr. Lucky's was a tiny white sandwich place that used to be a Tastee Freez. It sat beneath a huge oak Annie predicted would one day pitch forward and squash the place. Annie wanted to photograph the owner, a thin, cancerous man who did not seem all that lucky. He recognized Leigh, and by association, Annie, when the sisters leaned in to the tiny window to order. During Leigh's senior year, Mr. Lucky's son had strangled while swinging on a Tarzan rope at Blue Springs. Leigh recalled him fondly, and Mr. Lucky nodded, eyes welling.

After ordering, Leigh pulled out a wad of cash in a money clip shaped like a snake. "I'll get it," she said.

The offer to pay was reason enough to faint, but the wad itself nearly gave Annie a coronary. "Win the lottery, Leigh?"

"Something like that."

Leigh tipped Mr. Lucky generously. Annie wanted to ask more questions about the money, but knew she would get a lie. She took an oblique approach. "So you'll be able to pay half the room cost, then." Leigh pushed the money into a back pocket. "Seriously, where did you get all that?"

Leigh nodded at an oak whose thick, rambling branches dipped to the ground. "Let's sit over there."

The sisters sat in the shade beneath the oak, on two concrete benches curving around a concrete table. After three bites of her Mr. Lucky Burger, Leigh pushed the food aside and lit up a cigarette.

"Hey, I'm not done, here," Annie said.

"That's okay, take your time," Leigh said, missing the point. "Hey Annie, can I ask you something?"

"Sure."

"Has Dad—?" She stopped, drew on the cigarette, exhaled noisily. "You know, the way Mom used to communicate with you? Has Dad ever—?"

"Do I talk to Dad? No. Are you going to eat your fries?"

Leigh pushed them toward Annie. "What about Camp? Does he know about your—about mom?"

"I'm tired of this subject, Leigh. Let's drop it."

Leigh pulled a leg beneath her. "So, what did you and dad's girlfriend talk about?"

Annie popped a fry in her mouth. "She says she didn't do it."

"Bullshit," said Leigh.

"Yeah, well. That's what we talked about. She wants me to help her."

Leigh frowned. "Help her with what?"

Annie looked over her right shoulder. The sun was finally burning away, leaving pink ribbons in its wake. It wouldn't be fully dark until nine, but Annie could smell the gloaming. Ed had loved this time of day. He rode around in the truck, smoked, listened to music, ran over snakes.

"She says she's being set up. She thinks this local developer named Kingfisher Powell was after Dad's property, and when Dad wouldn't sell, the developer either killed him or had him killed." Leigh shook her head, a smirk growing. "So she asked me to look into it."

Leigh flicked ash with a snap of her wrist. Beneath the table, her foot jiggled. "And are you going to?"

"I'm thinking about it."

Leigh flicked again. Jiggle, jiggle went the foot. "Annie, do you realize if she's convicted, you and I inherit the house?"

"Yeah, she said something about that."

"So why, may I ask, are you trying to mess that up?"

"I'm not."

"Yes, you are. You just said you were going to help with her defense."

"No, I said I would think about it. She wants me to talk to Pete. He's defending her." Leigh's mouth dropped open. "It's weird, I know. He wants her to plead out."

Leigh paced erratic shapes in the cracked concrete patio, head shaking in tight bobble-head movements. Annie dragged another fry through a puddle of ketchup.

"Listen to me," Leigh said. She dropped the last of her cigarette onto the concrete, twisted on it. "I don't think you should talk to Della Shiftlet anymore."

"Don't worry. I've used up my prison privileges."

"Good, because you can't be objective. She's right that this is all about the house, but it's Della who wants the property. Della killed Dad for that house. Anybody can see that."

"That's the way it looks."

"No, that's the way it is."

"Innocent until proven guilty, Leigh. Remember that one?"

"Grow up, Annie. If this Kingfisher guy wants it, the house must be worth decent money, right?"

"I don't know."

"I think we should find out what we're talking about here— have an appraisal done."

"And who's going to pay for that?"

"We'll split it."

"Like the room?"

Leigh sighed, exasperated. "Yeah, okay. Like the room." Out came the money wad. Leigh peeled off several bills, slapped them in front of Annie. "Happy now?"

"I've never seen you with that much money before, Leigh. You want to tell me where you got it?"

"No. Are you going to help me get an appraisal or not?"

Well, at least she didn't insult me with a lie, Annie thought.

"Leigh, aren't you jumping the gun here? The house belongs to Della."

Leigh's expression turned hard. "Della is not going to need a house after she fries in the electric chair, Annie. Even if she pleads out, she'll go to prison, and we all know a murderer can't inherit her victim's property. That house is rightfully ours, and it's going to stay that way."

Mr. Lucky came out holding two cones piled high with swirling braids of chocolate and vanilla soft serve. The cones were the old-fashioned kind, with flat bottoms. Annie wondered if the ice cream machine was from the Tastee Freez days, when the tiny building was yellow and Mr. Lucky's cancer-free lungs were pink.

Mr. Lucky approached. "I brought you girls some dessert."

Leigh gave Annie a last look, then turned a full-wattage smile on Mr. Lucky. "We don't need dessert, Mr. Lucky. We're sweet enough as it is."

Leigh threw her arm around his shoulders, and pulled him to her, eyes blazing. Caught in Leigh's web of attention, Mr. Lucky giggled like a schoolboy. Leigh took a big bite of ice cream, then touched it to the tip of Mr. Lucky's nose. Annie brought camera to eye as Mr. Lucky giggled and blushed in the setting sun, so happy to be with Leigh, so lucky to be alive.

CHAPTER 11

Leigh passed out on the motel bed in the king's position: legs open, arms wide, belly up, a monarch confident of power and protection. Annie listened to her snore.

What about Camp? Have you told him about mom?

She might as well have asked, "How much longer do you plan to withhold your true personality from the man you intend to marry?"

The phone rang. Annie jumped. Where is it written, she wondered, that all motel room phones have ringers as loud as church bells? She picked up the phone.

"Annie?"

"Camp!" Annie's heart thrummed. "What time is it?"

"Late. Midnight. I thought you were going to call me."

"I'm sorry. I must have fallen asleep."

But Annie hadn't been asleep. She had tried, but images of Ed slithered in and out of the darkness behind her quivering eyelids.

"I miss you, Camp. I wish you were here."

"Really? Because I could come first thing tomorrow—"

"No, no, I didn't mean that. I just meant—I love you, that's all."

"I love you, too. How are things?"

Annie told Camp about identifying Ed, the prison visit, Leigh's arrival, and the singular charm of the Sha-D-Land Motel. She tried to keep her tone cavalier, even though the day had knocked her back.

"Did anybody meet you at the airport?"

"Oh, yeah! An old friend. Della's lawyer, in fact."

"That must have been weird."

"It was, at first, but I've known Petey Duncan since we were kids. He's just doing his job."

"You didn't tell me he was going to be there."

"I didn't know. Anyway, I'm having lunch with him tomorrow."

"Really? Huh."

Did Annie detect a jealous note in Camp's tone? "Don't worry, sweetheart. I told him I was engaged."

"Why? Did he hit on you?"

"No!" Annie sat up. "He just invited me to lunch, that's all."

"But you felt the need to tell him you were engaged."

"Camp, I tell everyone I'm engaged. I'm proud of it."

"Are you sure? Because at the airport I thought I felt a weird vibe."

"Camp, I want to be your wife more than anything in the world." Even if Kirsten was a pain, Annie was confident she would win the girl over in time. "You're just in a bad mood because I'm not there to rub your back."

"You're right. I don't like being apart. When's the funeral? I'd like to come down for that."

"I'm talking to the funeral home tomorrow. I'll let you know."

After Camp filled Annie in on his day, (Kirsten was mad because he was late picking her up; Dee Dee lost an alimony check and demanded he write another; an undetected nail in a support timber ruined one of the mill's saws), Annie found herself yawning. Appalled, she realized Camp must have heard it.

"I guess I should let you get back to sleep," Camp said.

"I wasn't bored, Camp; I'm just tired."

"I know. Oh, I almost forgot. The caterer called and wants a final count. And the tables-and-chairs woman needs a deposit. Do you want me to take care of it?"

"Oh, Camp, that would be great. Could you please tell her we've decided to seat six per table, instead of four? She'll argue because that means fewer tables, but be firm."

"I'll be a paragon of firmness."

Annie smiled. "Thanks, Camp."

"Sure. I really love you. You know that, right? And I want to live with you for the rest of my life."

"Me, too, Camp. I'll be home as soon as I can."

After a pause, Camp said, "Annie, is there something you need to tell me?"

"Tell you? No. I mean, like what?"

What about Camp? Have you told him about mom?

"I don't know. I just get this feeling."

Annie didn't want to open this door, especially not over the phone. Any talk of Helen would be face-to-face.

"No, Camp, I can't think of anything."

"Okay. Anyway. I love you. Call me tomorrow?"

"I will. I love you, too. Good night."

Annie hung up, completely spent. She didn't want to think about anything. She closed her eyes and emptied her head, concentrated on the too-soft mattress beneath. She felt a hand on her forehead.

One, one-thousand; two, one-thousand; three, one-thousand, breathe . . .

The tears came, warm and thick. They soaked the pillow and pooled in the shallows of the mattress. Helen sat on the bed. "Don't cry, little mermaid." Annie's tears flowed to the floor, sought the space beneath the door, ran into the parking lot where they filled cracks and trickled to level ground. Drop by drop, the earth drank the sorrow spilling from room number nine, where Annie Bartlett lay in a sagging bed, silently weeping for her father.

CHAPTER 12

The next morning, Annie struck out in search of breakfast. The nautically themed Pier Diner had once been The Boulevard Restaurant. Annie remembered a comfortably bland place with worn, red carpet and vinyl tablecloths. In her absence, the Boulevard Restaurant had changed hands and undergone a transformation that must have wiped out the Navy surplus store. Painted driftwood critters beamed from nails on posts and rafters. Fishnets hung from bright blue walls, colorful crabs and lobsters cheerfully tangled in its mesh. On the wall behind the cash register, an orange Styrofoam ring and a life vest were artfully arranged. At the end of a row of uneven pilings functioning as a room divider, stuffed pelicans collected dust out of the reach of children. Restrooms were designated Guys and Gulls.

Besides doing a brisk breakfast and lunch business, The Pier had an active nightlife. In the backroom bar, secluded from the dinner crowd, men raised glasses to the owner, an ex-exotic dancer named Florida Sunshine who mixed the weakest drink in four counties. Had she mixed stiff ones, the backroom would have been no more popular. Florida's frothy beehive, painted toenails, and wide, red smile could light up a lump of coal. Some placed the source of her popularity a little lower, on Florida's prize-winning ta-tas, shown to best advantage in clingy, low cut tops and custom bras from specialty catalogues. Others basked in the sight of Florida's shapely rear end, swaddled in a white miniskirt from whence tanned legs galloped, without stopping, all the way to the floor. Her delicate feet, no strangers to a vigorous pedicure, were stuffed inside tiny pumps topped with pom-poms, beckoning as befitted their X-rated nickname.

As the diner's indisputable hostess with the mostest, Florida dressed no more demurely during daylight business hours. Seeing her for the first time, men and children stared; women took notes. All called her Florida. Each time the bell clanged high on the diner door, Florida herself escorted hungry visitors to a table. The restaurant smelled good, the food came out fast, and the service was cheerful. As a result, the bell rang constantly, as did the register.

At a booth in back, Annie studied a menu. Leigh was to join her soon, after pulling herself together. Rousing Leigh had been difficult. Some things never change.

The bell clanged, and a beefy young man in baggy clothes entered, stopped with his back to Annie, and looked around. Annie thought him familiar. He was short, but big in the shoulders, and soft; his too-short arms hung slightly bowed from his body, as if repelled by his torso. Shifting from foot to foot, he slowly revolved until Annie saw his face—flattened features, short forehead, almond eyes.

"Eugene!" Florida Sunshine called. Bracelets clinked as she gestured. "You come on over here to me."

Eugene ignored Florida, moved to the counter. He pulled an old man's powder blue sleeve. "Dahll," he said, smiling broadly.

"I don't have a dollar for you today, Eugene."

Eugene moved to the next customer. "Dahll."

"Sorry, Eugene," said the woman, probably the first man's wife. "Fresh out." She did a double take. "What happened to your hand? Did you burn yourself?"

"Faaaa," Eugene said.

Florida clapped a hand on Eugene's shoulder. "Sorry, buster, out you go."

Eugene held out his hand for Florida to see. "Faaa!"

Florida steered Eugene to the door and gently nudged him through. "I told you a thousand times to leave my customers be. Now, you go on."

Annie watched Eugene lunge down the sidewalk and disappear around a corner. She wondered if Eugene's burned hand gave weight to Kingfisher Powell's accusation in the sheriff's office yesterday. How old was Eugene now—eighteen, twenty? The last time she saw him, he must have been six or seven. He had attended the same Catholic school as Annie, though later. Judge Lanier must have believed her son would have an easier time in a small parochial school, but Annie knew, in spite of his perpetual smile, Eugene didn't have an easy time of it anywhere. It was obvious to everyone that Eugene didn't fit; only Judge Lanier seemed in denial.

A pretty young waitress, who looked to be of Native American descent, approached.

"Good-morning-my-name-is-Sada-may-I-take-your-order?" she mumbled.

Annie was about to order when interrupted by a hoot from Florida, followed by a burst of applause. Sada swung her attention to the door, gave an excited expulsion of air, and clapped the air above her head in exuberant cheerleader fashion. Annie craned her neck to see what the fuss was about, but customers were getting to their feet now, forcing Annie to do the same.

"What's happening?"

Sada bounced on the balls of her feet. "It's Clyde Glenwood!" she said, eyes glistening.

"Who's that?"

"A firefighter!" Sada said, as if the question was insulting, then added, "I know him personally."

Annie saw him now, working past the crowded doorway, hand

high, acknowledging the applause with an embarrassed look. He looked like the lumberjack on the pancake box, only without the handlebar mustache: same sandy blond hair with sweeping bangs, same cartoon square jaw and buffalo biceps. The only difference was Clyde Glenwood had flaking red skin, as if sunburned too many times. His cheeks and nose looked especially well done.

Annie settled back in the booth, ready to order, but the spectacle wasn't over. Florida Sunshine, petite next to the tall, barrel-chested Clyde, rested one hip against Clyde's thigh, circled an arm around his waist, raised a hand. The diner went immediately quiet.

"I want all y'all to know," began Florida, "that Clyde Glenwood here," (anticipatory murmur from the crowd) "is a hero to the people of this town." (Cheers, whistles, pumped fists.) "Now wait a minute, wait a minute, I got more to say," ("You got more of everything, Florida!"—hoots, cat calls). "Settle down, Henry, or I'll short circuit your pacemaker." (Low laughter, gentle ribbing.) "Clyde Glenwood is a hero to the people of this town, and a hero to every man, woman and child in the United States of America!"

Wow, Annie thought, as water in her glass vibrated with the noisy applause. This woman can work a room. Florida raised her hand again. "For those of y'all who don't know, Clyde here has been battling the fires in the Bobcat Bay Forest, and if it were not for him—"

Here Clyde interrupted. "It's not just me; it's a lot of people."

"Oh see, and modest, too," sang Florida. (More applause.) "If not for Clyde and—" (nodding at him) "a lot of other brave people," (Clyde nodded back) "who knows . . . ?" (Florida paused for effect) ". . . who knows, what tragedies we might have endured?"

Annie was impressed. Florida Sunshine was one heck of a

public speaker. If she wanted to, she could beat the pants off any politician foolish enough to run against her. Even her name was perfect.

The diner was quiet as Florida's voice dove to its deepest register, resurfaced church-like and solemn. "Now, I want all y'all to remember Clyde Glenwood in your prayers, along with all those who have suffered from these terrible fires. And I want y'all to remember to thank God we have Clyde Glenwood, who will not only lead us through this trial of fire, but with courage and faith, extinguish it forever."

Annie's waitress placed two fingers beneath her tongue and blew a loud, shrill whistle, the kind Annie imagined would bring a wolf to her side. Annie applauded politely as Clyde Glenwood moved toward the counter. An older gentleman offered his stool to Clyde, who, after going through the required refusal/insistence ritual, accepted.

"Hey Clyde—" All turned toward the reporter at the counter. Annie recognized Jeb Barlow, still a scruffy, unshaven man in an ill-fitting seersucker suit. Jeb's dull gray hair, with comb tracks cutting through Brylcreem, grazed the tops of his ears.

"What's the scoop, Jeb?" said Clyde, shaking the reporter's hand. Onlookers chuckled at the pun.

"The readers of the DeLeon Sun News want to know if we're all going to get burned up." Jeb licked the tip of a pencil and poised it above a palm-sized pad. One huge, wiry eyebrow shot up in comic anticipation of the answer.

Clyde folded his hands on the counter like a schoolboy. "That depends on which way the wind blows."

Florida spoke up from the cash register. "That's what everything depends on!"

The breakfast crowd laughed with Clyde and Florida, and Jeb swiveled back to his sausage links and eggs.

Sada evidently forgot she was waiting on Annie and rushed

to Clyde's side. Annie smiled, mentally composing the story to replay later for Camp.

"I have a question for you, Mr. Fireman," boomed a voice from the backroom. Although closed during the day, the backroom seemed open any time to Kingfisher Powell, who filled its doorway as he emerged. Wearing jeans, a traditional patchwork shirt, and his dove gray Stetson, Kingfisher rotated from side to side as he walked.

"Hello, King," Clyde said. To Annie, the greeting did not sound enthusiastic.

"Clyde." King stuck out a paw. Clyde shook it without meeting King's eye.

"Tell me something," said King. "You've seen a lot of action since somebody started torching my houses."

"Actually, there's no proof of arson, yet," said Jeb Barlow.

King turned black eyes on the reporter. "A man who gathers facts leaves proof among stones."

Jeb's eyebrows shot up. "I have no idea what you just said, but I'm going to quote you, anyhow."

"What do you want, King?" asked Clyde, pulling King's stare from Jeb's smirking face.

A slow smile twisted King's mouth. "Why are you afraid?"

"Oh, Daddy, stop it," said Annie's waitress, Sada.

"Why am I what?" Clyde cocked his head as if he hadn't heard, but judging from his tone, he had.

"Afraid," said King, still smiling. "We all know you're a hero." King pivoted, arms open, suggesting solidarity with his audience. He grazed over Annie's face, returned to it, moved on. "And I, more than anybody, certainly appreciate what you and others have done to keep the fires from spreading beyond my construction sites. You have contained the fires, am I right? That is what you say? Contained?"

"What's your point, King?"

"This is my point. I have watched you contain the fires, but you do not seem in any great hurry to put them out. Smoke fills the sky outside this diner. My lumber, my land, my homes are being destroyed. Maybe you like the fires to burn as long as possible so you can be a hero. But no, that is not what we think. You are already a hero. So I ask you, Mr. Hero. Since you are not putting out the fire, what are you afraid of?"

Jeb Barlow took up his notepad. Riveted, Annie patted the seat in search of her camera, then realized she had not brought it. She could have knocked herself in the head.

Florida spoke up. "King, you take off your hat. You're not in a barn. And all you waitresses, get back to work. We got hungry people in here. I got a table over here, King."

"I'll tell you what I'm afraid of," said Clyde. He did not stand, seemed to know he didn't have to. As he spoke, Jeb Barlow scribbled.

"I am afraid of a hellish red light coming to meet me through a black tornado, heat so awful my sweat turns to steam inside my gloves, and before I can open it, I drop the nozzle on my partner's back. I'm afraid of a frightened child breathing smoke beneath a burning bed on the third floor of a house I'm told only has only two. I'm afraid of drought, lightning, and strong winds. I'm afraid of fire starters, rubber neckers, flashovers, backdrafts, gas leaks, Christmas Eve, New Year's Eve, and Prom night. Most of all, I'm afraid one day I will go in search of cooler air and turn my back on a huddle of honorable men because of ungrateful sons of bitches like you, who think I'm here just to cork your money-shitting ass. That's what I'm afraid of, King. Now, if you don't mind, I'd like to have some breakfast." Clyde turned to Annie's waitress. "Bring me some coffee, please, Sada. I got a bad taste in my mouth."

Sada scowled at her father and scooted. In The Pier Diner, a fork clinked against a plate, a chair scraped. Voices rose and fell, steady as waves. As the bell clanged high on the door announcing another customer, Kingfisher Powell faded like flotsam in fog, adrift on a sea of breakfast specials.

By the time Leigh arrived, Annie was ready to eat the décor. Leigh looked bad: ashen skin, dry lips, filmy eyes. "Why are you staring at me?" Leigh asked, drumming fingers on the table.

"Sorry."

"Which one's our waitress?"

"She hasn't actually made it over here, yet."

"You're fucking kidding me. You've been here, what, a half hour?"

"There was a distraction." Annie nodded her head at Clyde Glenwood.

Leigh dipped her head to see. "Wow," she said appreciatively. "Is there a lumberjack convention in town?"

"He's a firefighter."

"No shit?" Leigh pinched her cheeks. "I'll have to make his acquaintance before I depart this Vale of Tears."

Behind her, Annie heard a voice. She turned. Eugene stood staring at Leigh, his mouth agape.

"Dahl."

Leigh smiled. "Hey, I remember you. You're Eugene, aren't you?"

Eugene nodded. "Dahll."

"He wants a dollar," said Annie. "The owner already threw him out once."

Leigh extracted a crumpled dollar bill. "Here you go, Tiger."

Eugene took the bill, folded it twice, and put it in his pocket. Annie thought he would move along, but he seemed fascinated with Leigh's hair. He reached, and Annie saw an ugly pink burn on the flesh below his thumb and forefinger.

"You like my hair?" Leigh asked. Eugene nodded. "You want to sit next to me?" Leigh made room on her side of the booth, and Eugene slid in next to her. He smiled at Leigh as if she were Barbie, Blue Fairy, and the Good Witch, all rolled into one. Leigh lit a cigarette and Eugene's eyes followed the smoke.

"Faaaa."

"Can you understand him?" Leigh asked.

Annie shook her head. "Not very well."

"Eugene!" Florida Sunshine click-clacked toward them.

Leigh snickered. "Who the hell is this?"

"Shhh. The owner," said Annie.

"I'm sorry girls," Florida said. "I've asked his mother and the sheriff both to keep him away from my customers, but it's like asking for bigger tits."

"He's not bothering us," said Leigh.

"That's very sweet, but Eugene knows he's not to come in here and ask for money, don't you, Eugene?"

Eugene nodded, then showed Florida his folded dollar.

"He's the only person who's come over here in a half hour," said Leigh. "We don't even have coffee yet. Instead of tossing him out, maybe you should hire him."

Florida flushed. "You haven't been waited on?"

Leigh made a face that said, Nope, afraid not, and frankly, I expected to be treated better than this.

"Sada!" Florida snapped.

At the counter, Sada jerked around.

"Is this your table?"

"Oh, gosh!" Sada hurried over, wearing a look of abject horror. "I'm really sorry. What can I get you?"

"Breakfast is on me, ladies," said Florida. "And Eugene, you come with me."

Eugene slid obediently from the booth. "Buh."

"Bye," said Annie and Leigh. Eugene plodded to the door and exited without complaint. Hands on ample hips, Florida watched him go. Once satisfied, she turned her smile back on and greeted customers at a nearby table.

Annie ordered a full breakfast, including plenty of "pig body," as Camp called it. Leigh ordered coffee. Sada said, "It won't be long," and skittered away. Leigh puffed on a cigarette, eyeing Clyde Glenwood. As if pulled by her stare, Clyde looked over his shoulder. When he saw Leigh, he smiled.

"Houston, we have lift off," said Leigh, with a purr.

Annie thought of Camp, how excited she had felt when he first looked at her in the way Clyde now looked at Leigh. Nothing compares to that first phase of attraction, she thought, when the dance is non-physical, the transmissions nonverbal, the message unmistakable. Annie kicked Leigh's foot. "Hey."

"Hmm?"

"We're here to bury Dad."

"So?"

"We'll only be here a few days—get in, get out."

"I couldn't have said it better myself," said Leigh. "Excuse me."

"Wait. Can we talk first?"

Leigh's eyes searched the ceiling. "I'm thinking . . ." she swung them back to Annie, ". . . no."

"Just for a second, Leigh. Come on."

"Okay, make it quick. And just for the record, that is one thing I do not intend to say to that fire fighter."

Annie put one hand flat on the table, covered it with the other. "I guess there's no delicate way to ask this, so I'm just going to dive in."

"Oh, boy, this sounds promising."

"Are you . . . okay? You don't look healthy to me."

"I look healthy to me."

"I'm serious. You seem to live on cigarettes."

"I'm fine, Annie."

"Your color isn't very good, either. Last time I saw you, you looked a lot better. I'm worried about you."

"Well, don't."

Sada arrived with coffee, said, "Your order will be up in just a minute." As Sada left, Annie noticed Florida at the cash register, studying Annie and Leigh. A customer handed her a check, and the signature smile returned.

Leigh asked, "Are you finished?"

Annie hesitated. "How's AA coming along?"

"Oh, for the love of—. Fine. AA is fine. Anything else?"

"You're still going, then?"

"What are you, my parole officer?"

"You have a parole officer?"

"No—! Annie, I'm fine, really. And I can take care of myself. I've been doing it for a long time."

"Okay. It's just that—"

Leigh held up a palm. "Stop."

"Okay."

Leigh looked at Clyde, rapped knuckles on the table. "I'll be right back."

Clyde watched Leigh come toward him. Leigh squeezed into the space between Clyde's knees and the next stool, and rested her elbow on the counter. After they shook hands, Leigh lifted her hair off her neck and swung the mass over one shoulder. The ritual had begun.

"How is everything?"

Annie looked up. Florida Sunshine beamed down.

"Fine, thank you. Just great."

"In all that confusion before, I didn't introduce myself. I'm Florida Sunshine."

"I'm Annie Bartlett, and that's my sister, Leigh, over there. We used to live here."

Florida looked as though she'd just been told her g-string was around her knees. "Oh, my Lord in heaven." She placed a hand over her well-padded heart. "You're Ed's girls."

"Yes, ma'am."

"Oh, my sweet Jesus. I should have known that. I am so sorry about your father. Ed came in here all the time."

"Yes, I can imagine him here."

"And that's your sister talking to Clyde?"

Annie nodded. She sensed Florida winding up like a scoot toy and feared what might happen once she set herself on the floor. "Thank you for breakfast," Annie said. "It was nice of you, but you didn't have to do that."

"Well, that's what 'nice' is, isn't it? Doing things you don't have to." For a second Annie thought the diversion had worked, but Florida's hand was suddenly mixing the air over her beehive. "Everyone? Everyone? Can I have your attention, please?"

The diners quieted. Annie wanted to crawl under the table.

"I know all y'all know about this terrible tragedy that has greatly upset every single person in our quiet little town, but if you haven't heard for some reason, I'm sorry to be the one to tell you that Ed Bartlett was murdered a few nights ago." A low murmur rumbled through the diner. "That's right. It's shocking, just awful, and we are all deeply, deeply saddened by this terrible crime."

Leigh looked at Annie: What the hell?

"We have with us today Ed's daughters, Annie and Leigh Bartlett, who have come back to their hometown to honor the father they loved."

The applause made Annie's face hot. She didn't dare look up.

"Stand up, Annie," said Florida, leading the applause.

Annie shook her head. Florida swung toward Leigh.

"And this over here is Leigh Bartlett."

More applause. Leigh nodded, but Annie could tell she wasn't enjoying the attention either.

Tray held high, Sada approached Annie with breakfast, eyes pinned on Leigh.

"Y'all go back to your eatin', now," said Florida. "And I don't want to see any rubbernecking. Give these girls some privacy. They didn't come here to be gawked at. If you want to express condolences, leave a note in the comments box by the register. I'll see they get them."

Leigh borrowed a waitress's pen and wrote something on a napkin, which she gave to Clyde. On her return to the booth, she brushed a hand along Clyde's broad back.

"What was that?" asked Leigh, referring to Florida's tribute.

"Welcome home," Annie said.

Leigh looked at her coffee and addressed Sada. "I asked for black coffee. This has milk in it."

Sada held Leigh's eyes a tad too long, Annie thought, then reached for the coffee mug. The mug tipped, and coffee spilled toward Leigh, who plastered herself against the back of the booth.

"I'm so sorry," said Sada, her tone flat. "I'll go get a towel."

"It's all over my lap!" Leigh whined. "Damn. I didn't bring another pair of jeans, either. What's her problem, anyway?" She slid from the booth. "I'll be right back."

Leigh left for the restroom, and the front bell clanged. Annie turned to see a man in a black cowboy hat, a partially concealed tattoo licking his forehead. He drew stares as he swept the diner with a slow, steady gaze. Sleeves had been ripped from his green Army shirt, exposing fork-tailed creatures twined around his arms. He moved to the counter.

Sada arrived with Annie's food.

"Did I hear you say the Native American is your father?"

"That's what they tell me," Sada said. She finished wiping. "I'll be back with more coffee."

"Thanks."

The food smelled great, and Annie dug in. Maybe she could get Leigh to eat some toast when she returned. Annie bit into a golden brown triangle, slick with butter.

Outside, Sheriff Newcomb headed toward the diner. Eugene approached. Annie watched as the sheriff pulled a wallet from his pocket and gave the boy a bill.

CHAPTER 13

Judge Marguerite Lanier rarely banged a gavel. Her sixty-four year old voice, as imposing as the judge was diminutive, was a more effective method of restoring order. It soothed or struck dumb, as circumstances required.

Barely five feet, the judge boarded her chair by way of a four-inch soda box, which she carried in and out of the courtroom herself. Once seated, her tiny feet toe-hooked the chair's two front legs, and Judge Lanier was now ready to pass judgment on the proceedings below.

Beneath independently operating eyebrows, Judge Lanier's sharp brown eyes scanned the courtroom. They rested on the court's appointed attorney, Pete Duncan. To his left sat Della Shiftlet, the accused. Both listened to the State's Attorney, Matty Tatum, whose nasal voice grated like nails on a chalkboard. To the judge, this pink-eyed, pink-faced man would always be Little Matty Fatty, probably the only child in St. John's After School Program more reviled than her son, Eugene. But Matty got revenge. As a prosecutor, he took great satisfaction in putting many of his childhood torturers behind bars. Eugene had no such recourse, but his mother was a judge, and she, like Matty, had an excellent memory.

Matty Tatum recommended Della Shiftlet's bond set at $200,000. Pete Duncan shook his head. "My client has no felony arrests, Your Honor, and very little in the way of resources. She poses no flight risk, nor should she be considered dangerous to others. The bail request is unreasonable."

"This was a violent crime," Tatum argued. "Ed Bartlett was bludgeoned to death with an oar from his own boat. Della Shiftlet has not been analyzed by a court psychiatrist, so the defense cannot say she poses no threat to others."

Duncan countered. "Your Honor, Della Shiftlet has no history of violent behavior."

"A suspect need not have a history to be considered dangerous—"

"In all aspects, she has been an upstanding citizen—"

"Until now—!"

Judge Lanier did not bang her gavel. "Enough!" she said, at half vocal capacity. "Bail is set in the amount of two hundred thousand dollars."

Della Shiftlet looked up, shocked, murmured under her breath. "Jeez, you might as well make it a million."

"Done," said Judge Lanier. "Next case."

CHAPTER 14

When Judge Lanier left the courtroom, Sheriff Newcomb stepped quickly in pursuit. He had not expected Marguerite to come down so hard on Della Shiftlet. Pete Duncan was probably right—his client wasn't dangerous—but the flight risk thing, that was another story. Sheriff Newcomb doubted if a single person in DeLeon was on Della's side. If he were Della, he would be sorely tempted to light out at the first opportunity. He didn't think Della would do it, but you never knew. Dade Newcomb was past the age of surprise.

Yet something about Della Shiftlet bothered him. It wasn't her resemblance to the Barlett woman. Like he'd told Ed's daughter, that was yesterday's fascination. When Ed Bartlett introduced Della Shiftlet to the St. Johns Fishing Club ten years ago, the sheriff, like everyone else, had stared, but after a while, didn't notice anymore. Ensuing nonsense about Ed bringing Helen back from the dead amused a few, but that kind of ignorant talk was dangerous. Some holy rollers around here saw the devil's work in everything, and even when the devil took a holiday, it seemed to the sheriff, folks around here went looking for him. Della's resemblance to Helen Bartlett was coincidental, and if Ed wanted this woman because she looked like his dead wife, that was his business.

What the sheriff saw was a Man's Woman. Della drank like no woman he'd ever seen, played aggressive poker, and swore a blue streak when she lost. She loved a good dirty joke, mechanical bulls, and if tanked, an arm wrestle with anyone who slapped a fiver on the table. She wasn't popular with other women, but in Dade's experience, the Dellas of the world seldom were. Laugh a little too loud, show a little too much cleavage, and the pack turned its back, strange rules for a strange species.

What bothered Sheriff Newcomb about Della had more to do with her double nature. Beneath the redneck veneer lurked a complex intelligence, part instinct, part ambition. Della didn't laugh at Polish jokes because they were "racist." She bought books instead of checking them out of the library, then actually read them. She didn't cook, keep a clean house, or talk about babies. This was an odd fish Ed had on his hands, and Dade wondered more than once if Ed had his eyes fully open.

But he seemed to love Della, and Dade supposed that's all that mattered. Folks who disrespected Della soon found themselves denied Ed's company, and worse, the use of his rowboat. He and Della holed up on Widow Lake for the long haul and didn't care what anyone had to say about it. The sheriff stopped in a few times, killed a beer or two, jawed about pyramid schemes or some quick-money thing Ed always had going on, and life seemed hunky dorey. That Della could turn so violently against Ed over a piece-of-shit house didn't feel right, but that was where the investigation pointed. Now she was Pete Duncan's fish to fry. As for the judge, Sheriff New-comb now turned his attention to getting her on board with a little fire prevention.

Judge Lanier's chambers had become, over the years, a trophy room. The judge was one of few women to cross the gender line at the St. Johns Fishing Club, and any man was pleased to have her in his boat. What she lacked in muscle mass she made up for in competitive edge. Judge Lanier could coax a bass from a stand of lily pads with a half an earthworm. During competi-tion, she funneled her water overboard, never chit-chat, never got tired. Bass, marlin, barracuda, swordfish: black-eyed trophies lined the paneled walls of her chamber. Were it not for several framed pictures of Eugene, a visitor might think he had stumbled into a Hemingway museum.

The judge opened her door and encountered the sheriff, waiting patiently.

"Who let you in?" she asked, toneless.

"Clancy. He always lets me in. He likes me." The sheriff raised his eyebrows comically. "I'm not afraid to use my looks to my advantage."

The judge eyed him suspiciously. She hung her robe on a rack, sat, gestured for the sheriff to do likewise. "To what do I owe the pleasure?" No one but the sheriff would have known this beautifully modulated voice masked irritation at this unannounced visit.

"I got something to address, Marguerite." A fly buzzed around the sheriff's head. He waved it away. "It's Eugene."

"What's my little Frankenstein done now?"

"Don't call him that, Marguerite."

"Well, that's what most call him, isn't it?"

"All the same."

"He is, you know. A monster. Not because he's ugly, mind you, or mean, or dangerous; just the opposite. He's kind, loving, and oblivious to the shortcomings of others. What chance in this cruel world does a boy like that have? He's a freak."

"That's enough, Marguerite. I don't want to hear any more of that kind of talk."

The judge smiled, almost tenderly, at the sheriff. "Poor Dade. So sensitive." The smile disappeared. "Why are you here?"

"I think you know."

"Tell me anyway."

Sheriff Newcomb softened his voice as he came to the point. "If I find out Eugene has something to do with these fires, I'll have to act, Marguerite. You know that."

The judge lifted her chin. For a woman her age, her face had few lines. Dade's was a topographical map by comparison, and he was five years younger. She dyed her hair, of course, most women he knew did, and the jaw-length haircut was flattering, not the cap of tight curls favored by DeLeon's matronly elite. Marguerite's hair moved in graceful waves to her neck. Were he to touch it, it would be soft.

"He's got melted sneakers and a burned hand—" the sheriff continued, "—and with Powell stirring everybody up the way he likes to do, I'm feeling a lot of pressure to do something."

The judge raised an eyebrow. "Do something?"

Damn her, thought the sheriff. She knows what I'm talking about. "Have you thought any more about that place in Tampa?" he asked.

"No." The word came out clipped, final.

The sheriff had figured on that answer, but had to take the shot. Maybe, if she heard the question a few million times more, she might answer differently.

The sheriff nodded at a stand-up frame on the judge's desk. "Is that a new picture?" She handed it to him. He looked at Eugene's face: slanted eyes, flat nose, protruding tongue, and felt a tenderness that never failed to surprise him. The boy was programmed, had loved fire as far back as the sheriff could remember. Marguerite did her best, but she could not stop Eugene from carrying matches; no one could. It was only a matter of time before Eugene seriously hurt someone, or himself. The sheriff did not believe Eugene was behind the Bobcat Bay fires, but obviously he was up to something. For everyone's safety, including Eugene's, Dade had to convince his mother to give him up.

He handed back the picture "He looks happy."

"He's always happy."

"Now, listen here, Marguerite—" The fly dive-bombed. Dade swatted, missed.

"I won't discuss sending him away. He's my son, and I want him near me."

"Can't you see the wisdom of this—"

"It is not wise, Dade. It is cowardly and irresponsible, and I won't have this conversation again."

Sheriff Newcomb slapped his thighs. "Okay." He stood, heard a knee pop. The fly twitched atop an unfathomable law book, which lay on the desk before him. Knowing flies go straight up when they take off, Sheriff Newcomb clapped the air above, and sure enough, the fly flew right into the trap. The sheriff opened his hands, and the fly tumbled to the thick, Persian carpet. He sought the judge's approval, but she seemed oblivious to his victory.

"In that case," the sheriff said, "I'll have to ask you to keep him tied to your apron strings. You can't let him wander like he does, all over town, getting into things."

"You make him sound like a stray dog."

"Do as I ask, please, Marguerite? I will protect Eugene for as long as I can, but you have to do your part. He's starting to piss off a lot of people."

Judge Lanier smiled. "Not unlike his father."

"Well, that's your business."

Judge Lanier opened a thick appointment book. "Close the door after yourself, won't you, Dade?" She scribbled something without looking up. "Clarence has been letting in flies."

CHAPTER 15

Leigh's pupils whirligigged. The street had been so bright. The bar, even at nine-thirty in the morning, was dark and smelled of spilled beer and stale smoke. Her face felt stretched too tight, as if a scratch would cause it to suddenly split from the bone. She breathed deeply, trying to stop the pulse jumping in her neck.

She never should have taken Miguel's money. That was stupid. She nearly had a heart attack when she came out of the restroom and saw him at the diner. Of course he would come after her, of course he would. She remembered a back door to the place, had gambled it was unlocked. Thank God she hadn't let Annie talk her into leaving the car in front of the motel. Lucky so far, she would have to split before this luck ran out. She'd arrange for an appraisal on the house, go back to the motel and pack, leave Annie to take care of Dad's mess. She could be out of Dead-Leon by noon.

After a moment, eyes adjusted, she felt better. She was home.

Wedged between a restaurant and a dress shop on Woodland Boulevard, Red's had been Leigh's first real hangout. Owners were less concerned with checking ID's back then, and Leigh passed for twenty-one when she was sixteen. As long as she didn't give anyone reason to doubt, she could flirt, play pinball, pump quarters into the jukebox. The rattiness of the place appealed to her. Faded posters, cheap paneling, a rattling AC unit, even the heavy tables, their tops carved with switchblades, bottoms tiled with gum—this was what a bar was supposed to be, and in ten years Red's had changed little. Through one corner of a felt-covered window, a shaft of sunlight broke, glorious warrior angel, illuminating a single bar stool. Feeling guided, Leigh sat upon the chosen stool, spun toward the door, rested back and elbows against the bar. There was no one in the place. Probably someone in back, unpacking lemons or some such, in a dirty apron.

"Hello?" Leigh dug for cigarettes. Bars always had matches lying around, yet she saw none. She felt her heart begin to race and willed herself to relax. "Anybody home?"

From the back a good-looking man in his late twenties pushed through saloon doors. As Leigh predicted, he wore a dirty white apron, which he now used to wipe his hands.

"Hi. Help you?"

"That depends," cooed Leigh. "Are you open for business?"

"Sure. What can I get you?"

"Matches, for starters."

The man moved behind the bar, bent, placed a pack of matches in front of Leigh. "Something to drink?"

"A little early, isn't it?"

"I don't judge. I pour."

Leigh liked this guy. "I'll have a Bud—draft."

"Coming up."

Leigh lit her cigarette, reached for a plastic black ashtray, cozied her bottom into the stool. When the beer appeared in front of her, cold and frothy, she felt the palmetto bugs in her head skitter into a corner.

Leigh raised the beer mug, and her hand shook. She was coming down from the last of the black beauties, and unless she scored pretty soon, things were going to get ugly. She should have taken Miguel's pills instead of money. That would have been the smart thing, but when did Leigh ever do the smart thing? Annie was the smart one, and Ed had never let Leigh forget it. "Too much trash in your head," he once said. "No room for smarts, is that it?" Yeah, Dad, that was it. Too much trash, and not enough trash.

She couldn't believe Ed's timing. Why hadn't he lived for one more month, one more week? He had promised her money for rehab. She told him she could not kill on her own the thing crawling up her spine, could not sweep the bong water from her head. The beast had hold of her, and she had begged Ed to help her slay it before it tore her apart. If Ed had kept his promise, she wouldn't have had to steal Miguel's clip, wouldn't be in a town she hated hiding from a man she feared. She wouldn't have to keep the secret from her sister, too ashamed to admit she swallowed things that had teeth so sharp her life leaked from a million tiny holes she couldn't plug. Annie would look at her with Ed's disappointed eyes, and Leigh wouldn't be able to bear it. No, Annie must never find out. She was the only family Leigh had left. If she turned her back on Leigh, no twelve-step program could fill that void. And who was responsible for this whole, stinking predicament? Ed's murderer girlfriend! Well, Della Shiftlet would pay for this crime. Leigh's life depended on it. She pinched the bridge of her nose. Oh, what she wouldn't give for a Percodan.

Leigh asked the bartender his name.

"Robert. Yours?"

"Leigh." They nodded at each other, nicetomeetcha. "You go to school at Stetson?" Stetson kids rode the Gainesville drug train. Maybe he had something or knew how to get it.

"Not anymore."

"I don't suppose you know where I can score some . . ." She looked around as if someone could hear. ". . . You know."

" 'Fraid not."

The curt answer threw Leigh. "You sure?"

"Do you want to pay for that now? I have things to do in the back."

Oh Jesus, thought Leigh. A fucking health freak. "I thought you didn't judge."

"It's eighty cents."

"Run me a tab."

The bartender returned to the backroom.

Little did Annie know how wrong she was about Leigh drinking too much. Alcohol, never her drug of choice, was mere chaser to the stuff she really craved, but when the pickings were slim, a liquid high filled the hole. Twice arrested for DUI, she spent ten boredom-soaked days in a filthy city jail for the last one. The court also ordered abstinence from drugs and alcohol, that she attend AA meetings twice a week, group treatment (where she met Miguel), and a drivers' education course, all of which she regarded as an expensive, colossal waste of time. She'd come up dirty on her last urine test, and twice had driven to Florida on a restricted license, further violation of her court order. If caught, she was looking at serious jail time.

You see, Ed? You see how you left me?

The front door opened, a blinding announcement. Eugene stepped forward, blinking. Seeing Leigh in a celestial shaft of light, he slowly approached, awestruck.

"Hi, honey," Leigh said. "You want another dollar?"

"Haaar." Eugene lifted a hand, then withdrew it suddenly. He looked at Leigh, as if fearing reproach.

"You want to touch my hair?"

Eugene nodded, clapped. His tongue worked busily. What, wondered Leigh, must it be like, to be inside his head? As a little kid, Eugene loved everyone, wanted to touch, hug, hold. As an adult, his body had continued to mature while his mind had not, and the effect was far less cuddly. If Leigh let him touch her hair, would that lead down a path she didn't want to go?

When the door opened again, Leigh checked. Two figures stood in silhouette, both too thin to be Miguel.

"Haaar."

Leigh turned back to him. "Okay, but don't pull it."

Eugene gently stroked Leigh's hair. He looked at her, seeking approval. "Keee."

Leigh smiled. "That's right, just like a kitty." Really, the kid was sweet. Leigh envied his gentle nature; there was nothing innocent or gentle about her life now. Staring at Eugene's enraptured face, it occurred to Leigh that this might be as close as she would ever come to making someone happy. She closed her eyes, swallowed deep in her throat, lungs laboring for air. Someone had to sell uppers in this stupid excuse for a town. All she had to do was find him, and fast.

Eugene fixated on Leigh's curls, which spiraled like smoke. "Faaa," he said with reverence.

"Sorry, big fella, you lost me there."

Behind Leigh, a man spoke. "He said, fire."

Leigh's heart skipped. Her first instinct was run, but Eugene had a grip on her hair, and she wasn't prepared to drag him. Damn it! She looked over her shoulder.

Pete Duncan cocked his head. "Looking for me?"

CHAPTER 16

Finneran's Funeral Home occupied a Georgian building on New York Avenue. In 1928, Hulburt M. Finneran purchased and meticulously renovated the building to accommodate the special requirements of the family business. The polished and gleaming result, not unlike Mr. Hulburt M. Finneran III, was stately, formal and somber.

Annie paused at a coffin lined with ivory satin, the same fabric as her wedding dress. Indulging a macabre fantasy, she imagined herself in pearls and tulle, lying inside, eyes closed, expression serene. She looked at the price tag, and a sharp laugh escaped, scuttled beneath a row of waxed caskets smelling of lemon oil.

"That is our deluxe model," Mr. Finneran said. "Guaranteed twenty years."

Who would dig up a coffin to challenge such a guarantee? Annie wondered.

Mr. Finneran conducted his sales pitch from a don't-crowd-me distance. In gray suit and spit-shined shoes, the thin, middle-aged man looked every inch the dignified funeral director. Annie felt self-conscious in her cotton sundress and sandals. This was her first visit to a funeral home; had she known it was a dress-up occasion, she would have respectfully complied.

"Is this your family's business?" Annie asked, uncomfortable in this Room O' Caskets.

Mr. Finneran tilted his head to a forty-five degree angle, nodded. "My grandfather started it." He allowed a small, proud smile to crack his serious face.

"Oh, really? That's so interesting."

Where the hell was Leigh? She was supposed to help with this. When she hadn't come back from the bathroom, Annie had investigated, but couldn't find her. After over-tipping Sada, Annie made a quick exit. "Come back and see me!" Florida hollered behind her.

Annie turned to Mr. Finneran. "Could I have a moment or two alone? I had no idea how much this would cost, and I'm a little overwhelmed by all this."

"Of course. Would you mind if I assisted another couple in the meantime?"

"Not at all. Go right ahead."

Mr. Finneran gave a slight bow and withdrew.

"You're not actually considering a casket, are you?"

Annie turned. Helen strolled about the showroom, looking into each coffin as if expecting to come across someone she knew. She wore her white uniform, as always, and her hair rested in a loose bun at the base of her white neck.

"Why not?"

"Come, Annie, you can't afford a wedding and a funeral. Just cremate him. It's cheaper."

"I'm not sure if that's what Dad wanted."

"How would you know what he wanted? Besides, what does it matter? He's dead. Be practical, Annie."

"Cremation seems a little . . . I don't know . . . cheap, or something."

"I thought you were all about cheap."

"I was. I mean, I am. It's just that, maybe Dad deserves better."

"We all deserve better than death, but that's what we get. I hear you paid your father a visit."

Annie sat in a velvet chair the color of blood. The chair's back and legs were elaborately carved; the balled feet had toenails. "And you've come to give me a hard time about it, is that it?"

"You tell me."

"I don't know, Mom. I'm beginning to think it was a mistake, ignoring him all those years. Now he's dead, and I'll never see him again."

"Would you rather never see me again?"

Annie cringed, suddenly nine years old again and afraid of being alone. "No. Please don't leave me."

Behind Annie, the paneled wall split. Each side rumbled away from center, disappearing inside opposite walls. Annie jumped to her feet.

"Have you made a decision, Miss Bartlett?" asked Mr. Finneran.

She wanted the mahogany casket with satin lining the color of lake water at sunset. She could find a way to afford it, even if it meant a smaller wedding or civil ceremony with a justice of the peace. It would be nice if Leigh coughed up a share of the expense, but Leigh owed money in seventeen states. Leigh was not a well she could go to. Nor would she ask Camp. Alimony and child support had stretched him tight. He would offer, of course, but she would not allow it. No, this funeral was her responsibility.

She looked at the price tag on the mahogany coffin, sighed.

"May I say something?" asked Mr. Finneran.

"Of course."

"A lasting monument doesn't have to be expensive. Your father knows you love him."

Annie noted the use of present tense and looked at him. "Did you know my father?"

Mr. Finneran nodded. "Your father spent a lot of money on

your mother's funeral. I thought he would default, but he didn't. It took a while, but he paid every penny he owed, and it wasn't easy for him, as you probably know."

"Actually, I'm starting to feel guilty about how little I know."

"Will bankrupting yourself erase that guilt?"

"No."

Mr. Finneran leaned in, whispered conspiratorially. "Now, I'm not telling you what to do. Lord knows I'd love to sell you that casket, if that's what you want. I'm only suggesting there are many ways to honor a memory. Think about it creatively, and I'm sure you'll come up with something appropriate to celebrate your father's life."

"I don't see much to celebrate."

"Perhaps you should look again," said Mr. Finneran.

CHAPTER 17

When Annie was a third grader at St. John's, a thin-haired man in plaid pants and no shirt was rumored to have hung himself at the Sha-D-Land Motel. For two hours, his body dangled from a window in full view of passing traffic before police pulled him inside. Annie might have dismissed the story as the woven stuff of mischievous babysitters if not for the single, bizarre detail of the plaid pants. In her mind, they were the same plaid as her school uniform, red and navy blue. She could see the zipper's metal teeth, exposed by an improperly pressed fly. The pants hung low on the dead man's slender hips, slightly flared legs brushing the tops of scuffed, unlaced shoes. Toes pointed, mere inches from the ground.

Annie unlocked room number nine. She would be glad to leave this place in the morning. Memories like the man in the plaid pants were occupying too much space in her head. She pushed the door. Sunlight assaulted the dark room. Annie heard a muffled laugh and the rustle of sheets.

"Do you mind shutting the door?" came a male voice. Annie looked, straining. Leigh lay in bed with a stranger whose arm visored against the sun. "Seriously. I can see right through your dress."

Annie closed the door.

Leigh came into focus. "This is my sister, Annie. Annie, this is—" Leigh turned to the man next to her.

"Bill."

"This is Bill."

Bill extended a hand over the bed. "Pleased to meet you," he said with a hearty smile. From neck to waist, Bill looked like a fellow who liked to work out; from the neck up, he looked like a fellow who liked to drink. In fact, he looked like a fellow who had enjoyed a few quite recently.

Annie nodded at Bill's proffered hand. "You'll forgive me if I don't shake that."

Leigh nudged Bill with a foot. "Pass me my cigarettes, won't you, darlin'?"

Bill rolled to his stomach, felt the floor beneath the bed, came up with the pack. When he sat up, his eyes lost focus. "Whoa," he said. "Blood rush."

"Bill, here, is an appraiser," said Leigh.

"That's some place you and your sister have out there at Widow Lake," Bill said. "I used to trap gators over there to Lake Talmedge. Don't tell anyone, though."

Annie looked at Leigh.

"Bill has agreed to appraise the house for us."

"Oh, really?"

"Like I was saying to Leigh, it's a perfect time to sell. There's plenty of development going on over there."

Leigh nodded at Annie. "What'd I tell you?"

"Get out," said Annie.

Bill looked at Leigh, unsure which of them Annie was talking to.

Leigh exhaled a stream of smoke. "Oh, for Christ's sake, Annie."

"Put your pants on, and get out." Annie pinched Bill's pants from the floor, pinkie extended, and tossed them on the bed. Grasping now that he was the addressed party, Bill scooted agreeably into action. "I got to get going, anyway," he said, and wrestled with the tangled pants, managed to get his legs inside the proper holes. Facing the wall, he stood, pulled his pants up and over his white rear end.

"Pass me that ashtray, hon." Bill zipped as he fetched, glancing at Annie to gauge his progress against her tolerance level. He shrugged into a T-shirt, which left him momentarily off balance, then leaned over the bed. After a quick puff, Leigh obliged with a smack on the lips.

"I'll call you tomorrow." Bill stepped into ratty Nikes, then saluted Annie. "Always nice to meet the family." Annie opened the door. "Y'all have a good day." Bill waved, staggered into sunlight, and was gone.

Leigh's foot jiggled. "Nice guy, huh?"

Annie tossed her purse into a chair. "What are you doing?"

"What does it look like I'm doing? I'm smoking a cigarette. Did you make the funeral arrangements?" Leigh picked a pat of tobacco from the tip of her tongue.

"There's not going to be a funeral."

"How come?"

"Because I can't afford it, Leigh, and I don't see any help coming from you."

"Don't make me sound like a parasite, Annie. I bought you lunch and paid for half this room."

"Did you pay that guy to appraise the house?"

"In a manner of speaking."

"Oh, so you're a prostitute now, is that it?"

Leigh flung covers. "Screw you." She bounced out of bed toward the bathroom.

"The house belongs to Della, Leigh."

"Not for long!" She slammed the door.

The sound of Mrs. Voorhis's television suddenly burst through the wall. Annie rapped on the bathroom door. "I want to talk to you."

"Too bad."

Annie gave up and snatched clothes from the floor, bed and furniture. A black film canister, its contents rattling, fell to the floor. Annie retrieved the canister and opened it. It was full of small white pills, and Annie knew instinctively they had come from Bill. Annie beat on the bathroom door.

"Leigh, are you taking drugs?"

"I'm not talking to you."

Shoulder against the bathroom door, Annie rattled off the evidence. "You don't eat, you chain smoke, and I suspect you're stealing. Where did you get that big wad of cash?"

"None of your goddamn business!"

"And another thing! If you want to sleep with strange men in exchange for drugs, do it somewhere else. I don't want to watch you degrading yourself."

Leigh opened the door. Clutching a towel wrapped beneath her arms, she sneered. "You crack me up, you know that? You're all over my shit, but do you ever aim that razor-sharp insight at yourself?"

"I'm not the self-destructive one, here."

"Oh, that's good, coming from you. You want to talk about self-destructive? What about your psycho relationship with a dead woman? What do you call that?"

Annie, feeling impaled, waited for Leigh's expression to soften, the knifing words to dislodge themselves from her chest. For years, Leigh had fought like this with Ed. How ugly they had been, bent at the waist and screeching, calling each other names they could never take back. In the end, both hearts lay shredded.

"We can't do this," Annie whispered.

"Well, we're doing it."

For a brief moment, Annie didn't recognize her sister, chin lowered, muscles rigid, a hard, black shine in her eyes. A wall descended, and Annie moved back to keep from being crushed.

CHAPTER 18

The phone booth smelled like peanut butter.

"Camp?"

"Hey, sweetheart. I was just thinking about you."

"I miss you, too," said Annie, then realized Camp hadn't said he missed her first. "I mean, how are you?"

"I'm fine, Annie, but I'm worried about you. How's everything going down there?"

"Not too well. In fact, I'm coming home tomorrow. Can you pick me up at the airport?"

"Of course. What's happened, Annie? You sound upset."

Across the street, the bell on the front door of The Pier Diner tinkled.

"Leigh and I had a fight."

Annie recounted the details of the fight, minus one. She didn't tell her fiancé about Leigh's last, stabbing remark. She wanted to, but was afraid. Who would marry a woman who, as Leigh had so succinctly put it, had a psycho relationship with a dead woman?

"Anyway. I didn't mean to dump all over you."

"You can dump on me anytime you want. That's what I'm here for."

Annie sighed. "You are the most amazing man."

"I know."

Annie smiled, feeling better. She should take lessons from Camp, who listened with compassion, withheld judgment. She knew, suddenly, that she could trust him to listen compassionately as she explained about Helen, how she knew her mother was dead, that these "visits" were left over from childhood, and no more significant than if Annie still sucked her thumb from time to time. He would understand that. He would still love her.

"When's the funeral?" Camp asked.

"I made an executive decision. No funeral."

"Why did you do that?"

"It's complicated, but I was thinking, maybe there's a way to incorporate a wedding celebration and a memorial service into the same ceremony. Maybe the memorial part is as simple as a moment of silence, or I don't know, lighting candles, or something like that. What do you think? Does that sound too bizarre?"

"Um . . ."

"I mean, I want a wedding, Camp, I do. When I realized how much a funeral would cost, I thought about just getting hitched in the courthouse, but that doesn't feel right. I want to share our vows with the people we love, and who love us. If I could, I'd tell the world how much I love you. It sounds stupid, but Camp, I want to declare my love for you."

"Annie—"

"So let's not put ourselves through a lot of financial stress right off the bat. Let's just, I don't know, do this our own way, without letting all these complications trip us up. We can figure it out, I know we can." She pressed the phone tight against her ear. "Here it is, plain and simple: I love you, Camp, and I can't wait to be your wife."

She could hear room noise, but Camp was silent. After a moment, he said, "I love you, too."

"Camp?"

"Annie, I—" He stopped.

"What is it?"

In the short time it took for Camp to arrange his thoughts, Annie's imagination rode through a dark tunnel. She knew she was being stupid, but she closed her eyes anyway, and waited for sunlight.

"I think we need to postpone the wedding."

The tunnel stretched, black as ink. Annie's chest filled with heat. "Why?"

She heard Camp rearrange himself. She could see his chair as if in the same room. He'd made it himself, from a black locust tree that had fallen on his land during a bad storm. The chair's arms were gnarled, curled in primitive yet elegant loops which made Annie think of Middle Earth.

"It's Kirsten," said Camp.

Annie wished she could sit. "Go on."

"It's just that—she's really not taking this well, Annie."

"Taking what well?"

"The fact that her father has a girlfriend."

"You mean fiancée."

Camp's mouth was dry. Annie could hear the telltale noises through the phone. "She's upset, Annie. She seems to think everything is going to be different for her."

"She's right. It's going to be very different."

"Right, I know, but Dee Dee—see, instead of helping Kirsten through this, is being—well—"

"A bitch?"

Camp laughed uneasily. "Well, yeah."

It was uncharacteristic of Annie to speak this way about Dee Dee. Usually, she let Camp do the disparaging, stayed outside the he-said/she-said imbroglios. It was beyond difficult, having no say, yet remaining vulnerable to Camp's ex-wife and daughter. Annie felt most helpless against Kirsten, who was free to flex her own power, grind into the core of Annie's life.

"Believe me, it's not that I don't want to get married," said Camp. "I do. You know I do. But with Kirsten so upset, and Dee Dee encouraging her insecurities just to punish me, I don't see how I can. Get married. Right now, I mean."

"Camp, you're letting Kirsten manipulate you."

"Wait, now, that's not entirely fair. Kirsten's feelings are valid. She's scared and threatened. She thinks I'm ruining her life, and her mother's life."

"God." Annie dropped her face into a hand.

"Can you be patient for me, Annie? Just until we get through this?"

"I want to get married, Camp."

"Oh, sweetheart, so do I! And we will, I promise. Just . . . not now."

She wanted to say, when, then? But did it matter? Wouldn't Kirsten detonate another well-placed temper bomb a couple weeks before that date, too?

"I've sent invitations, Camp. People have RSVP-ed. The wheels are in motion."

"I know, and I'll take care of that. You won't have to do a thing."

"That wasn't my point."

"I know it wasn't. I'm sorry. I'm just trying to . . . to . . ."

"Cancel our wedding."

"No, Annie. Not cancel. Postpone. I realize I'm making a mess, but I don't see how I have any other choice. Kirsten is so upset right now. Just give me some time to help her over this, okay? Please?"

She pushed the door. Air, thick with cooking oil, entered.

"I love you, Annie. I want to live with you for the rest of my life."

"Live with me? Or marry me?"

"Try to put yourself in her shoes, can't you?"

"Sure," Annie said, voice dead.

"Are we okay, then?"

Annie drifted. They were plaid pants. The man who hung himself had worn plaid pants, blue and red, like her school uniform.

"Annie?"

The toes of his black shoes pointed down, sock exposed, knees turned in.

"Annie, are you there?"

He'd worn plaid, Annie decided, because he hated plaid, and thought these the perfect pants to die in.

"Annie?"

"I'll talk to you later, Camp."

"Please don't be mad."

Annie hung up the phone and cried.

He knew that poor, doomed guy, even as he pulled on those pants, that once buried in them, he would spare others the sight of their artificially hopeful weave.

Chapter 19

Miguel could almost smell her. She was near, and he would find her. It was just a matter of time. *Nobody steals from Miguel Vedra and gets away with it. Nobody.*

Miguel threw several bills on the diner's counter, washed down the last of his coffee. He tipped his waitress—a skanky little piece named Marlene—two cents, exactly what she was worth. When Miguel asked Marlene if she knew Leigh Bartlett, she said no, but Miguel didn't believe her. He then asked if she knew anything about the Bartlett murder, but might as well have been talking to the wall. Maybe two cents was too much.

Miguel had driven his black El Dorado to the Bartlett place in search of Leigh. The house and yard were enclosed in a yellow spiderweb of police tape. A couple police types milled around, but Miguel stayed out of sight. Too many questions, and someone might wonder why an out-of-towner with a tattoo on his forehead would have so much interest in a local matter.

Now, where could she be? he asked himself and zeroed in on the diner. He scanned the place as he headed for the door and caught the eye of a woman sitting alone in a booth, peering at him over her coffee cup. She wasn't bad looking, but she wasn't great looking, either, not like Leigh. Then again, few women measured up to Leigh. Miguel gave the woman a wink, but she either didn't catch it or ignored it. Miguel's spleen boiled. Worse than your garden-variety rubberneckers were women who pretended not to see him, like this yanker in the booth. Miguel took another look, wondered what she'd do if he sashayed over and slid opposite, if she'd stop stuffing her face long enough to look at him then.

Christ, Miguel, let it go, he said to himself. You got bigger fish to fry, eleven hundred fish, to be exact, in a snake-shaped money clip. Time to bait the hook.

Outside the diner, Miguel slipped a dime into the newspaper kiosk and pulled the door. The hinges made a sound that instantly placed him inside a jail cell. He shook that off, but not before liberating all the newspapers into a sidewalk trashcan. Information should be free, he thought, smiling. The kiosk's spring loaded-door snapped shut with a metallic whang. Miguel cringed, picked up a paper, opened it.

Very little about the murder. An article on page one, below the fold, lamenting DeLeon's loss of innocence, but nothing about the incident, specifically. Judging from the big headline, DeLeon had a serious firebug on the loose. Miguel's skin convulsed. A while back, his clothes had caught fire in a prison riot, and he recalled the heat, the panic, flames whip-snapping his face. No, sir, Miguel would rather be cut to ribbons with his own switchblade than die by fire, not that he intended to die anytime soon. Arson, he wasn't into; maybe the only thing he wasn't into. What kind of fucked-up whack job would purposely set buildings on fire?

"Daahl."

Miguel lowered the paper. Before him stood a retarded guy with simian arms, slanty chink eyes, and a wet, darting tongue.

"Dahl."

Miguel stared. "What's your name, Hoss?" He watched the retard's eyes light on him for an instant, then flit, restless as black bees. Eugene licked his lips, made a tee-pee of fingertips touching.

"Dahl."

A light came on in Miguel's head. He reached behind for his money. He remembered this kid, now. Sure, this was the same guy he'd seen in the diner the last time he was here, the town Pain in the Ass, a half-step up from Village Idiot. Maybe it was time the kid made himself useful.

"Your name is Eugene, right?" said Miguel, opening his wallet.

Eugene's eyes widened as Miguel withdrew a dollar bill. His feet shuffled in an awkward dance, head bobbed. He reached for the dollar.

"Hold on there, Hoss. You got to do something for me, first." Miguel pulled the dollar back.

Eugene stopped dancing. Slowly, his face changed to something that, until now, Miguel had seen only in prison. The extruded veins in Eugene's forehead, the vessels in his eyes, the skin on his plump cheeks all pulsed with hot, homicidal fury.

Miguel thrust the bill at Eugene. "All right, all right, take it then. No need to get your panties in a twist."

Eugene's rage drained as if Miguel had pulled a plug. He reached eagerly for the dollar.

"All right, then. You got your dollar. You happy, now?"

Eugene shoved the bill into a pocket and shouldered past Miguel, head down.

"Thaaak."

"You're welcome, but hang on." Miguel pulled out another bill. "How would you like to have this one?"

Eugene reached for the bill. This time, Miguel stepped to a safe distance should Eugene decide to lunge. "I gave you one already, Hoss. I'll give you this one, too, but not for free. I want you to tell me something."

"Dahl!"

"I know you want the dollar. And I'll give it to you, after you answer my question. I'm looking for somebody named Leigh.

Do you know Leigh?"

Eugene flapped his arms, brayed like the hairy Chewbacca in that Star Wars movie.

"That's right. You gonna earn it, ain't ya'?" Miguel waved the dollar, showed coffee-stained teeth.

Here, fishy, fishy, fishy.

CHAPTER 20

The mammoth pine, branches sagging with cones the size of cucumbers, scratched the sky. Annie craned her head, marveled at how much it had grown since last she was here. She wrapped her arms around its trunk, tried to touch fingertips, couldn't do it.

This had been "her" tree, and Annie had played with it as other girls played with dolls. She lashed Leigh to it with red and white cotton rope, danced around, whooping. Later, she sat beneath it and read every library volume of *The Happy Hollisters,* getting lost inside that large, convivial family of child detectives. At sixteen, she scraped a section of bark from its trunk, and with her father's hunting knife, carved the initials, AB+PD. The wound had healed somewhat in ten years, but the initials had not closed completely. She ran her fingers over them now, remembering.

Annie had heard it said that nothing compares to first love, and she believed it. Would she ever feel that reckless again? With Camp came safety, serenity, security, all well and good, but hardly corset-ripping. She smiled. Not that they lacked for corset-ripping moments. Annie had no complaints in that department.

Pressing against the pine's trunk, she stood on tiptoe and reached. Fingertips found the hole, which used to be at eye level, and gingerly explored. She pressed down the thought of a scaled or furry creature skittering over her hand. Beneath pine needles and moss, she touched the key, scooped it. Still here, after all these years.

Inside the house, the air smelled medicinal. A forensics team had come and gone, leaving signature detritus. Police tape littered the floor, lay snarled on cheap furniture. Fine, black dust from a fingerprint kit peppered the length of the kitchen counter. Annie dipped her index finger in the dust, rolled it on the countertop, lifted. A whorled imprint stayed behind.

A jolt ran through her. Should she even be here? Maybe that wasn't so smart, leaving this calling card. Annie looked for a dishrag, then settled on her shirttail. She spat on the imprint, rubbed until it disappeared.

Hands in pockets, Annie walked from room to room, and tried to relax. In places, the wallpaper hung in precarious curls where roaches and silver fish had eaten the glue. Trails of tiny holes swirled about the walls in the dizzy pattern of a diseased leaf.

In each room, Annie felt assaulted by evidence of her father's life; her own had been long swept away. A bottle from treasure hunting days, unearthed when Annie fell beneath Ed's spell, stood upright in the window above the kitchen sink, sunlight through amethyst glass. Ed's boots, caked with earth and dried fish slime, sagged in a corner. His fishing pole, the one Annie mangled in Key West when she was eleven, pointed at the acoustic tiled ceiling. Scattered like landmines: a pair of stained workpants, a Boy Scout knife, a pack of cigarettes. Each familiar object blew her back to another time, when Ed was alive and she, another person, had loved him.

An open desk drawer drew her. Inside, a jumble of paper and photos, recently riffled. Annie withdrew a cracked photo of Ed, one she had taken as a child outside Otis's Bar and Grill, on the edge of the St. Johns River. He had not wanted his picture taken, Annie remembered, and had raised a hand in protest, but the picture suggested "come here," rather than "don't," and his expression looked amused instead of annoyed. It was Ed, and it wasn't, a disconnect Annie knew all through childhood. She slid the picture into her back pocket.

A hand clapped Annie's shoulder. She screamed and swung around.

"Jesus!" Leigh yelped.

"Don't do that!" yelled Annie.

"You scared me!" Leigh's eyes zoomed in their sockets.

"Sorry." Annie placed a hand over her heart. "Why didn't I hear you drive up?"

"I parked down the road, didn't want to advertise I was here."

This was the second time Leigh had taken pains to park her car at a distance. "Advertise to whom?"

"Oh, I don't know. Police, I guess. I'm really not supposed to be driving. Jeez, this place gives me the creeps."

"It's a boogie stew, all right. What are you doing here?"

Leigh slid hands in the front pockets of clinging jeans, and shrugged. "I took a chance you might be here. I came to tell you I'm sorry, and that I'm going back to Atlanta."

"Why?"

"Why am I sorry?"

"No, why are you leaving?"

"If we're not going to have a funeral, I don't see any reason to stick around."

"What about the appraisal? I thought you were fired up about selling this place."

"I still am, but I can't do anything until after Della is convicted. Besides, I got places to be, people to see. Time's a'wastin'. Gotta go, gotta go."

Annie peered into her sister's eyes. Something was wrong. Leigh seemed jumpy, as she had in the diner. Annie didn't want to believe her worst fear, that her sister was not only using again, but addicted and in trouble. That might somehow explain this sudden departure, which didn't make sense. Then again, nothing about this trip made sense: Ed's murder, Della's claim of innocence, Camp's postponing the wedding. Where was the logic in any of it?

"What about you? When will you go home to that fiancé of yours? What's his name? Scamp?"

Annie didn't smile at Leigh's intentional blooper. "I don't know. Sometime. Later. Never."

Leigh's eyebrows rose. "Something wrong?"

As she replayed in her head the last conversation with Camp, Annie's breathing turned shallow. "Can we go outside? It smells like death in here."

Widow Lake, still as a mirror, reflected smoke from a not-too-distant fire, which seemed to burn a slow but perpetual path toward them. The lake was obscenely beautiful. Annie's mother had drowned in this black womb, her father had been murdered at its shore. Here also, Annie had learned to swim, and beneath its surface, kissed Petey Duncan for the first time. The lake had been solace, refuge, companion, and for its trouble, had taken her innocence.

Leigh side-armed a flat rock over the surface, and the dark mirror shattered in three places, twenty-one years bad luck.

"See if you can beat that."

Annie picked up a rock, wrapped her index finger around its perimeter, drew back and snapped her wrist. The rock hit the water heavily, but managed to skip once before disappearing, another swallowed victim.

"I win!" said Leigh.

Instead of redeeming herself, Annie sat on the grass. A short distance away, Ed's rowboat lay upside down in the sand. Leigh threw one more rock, then sat, wrists rested on knees.

"I wouldn't worry about Camp, Annie. He'll probably call back tonight and put everything back the way it was."

Can he? Annie wondered.

"Maybe you should cut him a break. It must be hard for the daughter—what's her name?"

"Kirsten."

"Ew."

"I know."

"It must be hard for Kirsten to like the idea of her father's girlfriend becoming her stepmother. Look how hard it was for us to adjust."

"Oh, did we adjust? I missed that."

Leigh threw back her head and laughed. To Annie, it was a wonderful sound. In the late morning sun, Leigh's curls were flaxen, nose already pinking, and Annie thought her beautiful again. She was sorry Leigh was leaving so soon. With this thought came an image of a helium balloon floating off, dangling string out of reach, destination unknown.

"God, do you remember Lucy?" Leigh asked. "The barfly? She used to hang out with Dad at Otis's. Skinny legs, teased hair? What a lush. I wonder if she's still around."

"Probably. Seems like the whole town's still around."

"The thing about ol' Ed," said Leigh in the voice of an Ed expert, "he went through girlfriends like socks. Seemed like there was a new one every Sunday morning, hogging the bathroom. What the hell did they see in him?"

Annie thought for a moment. "Themselves."

"Thank God he didn't marry any of them."

Annie wanted to ask why Leigh was glad about that, then stopped herself. If related to their inheritance, she wasn't in the mood to rehash it.

"What's that?" asked Leigh, pointing. "On that tree." Leigh stood, walked to Annie's tree, peered at the initials carved in its trunk. "Wow. You really had it bad for the Pete-ster, didn't you?"

"When I gouged those initials into Dad's boat, he switched the back of my legs and made me clean fish for a week."

"Sounds like him."

"That didn't stop me, though. I carved tables, baseboards, doors. It's a wonder I didn't cut it into my own flesh. Boy, Dad was angry."

"Dad was always angry. Glad I wasn't there."

How Annie wished Leigh had been there. Together, they might have warded off his insults, or worse, his obliviousness. But Leigh left, and Annie lived with Ed for four more years until she saved enough money to light out herself. She often wondered how long it took Ed to notice she was gone.

"Was he as bad as I remember?" Annie asked.

Leigh looked away. "Probably not."

Annie stared anew at Ed's rowboat. Something gnawed at her. What was it?

"I have to get back," Leigh said. "You want a ride?"

"Leigh, do you see anything strange about the boat?"

"Besides the fact he died in it?"

Maybe that was it. Anybody would get weird vibes, looking at the place their father was murdered.

Leigh squinted at the horizon. "I hope she fries. Come on, let's go."

Annie stood, took one last look at the rowboat. "Can you drive me to the sheriff's office on your way out of town?"

"Sure. Why?"

Annie turned her back on the rowboat, walked briskly toward the road. "I want to see the murder weapon."

"What for?"

"I'm not sure."

"You're a goon girl, you know that?"

"Takes one to know one."

CHAPTER 21

The evidence room, devoid of aesthetics, smelled of dirty hairbrushes. A burly officer with a salt-and-pepper beard emerged from the labyrinth of gray industrial shelving. In both hands, he cradled an oar. At the base of the oar's shaft an evidence tag hung from a noose. Annie straightened, and the clerk placed the oar onto the counter.

"Thanks, Rocky," Salceda said.

Annie looked at the oar that had killed her father, as familiar to her as her own arm. "Can I touch it?" she asked Salceda.

"Sure. The lab's through with it. You can't take it out of here, though."

It was Ed's oar, all right. No mistaking it. She had held it a million times, although never with Ed's image so brightly seared in her mind, face flashing from smiling to bludgeoned. Annie rolled the oar in her hands, fingered its flat, worn surfaces, held it to her nose. The smell of mud flash-popped a memory picture: scooped minnows in a tin can. She ran a palm down its length, then set it on the counter. "Thank you." She gave Rocky an appreciative smile.

"Sure thing."

Deputy Salceda nodded to Rocky that she was through with the oar, turned back to Annie. "Do you have any questions?"

"Just one."

"What's that?"

Annie paused. "Where's the other one?"

"The other—?"

"Oar."

Salceda blinked, looked at Rocky. "Not in the book," he shrugged. "One oar. Tagged. This here's it."

"The other one is not with the rowboat," said Annie. "I checked."

"If it's not evidence, it wouldn't be in here," said Salceda.

"I guess not." Annie thrust a hand at the deputy, then said sincerely, "You've been really nice to me, and I appreciate that very much. If I can ever return your kindness, I'd consider it an honor."

Salceda gave Annie's hand a firm shake. "Forget it. Just doing my job."

"Can I use the phone?"

"Sure. Right over there. Just dial nine first."

Pete answered on the second ring.

"I'm hungry," said Annie. "Feel like feeding me?"

"Leigh?"

Thrown, Annie hesitated. "No, it's me, Annie."

There was a pause, then Pete said, "I was just kidding. Sure, I feel like feeding you. Where are you?"

"In the evidence room."

"What are you doing there?"

"Looking for evidence."

"Hey, that's my job."

Then why aren't you doing it?

"I'll pick you up in fifteen. That good?"

"Sure."

By the time Pete and Annie arrived, the Country Club's lunch crowd had thinned, freeing tables overlooking the St. Johns River. Annie could scarcely believe she'd never been inside these hallowed walls, a far cry from The Pier Diner. Pete had stopped by the motel so she could change and grab her camera. Her tan cotton slacks and crisp linen shirt made her feel appropriately Floridian. The tortoise shell clip, a gift from Camp, held her dark hair at the base of her neck. A slender young woman neatly poured into a white silk blouse and black skirt approached. Her pencil-straight blond hair stopped just above her waist.

"Hello, Mr. Duncan," she said with a sultry smile.

"How are you, Denise?"

"Fine, thanks. Table for two?"

Annie, aware of Pete's hand on her lower back, followed Denise to a two-top by the window. She scanned the diners, recognized Judge Lanier sitting with a man whose pink complexion made him look freshly steamed. The judge caught Annie's eye, stopped mid-sentence to take her in. Annie nodded, not sure if the judge remembered her.

Denise led them to a table by a window. Enchanted with the view, Annie pulled a chair, sat, and had removed her camera from its leather case before realizing Pete was eyeing the picnic tables on the dock.

"What do you say, Annie? In here with the stuffed crabs, or outside, with the sea and the air?"

"Lead the way, Mr. Duncan."

The dock had been built to accommodate a thick, Carolina oak, rising from its center. The crotch was low and ample, an excellent climbing tree that would have been irresistible to Annie as a child. Meandering branches swathed with Spanish moss dipped over the water. How tempting to scoot to the end of a waist-thick branch, and, with an Indian battle cry, hurtle into the river below.

Annie swung a leg and settled herself at the redwood picnic table. The water was blinding, as if its gilled occupants worked tiny mirrors above the surface to reflect the sun. Annie sniffed the air, testing for smoke. Nothing.

"How's this?" Pete asked behind sunglasses. "Not too hot?"

"Oh, no. It's nice."

Denise arrived with menus. "Wow. You two are diehards. I can't live without air conditioning, myself."

"You get used to it. You must be a northerner."

Denise opened a menu, handed it to Pete. "In fact, I was born just down the road, in Oveido, and nobody gets used to it. You just run out of people to complain to. That's why I like working here." She handed Annie a menu. "Fresh blood."

Pete gave an appreciative little laugh. Annie wondered if she'd just been insulted.

"Philip will be your waiter. Nice to see you again, Mr. Duncan."

"You take care."

Annie scanned her menu, watched Denise disappear into the air conditioning. Chanel No. 5 lingered in the humid air.

"Nice to see you, Mr. Duncan," Annie mocked.

"Now, now, mustn't be jealous."

"Who said I was jealous? She was practically in your lap. Hardly becoming to a man such as yourself."

"Really? And what kind of man might that be?"

"I haven't decided yet."

"Chicken."

"I am not chicken. I just think you're fishing for a compliment, and I'm not taking the bait."

Pete peered over his sunglasses. "No," he said, tapping the menu. "I mean, chicken, as in 'I'm having the chicken.' "

"Oh. I knew that."

Philip came to the table with water, made obligatory remarks about heat and humidity, and took their orders. When he was gone, Annie said, "Is Judge Lanier the reason we're sitting out here? I saw her inside, and noticed you gave her a wide berth."

"Yeah, well. I'm on my lunch break. I don't want to talk shop."

Annie filled her lungs with river air. This was the smell of Florida: salt mixed with algae, Earth's seminal fluids, the pungent bouquet of creation itself. Nearby, alligators snorted courtship songs in lily pads and reeds.

Pete followed her gaze. "Incredible, isn't it? It's all private property, though. One of these days . . ." Pete drew a finger across his throat, made a gagging sound. The gesture chilled Annie. It was unthinkable this natural beauty would be gouged from existence.

"Speaking of private property," Annie said. "I met Kingfisher Powell yesterday. I saw him again at the diner this morning. He's connected to Della's case, isn't he?"

"Who told you that?"

"She did."

Pete leaned back. "Yeah, I heard you two had a little chat." He cleared his throat, as if holding back a reprimand. "Kingfisher Powell is Council Chairman for the Seminole Tribe."

"Meaning?"

"He's the big swinging dick."

"How vivid."

"He opened the first casino on the reservation a couple of years ago and is overseeing the development of several more. He makes a lot of money for the Tribe."

"Is that what burned down, a casino?" Annie asked.

"No, no. Casinos are legal only on the reservation. His latest project is a housing development. That's what burned down— one of his houses."

"How does a housing development benefit Seminoles?"

"It doesn't, that I know of," said Pete. "I think this one just benefits King."

"Why is somebody burning down his houses?"

"Nobody knows," said Pete. "And no, he is not connected to Ed's murder. Della just thinks he is."

"She says he's setting her up, that he wants my father's property."

"If Kingfisher Powell wanted your father's property, he'd have it by now. And there are easier ways of getting it than murder."

"Like what?"

"Like buying it outright. The guy's made of money."

"He tried that. Didn't work."

Pete opened his hands. "King has nothing to do with Ed's murder, Annie. Della is desperate, just pointing fingers, that's all."

"So you're convinced she did it."

"I am Della's defense attorney. It is my job to get her the best deal I can."

"But isn't it also your job to prove her innocence?"

"No, it's the State's Attorney's job to prove her guilty. And if we go to trial, he'll more than likely succeed."

"What if she didn't do it?"

"I'm sorry, Annie. I can't discuss this case with you any further."

"Do you realize there's an oar missing?"

"A what?"

"An oar. The murder weapon is tagged, but where's the other oar?"

"What does it matter?"

"I don't know if it matters, it just seems strange. Doesn't it seem strange to you?"

"We have to change the subject, Annie."

"Why?"

"Confidentiality."

"But, Pete—"

"Enough."

Annie strained against Pete's abrupt cut-off. If she pushed, he would shut her out and ruin their lunch. Better to respect his wishes. For now.

Annie leaned on the table and held her elbows. Herons high-stepped in shallow brine. Dragonflies hovered an inch above the water, dipping the tips of their abdomens as if to cool them. "I'm glad we came out here."

"Yeah. I like it, too. Peaceful." Pete's voice contained a note of conciliation. He would not brood, it said. Everything was okay.

Pete's chicken looked delicious, and Annie secretly wished she had ordered it as well. Her Caesar salad was crisp and nicely dressed, but she had ordered it only because it was the only thing under ten dollars, a fortune to spend on lunch in Annie's book. Then again, Pete could afford it, so why was she depriving herself?

"Are you going to eat the rest of that?" Annie nodded at Pete's plate.

"You want my scraps?"

"I live for your scraps."

"Have at them, woman."

Annie helped herself, enjoying this intimacy. In high school she was always pinching his food. That he had kept his good humor after all these years felt warm, cozy, and God knew, Annie hadn't had much warm or cozy in the last few days. She sighed, content.

Pete smiled, regarding her. "You look good, Annie."

"As good as Leigh?" Annie stopped chewing. "Gee, I wonder what I meant by that? Where's Freud when you need him?"

"Dead."

"Right. Oh well." Annie pushed Pete's plate away. "I think I just spoiled my own appetite."

"Alert the media."

"Do they serve ice cream here?"

"I was messing with you on the phone when I called you Leigh."

"I've forgotten all about it."

"I was kidding, Annie. I knew it was you."

"Nuts."

"No, really. I was expecting your call."

Now Annie peered down her nose. "No, I meant nuts, as in 'I'd like nuts on my ice cream.' "

In the plump seconds it took for Pete's smile to reach full wattage, Annie felt a warm wave roll though. She felt pretty, and witty, and bright, and would embrace the cliché for however long the feeling lasted.

Annie raised her arm, signaled to Philip. "Let's have champagne. What do you say?"

"You go ahead. I still have work to do."

"Oh, come on, Pete. One glass."

Pete put up a palm. "Sorry."

Philip arrived at the table. In his best James Bond voice, Pete said, "The lady will have a glass of champagne."

"No, no—not if you're not going to have one," Annie protested.

"No, go ahead." Pete nodded at Philip.

Annie addressed the waiter. "Tell you what. Bring me ice cream instead. Chocolate. Two spoons."

"And nuts," said Pete.

Philip gathered their plates, then swept himself away. Annie lifted her camera into her lap. "Do you mind if I step away for a minute and take some pictures?"

"Of course not. Don't fall in."

The flip warning rang a distant bell. Ed said that to her all the time, only it was not a joke. Around water since birth, Annie thought her name was Don't Fall In until age four.

Annie's camera framed a half-tropical forest shadowing the low shore. The river carried a perfume of cypress, myrtle and magnolia, flowed into fingers harboring egrets, ducks and whooping cranes. She zoomed on a bald eagle, gliding atop a thermal pocket. The eagle suddenly flattened its wings against its body, swooped, then rose again, a rodent squirming in its beak. As it flapped to a distant stand of trees, no doubt to feed the chicks, Annie marveled at the beauty, grace and uncompromising instincts of this impressive bird of prey.

"Excuse me."

Annie turned. Judge Lanier stood, squinting up at her.

"So sorry to disturb you, but I know you, don't I?"

"Yes, ma'am. I'm Annie Bartlett."

The judge's face lit with recognition. "Of course. I was very sorry to hear about your father. Please allow me to offer my condolences."

"Thank you."

Annie found herself trying to guess the judge's age—bright, alert eyes, high cheekbones, discreetly applied make-up. Auburn hair, swinging to her jaw, was streaked from the sun. She dressed simply, but smartly, in lightweight cotton pants and a loose button-down shirt that skimmed her hips. Her small frame stood ramrod straight. It seemed unreal that this was Eugene's mother. The contrasts between mother and son, physical and otherwise, were stark. She was what, fifty-five? Sixty-five?

"You must forgive me for interrupting your work."

"Oh, no, that's all right. Would you like to sit down with us?" Annie looked at Pete who watched behind sunglasses.

"No, no, I've intruded enough. So lovely to see you, although I wish your visit could have been under less painful circumstances." Annie lowered her eyes in silent acknowledgement. "And congratulations on your photography career. You've made us all very proud."

"I'm afraid it's not much of a career yet."

"Nonsense. I've seen your photos in magazines. You're very good."

The compliment pleased Annie. She had not realized anyone outside her small circle knew her work. "Thank you."

"You must get your talent from your father."

What a strange remark, thought Annie. Ed was never into photography; in fact, he groused about Annie's hobby all the time. On her thirteenth birthday, her new stepmother had bought Annie her first camera, an Instamatic with pop-on flashcubes that, immediately after firing, were irresistibly pliable. Even though it burned, Annie loved finger crushing the cube once the last bulb was spent, and shot picture after picture to bring on this pleasure. Ed had not been so amused. After tolerating Annie's frenetic picture-taking for a few days, he announced, "Enough with the camera," and placed his own gift into her adolescent hands—a .33 rifle. Annie went deer hunting the next morning, had hated it, and never looked at the rifle again. The camera, on the other hand, became a part of her.

"I need to get out of this sun," said the judge. "We must go fishing sometime, do some catching up."

"Yes, ma'am. I'd like that."

"How long will you be in town?"

Pete was suddenly at Annie's side. "She's heading back to Michigan soon," he said.

"Actually," said Annie, "I'm thinking about staying for the trial."

The judge cocked an eyebrow. "Trial?"

"Della Shiftlet's trial," Annie said.

Judge Lanier looked at Pete, eyes flashing, face pinched. This is how she must look in the courtroom, Annie thought. It was a look Annie would not want directed at her.

Pete shook his head. "Annie means arraignment."

"I see," said the judge. "And how's my favorite public defender doing?"

Pete took Annie's elbow. "I don't know," he said, gently pulling. "Why don't you ask him?"

Annie allowed Pete to extricate her from the judge. She said good-bye, then walked with Pete to the picnic table. A melting mound of chocolate ice cream, topped with nuts, swam in a dark puddle.

"What was that all about?" Annie asked, sitting.

"Better eat your ice cream before it all melts."

"I don't think I want it anymore."

"Then let's get out of here."

"Pete?"

"What?"

His look was a challenge and a warning. With Leigh leaving, and Camp withdrawing, she did not want to alienate her oldest friend. This was not the time to pry.

"Nothing," said Annie. "I'm finished." She gathered her belongings as the lie, in concert with the sun, flushed her cheeks.

CHAPTER 22

Thou sHaLT NoT RaPE God'S Good eaRTH

Sheriff Newcomb studied the erratic handwriting on the note, printed with a felt marker of some sort. No punctuation, no misspellings.

"That sound like a Bible thumper to you?" asked Bureau Chief Phil Huffman. He stood, arms crossed, looking down at the note inside an evidence bag. Dark mustache twitching, his square jaw slid back and forth, working a stick of Juicy Fruit. A Miami Dolphins cap covered neatly trimmed dark hair.

"You found this where, exactly?"

"Perimeter of the property, tacked to a tree."

"Any footprints?"

"We got a team out there now. The graphologist and profiler show up tomorrow."

Sheriff Newcomb sucked his teeth, hated to think what this arson investigation was costing the taxpayer. The investigation already included an impressive bouillabaisse of local resources: the DeLeon Police Department, the Fire Department, Volusia County Sheriff's Office and the Division of State Fire Marshal. Well, at least they'd have something to look at now. In the absence of a real suspect, this note would keep them buzzing for a while.

Chief Huffman hooked thumbs in his belt, sniffed. "I think we've got one serious hombre on our hands, Sheriff."

This mustached blowhard had seen too many Westerns, the

sheriff thought. "You think so?"

"Oh yeah."

"You see anything at the site besides the note?"

"Like what? Somebody walking around with a magic marker?"

Sheriff Newcomb felt his blood pressure creep. This was exactly the kind of pissing contest he had hoped to avoid. That was the trouble with guys like Huffman—no regard for boundaries.

The sheriff stayed calm. "How about a little respect, hombre?"

"Listen, Sheriff. You and your deputy have done a bang-up job cooperating with my bureau so far." Chief Huffman sliced the air with the edge of his hand. "A real bang-up job. And we want to continue working with you in every way we can."

"Uh huh."

"I know it must be hard to see all us Fire Marshal types swoop in here with our fancy equipment and newfangled ways. Naturally, you're going to resent that."

"Naturally."

"But we all have the same goal here, and the sooner we put the squeeze on this guy, the sooner we're gonna pop him out."

Evidently, Chief Huffman believed the arsonist was a pimple.

Huffman sat on the corner of the sheriff's desk, extended a pack of Juicy Fruit. "Gum?"

"No, thanks, I'm trying to quit."

Huffman unsheathed a stick, inserted it like a tongue depressor into his mouth. All wrist, he over-handed the wadded wrapper, bounced it on the bottom of a trashcan across the room. Huffman punched the air. "Two points!"

Pretty newfangled, all right.

In truth, Dade Newcomb was as anxious as anyone to catch this arsonist, who was making them all look foolish. After the second fire, Kingfisher Powell had hired a private security outfit to babysit his properties. The guard's schedule was 5:00 P.M. to 5:00 A.M. One early morning in May, in that last shrug of darkness before dawn, the arsonist struck. A fire was called in from Seminole Estates at 5:30 A.M., thirty minutes after the guard had left.

The third and fourth fires were on top of each other. One was called in at 11:30 P.M., the other, two hours later. It seemed the arsonist waited for the firefighters and the media to become "fully involved" with the first, then struck again while backs were turned.

This last fire was the fifth, and this note, the first substantial clue. In his own defense, the sheriff reminded his constituents that the Bobcat Bay State Forest covered about twenty thousand acres. Rima Ridge added another three thousand. Most of the acres were wetlands, some developed, some under construction. King's latest house, in fact, was literally rising from the ashes. It had been the first the arsonist burned down, and was now going up again, like a defiant phoenix.

As residents had pressured him to do, the sheriff added patrols in Seminole Estates and other outlying developments, which made the surveillance operation the largest of all time. The expense was choking the municipal coffer. As much as Newcomb hated to admit it, Chief Huffman was right. They needed to nail this guy fast, and not just because he was expensive. It was only a matter of time before someone got killed.

Thou sHaLT NoT RaPE God'S Good eaRTH

Rape. That's a female word, he thought. Would a man say "rape?" Not destroy, demolish, mangle—but "rape." Was this significant? Newcomb turned the note over, held it to the window. Maybe a watermark. Something.

"What do you know about this Powell feller?" Chief Huffman asked. "Would he stand to gain anything from torching his own construction sites?"

"I doubt it." Christ, Newcomb thought, if they're sniffing King's asshole, this investigation could take a while. "King's losing money hand over fist. He wants this guy racked and separated."

Chief Huffman cracked his gum. "What about the slow kid, wassisname, Eugene?"

The sheriff's blood pressure ticked another notch. "What about him?"

"I hear he likes to set fires."

"And I like to make love to women. Does that make me a rapist?"

Huffman's eyes narrowed. "Look—"

"No, you look. That dog don't hunt. Eugene can't read, much less put together a note like this. He doesn't understand people being unkind to him, and I don't want you, or any of your beef jockeys riding him, you understand me? If Eugene needs to be questioned, I will do it myself, and if you cross me on this, I will pull your plug, Chief Huffman. You mark me."

Chief Huffman removed his sunglasses, folded them slowly. "All right, Sheriff. But if my men come up with anything at the burn site that points to him, you're going to have to bring him in."

"Don't tell me my job."

"I believe you just told me mine."

As long as Sheriff Newcomb stayed seated, he would not force this guy's gum down the wrong hole.

"This was a courtesy call, Sheriff. I could have sent this note straight to the lab, but I didn't. I brought it here, first."

The sheriff took a deep breath. "I know. And I 'preciate it."

"I know I don't need to remind you that this stays out of the media."

Yet, you just did. The sheriff cleared his throat. "I think we should tell them we found a note. People around here need to hear something positive."

Chief Huffman rose. "Correction. I found a note, and I intend to release that much, myself. As far as the content goes—"

Newcomb put up a hand in agreement. He'd keep it to himself. Any whack job with a black marker could muddy the water with counterfeits, false confessions, copycat stunts.

"Well, let me get this thing to Tallahassee." Chief Huffman picked up the note. " 'Thou shalt not rape God's good earth.' " He chewed, concentrating. "Still sounds like a Bible thumper to me."

Newcomb kept quiet. The Bureau of Fire and Arson Investigations could think what it wanted. At least he had moved Huffman off Eugene. He had kept his promise to the judge—so far—but protecting Eugene was only going to get more difficult. Marguerite was going to have to keep him indoors, just long enough to eliminate him as a suspect. At the prospect of having that conversation, Newcomb's blood pressure pulsed a third time. This day was swiftly turning to shit. One of these days, he was going to turn his back and walk away from this job.

"Sheriff?" said Huffman.

"Hmm?"

"Did you hear what I said?"

"No, don't believe I did."

"I said, 'Have a nice day.' "

CHAPTER 23

In his cubicle, Jeb Barlow, reporter, passed gas. As much as he loved The Pier Diner, he'd have to give it a break. Barlow pulled broken reading glasses from a breast pocket and settled them. He picked up a neglected pile of mail from his desk, sorted absently.

Who was he kidding? The Pier was his office. He picked up more news in that place than he ever did chasing politicians. This morning, for instance, when Florida Sunshine gave that tribute to the firefighters, what was it Clyde Glenwood had said to King Powell? God, it was classic. Barlow pulled out a small spiral pad. Oh, yeah; here it is. "I'm afraid one day I will go in search of cooler air and turn my back on a huddle of honorable men because of ungrateful sons of bitches like you, who think I'm here for no other reason than to cork your money-shitting ass." Where else would he get stuff like that? Classic! He'd have to clean it up for the paper, but that was all right.

Barlow lifted a buttock, felt heat as gas expelled. He thought of fires scathing the local landscape. Up close, a flatulent man wouldn't stand a chance, go up like spent ash in a chimney. What the hell. At least he'd die happy. At The Pier, the scenery alone was worth the gastrointestinal distress. Florida hired young, pretty waitresses, but none could hold a candle to Florida herself. She was the headliner.

Barlow remembered the first time he saw her, five or six years ago, fixing up her place: shirt tied beneath her tom-toms, Daisy

139

Duke cut-offs, paint on her toenails. When Jeb introduced himself, she turned a smile on him he didn't deserve. A man could drown in a smile like that. She made him forget he was a soft, overweight schlub in size thirteen shoes. Jeb interviewed her, asked about the profession from which she was now retired ("The only stripping I do now involves turpentine"); what brought her to DeLeon ("A 1979 Cadillac"); and her plans for the restaurant ("To make more money than I spend"). Once he got beyond the glib answers, he learned she had been involved in an abusive relationship with a rich, Cuban man she met in the Bahamas. He'd wanted to stash her on his sailboat and take her home to Mama, but one black eye and a loose tooth later, she decided that Emilio, money or no money, wasn't a keeper. She discovered DeLeon while attending a graduation ceremony at Stetson University for a friend's daughter, fell in love with the sleepy security of the town, and decided to, as she put it, hole up. Jeb scribbled in his spiral pad, left out the abusive relationship at her request, then invited her to have a drink with him. She'd been sweet about it, but he could tell the answer would always be no. Jeb was not in her league, not even close.

Barlow pulled a bottom drawer, wrapped fingers around a half-killed pint of Jack Daniels. The smudged rocks glass was from Red's—another place he frequented too often. He kept meaning to return the glass, but after all this time he supposed he'd just keep it. He pulled off his glasses, tossed them on the desk.

The whiskey cut through the crap he swallowed working for this third-rate newspaper. He'd filed two good stories this week, one about Ed's murder, the other about the Bobcat Bay fires. Did Rip Kirby, his editor and brother-in-law, print either of them? No. And why not?

You're sloppy, Jeb. I have to run behind you checking facts and crossing T's. You're killing me.

Barlow tossed back a shot. Okay, so maybe he didn't check every single detail. That's what copy editors were for. It wasn't like he didn't research. He'd gone to the county records office, pulled the plats to confirm Kingfisher Powell wasn't building on protected land (he wasn't), had tried to find a pattern to the location of the fires. But the plats had not been filed properly, and he wasted a lot of time looking at properties unrelated to his story. Sure, his facts got knotted. He had been rushed. With a serial arsonist on the loose, who has time to reorganize the county records office? And sure, maybe he was a little careless sometimes, but did Rip really think readers cared if he misspelled Della Shiftlet's name? Hell, no. They wanted to know about the fight they had, blood on the oar, the crack in Ed Bartlett's skull, and that's the stuff Jeb Barlow delivered. What was Rip saving him for, Armageddon?

Jeb, you're a lawsuit waiting to happen. If you weren't Clara's brother, you'd have been gone years ago.

Clara was Jeb's younger sister and only living relative until, at thirty-two, breast cancer took her. Before she died, Clara asked her husband to look after her hapless, unemployed big brother, who always had a novel-in-progress, but never a chapter to show. Rip promised, and after Clara died, wouldn't let Jeb forget how lucky he was to have this job.

Barlow poured more JD into the rocks glass, tossed it back. He resumed sorting mail as liquor warmed its way to his fingers. He came to a large brown envelope addressed in loopy, feminine handwriting, tore the flap, reached in.

If Rip didn't print Jeb's next story, Jeb was going to quit. The *Orlando Sentinel* would snap him up. First thing tomorrow, he'd check it out. He didn't need this crap.

Barlow's hand closed around the contents of the envelope. He removed a small stack of three-by-five snapshots bound with a rubber band.

What the hell?

He slipped off the rubber band. As he sifted the photos, their significance dawned. He picked up the brown envelope, looked at the return address.

Ed Bartlett.

He looked at the postmark. Friday, July 10, 1981. The day before Ed was murdered.

Holy mother of pearl.

Breathing audibly, Barlow went through the photos again, more slowly this time. There was no mistaking Eugene Lanier, no mistaking what he was doing. In picture after picture, he steadily built, lit, and fanned a brush fire.

Jeb's intestines spasmed. The emission was so potent he could have seen it had he been able to lift his eyes.

CHAPTER 24

"What is that smell?"

Leigh fanned the air with one hand, clutched a mascara wand with the other. "It smells like something's burning."

Annie looked briefly away from the local news anchor, a young man with brown bangs rippling across his forehead. "I think it's the TV."

Leigh pressed close to the bathroom mirror. "Turn it off! It smells like it's going to blow up."

"Probably dust," said Annie. Without unwrapping her legs from their lotus position, she butt-walked to the edge of the bed and turned up the volume. The news anchor was talking about a note found at the scene of the latest fire.

"Channel Six News has learned the contents of the note. It reads, 'Thou shalt not rape God's good earth.' Neither the sheriff's department nor the Bureau of Fire and Arson Investigations will speculate as to the meaning of this note or who might have left it. In fact, Bureau Chief Huffman expressed dismay that the note's contents were made public. Channel Six News caught up with Chief Phil Huffman about an hour ago."

The scene cut to a head-and-shoulders shot of a mustached man whose dark glasses reflected constant camera flash. A tide of reporters surged and receded, microphones jostling.

"The media has seriously crippled this investigation by releasing the contents of this note. When I find the hombre who's

143

behind this leak, I will take the appropriate legal or disciplinary action."

From within the tide, a muffled question rose. "Were there fingerprints on the note?"

Huffman's jaw slid back and forth as he spoke. "We haven't received the lab results, but when we do—" he flashed a mean smile, "you'll be the first to know."

Annie shivered. Passive/aggressive people made her nervous. Her father had smiled when he was angry, gone quiet when he raged inside. Annie seldom knew where she stood because the emotional truth was hidden, coiled beneath sarcasm and calculated smiles, a rattlesnake ready to strike, and when it did, she rarely saw it coming.

"Look, there's Clyde!" Leigh pranced into the bedroom, knees high. "Is this live?"

"Not this part."

"It better not be because he's supposed to be here in five minutes." Leigh adopted a stance Annie had seen all her life; left hand on jutted hip, right leg bent, finger wagging. "And he better not be late."

"What's the difference? You won't be ready anyway."

"That's on purpose. A lady is never caught waiting for her date to arrive. It makes her look too anxious."

"What if she's not a lady?"

"I wouldn't know," Leigh said and, nose in the air, minced comically back to the bathroom.

A tall, thin weatherman whose arms were too long for his suit jacket had replaced the wavy-haired reporter. Each time the weatherman pointed, he exposed a wrist white as beach sand.

Annie moved from the bed to the bathroom doorway, watched Leigh attack her hair with a flat-back brush.

"Where are you and Clyde going?"

"We'll start out at The Log Cabin, but if I have anything to do with it, that's not where we'll end up." Leigh made eye contact with Annie's reflection in the mirror and winked. How familiar this felt: Leigh getting ready for a big date, Annie watching with a mixture of envy and something else, something not good.

"What do you know about this Clyde guy?"

Leigh applied lipstick, talked through lips stretched taut. "He's sexy, he's employed, and he likes me. What else is there to know?"

"Is he married?"

"Oh, come on, Annie."

"Is he?"

Leigh pressed her lips, setting the lipstick. "No."

"And you know this because . . ."

"He's not wearing a wedding ring."

"Dad never wore a wedding ring."

"Clyde is not Ed, okay?"

"You're sure?"

Leigh turned a cold stare on Annie. "What's that supposed to mean?"

Annie shifted. "Nothing."

"No, come on. What are you trying to say?"

Annie shrugged. "You fall for men like Daddy."

Leigh's eyes widened, then froze. She turned to the mirror. "You don't know what you're talking about."

Annie could hear hurt in her sister's voice. "Hey, I didn't mean . . ."

"Yes, you did, Annie. You'll say anything to bring me down. Why is that? Why do you always do this to me?"

"I don't."

"Ever since I was in high school, you've been jealous of me. I'm getting ready for a date, and here you come to put me down, put down the guy I'm going out with, make fun of his

145

car, his hair, his cowboy boots . . ."

"I wasn't jealous."

"What then?"

"I was—scared."

When Leigh was seventeen, her boyfriend du jour brought her home at one in the morning with a broken jaw, then simply left. Leigh knocked on Ed's bedroom door and calmly told him she needed to go to the hospital. Leigh had been, as she put it, "fooling around" on the hood of the guy's car, slipped off and cracked her jaw on the bumper. On the ride to the hospital, Annie sat in the back seat, listened to Leigh whimper each time the car hit a bump. Ed drove in silence, face and knuckles white in the moonlight. That boyfriend was out of the picture after that, but the parade of losers was just beginning. Time after time, Annie slouched in the bathroom doorway, keenly aware of Leigh's pungent sexuality and her own lagging pubescence, and watched her sister's transformation into a brightly colored lure. If someone was coming to pick Leigh up, Annie worried less for her fate; but if she was going to a bar alone, "trolling" as she called it, there was no telling what predator from the deep might snatch her from the swirling blue smoke. Awaiting Leigh's return, Annie's nightmares were filled with grotesque fish shapes, long spindly teeth, Leigh's faint laughter, and darkness. After a date, Leigh sometimes slipped beneath the covers with Annie, smelling of smoke and beer. Sometimes Leigh told about the man she had been with, how old he was, if he was handsome or nice, if she had kissed him, or gone further, if she would see him again. Annie listened, imagining Leigh atop a barstool, long legs crossed, commanding subjects with a come hither look, discouraging them with an abrupt wave of her hand. In these fantasies, Leigh was always in control. In reality, more than once, Leigh woke with pink and blue bruises on her arms and thighs. They faded, only to be replaced weeks later with fresh evidence of an evening spent snagged and squirming at the end of a money-baited hook.

The phone rang, loud as a fire alarm. "I'll get it!" Leigh dove across the bed. She let it ring a second time, then lifted the receiver. "Hello, lover boy," she cooed. Annie watched Leigh's expression sink. "Just a minute." Leigh tossed the receiver on the pillow. "It's for you."

"Who is it?"

"Fucking Santa Claus. I don't know."

"What's the matter with you?"

"Nothing!" Leigh stopped, then sighed. "It's just that I don't fall for men like Daddy. And you don't have to be scared. Don't talk long. Clyde might be trying to call."

Annie pressed the phone to her ear. "Hello?"

"Miss Bartlett, my name is Jeb Barlow. I'm a reporter for the DeLeon Sun News. About your father . . ."

"I'm sorry, but I don't want to talk to a reporter."

"I'm not just any reporter, Miss Bartlett. I'm the reporter your father chose to contact from the grave."

"From the—? I don't understand."

"Can we meet somewhere? I have something I think you should see."

CHAPTER 25

"It's all about asking the right questions."

Jeb Barlow arranged photos like Tarot cards on the formica table, one beside the other in straight, tight rows. The Pier's dining room was quiet, the supper crowd long gone. Only the back room, and Jeb's gastroenteritis, emitted signs of life. Pretending not to notice Jeb's distress, Annie watched the photographic tableau unfold: Eugene assembling twigs, Eugene striking a match, Eugene fanning a small blaze, Eugene feeding palmetto fronds to a blur of smoke and flame.

"Who took these?" asked Annie.

"Your father."

Annie looked up, shocked. "My father? Why?"

Barlow shook his head. "Wrong question." Peering at Annie beneath wildly untrimmed eyebrows, he wagged a meaty index finger. "A better one is, 'when?' " He produced a large brown envelope, tapped the postmark. "Here's what I think. I think your father took these pictures last Thursday or Friday, had them developed at some one-hour place out of town—"

"Why out of town?"

Barlow held up a finger. "One question at a time. We're still on 'when.' So, he gets these pictures back, sticks them in an envelope, sends them to me on Friday, July 10. Only I don't get them until today, July 14." Barlow leaned back, watched Annie as he tucked a cigarette between his lips and lit it. "You smoke?"

Annie shook her head.

148

"Mind if I do?" asked Barlow, already exhaling.

"No, go ahead. So, why out of town?"

Barlow lifted one shoulder to his ear. "He didn't want anyone to recognize Eugene."

"But why did my father send these pictures to you?"

"Because he knew I would look for the story behind the pictures." Barlow twisted his mouth to one side and exhaled, an ineffectual attempt at etiquette. Annie waited for him to resume, then realized he was waiting for a response.

"So what's the story behind them?"

Barlow's eyebrows shot up. His cigarette, wedged between knuckles, pointed. "Nah ah ah. Wrong question."

"Mr. Barlow—"

"Call me Jeb—"

"Jeb—I don't have time for games. If you have information about my father's murder, please tell me what it is."

Barlow looked over one shoulder. "All right," he said, head bobbing between hunched shoulders. "I have a question for you."

"I don't want questions; I want information."

"I'm getting to that." Jeb set an ashtray between them, tapped his cigarette. Annie could tell he relished the spotlight, one she guessed did not shine on him often. She remembered him from the public library, where Annie did homework each day after school. He sat behind newspapers held close to his face, and turning a page, revealed pockmarked cheeks, red nose, small eyes.

"What's your question?" Annie asked.

Jeb's eyes flicked, widened at something over Annie's shoulder. He wedged his cigarette between gapped teeth of the black plastic ashtray, and, using his forearm, swept the photos from the table into his lap. Annie turned to see Florida

Sunshine's beehive hairdo coming her way. Beneath it, Florida smiled.

"What are you two whispering about over here?"

Florida tilted her head for a better view of Jeb's lap, but the reporter had been quick; the photos found a pocket.

"Whatcha' hiding under the table there, Jeb?" asked Florida in sing-song.

"I'll show you mine if you show me yours."

Florida cocked a hip and looked at Annie with a wry, man-weary look. "He never stops," she said, deadpan.

"Can you blame me?" Jeb said, showing nicotine teeth.

"Oh, you. Can I bring you two another beer?"

"Not for me, thanks," said Annie.

"Got any JD?" asked Jeb.

"I do," said Florida. "Why don'tchall come on into the back room with the rest of the boozers?"

By Jeb's reaction, Annie gathered this was not a frequent invitation. She watched him wrestle the moment before answering. "Any other day, I'd beat a path, Florida. But today, duty calls."

"What duty?" Florida looked from Jeb to Annie. "Something about your father?"

The last thing Annie wanted was Florida knowing her business. She could hear the dining room announcement now: "All y'all listen up! Ed Bartlett took pictures of Eugene Lanier setting a forest fire, and Jeb Barlow's got them!"

"Not really," said Annie. "We were just doing some catching up."

Florida shifted her hip within inches of Jeb's shoulder, torturing him with her proximity. "Are you staying in town for the Shiftlet woman's trial, Annie?"

"Pete Duncan says there might not be a trial."

"Why's that?"

"He's counseling her to cut a deal."

Florida drew red lips into a contemplative pucker. "That so. This all must be so awful for you and your sister. I'm so sorry for you both. The whole town is." Annie nodded her appreciation. "Well, I'd best get back to the back room before somebody helps theirselves to the bar. You give my best to your sister."

"I will."

"And you," said Florida, pointing at Jeb with a long, painted nail, "you behave yourself."

"I always do." Jeb glanced in the direction of the back room. "Can I still have that JD?"

"Well, I usually insist the hard stuff stay in the back room, but since it's you, I'll have one of the girls bring it out."

"You're a wonderful woman."

"Don't go tellin' everyone I let you drink in the dining room. I don't like doing for one what I can't for everybody."

"My lips are sealed."

Florida grinned. "You mean, your lips are seals!" She slapped Jeb's shoulder, laughed uproariously. "Good one!" Heels click-clacking, she retreated to the back room, rear end ticking—left, right, left—in metronomic precision.

"That was close," breathed Jeb. "She'd have the sheriff all over these pictures."

"I think going to the sheriff is the right thing to do."

"No can do. There's a story here. You know what I mean, a story? A beginning, middle and end stitched together with a moral truth. I owe it to your father to write this story."

"Mr. Barlow—"

"Jeb."

"Jeb—you're withholding evidence."

"Just the opposite. I'm going to blow this whole thing wide open. And the sheriff can read about it in the paper like everybody else. That's what your father wanted, and that's what

I'm going to give him."

"How do you know that's what he wanted? Did he include a note?"

"I don't need a note." He tapped his temple. "Some things, a man knows."

It dawned on Annie that Jeb Barlow might not be dealing with a full deck. "Mr. Barlow—"

"Jeb—"

"Jeb. What do these pictures have to do with my father's murder?"

The cocktail waitress arrived and set a shot of Jack Daniels in front of Jeb.

"Thank you, darlin'."

The waitress left, and Jeb removed the pictures from his pocket, set the stack on the table, tapped as if passing an opportunity to cut cards.

"Are you aware your father was planning on selling his property?"

Annie stared, blindsided. "No. I had no idea. How do you know that? And please, don't tell me that's the wrong question."

"There was a survey ordered."

"Who ordered it?"

"I only saw the plat, and it doesn't say who ordered the survey, just that it was done."

"The plat?"

"I pulled some plats from the records room. I was trying to pinpoint the location of the fires, see if I could identify a pattern, a clue, something. But it's a mess over there, and when I accidentally pulled the plat showing your father's property, I noticed a survey had been done."

"When?"

"Ten days ago."

Annie let this news settle like coins in a money counter, but the facts wouldn't stack. "Have you told this to anyone?"

Jeb shook his head. "Only you. I figure I owe you that much because tomorrow morning, my story will be on the front page of the paper, above the fold."

"And you're going to say he was about to sell his property?"

"I'm going to say a survey was done."

Annie sat forward, and concentrated. "Okay, let's say my father was planning on selling his house. What's the link between that, his murder, and these photographs of Eugene?"

Jeb Barlow fixed such a steady gaze on Annie, she realized, for the first time, one eye was larger than the other.

"Now that, Miss Bartlett, is a very interesting question."

CHAPTER 26

Pete Duncan, Public Defender, poured champagne into a tall, crystal glass. Its perfume came to him first, then the electric current, pumping his desire to empty the contents of the entire bottle down his throat. He'd come to accept his craving for alcohol would never go away, only wax and wane, a siren's lure. For three years, two months, fourteen days, he had been, as he said in AA, "a grateful, recovering alcoholic." It seemed unfair, how each triumph over temptation did nothing to alleviate the pull of the next encounter. This small victory would have no effect against the next glass of champagne poured for a beautiful woman sitting on his camelback sofa, do nothing to ease this current of desire more powerful than the promise of sex. Pete Duncan lifted the glass by its stem, waved it beneath his nose, and silently pronounced himself no more recovered than the lowliest park bench indigent.

"Thank you, counselor," said Pete's date, the tall restaurant hostess named Denise. She coaxed blonde hair from front to back with a shimmy of her tanned shoulder. Her dress, held up by two thin straps caressing her collarbone, revealed tennis thighs smooth as the deer-skin pillow she leaned against.

"My pleasure," Pete said.

"Aren't you having one?"

"I have a drink here." Pete raised his glass in salute. He'd found, much to his relief, he could seduce a woman while drinking ginger ale just as long as she believed it was scotch. Women didn't like to drink alone, particularly on dates. In the past, when Pete admitted he was drinking a soft drink, the air lost its sexual charge. The women seemed to swing from ready to wary, as defenses kicked in—*what are you trying to do, get me drunk?* It confounded Pete, how intentions and motives alchemized from mutual to self-serving in the popping of a soda can tab.

"How about some music?"

Pete moved to his stereo, an expensive setup he could operate but knew nothing about, except that it was top-of-the-line and, according to the salesman at Montgomery Ward, the system of choice among young professionals.

"What would you like to hear?"

"Do you have Kenny G?" asked Denise.

"Uh, I think so. Just a sec."

Kenny G?

Pete's brother-in-law had given him a Kenny G album one Christmas. Pete hadn't removed the cellophane—it was filed with other outcasts, denied the dignity of alphabetization.

"I just bought it. This will be its virgin spin."

Denise sat back and crossed one long leg over the other. "Ooh, I like virgin spins."

Pete cued the record and sat next to Denise, twisted himself toward her. "You look very pretty tonight."

Denise smiled, studying him with intelligent, brown eyes. "As opposed to other nights?"

"I wouldn't know. I wasn't there."

"But you're here now."

"Yes, I believe I am."

"I'm here, too."

"Here's to being here together," said Pete, raising his glass.

Denise met the toast, eyes burning. "Here's to the youngest criminal defense lawyer in Volusia County."

"Actually, I believe in the state of Florida."

"My mistake, counselor," purred Denise. "I'll make it up to you."

God, how many times had he fantasized about this moment? The cool, unattainable Denise, languid after a heavy dinner of Oysters Rockefeller and Cote du Rhone, one leg switching back and forth, setting the rhythm of seduction. Pete removed the glass from her hand, placed it on the coffee table, and slid his hips toward her.

"Don't you just love Kenny G?" Denise murmured.

The doorbell buzzed, a grinding, mechanical intrusion, and Pete cursed whoever was on the other side for their exquisite bad timing.

"Who's that?"

"I don't know."

"Do you have to answer it?"

Pete's hopes soared on the question, were just as quickly dashed as the buzzer sounded again, a long, insistent demand, punctuated by pounding. Pete had a sudden, discouraging thought: "You're not married, are you?" Denise gave him a withering stare. "Of course not. I knew that. Sorry. I'll get rid of them, whoever it is. Would you excuse me for a moment?"

Pete left Denise with champagne for company, and went to the door. In all the years he'd lived in DeLeon, Pete Duncan had never opened his door to someone he did not care to see—until now.

"About time, Duncan," said Annie. "My knuckles are practically raw. Let me in. I have to talk to you—" Annie stopped short, her brow creased. "God, what is that—not Kenny G?"

"Haven't you heard of the telephone?"

"I need to talk to you in person. It's about my father."

Pete's voice was as flat as his stare. "Your timing absolutely sucks."

"It's late, I know. Sorry about that, but Jeb Barlow just

showed me two dozen photos of Eugene Lanier setting a fire. He said my father sent them to him the night before he died."

"Can we talk about this tomorrow?"

"Barlow says my father wanted him to write a story for the paper, but that's not the weirdest part."

"Of course not."

"Can I come in?" Annie asked. "I don't have leprosy."

He had to let her in. It sounded like Annie had stumbled across something pertinent. With luck, Denise would understand. He swung the door back. Annie entered, talking.

"Jeb Barlow saw the Widow Lake plat and said there was a recent survey done on the house. Did you know my father was planning to sell?"

"Why was Barlow looking at land plats?"

"Something about researching fires. I don't know. Did you hear what I said?"

"Go on."

"My question is, why would my father sell? According to Della, he turned down King Powell, and he offered the moon."

"I don't see how any of this matters, Annie."

"You don't see how—Pete, this could be important. You have to talk to Della, find out what she knows about this."

"She doesn't know anything. Now, if you don't mind, I'd like to get back to what I was doing."

"What could be more important than this?"

"Hi there," said a voice.

Pete looked at the floor, and began a silent countdown in anticipation of worlds colliding.

CHAPTER 27

Annie gaped.

Standing at the archway leading from the foyer to the living room was a long, blonde drink of water, wearing a short, black cocktail dress. Her slender fingers caressed the rim of an empty champagne glass, which dangled almost to her knees.

"Denise, you remember Annie—" Pete began.

"From the restaurant, yes," said Denise. "Nice to see you again."

Annie's eyes sought Pete's. He gave her brief contact, then looked away. Annie drew a hand to her chest. "I'm sorry. I didn't realize—"

"Of course you didn't," said Denise. "Pete, shouldn't you offer your guest a drink?"

"Annie was just leaving. Weren't you, Annie?"

Annie tried to account for a sudden sinking feeling, as if, lungs empty, she was about to hit lake bottom. Denise had called Pete "Mr. Duncan" at the restaurant. Chances were pretty good they were on a first name basis in the living room. The thought made her want to turn heel, yet why did she care? Even though her wedding to Camp was "postponed," Annie was still engaged to Camp (wasn't she?), and Pete hadn't been her boyfriend for over ten years. He had every right to entertain women in his home. Still, the sight of Denise—tall, gorgeous, one hundred and ten-pound Denise, lifting a toned, white arm as she coaxed a fallen strap onto her shoulder—made Annie feel suddenly unattractive and unwanted.

"I'll come back tomorrow," said Annie.

Denise stepped forward. "Please, stay. I heard about your father, and may I say I'm very sorry for your loss?"

"Thank you."

Denise handed her glass to Pete. "Well, you two obviously have things to talk about. I should be going, anyway."

"Denise—"

"It's okay, Pete." Denise smiled. "I get it. I really do." To Annie, she held out a slim hand; Annie took it, marveled at its softness. "Take care."

"You, too."

Denise turned to Pete. "Call me tomorrow?"

"I'll walk you."

"No, I'm parked right outside the door. I'm fine, really." Denise squeezed Pete's wrist. "Thank you for dinner. I had a wonderful time. Good night." She kissed the side of Pete's mouth. Annie looked away.

Pete closed the door behind his date. The look he gave Annie would scale a fish.

"Hey, you're the one who let me in."

Without a word, Pete moved to the coffee table, picked up a glass, and headed for the kitchen.

"So, can I have a glass of champagne?"

"No."

Annie followed Pete into the small, efficient kitchen. Beige tiles, twined with painted ivy, lined the wall above the sink and stove. The beige linoleum floor with specks of white shone as if just polished. Appliances gleamed.

"Wow. It sure is beige in here."

Pete placed glasses in the sink, turned to Annie, his face serious. "What does Jeb Barlow intend to do with this information about Ed selling his house?"

"He's writing a story."

Pete emitted a sound—a chain saw sputtering to a stop.

"Pete, what's going on?"

"That information is extremely harmful to my case. If Matt Tatum learns Ed intended to sell his house, the state could argue the murder was premeditated and refuse to plea bargain."

"Matt Tatum? Matty 'Fatty' Tatum?"

"He's the State's Attorney."

Annie shook her head. If stuttering Petey Duncan and Matty Fatty Tatum could make something of themselves in DeLeon, maybe she could have been a big fish in a small pond, too. No, she decided. If she had stayed, she would have gone mad.

"But if Kingfisher Powell ordered the survey," she said, "then maybe Della really is being framed, like she says."

"For the last time, Annie. Della is not being framed."

"You don't know that!"

"I do!"

"Pete, what are you hiding?"

"There's no way I can share confidential information with you, sympathetic as I am to your father's death. I'm sorry. Please don't ask me again. All I'm trying to do is save my client from the electric chair."

"Oh, come on. Florida doesn't execute women."

"Yes, Florida does. It's been almost thirty years, but that doesn't mean Della is safe from death row." Pete walked to the front door. "Now, if you don't mind, it's late."

"You're throwing me out?"

"I'm asking you to leave."

"Pete, I'm sorry I crashed your date, but you don't have to—"

"It's not personal. I have to protect my client. This case cannot go to trial. The information you just shared with me will almost certainly make things worse for Della. I can't stop Rip

Kirby from printing Jeb's story, but Annie, I'd be very suspect of anything Jeb Barlow tells you. He loves conspiracy theories and has been known to twist facts to support them. If Rip Kirby didn't keep him clamped, Jeb would have us believe 'dog bites man' is a canine insurgency plot."

"Where's the other oar, Pete?"

"What?"

Annie crossed her arms. "I was at the house. My father had two oars. There's only one in evidence. Where's the other one?"

"That's irrelevant. The murder weapon has been entered into evidence."

"I don't think Della swung that oar!" said Annie, voice rising.

"It doesn't matter because a jury probably will."

Annie stared into Pete's face, once so familiar, now that of a stranger. Maybe Pete was too inexperienced to provide adequate defense for Della. How could he ignore evidence that might prove Della's innocence?

"Della is right to want a new lawyer," Annie said calmly. "She thinks she's being set up, and you don't seem to care."

"Get some sleep, Annie. You've had rough couple days. You'll feel better in the morning."

Pete's patronizing tone cut through Annie's disappointment. Fury welled, but yelling would do no good. Pete was resigned to a passive defense.

"I think I'll pay a little visit to Judge Lanier. Someone should know you're not willing to do your job."

"Knock yourself out." He opened the door. "Drive safely."

"I walked."

"Walk safely, then."

Annie stalked through the doorway, then turned, determined to have the last word. "And just for the record, your taste in women stinks."

Pete smiled, gave Annie a knowing look, and shut the door.

As Annie reached the sidewalk, she realized she had just insulted herself.

CHAPTER 28

Leigh rested chin in hand, gazed up at her date. "What's the worst fire you've ever been in?"

Clyde took Leigh's cigarette from her fingers, inhaled, gave it back. "I get this phone call. Forest fire in the Tomoka Preserve. Drought conditions, no rain in the forecast, gusting winds. I got to the station, pulled on my turnouts, grabbed my coat and helmet, hopped on the truck. Another day, another forest fire, right?

"Here's the thing they didn't tell us. It was a crown fire, know what that is? It's a fire that moves across the treetops rather than on the ground. In high winds, crown fires travel fast.

"So we get out there, and I hear this roar, and I turn around and from out of nowhere, here it comes. We hadn't even got pressure on the hoses before it's dead on us. I'm screaming for everyone to get back in the truck when I notice this new guy take off through the woods. I yell at him to come back, but he's out of his head with panic. I mean he's gone. Fire is dropping from the sky, igniting underbrush—it's like he's being chased by demons. Trouble is, he's running uphill. Fire travels fast uphill, and he hasn't got a fire shelter with him. Right away, I could see he was going to get cut off. So, I grabbed a shelter and took off after him."

"Oh my gosh," said Leigh, awed. Then, "What's a fire shelter?"

"It looks like a rectangular pup tent, made of fire retardant material. It can save your life on a fire line if you can get it out and crawl under in time. Without a shelter, I knew this guy's chances were nil. So anyway, I grab the shelter and I go after this guy, and I'm running, and I'm yelling, and I'm telling him to run down the hill, but he either doesn't hear me, or he sees the fire coming up the hill and thinks I'm crazy, telling him to run towards it, so he keeps going. Already I can feel the heat, intense on my back, so I pull the flap on my shelter and let it drag behind me to shield me from the heat. It's working, but it's also slowing me down. If the shelter snags on something and tears, it's not going to be worth a shit, and then we're both toast. In the meantime, this guy is making progress up this hill. I'm going to have to haul ass if I have any chance of catching him.

"Then the wind shifts, and just like that, I've got a bigger problem."

"What?"

"I'm cut off. Fire in front of me, behind me, to the left, to the right. A bobcat comes screeching out of the trees, then moves past me so close I can smell burning fur. I drop my pack. I have to deploy this shelter now or never. These things are awkward in the best conditions, but with wind catching it like a sail, I'm struggling to get tab A into slot A, you know what I mean? Finally, I get it set up and crawl inside, lay on my stomach, face down. The only thing I can do now is wait and not move, no matter how hot it gets."

"Why can't you move?"

"Heat rises, okay? So the coolest place is going to be the ground. But once you make the commitment to wait out an entrapment in a fire shelter, you can't change your mind. Once you're off the ground, hot gases can come under the shelter and right into your face. If you stand up, you become a chimney.

I've seen firefighters panic, and when they try to make a run for it, whoosh! So I'm nose to the ground, no matter what."

Leigh squashed her cigarette butt in the ashtray. "Clyde, that's so brave."

"Just the opposite, really. There's nothing brave about pure survival instinct. In the worst situations, it's usually knowledge that saves you, not courage."

"So what happened to the guy who took off?"

Clyde shook his head. "The windshift must have sent him back down the hill. I could hear him, screaming in that wild, high way, like he's being ripped apart, but there's nothing I can do. Pretty soon it's getting hotter and hotter inside my shelter, so I lay there, nose in the dirt, praying to God to have mercy on this guy. It is, by far, the lowest moment of my life."

"I can't imagine."

"A few seconds later, I feel the edge of my shelter start to lift. Hot gases rush into my face. Just like that, I'm in big trouble. I can't hear anything because the flame front has arrived and the turbulence is loud as shit; I can barely see because my eyes feel like ragged glass in my head, but my hands find the problem, and force the edge back down on the ground. Then another edge lifts, and I'm burning up. I spread eagle and hold the corners down tight. The winds that accompany the arrival of a flame front can be intense, but I never heard of it stripping off anyone's shelter. All of a sudden, it hits me what's happening."

Leigh's eyes went wide. "The guy?"

Clyde nodded. "He's made his way through the flames, and now he's trying to get in my shelter."

"Oh, shit."

"Now, I've got to make the toughest decision I have ever had to make. I have two choices. One, I can lift the shelter to let him in, and almost certainly burn to death, or two, I can refuse to aid a fellow firefighter, who is undoubtedly severely burned by now and seconds away from total engulfment."

"Which one did you do?"

Clyde paused, gave her a guarded look. "Which one would you do?"

Leigh shrugged. "I don't know. I've never been in that situation."

"Exactly," said Clyde. "You've never been in that situation. You don't even think about the choice you make. An essential part of you takes over. In an instant, all your experiences, your world view, genetic make-up, psychological whatevers, everything and everybody that ever touched your life gets burned down and boiled away, until all that is left is what you would do in that situation."

"So, what did you do?"

Clyde smiled, shook his head. "Nuh uh."

"What do you mean, 'nuh uh'?"

"I mean, nuh uh, I'm not going to tell you."

"You son of a bitch. You tell me a story like that and you're not going to tell me how it ends?"

"Nope."

"Why the hell not?"

"Because I don't know you well enough to tell you who I am."

After a moment, Leigh rose and swung her fringed bag over one shoulder.

"Where are you going?" Clyde asked.

Leigh held out a hand. "To your place."

"My place. How come?"

"You won't tell me the end of that story because you don't know me well enough, right?"

"Yeah."

"Well, I'm leaving in the morning, so I suggest we put this relationship on fast forward."

"How fast?"

Leigh's eyes dropped to half-mast. "Real fast."

Clyde stood. "I have to warn you," he said, pressing close, "there are some things I don't do fast."

"Not a problem, fireman," said Leigh. "Because this is one fire you're going to enjoy putting out."

Leigh waited outside while Clyde paid the bill. On summer nights like these, mischief filled the air. It had been a long time since she felt this way, and she couldn't wait to get in bed with Clyde. Leigh dipped her gaze beneath the glare of the parking lot lamps and noticed the waitress who had spilled coffee on her leaning against a car. Her mood generous, Leigh waved. The waitress moved back until she became part of the night.

Leigh shook her head, amused at the snub. If there was one thing Leigh had learned after years of on and off waitressing, it was this: Don't bite the hand that tips you. Clyde emerged from the restaurant and slid an arm around Leigh's waist. Together, they headed for his truck. Leigh glanced back at Sada, but she was gone.

CHAPTER 29

Marguerite Lanier woke herself each morning at the precise time she mentally programmed the night before. Since she was a little girl, she could make her eyes fly open at 4:22, or 6:37 or 7:01. Amazing, what the mind can do, she thought, recalling the words of the Bard: What a piece of work is a man, how noble in reason, how infinite in faculties.

Well, not every man, of course. No one would say her son, for instance, was infinite in faculties. Eugene could no more control his subconscious than he could his speech. He required physical rousing lest his bladder release while still in bed. Marguerite padded to her son's bed, shook his shoulders until his almond eyes creaked open.

"Maaaaa."

"Good morning to you, too. Time for cereal."

Eugene's erection made a teepee of the sheet. The judge turned away, allowed her son his morning pleasure. Now that he was awake, he would not wet the bed, and Justinia would be here shortly to do laundry. In the kitchen, the automatic coffee maker gurgled. It, too, was programmed to wake itself and start cracking.

Eugene's sexual awakening had begun earlier than most boys. At ten, he discovered his penis operated independently of will, and he watched, fascinated, as if it might be a pet that did tricks. During this stage, Eugene shed clothes in public to see what his pet would do next. The judge talked and talked, but

Eugene was slow to understand the social disgrace of stripping to pleasure oneself.

Eugene's principal, a young, idealistic woman fresh from the Peace Corps, suggested the judge purchase adult diapers and drawstring-waist pants, and knot the pants close to Eugene's stomach. It was worth a try. As predicted, Eugene's plump fingers were helpless against knots, and in spite of thrashing and wailing, the pet stayed confined. After a week, Eugene was fully penis trained. The judge was delighted. Off came the diapers, and up went the school's subsidy fund.

But the judge knew her money would yield results for only so long. Dade Newcomb urged her to send Eugene where there were others like him, where he would be cared for by people trained to enrich his life, not punish him for it. The judge visited a few such places in Tampa, Orlando, Miami; and yes, the facilities were clean and modern, and yes, the residents seemed happy and healthy, and yes, she could afford to send Eugene to any of them. But when it came time to hand him over, hard steel clicked, shifted, locked inside her, and Judge Lanier couldn't do it. Eugene was her son, her responsibility, her late father's grandchild. Giving him up, even if "for the best" went against her every instinct. No, she would accept what had been given and devote herself to her boy.

Marguerite cut work hours. At night, she talked to Eugene about his body, read to him, told him about his grandfather, whose name had also been Eugene. Hand in his, she sat beside him on the bed until sleep claimed him. After six months, Eugene exhibited improved attention at school. Playground behavior mellowed, and a few children ventured friendships.

But they weren't out of the woods.

One morning, the maid, Justinia, approached Marguerite with face creased, two fingers hooked into the heels of Eugene's high-top sneakers.

"What is it, Justinia?"

"These here sneaks. They're melted. I was about to chuck 'em in the washer when I saw the bottoms. Look here."

Justinia turned them over. The rubber soles were indeed melted and black with soot. The judge sniffed. "Smoke."

"That's what I thought, too. What's Eugene up to, Miz Marguerite?"

"Have you washed the laundry yet?"

"Just about to."

"Where is it?"

"In the basket, on the washer."

In the washroom, the judge pulled Eugene's pants from the pile and from a pocket withdrew a matchbook. She turned to Justinia. "Have you found many of these?"

"A few. I didn't think nothing of it, except maybe he was smoking cigarettes, like boys do."

"Will you let me know if you find any more?"

"Yes ma'am. What you want me to do with them sneaks?"

"Throw them out."

"Yes, ma'am."

At bedtime that night, the judge told Eugene about Smokey Bear. "Only you can prevent forest fires," she said in a comic growl.

Eugene laughed. "Faaaa."

"That's right. Smokey Bear doesn't like fires. Fires burn up the forest. You must never set a fire in the woods, Eugene. Do you understand?"

Eugene nodded, eyes wandering.

"Look at me." Marguerite locked eyes with her son. "I found matches in your pocket. Where did you get them?"

Eugene's hands went below the sheet. Marguerite pulled his wrists above the covers. "Smokey Bear won't be your friend if you set fires, Eugene. The next time I find matches in your pocket, I'm going to tell Smokey Bear."

"Nooo," whimpered Eugene.

"Yes. And he will be very upset with you. No more fires. Do you hear?" Eugene nodded. "Good. Time to fall asleep now. I'll hold your hand."

That had been five years ago. Under his mother's constant supervision, Eugene's fire setting stopped, replaced by an obsession with one-dollar bills. Eventually, Eugene demonstrated a degree of responsibility and life-skill proficiency, and Marguerite returned to work, part time.

Then, yesterday, the sheriff had come into her chambers and talked about the home in Tampa again. Why did others so quickly blame Eugene for the town's misfortunes? They had no proof he had set those construction fires. Why did they fear him so?

Marguerite carried a cup of coffee to the front steps, picked up the paper from the stoop and settled at the breakfast table, toes barely touching the floor. She skimmed off the rubber band, opened to the front page.

Hot coffee spilled into her lap, but Marguerite barely felt it. There, on the front page of the paper, above the fold, was a picture of Eugene setting a fire in the woods. It almost stopped her heart. Marguerite gasped as her carefully contrived world collapsed.

"Eugene!"

She caught him still in pajamas coming from the bathroom. He looked at her, smiled. Marguerite sat on his bed.

"Sit on the bed with Momma," she said, patting the mattress, corralling her composure. Eugene's smile faded. He shook his head. "Come on, son, I want to talk with you."

"Taaab."

"No, son, you're not in trouble. Where are your matches? Hmm? Where?" Marguerite watched Eugene's eyes. "Where,

Eugene? Smokey Bear is going to be very upset if you don't give them to me."

"Nooo!"

"Are they under your bed?" Marguerite looked. She saw a shoebox, pulled it toward her. Eugene snatched the box from her, crushed it to his chest.

"Are they in that box, Eugene?" Marguerite held out her hands. "Give it to me, then."

"Nooo."

"Eugene, you must give me your matches. People will be watching you, now. Do you understand me? We have to be very careful. No more fires, ever. Now, give me that box."

Marguerite stepped forward; Eugene rocked and moaned. "Give it to me, son." Finally, head dropped, Eugene gave up the box.

Marguerite opened it. Not matches, but notes, cobbled from headline newsprint.

"STOP UrBan SpraWL"

"FeeD tHe LanD, EaT the RiCH"

"YoU BuilD It, I BuRN It"

"GoD iS FiRE"

Marguerite looked into her son's tear-streamed face. "Where did you get these?"

"My haaaart."

"Eugene, I asked you a question."

"My haaaaaaaaaaaaart!"

With rage and grief in equal measure, Eugene's scream blew from his mouth like a black, monstrous thing, ropy with spit. Marguerite had seen fits and histrionics, tantrums and displays, but she had heard nothing like this. Predatory and merciless, the scream rose, ripped the air with ragged teeth.

"Stop it, Eugene! Calm down this second!" Slowly, Eugene's distorted face unknotted as huffs of air moved his man's chest up and down.

"Myyy."

"Yes, yours. I know. Settle down."

Eugene's attachments to objects were usually short-lived, but what Eugene now crushed to his chest was too dangerous to wait out. She had seen the news. There was no mistaking the similarity of these to the note left with the Bobcat Bay fires: pasted letters, reference to God, admission of willful destruction. Eugene could not have constructed such things, but possession placed him at the scene. Had Eugene been an accomplice, or simply a spectator? Whatever the truth, this could not be ignored.

"It's all right, Eugene. I'm not going to take your notes, but we can't keep them under your bed. They're bad."

Eugene's eyes tracked back and forth. "Nooo."

"Yes, they are. A bad man made them. We can't let anyone see them, or they'll think you're bad, too." Eugene shook his head. "No, we can't. If someone finds them, they'll be very angry with you, won't they? They'll take them away." Eugene looked frightened, closed his body off. "But we're not going to let them, are we, Eugene?" He checked her face for sincerity. "No, we're not. We're going to send those notes some place no one will ever, ever find them." Eugene whimpered, his gaze floating to the ceiling. "Let's burn them, Eugene."

She had to appeal to his pyromania. It was the only way he would give up the arsonist's notes. Let him light one more fire, under her supervision, and it would be done.

"Faaaa," cooed Eugene, face awash in ecstasy.

"Yes, son. Fire."

He unfolded himself from the corner. Never had his eyes seemed so alert. The thing most forbidden was now allowed, and his mother, the prior obstacle to his total immersion, now took his hands.

"We need matches, Eugene. Do you have matches?" The boy's guilty look said it all. "Go get them, son."

Eugene lifted his bed. Beneath one leg, a book of matches, serving innocently as a shim. Marguerite led her son to the kitchen sink. Eugene's breathing became heavy as he struck a flattened match across the strike pad. A flame sparked, sputtered, came to life.

Marguerite told Eugene this was a special occasion, that he was never to do this himself, but she knew she wasn't getting through; her son bounced from foot to foot in anticipation of touching flame to paper. Wretched, Marguerite listened intently for the trilling of an alarm clock from some dark, far away place, but she knew this was no dream, and even if it was, she, not an alarm clock, would have to control its ending.

CHAPTER 30

A rolled newspaper slapped Rip Kirby's desk, the sound sudden, flat and loud. Kirby jumped, looked into Sheriff Newcomb's face, and reached for the phone.

"Don't," Newcomb warned.

Feet scrabbling, Kirby rolled his chair back. In an instant, Newcomb had pinned him, vise-like hands clamped on either side, preventing him from rising. "Take it easy, Dade."

Newcomb grabbed Kirby by the shirt front, pulled him up. On tiptoe and nose to nose, the editor could smell the sheriff's anger, a mix of onions, ash, and stale coffee.

"I'm past taking it easy, Rip. Way past."

Kirby clamped the sheriff's wrists and pushed. Grip broken, Newcomb shoved the editor into a half-sitting position on the desk. Flailing, shirt pulled from his pants, Kirby realized half the newsroom was witnessing his humiliation. Familiar gorge rose. As an ex-Major League umpire, he knew how to handle physical bullies. Balance restored, he pushed himself up, and leading with his still-impressive chest, got in the sheriff's face. His voice roared with stadium volume.

"You may think you make all the rules, Sheriff, but last time I looked, freedom of the press was still a constitutional right! Now back off before I call security!"

"I am security, you peon," the sheriff spat back. "And you do not have a right to try Eugene Lanier in your paper."

"I print news, whether you like it or not."

"This isn't news. It's incendiary garbage."

Kirby's impossibly thin secretary poked her head in. "Mr. Kirby . . . ?"

"It's all right, Sherry. The sheriff had me confused with someone he could push around."

Sherry's bulging eyes blinked twice, then withdrew. Dade Newcomb unrolled the newspaper baton and batted the front page with the back of his hand. "Look at this headline: ED BARTLETT SPEAKS FROM THE GRAVE. What kind of shit-pulp is that?"

"The article holds up. I checked the facts myself."

"I don't care about facts. We're going to have every redneck from here to Deltona marching down Woodland Boulevard with torches and pitchforks, demanding Eugene Lanier's head on a platter. In the meantime, there's an arsonist out there getting away with murder—"

"There's no proof the arsonist murdered anyone."

Sheriff Newcomb exploded. "Goddammit, Kirby, are you intentionally missing my point, or are you as stupid as the rest of the flotsam around here? Get Jeb Barlow in here right now, or you'll be joining your wife a lot sooner than you thought."

With this disrespectful mention of his wife, Rip Kirby felt dangerously close to losing control. With hands curled into fists, one finger punched the air in a frenetic, upward trajectory. "You're out of here!" the editor yelled.

"I hope I'm not interrupting something important."

In the doorway, smiling with sharp, feral teeth, Kingfisher Powell stood. He, too, held a newspaper in one large, brown hand.

"This is none of your business, King," the sheriff said.

"I disagree. It is all about my business." King lowered himself into a chair, which groaned in protest.

"Don't make yourself comfortable, King," said Kirby, then

swung accusing eyes on the sheriff. "I've had enough enlightened opinions for one day."

The sheriff pointed at Kirby's chest. "Why the hell didn't you come to me with these pictures, Rip? We could have investigated quietly, instead of ruining this poor boy's life."

"You need to face truth," said Kingfisher, leaning back. "That boy's life was ruined before he was born. You've been looking the other way ever since that kid picked up his first book of matches." King displayed the picture of Eugene. "There's no turning from this, is there?"

After a moment the sheriff spoke, his voice a controlled growl. "Rip, how many pictures do you have?"

"About a dozen, I guess."

"Give them to me."

Kirby clicked his tongue. "No."

Sheriff Newcomb's glare was full of menace. Kirby had never seen him like this. The sheriff must be under some serious pressure from the judge, he thought. He smelled a story but knew pursuing it would be dangerous. Backdoor politics opened a many-chambered den of snakes, and Kirby didn't feel like getting bit. He sat hard in his chair. The sheriff was right about the article—links would be drawn, Eugene vilified. Still, Kirby knew he didn't have to give up the pictures. They were the property of the paper, and Barlow's story had stuck to facts. His brother-in-law had violated no laws in writing the story, and Kirby none in printing it. In fact, they had done what every paper in the country is duty bound to do—report the news.

"We won't print any more of them," said Kirby. "You've got my word."

The sheriff held out his hand for the pictures. "You heard what I said."

Kirby stared at the sheriff's open hand. After a beat, he shook his head.

The hand curled into a gun-shaped point. "This isn't over, Kirby."

Kingfisher grunted, his face lit with a self-satisfied smirk. "My people have a saying: 'Only the toothless dog barks at the thief leaving the house.' "

Newcomb turned a dark look on the hulking Seminole. "You'll get yours, King. You can take that to the bank."

"I already have," said King. "Five times. The bank is a little tired of seeing me come through the door. It seems they don't like it when their investments burn to the ground." King dropped the newspaper at the sheriff's feet. "Pick up the boy before the Fire Marshal does, Sheriff. It is no longer safe for him. You said so yourself."

Sheriff Newcomb shouldered past Powell without another word. Kirby felt instant relief, but knew it wouldn't last.

CHAPTER 31

The television in the motel office blared, but Leigh took no notice. Distracted by the memory of Clyde's body against hers, she threw clothes into grocery bags. It was past time to get out of here. Miguel could be around the next corner. She had lingered as long as she dared.

Yet, it might be worth the risk to spend another night, even another day with Clyde Glenwood. Leigh couldn't remember ever falling so hard for a man. He at once fascinated and repelled her. The story he told at dinner—had he saved himself while a man burned to death right beside him, or had he risked almost certain death to aid the doomed firefighter? His refusal to tell her the answer aroused her so much she would have dragged him to bed had he not come willingly.

I don't know you well enough to tell you who I am.

He certainly knew a thing or two about her now.

How lovingly he had traced her body with callused fingertips, how shy about accepting the gift unwrapped before him. Afterward, he lightly touched her face, as if to memorize it. Later, in the bathtub, Leigh lay back against his chest as he soaped her breasts, kissed her neck, told her she was beautiful.

"Your turn," Clyde said.

"To do what?"

"Tell me a story."

Leigh twisted to see his eyes. "What kind of story?"

"The one you haven't told anyone else."

Leigh held his gaze for a moment, working the fuller meaning of the request. Was he after something in particular, or was this a game he played with all his tub buddies?

"Hey, what you see is what you get," said Leigh. "I'm an open book."

"No, you're not."

The truth was, and apparently Clyde sensed it, she had more stories than time. "Okay. You want to hear about sex, drugs or rock and roll?"

Without hesitation, Clyde said, "Drugs," and Leigh's defenses went up.

"What about drugs?" she ventured.

"Are you an addict?"

In the moment it took to answer, Leigh saw her father's sad, despairing eyes. She thought of her mother long ago in white uniform and shoes, saw her open the locked narcotics cabinet in the infirmary, slip a small bottle into her pocket. She thought of crooked doctors, clinicians, pharmacists, all avoiding her eyes as they surreptitiously took her money and placed brightly colored tablets into her hand; of needles, rolled dollar bills, boiling vomit; of boyfriend after boyfriend, apartment after apartment, each seedier than the last, strangers asleep on the floor; of Annie, who cared about her, and everyone else in the world, who didn't.

"Why did you ask me that?" said Leigh.

"I've been asking around about you."

"Asking who?"

"Doesn't matter. They knew you ten years ago. People change. I was just wondering if you have."

Leigh jiggled a foot. Tiny bubbles formed, swirled and vanished. Once he knew the truth, Clyde would vanish also. She sighed with the loss.

"No," said Leigh. "I haven't changed."

"That must be very tough for you."

Leigh teared up. "Yes," she whispered, shame wrapping her in its damp towel.

"Poor Leigh," Clyde said, and drew her closer.

With Clyde's arms around her, Leigh surrendered to the tears that had been crawling at the edge of her terrible need. Her father, the only person who would help her, was dead. After promising to sell the house, he hadn't done it, and now, if acquitted, Della stood to inherit everything. Treatment centers cost money, lots of it. Without that house, Leigh felt doomed to loneliness and certain self-destruction. Flooded with defeat, she clung to Clyde.

"Please don't tell my sister," she breathed into his warm neck. "She still loves me."

Now Leigh sat on the bed, looked at a grocery sack stuffed with her belongings. On top was a T-shirt belonging to Clyde, "borrowed" so she would have an excuse to stop by his place before leaving town. She had found something else stuffed behind the T-shirt drawer, which struck her as odd. It was a latex Richard Nixon mask, the pull-over kind, more grotesque than comical. She poked fingers through its eye holes. Probably a leftover Halloween joke. She was tempted to pull it over her head and scare Clyde, but she didn't want him to think she was snoop. She picked up his T-shirt and pressed it to her nose, breathed in.

What the hell was she doing? Clyde was the best thing that had happened to her since leaving home. These feelings were not the fleeting residue of a great one-night stand. Something was happening here.

The phone rang. Leigh jumped on it. "Hello?"

"Hey Dollface, how yew?"

Leigh's heart sank. "Who is this?"

"Bill! You forget me already?"

"Oh, yeah," said Leigh, without cheer. She had forgotten the appraiser. "How you doin'?"

"You don't sound very happy to hear from me. What's the matter? Did I catch you in the middle of someone?" Bill guffawed.

"You got an appraisal for me, Bill?"

"I surely do. Let me bring it by. We can go over it together."

"Actually, I'm getting ready to leave here in a minute. Can you mail it to me?"

"It won't take but a minute. Then I can collect the rest of my fee, if you know what I mean. Don't bother changing the sheets. We're just gonna mess them up again."

Leigh blocked the image. "No, really, Bill, just tell me the bottom line."

"Your sister's not there, is she?"

"No, but—"

"Good. Don't start without me."

"Bill?" She replaced the receiver. "Shit."

Leigh picked up her pace, determined to leave before Bill arrived. She peeled off three fifty-dollar bills, stuffed them in a drawer, scrounged for paper and pen, and scrawled a hasty note:

Annie,
I left some money in the nightstand for the appraiser. Sorry I couldn't stay. I love you.

Leigh

Finally, everything together, Leigh checked the bathroom one last time. Seeing nothing left behind, she slung her fringed bag over her chest, commando style, and dug for keys. She would drive by Clyde's before heading on, let him have one last look at her; that is, if he wasn't out fighting a fire. Maybe she should call first. God, she didn't know what to do. She had always been the one in control, able to get what she wanted by crooking a finger. With Clyde, she felt vulnerable, and it scared as much as excited her. Now she regretted telling him anything. How stupid can you get? Yet, he had been so sympathetic. Would he want to help her, really, or was he even now glad to be shed of her? Had he checked his wallet, pockets, secret hiding places after she left?

A knock came at the door.

Dammit!

Leigh removed the money from the bedside table, steeled herself for a battle with Bill, who expected sex in payment for his appraisal. Well, tough. He'd have to take the money or leave it. If he laid a hand on her, he'd withdraw a bloody stump. Leigh walked to the door, placed her own hand on the knob.

Wait a minute. Be smart, Leigh.

She looked through the peephole.

Eugene's distorted face loomed large, mouth open slightly, tongue working. What did he want? Whatever it was, she would have to disappoint him. Leigh opened the door. From the office, Don Pardo hollered for Nola Huber to *Come on down!*

"Eugene, honey, I don't have time—"

Miguel appeared from nowhere and stepped in front of Eugene. Leigh retreated, but not in time. She slammed the door on a steel-toed boot. As Miguel pushed himself in, silver handled switchblade gleaming in one hand, Leigh screamed.

You're the next contestant on The Price is Right!

Shifting from foot to foot, Eugene stared at the door just slammed in his face. The man with the pictures on his skin had promised him a dollar. Eugene knocked.

"Dahl?"

Leigh screamed again. Eugene tried the door. Not locked. He pushed it open.

CHAPTER 32

Annie watched Della shuffle into the visiting room. Still in oversized togs, hair haphazard, she looked like a mental patient. Under fluorescent lights, Della's skin seemed gray, eyes raccoonish. A large bruise highlighted her cheek. Della stopped short when she saw Annie at the table, and bumped from behind, spun on the woman at her heels. Annie stiffened, anticipating a confrontation, but Della caught herself, as if counting to ten. She obviously wasn't sleeping well. Was she afraid to close her eyes?

Della sat, posture slumped, eyes curious.

"What happened to your cheek?" Annie asked.

"Nothing." Della gave a sick smile. "If a fight breaks out, and nobody 'sees' it, does it make a bruise?"

A disheveled man at the table next to Annie hollered at the young woman opposite for getting herself arrested. Beyond them, an elderly black woman, spine curved with osteoporosis, stared motionless at the crying young woman opposite, no older than eighteen. Smokers filled the air with a toxic cloud. A clueless young father changed a baby on the floor, contorted his face, said, "Yuk!"

"It's a little different in here since the last time I saw you," said Annie. "Is it always this loud?"

"Is that what you came here to ask me, or are we making nice, or what?"

Annie dropped her eyes. "I'm sorry, I was just—"

"Did you talk to Pete?"

"Yes, but he wasn't much help."

Della seemed to shrink. Any smaller, her shoulders would come through the neck of the jumpsuit.

"I need to know something," said Annie. "And I want the truth."

"I already told you the truth. I can't help it if you don't believe me."

"Did you know my father was going to sell his property?"

"Yes, I did."

Annie straightened, her senses heightened. "Who was the buyer?"

"I don't know."

"He didn't tell you who was going to buy the house?"

"He didn't tell me anything. I found out."

"How?"

"Why do you want to know?"

"You asked me to help you, Della. That's what I'm trying to do."

Della's eyes narrowed. "Why?"

It was a good question. Annie wondered why she hadn't lit out of here like Leigh, returned to her own life, left Della's problems for Della to solve or not. And that had been her plan: chuck her father in an urn, scatter his ashes, go home. Then a series of events waylaid her: her father in the morgue, brutally beaten; a postponed wedding; Jeb Barlow with photos and proof of a survey; and Pete Duncan's stubborn refusal to believe Della might be innocent. Overshadowing all was the Widow Lake property, ownership to be determined upon Della's fate. Her conviction seemed, in Annie's mind, to benefit too many people.

"Because I want to know what happened to my father," said Annie. "It's like you said. I owe him that much."

Della's eyes softened. "Thank you," she whispered.

It was during an argument that Della learned Ed planned to sell the house.

"Ed was cheating on me. I confronted him; he denied it; I threatened to leave. That's when he said he had a buyer for the place, and I was welcome to leave any time."

"Was this the night of the murder?" asked Annie.

"Yes. I assumed Ed was going to take the money from the sale and run off with this other woman."

"How did you know my father was cheating on you?"

"I followed him to a hotel in Daytona and saw them."

"Did you recognize her?"

"I didn't get a good look. I was in the parking lot. She wore big sunglasses and a baseball cap. Either her hair was real short, or she had it pulled back or under the cap, I'm not sure. I recognized Ed, though. The two of them went into a room and closed the door. They came out about thirty minutes later, arms around each other. I wanted to kill them both."

Annie's eyes darted. "You might want to keep that to yourself," she said.

"Won't do me any good. Pete Duncan's got me guilty anyway."

"Does he know about the other woman and that you saw them together?"

"I told him right off."

"Did you also tell him Ed was selling the house?"

"Yes. He told me not to tell anyone because it would damage my case. Why? Do you think it means something?"

"I'm not sure yet, but I've been thinking about what you said about King Powell framing you. Do you think it's possible my father was finally going to sell to King?"

"Absolutely not," said Della. "Ed hated King. He called him a greedy, red-skinned scalp fucker."

Annie winced at the racist remark, so typically Ed, and

glanced around to see if anyone else had heard. Della continued, oblivious.

"Like I told you before, I think King's behind Ed's murder. Maybe he knew Ed was planning to sell to someone else, so he had him killed. And with me sitting in here, he'll get exactly what he wants."

To gauge the probability of Della's conspiracy theory, given the woman's desperate circumstances, was difficult. As Pete said, she would say anything to save her skin. Still, there were unexplored avenues here, and someone had to stroll them.

"Did you tell the sheriff any of this?"

"I tried. He said he'd look into it, but frankly, I think he sees me guilty, just like everybody else. 'Sides, he's up to his whatzits with these fires around here. I'm not exactly what you'd call a priority."

Annie shuffled facts. "Okay, help me out here. You followed my father to a hotel in Daytona. What time did you leave your house?"

"About six in the evening, I guess."

"So you got to the hotel around six-thirty, left around seven, got home at what, seven-thirty?"

"About that. Maybe eight."

"When did Ed get home?"

"Nine, something like that."

"So there's an hour between eight and nine where he's unaccounted for."

Della shrugged. "He wasn't with me, if that's what you're askin'."

"What did you do in that hour?" asked Annie.

"I drank."

"Alcohol?"

"It wasn't holy water."

"Then what happened?"

"Ed came home, and I lit into him."

"And that's when you found out he was planning to sell the house?"

"What can I say?" Della shook her head, eyes downcast. "I just . . . lost it."

"What did my father do when you blew up at him?"

"That's the funny thing: he just stood there and took it. Didn't deny anything, didn't admit anything, just stood there. Never did tell me who the woman was. Finally, I smacked him one, and that's when he left."

"You hit him?"

" 'Course I hit him."

Annie blinked. "With what?"

"My fist. I wasn't trying to hurt him, I just wanted him to fight back. I punched him on the arm."

So Della was a hitter. Could she have crossed the line that night, drunk and angry enough to pick up an oar and swing it with all her might?

"Where did Ed go after you hit him?"

"I assumed he went back to his girlfriend. I had a few more drinks, threw some things against the wall. That's about all I remember before I passed out."

"From drinking?"

Della's eyes narrowed. "Oh, like you never have."

"I'm not judging you, Della. I'm just trying to get the lay of the land here."

"I'm sorry. It's just that nobody's listened to my side without coming after me in some way. They're saying I killed Ed in a drunken rage, and I suppose I could have, but I didn't. I was passed out on the couch."

"For how long?"

"I swear, I don't know. Might have been five minutes or five hours. All I know is, when I woke up, it was dark. I called for

Ed and when he didn't answer, I went outside to look for him."

"Why did you go outside? I thought you said he drove off in the car."

Della's eyes tracked back and forth as she considered the question. "I heard something." She turned her head sharply, as if listening in the distance. "I don't know," she said faintly. "It was dark. My head was full of cotton. But I heard it. Something."

"That hotel in Daytona, where you saw my father. What's its name?"

"It was a Comfy Inn, right there across from the racetrack."

Annie knew the one. She'd have to rent a car.

"One last thing. Did my father own a camera?"

"I don't think so. Oh, wait. I think he had an old Instamatic. You know, the kind with the wrist strap. Why?"

"Just wondering." Annie gave Della a reassuring smile.

"Are you going to visit me again?"

"I'll try."

Della explained her pod was scheduled to receive visitors at this same time once a week. She leaned in, eyes full of hope, and held Annie's hands until it was time to let her go.

CHAPTER 33

What a morning! Jeb Barlow's story hit the front page, and suddenly, he was man of the hour. Other reporters came by his desk, wanted to know how he managed to get those photos of Eugene. Even that tight little package from sales, the one with the red hair, Kelly something, walked by twice this morning, and she wasn't after coffee. True, his desk was next to the break room, but she had smiled at him both times, he was sure. Even his brother-in-law said it was a good story. Maybe this was a good time to hit Rip up for a raise. Jeb could say the *Orlando Sentinel* had called, even though they hadn't. No harm in running it up the flagpole, right? He'd have to be careful how much he asked for—not too little, not too much.

Jeb tucked a newspaper under his arm. It was a bit early for a break, but he couldn't wait to show Florida his byline. By lunchtime, she'd be too busy to talk to him.

Listen up, everybody! I want all y'all to know that our own Jeb Barlow got himself a Pulitzer Prize story, right here in the DeLeon Sun News!

Maybe she'd pick up his tab. Maybe, this time, she'd let him buy her a drink.

Once outside, Jeb lit a cigarette. To reach the diner, he'd stroll the New York Avenue sidewalk, which would take him by a stretch of storefronts and a bank or two. His step light, Jeb whistled and nodded at strangers. To people he knew, he stopped, pulling the paper from beneath his arm to stab at his article. They told him to keep up the good work, then hurried away. Jeb moved on, Andy of Mayberry, avuncular protector, beloved by all.

Jeb crossed the boulevard and tossed his cigarette into the gutter next to the jail where Della Shiftlet had been detained. They'd since moved her to county. He liked Della Shiftlet. She wasn't as sexy as Florida, but she had a nice smile. People around here steered clear of Della, said her resemblance to Ed's late wife was unholy, or somesuch. But Della always said hello, didn't treat him like he stank, which, most of the time, he admitted, he did. Della's temper was documented, but Jeb could never believe her capable of murder. He had his money on Eugene Lanier. He didn't say that in the article, of course, but it seemed clear that Eugene whacked Ed to keep him from making those pictures public.

But if that was the case, why had Ed mailed the photos? Why not bring them directly to the paper?

Questions, questions. Group, prioritize, see the big picture. Then think about it later.

With the diner in view Jeb could smell today's lunch special: meatloaf. He loved Florida's meatloaf, even if it didn't love him. Too early for lunch, he reminded himself. He'd just have coffee, show Florida the paper, come back later for meatloaf. On the other hand, there wouldn't be many people in the diner right now; Florida's announcement would not have maximum effect. Maybe he should return to the office, come back later. Then again—he looked at his watch—noon was only two hours away. Nobody would miss him at work. He'd have coffee, shoot the shit, and when the place was full, show off the paper. Perfect. Jeb headed for the front door.

A noise like crying stopped him. Jeb stepped around the corner, but saw nothing out of the ordinary: dusty cars, a big green Dumpster on a concrete slab, its side door open like a service window, beyond it the alley. Must have been a cat, thought Jeb.

He heard it again, louder this time, from behind the building.

"Hey, are you all right back there?" Jeb called, hoping to God the woman would say she was fine, freeing him of further responsibility. Probably some chick had a fight with her boyfriend. None of his business.

But the woman did not say she was fine. He moved along the side of the diner. "Miss?"

Another whimper, high pitched, like a child. Jeb turned the corner. Kingfisher's daughter, Sada, squatted against the building, hugging her knees. Her body jerked as she snuffled and huffed for air. Jeb thought of a whipped puppy.

"Hey, what's wrong?" He moved toward her. "Did Florida say something to you?" Crazy as he was about Florida, Jeb knew she was tough on her waitresses.

The girl looked at him with tearful brown eyes. "No," she said, then slid her back upward against the wall. She wiped her eyes. "I better get back."

"Okay," said Jeb. He didn't know if he should walk with her. "You're all right, then?"

Sada shrugged, then gave Jeb a shy smile. "Thanks."

"Don't mention it," said Jeb. He watched Sada return to the diner through the back door. A blurred movement over his left shoulder spiked his adrenaline and instinctively he stepped back, threw up an arm. The newspaper hit the gravel. Jeb felt the first blow over his eye. After another, he didn't feel anything.

CHAPTER 34

Annie reined in the cherry-red Ford Mustang. The car wanted to fly, but Annie was determined to stay on the ground and, as Della had done, within the speed limit, a stingy fifty-five. So the Mustang took the seams in the road with a hypnotic thuh-dump, thuh-dump, thuh-dump.

Annie felt guilty for not returning to the motel, but perhaps Leigh would wait. If the sheriff was too busy, and Petey too lazy to check out Della's story, Annie would do it herself. If her father had planned to sell his house and run away with this woman, as Della suspected, that would make the woman in the baseball cap a worthy suspect.

She could hear Petey's voice now: *Annie, leave this alone. You don't know what you're doing. Maybe she didn't, but at least she was doing something.*

Annie pulled into the Comfy Inn, looked at her watch. The drive took twenty-eight minutes. Climbing from the car, she noted her distance to the hotel. The salmon-pink building had three stories with a waist-high concrete wall surrounding each. As she looked, a maid with a cart emerged from a room on the second floor, her top half visible from the ground. Annie could make out the maid's size and race, but not facial features. So far, everything Della told her added up.

The reception area, blissfully silent, was nothing like the Sha-D-Land Motel. Tiled floors, waxed furniture and freshly painted walls coordinated with the salmon-colored sofa and chair. A large painting of a sailboat hung over the reception desk. Everything was spotless. Annie did not patronize franchises as a rule, preferring to support Mom and Pop outfits. Between the Sha-D-Land and this place, however, no contest. Some Mom and Pops deserved to die.

No one sat at the reception desk. Annie cleared her throat, called, "Anybody here?"

The sharp squeak of a chair, a sudden thump. Oops, thought Annie. Somebody's napping. The clerk emerged, blinking, from a room behind the desk. He looked to be in his teens, all legs and arms, thin with unruly dark hair and brown eyes, whites pink.

Not napping. Imbibing.

"Help you?" said the clerk, scratching the back of his head. "Heh, heh," he muttered, a silly smile on his face.

"Yeah, hi. I wonder if you could answer a few questions for me?"

"You need a room?"

"No, I—"

"That's good, heh heh, because we don't have any ready, heh heh." The clerk placed elbows on the counter, leaned in. "What kind of questions?"

"I'm trying to find out if this man was a guest at this hotel." Annie extracted her father's picture from her wallet, handed it to the clerk.

The clerk looked at the picture. "You a cop?"

"Me? Oh, no."

"I didn't think so." The clerk narrowed his bloodshot eyes. "Hey, I know. Private investigator. The guy's got a wife, doesn't he?"

"Why do you say that?"

"Well, because he—" The clerk stopped, then grinned from ear to ear. "Wow, you almost got me to spill." He slapped the counter, pointed at Annie's chin. "You're good! Heh heh. How do you do that?"

"You recognize him, then?"

The clerk looked to the side, a stupid grin splitting his face. "I don't know, man. That sounds like primo info to me. What do I get in return?"

Oh, brother, thought Annie. In your dreams. "Never mind," she said, picked her father's picture from the clerk's fingers. "I'm sure I can get what I need from the manager. Is he around?"

"Oh, come on, man, I was just messin' with ya. Lighten up, heh heh heh."

"When did you last see this man?"

"Hey, how do you get a job like this? I bet I'd be good at it."

Annie tamped her rising ire. This kid obviously knew something about Ed and if it took a little chitchat, that was little enough to invest. "You have to pass some tests," she said.

"What kind of tests?"

"Drug tests."

"Seriously?"

Annie nodded. "Oh yeah. All the time."

The clerk seemed to deflate, then brightened. "What about an informant? How do I get to be one of those?"

"By answering questions," said Annie.

"Riiiight, heh heh," said the clerk, head bobbing. "Okay, shoot."

"When did you last see this man?"

"Yeah, yeah, let me think." The kid contorted his face. "I think it was last week. I'm not sure of the day."

"Do you remember seeing anyone with him?"

The clerk's face morphed into a salacious leer. "Oh yeah," he said, nodding. "So I was right, right? The guy's married, and you're working for the wife."

"You got me!" said Annie, replacing Ed's photo.

"I knew it! See? I'm good at this."

"Can you describe the woman?"

"Oh, man, can I ever! She was about your height, skinny, long blonde hair, nice tits—" He glanced at Annie's chest, pupils dilating.

"Hello?" said Annie.

Eyes rose to meet Annie's. "What?"

"What else do you remember about her looks?"

The clerk studied Annie's open wallet. "Oh, I get it. You're testing my powers of observation or whatever, right?"

"What do you mean?"

"That's her, right there!" The clerk pointed to a picture inside Annie's wallet. He clapped, flexed biceps. "Woo hoo! Am I good at this, or what? I passed, right?"

Annie stared. She had taken the photo herself, last Thanksgiving, a close-up that caught light from within.

"Man, she's so hot she glows," crowed the clerk.

Annie grabbed the edge of the counter to steady herself.

"What's her name?"

"Leigh," she whispered.

"Can I have her phone number? I mean, this guy's done with her, right? The gig is up, right?"

Annie closed her wallet, tucked it into her purse. "Yeah," she said. "The gig is up." She stumbled toward the door.

"Wait! I helped you out, right? Aren't you going to give me her number?"

Outside, Annie couldn't remember where she had parked the car. She scanned the lot, not seeing, lost.

CHAPTER 35

"It doesn't surprise me one bit," Helen said, riding next to Annie in the Mustang. "There was always sexual tension between Ed and Leigh. They whipped each other with it."

"Don't be absurd," said Annie. The traffic west to DeLeon was light. With an eye to any police cars lurking in the brush, she pushed her speed to sixty-five. "There's got to be a reason Dad and Leigh were at that motel together."

"What reason?"

"I don't know, but it's not what you're thinking." Still, Annie struggled with the secrecy aspect. Why hadn't Leigh told Annie she'd seen Ed the night before he died? Could Leigh have had a hand in Ed's murder? As soon as the thought formed, Annie pushed it away.

"Your father undermined everything Leigh accomplished, told her she was worthless in a hundred different ways," Helen continued. "She played softball one summer when she was about twelve, brought home a little team trophy. She was so proud of that thing. Ed took one look at it and said, 'Where'd you pick that up, Woolworth's?' That little girl's face fell right through the floor."

"I remember," said Annie. She had pulled the trophy from the trash, where Leigh, devastated, had chucked it.

"Leigh craved her daddy's attention so badly she became what he desired in other women—a loose, foul-mouthed slut."

"Mother!"

"It's true. She saw the way he looked at other women. She knew what was going on. She fashioned herself after those floozies to get Ed's attention, but it backfired. What he liked in other women he couldn't stand in his own daughter. The harder Leigh tried to get Ed's attention, the more he pushed her away. But you know he wanted her."

"That is really sick, Mom."

"I'm just trying to be helpful."

"Dad and Leigh did not do what you're suggesting."

"You're just afraid to look at it."

Annie rolled down her window. Hot air roared and whipped hair about her face.

"That's a little windy for me, dear."

Annie reached for the handle, then stopped. How adolescent she felt, eagerly doing as told. Since coming to DeLeon, Helen had offered nothing supportive, and with this latest "helpful" suggestion, Annie had enough. She left the window down, and if her mother was sucked out the window, that would be fine.

"Mom, I need you to do something for me."

"Of course, dear, after you roll up your window."

"I want my window where it is. And I want you to stop running down Dad. I need to draw my own conclusions without your commentary."

"My marriage to your father was a disaster!"

Annie gripped the wheel. "So you've said. But I wasn't married to him, Mom, and I'm tired of carrying your cross."

"What's that supposed to mean?"

"The problems you had with Dad were real. I get that. But I never got to know my father outside your influence, and now I never will. I've been trying to piece together the details of his murder, and the picture that's developing is different from the monster you painted for me all these years."

"You need to stop talking."

"He was a flawed human being, yes, but so am I. So were you. I've got to start listening to the voice in my own head, Mom. I think it's time for you to leave."

"I said stop!"

The air in the car thickened, swirled. Each crack in the road seemed to widen. Annie glanced at Helen, ramrod straight against the seat. They passed an unfenced cow, then another, no doubt nosing for water in the parched drainage ditch. Annie half expected them to leap, deer-like, before the car.

"I'm sorry, Mom, but I don't want to see you, anymore."

Annie braced for a lightning bolt, but all she felt was her mother's shock and hurt. She had spoken from the heart but wished now she could take it back. Instead, she rolled up her window.

Helen sat arms crossed, jaw clamped. They drove in silence until I-17, where Annie turned left toward town. Finally, Helen spoke.

"I know who murdered your father."

The announcement hit Annie in the chest. Helen looked straight ahead, face stony.

"Who?"

Helen smiled. "See? I knew you still needed me."

Furious, Annie pulled to the side of the two-lane road. "First of all, I don't appreciate you trying to control me by dropping bombs."

"What bomb? All I said was—"

"Second, you're a projection of me. If you know who killed my father, that means I know, too."

"Are you sure? Can you tell me, right now?"

Annie sputtered. "Of course not."

"Right. You don't have access to repressed knowledge."

"And you do?"

"Yes."

Annie shook her head to clear it. "Are you saying that, deep down, I know who killed my father, but can't access that information without you?"

"Yes."

"That is total bull."

"It was your father's girlfriend."

"What, am I supposed to be impressed? You'll say anything to stay with me!"

"Since you were nine years old I've been whispering in your ear, showing you the truth, lighting your way."

"You sound like the writing on a holy card. What's wrong with you? It was me the whole time."

"No, Annie. It was me. And if you think you can replace me with Della Shiftlet, you're mistaken."

So that was it. Helen was jealous of Della Shiftlet. Annie felt foolish for not seeing it before. Her attitude softened, but Annie knew she must not get sidetracked. "I know no one can take your place, mom. That's why I've clung to you for so long."

"Then please," Helen whispered. "Don't send me away."

The plea threw Annie back to the bank of Widow Lake where Helen lay cold and dead. How could she turn out her own mother? Hadn't she suffered enough? Annie knew it had never been Helen's intention to rob Annie and Leigh of a father; she simply needed an ally. Recruiting Leigh had been easy, but Annie was drawn to her father. For Annie she had to lobby hard. And then, to keep Annie on her side—

A sparkling stream suddenly cleared the opposing banks in Annie's mind. Growing up, she had been torn between her father on one side, her mother and Leigh on the other. Now, she finally understood. To keep Annie on her side forever, Helen had to make the ultimate sacrifice. She had to die.

Annie watched cars speed past on I-17. She would give almost anything to be inside one of them. "Mom? Did you kill yourself to punish Dad?"

Helen brushed her clothes. "We should get moving, before we're rear-ended."

"Answer me, please."

Helen sighed. "You know what happened that morning, Annie. You were there."

"I know you drowned. But you've never told me how."

"My lungs filled up with water—"

"You know what I mean. Was it suicide?"

Helen adjusted the vent in the dashboard to direct cold air into her face. Hair lifted from her neck. "I can't tell you what you don't know," she said.

"The thing is, I do know. Don't I?"

Helen wiped beneath her eyes with fingers, and sniffled. "I'm sorry I had to leave you so young, Annie."

"But you stayed with me all these years to keep me away from Dad, didn't you?"

"You wanted me here."

"You knew I would be alone once Leigh left. You knew how lonely I was, but still, you would not let me have my father."

"It was you clinging to me. You just said no one can take my place."

"And no one will. You're my mother. You'll always be my mother." Helen began to cry. "But Mom, I needed my father, too."

"Oh, my," Helen breathed. "Oh, my, my, my."

Annie put a hand on her mother's shoulder. "You okay?"

Helen shook her head. "You'll visit me?" she asked, voice cracking.

"I don't think so."

After a moment, Helen nodded. "Say goodbye to Leigh."

"I will."

Helen leaned in, kissed Annie on the cheek. "Are you ready?"

Annie nodded.

"Close your eyes."

Annie sat back, closed her eyes. Helen's voice was soothing, rhythmic as more cars sped past.

"First, take a big gulp of air so you can stay under water a good, long time. Then, let the air out while you're underwater, until your lungs are empty and you sink to a sitting position on the lake bottom."

Annie expelled air.

"Count to three, then inhale through your nose—not enough to pull the water into your head, but just enough to feel it begin to travel up your nostrils. Now, breathe out."

Annie exhaled.

"Then try it again. One, one-thousand; two, one-thousand; three, one-thousand . . ."

The rhythms came together as Annie drove: her breathing, the road, the beat of her breaking heart. She would miss her mother, almost as much as she missed her father, but she knew she had done the right thing. At the light, Annie sensed a presence and turned to the car next to her. The driver, no one she knew, gave a friendly wave. Annie waved back, not sure if to say hello or good-bye.

Turning into the parking lot of the Sha-D-Land motel, Annie saw an ambulance, then recognized Deputy Salceda's car. "Now, what?" she breathed, just as a thousand hooks picked her skin, and she knew. *Leigh.*

CHAPTER 36

Deputy Salceda, knees shaking, stepped from room nine of the Sha-D-Land motel, and leaned against the door. The sight of Leigh Bartlett lying in her own blood had made the floor tilt. Leigh's sliced face peeled away in places like old wallpaper. Through Leigh's fingers, pressed to her face as if to keep it from sliding off, Salceda made out one eye, wild with shock. Who knew what the other looked like, if still there. Salceda had to get out of there, let the paramedics do their thing.

Outside, Salceda bent at the waist and rested her hands on her knees. What kind of monster did that?

"Excuse me," said a gritty voice. Salceda straightened. A gray-haired woman in a shapeless housedress shuffled toward her. "Is she going to be all right?"

"And you are?"

"Edna Voorhis. I own this place."

Salceda nodded. "The paramedics are getting her to the hospital now. We won't know anything for a while yet. Ma'am, were you here when this happened?"

"Yeah, but I didn't hear nothin'. I had the TV on."

"Did you see anyone, anything out of the ordinary?"

"I might have done. My eyes aren't so great any more, but I did see this motorcycle-looking feller leave out of here in a hurry. We get lots of motorcycle people down here, so I didn't think nuthin' of it until this here." She waved a limp hand toward room nine.

"What do you mean, 'motorcycle-looking'?"

"Black leather, got them tattoos, nekkid women, snakes and such."

"Can you describe him?"

"I just did."

"Yes, but did you see his face?"

"No, I told you, I don't see so good."

"But you saw tattoos."

"Kinda hard to miss."

Salceda shifted her weight. "Did you see anyone else?"

"I thought I saw that slow kid, wasisname?"

"Eugene Lanier?"

"Yeah, but I didn't pay him no mind."

"Mrs. Voorhis, I need to find the victim's sister, Annie Bartlett. Any idea where she might be?"

"I don't pay attention to what ain't my business," the woman scolded.

"Who called this in?"

A wiry man stepped forward, white as a sheet. "I did."

"Hey!" Mrs. Voorhis shouted to one of the paramedics. "Don't step on my azaleas!" She scurried to the bush's aid.

"What's your name?" Salceda asked the man.

"Bill."

"Last name?"

"Do I have to give it?"

"What's the problem?"

"Well, see, I'm married, see, and Leigh and me, we sort of . . ." He gestured awkwardly.

Salceda nodded. "I think you better tell me, anyway."

"Ah hell. It's Castle." Bill Castle twisted an absent ring on his wedding finger, eyes on the ground. "Why did this have to happen to me?"

"It didn't happen to you, sir. It happened to Leigh Bartlett."

Bill looked off. "So, you found the victim?"

"Yeah. I knocked on the door, and when she didn't say nothin', I went in."

"The door was unlocked?"

Bill nodded. "The place was a wreck, and she was on the floor, all cut up. I seen she was still alive, so I called 911."

Allegedly, Bill Castle had come to the motel with an appraisal. He had talked with Leigh Bartlett before arriving, so she was expecting him. In the time it took for him to arrive, Bill said, someone must have entered the room. "I had nothing to do with this, I swear."

"Did you see anyone suspicious?"

Bill Castle tucked hands into armpits. "I was too freaked out to notice much of anything."

"We're going to need to talk with you again, sir."

"Yeah, I figured that."

As he moved off, Bill's shoulders shimmied, as if cold. Salceda knew the feeling. Whatever evil moved among them had stripped the town's warm aura of safety, forced eyes open to what they didn't want to see. First fires, then murder, now mutilation: what was happening to this town?

Paramedics pushed a stretcher out the door. Leigh's bandages, around her head and face, were already turning red. At least she was quiet now, and, if lucky, unconscious.

From the parking lot, Salceda heard several raised voices talking at once. She stepped around the ambulance to see what was happening. Annie Bartlett strained against uniformed arms holding her back. She scream-shouted, voice garbled with tears and anger. Salceda ran toward her.

"That's the sister! Let her go!" Salceda reached the clot of bodies and shouted over Annie's wailing. "It's the victim's sister. Let her go!" The uniforms seemed reluctant. "Now!" ordered the deputy. Annie shook off the loosened grip and ducked

beneath yellow tape, appealing to Salceda with fear-filled eyes.
"She's in the ambulance. She's alive."

The ambulance moved forward. Salceda stepped in front of
it, lifted her arms and yelled, "Stop!" The window rolled down.
"The victim's sister is here. Let her in."

The back doors opened, and Annie climbed inside. The
ambulance bounced into the street, lights flashing, siren pitched.
Salceda shivered in its wake, then made the sign of the cross.

CHAPTER 37

Glued to the gurney, Annie chanted alongside her sister: "I'm here, Leigh. You're going to be all right." Outside the operating room, Dr. Neeman, short, and authoritative, peeled Annie away, made promises, nodded instructions. Annie listened, head full of scratching wings.

Follow the blue line.

Down the airless, L-shaped hall, the blue line veered to the left. In the waiting room, *hot in here,* a phone smelled of disinfectant. Annie dialed Camp's number, got his answering machine.

. . . your call is important to me . . .

She left an incoherent message and hung up, light-headed. She sat, and the trembling began, shoulders first, then down her arms. Never had she felt so scared and alone.

Deputy Salceda pulled a chair, sat facing Annie.

"Do you have any idea who might have done this?"

Annie shook her head. "None."

"Does she have a boyfriend?"

"Leigh always has a boyfriend. The latest is Clyde, the fire fighter guy."

"Clyde Glenwood?"

"Yes."

Salceda asked questions about Clyde as Annie dredged something mired in her still muddy brain. It was stuck, whatever it was, like old bottles she and Ed used to pull from the mud at the St. Augustine dump. Some gave themselves up with a wet, sucking sound; others came reluctantly, slick with silt and slime. Annie lifted the hair from her neck, interrupted Salceda. "Is it hot in here to you? I'm dying."

The deputy looked taken aback. "Uh, yes, it is a little warm, I guess."

"Sorry. I'm having trouble concentrating."

"That's understandable."

"I was trying to remember something . . . on the periphery."

"Does it have to do with what happened to Leigh?"

"That's just it. I—I don't know. I think so."

Salceda looked at Annie with kind, honey-colored eyes. "It'll come to you," she said, then offered a small smile. "Can I do anything for you right now? Get you anything?"

As a child, Annie didn't often cry at movies, but when she did, her tears filled buckets. The parts that got to her were not the dog-recovers-from-coma moments that slayed Leigh. Rather, unexpected kindness: a child smiling at the isolated, creepy-but-benign neighbor; a soldier giving sustenance to a wounded enemy; a teacher, seeing the redeemable in a delinquent student. Such acts inspired Annie to goodness. Before a mermaid, she had wanted to be a nun, like Julie Andrews in *The Sound of Music*. Then Annie wanted to live among lepers, like selfless Father Damian, take on the fate of the walking damned with stoic acceptance. Locked in prayer, nose falling off, she would give thanks for her temporal whole heart, which beat with selfless love for those without faces.

Looking into Deputy Salceda's eyes, Annie cried.

The surgery took six hours. When Dr. Neeman shuffled into the waiting room, Annie jumped to her feet.

Machines emitted beeps and muffled wheezes while Annie's world dimmed. With wet eyes and chewed lips, Annie willed

Leigh to wake, dreaded it at the same time. Her sister would want to know how bad it was, if the doctors had saved her eye, would there be scars?

Bad, no, yes.

Annie slipped her hand beneath Leigh's, massaged her sister's fingertips. A needle, tip in a vein, rested atop Leigh's hand, secured with white tape. The tape comforted Annie, reminded her of the cylinders she often found in her mother's uniform pocket, white metal with a red cross on them. Unlike cellophane, the cloth tape dispensed only after a struggle. It smelled like an empty prescription bottle and was not to be used for wrapping presents.

Leigh's finger joints seemed enlarged. Did she still crack her knuckles? She still chewed her nails to the quick, that was clear. Cuticles were red and ragged, as always.

Ed's hands were huge, fingers thick as pickles. At age five, Annie's head and Ed's hands met at the same level. She grabbed them constantly, jumping when they fluttered out of reach. If she got a grip, Ed locked on. Annie lifted her feet, then swung, a child-shaped tote at her father's side. Ed's hand steered her head through a crowd, go this way, go that way, or rested possessively, a scalp yoke. Formidable weapons, Ed's open hands made bare flesh sting, or closed, blasted holes in drywall. When hidden in front pockets, they made music with keys or coins and were restless in the dark.

Leigh's hand stirred. Annie stood, moved so Leigh could see her through the gap in her bandages. "Leigh? You're in the hospital, and you're going to be fine." Blood clots pooled in Leigh's unfocused eye. "Can you see me? I'm right here."

The eye rolled. "Daddy," Leigh rasped.

"No, it's me. Annie." She stroked her sister's hair. "Somebody attacked you with a knife, Leigh. You're cut up pretty bad, but the doctor says you'll be fine."

Leigh's eye closed, slowly reopened.

"Leigh, who did this?"

Leigh's lips parted with a dry, cracking sound. Annie reached for the cup of melting ice beside the bed, fed Leigh a transparent sliver. "Can you hear me?" Leigh gave a slight nod. "Who did this to you?" Annie asked again and placed her ear close to Leigh's mouth.

"Miguel." The word was slight as air.

Annie lifted her head. "Miguel? Miguel who?"

"Ved . . . ra."

A single tear filled Leigh's eye, overflowed. A salty flood broke, stung its way down the ruined landscape of sliced flesh. With a tissue twisted into a cone, Annie wicked Leigh's tears into her hand, wished with all her heart she could do the same with the pain.

Clyde Glenwood was suddenly at Annie's side, breathing audibly, his face a roil of shock and anger. "Jesus Christ," he said. He ran both hands through his hair. "Oh, God."

"Clyde?" rasped Leigh.

Clyde composed his face, and leaned in. "Yeah, baby. It's me. Don't you worry. I'm going to get this guy. He's going to pay for this."

A nurse stepped into the room. "The police need to come in, now."

Outside the room, Annie saw Deputy Salceda and some officers she didn't recognize. "We have to go, Leigh," she said. "I'll be back in the morning, okay?"

Leigh whimpered.

"Don't worry, baby," said Clyde. "I'll be back. And I'll find this creep. I promise." He kissed Leigh on the temple, said good-bye. When he turned around, Annie saw his face shift into a hard, cold mask. He took the hallway in five giant steps, missed the elevator by seconds, and smashed the door with a fist. Instead of waiting, he pushed the door to the stairs. It banged the wall, then slammed after him.

As she passed Deputy Salceda, Annie related the name Miguel Vedra, extracted a promise he would be found. Mrs. Voorhis had provided a vague description of a tattooed man she saw leaving the premises, Salceda said. He wouldn't get far.

Annie waited for the elevator, and the mudstuck bottle in her mind came loose with a wet, sucking sound. A tattooed man, Salceda had said. Annie had seen such a man at The Pier Diner. When he came in, Leigh slipped out, left Annie alone. So Leigh had known she was in danger, yet stayed in DeLeon, ostensibly to keep a date with Clyde Glenwood. Good God, was she that desperate for sex, or was it loneliness, like her own, that had trumped her self-protective instincts?

Annie shuffled toward the hospital exit, wondering where she got the energy to put one foot in front of the other. She heard someone make an explosive entrance, moved to give a wide berth. She looked up, expecting Clyde. Pete Duncan barreled toward her, saying her name. Annie went limp in his arms, body wracked with exhaustion. She was beyond tears, could barely speak.

"I thought she was . . . I thought . . ."

Pete held her close. "Shhh," he said. "She's going to be all right." He pressed her head into his shoulder, rocked her back and forth.

"I want my mother," Annie cried and buried her face.

CHAPTER 38

In all her configurations, Annie Bartlett always loomed large in Pete Duncan's life, whether as childhood nemesis, adolescent crush, or contentious pest. Yet, she had felt small in his arms, diminished by fear and grief. When Annie asked to rest at his apartment, he took her there right away. Entering, he switched on the lamp.

"You can have the bedroom," Pete said. "I've slept on the couch before; it's comfortable."

"Oh, I don't want you to—"

"You've had a rough day, Annie. Let's not have a debate. You'll take the bed; I'll take the couch. Now, what can I get you?"

Annie sat on the sofa, toe-heeled her sandals off. "Do you have any whiskey?"

"No, sorry. I don't drink it."

"What do you drink?"

"I have most everything else," said Pete, peering into his liquor cabinet. The indirect answer was a courtroom favorite: tell the truth, just not to the question you were asked. "How about vodka and tonic?"

"How about just vodka?"

Pete smiled. "You got it." He mixed her a martini, filled his own glass with water, topped both with an olive.

"I'm sorry to burden you like this," said Annie. "I just couldn't go back to that motel."

"Of course you couldn't. And you're not a burden. Cheers."

"Yeah, right. Cheers," Annie repeated, downhearted, then sipped. As she savored the liquor she held her glass at eye level, peered through it.

"So, are you and Denise an item, or what?"

The question seemed out of the blue. Curious as to her motive, Pete answered. "No. Not an item. Friends. Why do you ask?"

"Maybe you should be more than friends. She seems nice."

"I can do my own matchmaking, thank you very much."

"So what's stopping you?"

You, he almost said. *You're stopping me. Nobody else challenges me, shares my past, makes me laugh like you. Only when you leave again can I return to the business of manufacturing a prefabricated happiness, one without excellence, passion, or you, one I will eventually convince myself is as good as it gets, and probably more than I deserve.*

"How's your drink?" he asked.

"Good. Just what the doctor ordered."

Pete sipped water with an olive, also what the doctor ordered. Three years ago, a sardonic, triangle-eyed doctor told him that alcoholic fatty liver was the first stage of liver damage, and he was way past that. His alcoholic hepatitis would lead to cirrhosis and death unless he had an attitude transplant, and, the doctor droned, replaced the alcohol in his veins with blood. The news had come as no surprise. Pete Duncan never did anything halfway; even his cover-up was top drawer. Pete, a "high functioning drunk," got to court, not always clear-headed, but on time; put in the hours, not always productive, but documented; submitted the paperwork, not always accurate, but as required. Once home in front of the television, he drank himself unconscious. If he went out with others, he left the table periodically, slipped to the bar, threw back shots that he paid for on the spot and did not appear on the dinner bill. If alone, he treated the next town to his hard-earned drinking money, drove home with one hand covering his right eye to reduce the number of center lines coming over to his side of the road. He occasionally hit a dog or some nocturnal thing—regretful, but he could live with it—his only collateral damage. In the morning, after a hot shower, eye drops, and a little hair of the dog, Pete was back in the saddle, mind on quitting time. What errors he made were explainable, and his cover-up fooled everyone, for a while.

"You don't fool me, Pete Duncan," said Annie.

Pete, jolted, looked at Annie looking at him. God, he was sick of this subterfuge. Would it never end? After the drunken nights, hangovers, lies, self-abuse, he was still covering up, not alcoholism, but sobriety. Pete wanted to share the irony, but even if Annie understood his disease, he could not risk the disclosure getting beyond his living room. The good people of DeLeon would not tolerate a recovering alcoholic in a position of legal responsibility, just as they would not have tolerated a practicing one. Pete's past was just that, and he had sold his soul to keep it that way.

Annie raked her mussed bangs. "I mean, you act so big and tough all the time, you know? Pete Duncan, Public Defender, all that macho Perry Mason stuff. But inside, you're just a big pussycat, aren't you?"

"Funny, I was just thinking the same about you." Annie smiled, and Pete raised a finger. "That's what I've been waiting to see."

So, she hadn't seen through his ruse, after all. As far as Annie knew, Pete was a normal adult, enjoying a martini with an ailing friend. He watched her sip vodka, wished he could have one swallow, just one, to settle his nerves. He had a lot of experience with vodka, knew how it would feel going down, how long it would take to raise his temperature, loosen his libido, then, in a cruel twist, paralyze his dick.

"Feeling better?" Pete asked.

"A little."

Annie swirled her drink. Pete remembered doing that, too. He set his world spinning, hoping to be sucked into the vortex. He used to make a game of it, rewarded himself with another drink if he successfully reversed the swirl with one wrist movement. If not successful—

Hey, Andy, top me off over here.

Annie set her empty glass on the table. "I was supposed to go back to the motel this morning, but I didn't. I went to Daytona because Della told me she'd seen my father at a hotel with another woman, and I wanted to find out who she was. If I had gone back to the Sha-D-Land like I said I would—"

Her shoulders shook. Pete placed his hands on Annie's back. "None of this is your fault."

"I hurt so bad," Annie sobbed into her hands.

"Come here."

The dam broke, soaked Pete's shirt with tears, mascara, saliva. He did not try to quiet her.

"I found out the other woman was Leigh. My father was at a hotel with Leigh the night he died. Leigh never told me she was probably the last person, besides Della, to see him alive. I don't know what's going on, Pete. I'm so scared."

"Of what?"

"I think Leigh might have something to do with his murder."

Pete hugged her closer. "No, Annie."

"She's hell bent on getting his house. She has as much motive as Della. If she sells to Kingfisher, she'll have more cash than she's ever had in her life."

Annie pulled back, looked at Pete with pure pain. "I wish I had never come back here. Everything is gone."

"I'm not gone."

"No," Annie admitted, wiping her face with her palms. "But sometimes it feels like you are. I don't know who you are, anymore."

The comment tore through him with the force of a cannon ball. He wanted to scream.

It's me! Petey Duncan! I am your childhood, the first boy to see you naked, the one you left behind. I am the one who finishes your sentences and knows the exact date you got that scar on your arm. I know you better than anyone else ever could, and you know me. Look harder! I'm here!

But he didn't say those things because Annie was right. He wasn't that Petey Duncan anymore, not since she left. In that time, he had lied and betrayed as much as Leigh, probably more. He had burned bright, then burned out, glimpsed the abyss, but did not jump. For three difficult, sober years, Pete struggled, with the help of his sponsor, to redefine himself without alcohol and still didn't have a clue.

It was time to tell Annie. He'd been keeping things from her that she had a right to know, things about Leigh, her father, the lake property. When she arrived in DeLeon, Pete thought Annie would bury her father, then return right away to her fiancé. Who could have anticipated she would visit Della in jail, stir this muck with talk of Della's innocence, and end up on his doorstep, grieving and alone? However indirectly, this was all his doing. He was tired of keeping secrets—his own and other people's. It would end now.

"I think I'm melting down," Annie said. "I don't know half of what I'm saying."

"Annie, there's something I have to tell you."

His tone—somber, sincere—gave warning. Annie sighed, shook her head. "Nothing bad," she said. "No more."

"It's important."

"Tomorrow," said Annie, and rested her head on his chest.

"Whatever it is, it can wait until tomorrow. I can't handle more bad news. Let me rest first. Please?"

He smoothed her hair, kissed her head. She was quieter now, allowing herself to relax. Reluctantly, he agreed to wait until tomorrow. "Annie?" She lifted her face, sad eyes questioning. Pete had loved this face since the first time he saw it, over twenty years ago. Her life, like a flat-sided rock, skipped from tragedy to tragedy. Yet, through it all, Annie managed to avoid the behavioral traps he and Leigh had fallen into. She left DeLeon and its bad memories as soon as she was of age, nurtured a career, built a life, fell in love. How he wished he had been there to see it. Annie Bartlett was a force, Pete Duncan saw, the most dynamic and beautiful he had ever known.

"What are you doing?" Annie whispered.

Pete realized he had been about to kiss her and pulled back. "I don't know."

Annie searched his eyes. "Me neither," she said, then wrapped her arms around his neck.

The kiss was long, passionate, probing. Pete wove fingers into her hair, kissed her eyes, tears, and neck, inhaled the air she exhaled, hungry for every molecule. Suddenly, she broke away.

"I can't do this," she said, voice thick.

Pete, in agony, released her. "Okay." He knew what would happen next. Annie would leave, and he would have to let her go. Breathing heavily, he waited for her to move from the couch, but she didn't, and when she looked at him again, his heart combusted.

Annie moved to the end of the couch, lay down, and reached for him. They melted into each other as they never had done as teenagers, a time when they fished in the same lake, read the same books, loved with the same heart. Flailing blindly, Pete found the lamp switch, and doused the light. In the dark, with Annie, he found his way.

CHAPTER 39

Headlights burned holes in the night. The sedan screeched to a halt; a door opened. A large body hit the grassy bank, then rolled into the drainage ditch. The car sped away, engine roaring.

As instructed, Jeb Barlow waited several minutes before moving. He was dry; the ditch hadn't had anything to drain since March. He counted out the minutes; then, certain it was safe to move, sat up. He wobbled to his feet, lost balance, fell into the shallow ditch. Jeb rolled to all fours, worked his legs into a wide stance, then, balanced, pushed himself upright.

He knew he was banged up, but everything seemed to be working. He looked around, trying to gauge where he was. No phone or gas station for a ways, but he could walk. Covered in mud, bent slightly at the waist, Jeb Barlow crawled up the bank to the edge of the road and limped south in darkness, head throbbing with a story no one was going to believe.

CHAPTER 40

Thursday, July 16, 1981

AN EXCLUSIVE INTERVIEW WITH THE BOBCAT BAY
ARSONIST

"He knows he is a criminal. He says he is doing us a favor."

By Jeb Barlow

The arsonist claims to be a public servant.

His self-assured demeanor and articulate speech suggest an
educated man accustomed to public contact. He is tall and fit
with sun-bronzed hands always in motion. Although I have no
real way of knowing, I place his age at mid-thirties. He says the
woods are his home, and preserving the environment is his
religion.

And urban sprawl is threatening both.

The day it began, the arsonist says, he was hiking through his
favorite wilderness, the Bobcat Bay State Forest. Through a trail
in the scrub, he came upon a construction site that looked as if
it had "slouched" from the new suburban development,
"Seminole Estates," which abutted the forest.

The house under construction was an ugly, many-winged
"obscenity" that bit into scrub, displaced wildlife, ruined the
arsonist's view. Worse, other foundations were poured in the
vicinity, more homes poised to block the sun. This was the first
indication of a "cancer" spreading to healthy muscle. Un-
checked, it would spread further.

The arsonist thought, "Somebody ought to burn that down." Then came the rationalization.

"It would be a public service."

On July 15, I was abducted, blindfolded, and taken by car to a dim warehouse in a location still unknown to me. Unknown to me no longer is, why: I made the arsonist angry.

I do not know the arsonist's name, nor can I describe his features. When my blindfold was removed, he stood before me in khaki pants and nylon jacket zipped to his neck. He wore an absurd Richard Nixon mask, the rubber kind that goes over the head and conceals to the shoulders. He spoke in a false, falsetto whisper, oh-so-disconcerting for a man of his size and tenacity.

"I am the Bobcat Bay arsonist," was all he said in the way of introduction. He was more interested in telling me who he is *not* than who he is.

He is not Eugene Lanier.

The day before, the *DeLeon Sun News* ran a photo in which Eugene Lanier, son of Judge Marguerite Lanier, appeared in a wooded setting kindling a fire. The photo, one of many, had been mailed to me by Ed Bartlett, who was murdered one day before the envelope's postmark.

While my story never accused Eugene Lanier of arson, the arsonist claims it strongly suggested that Lanier was responsible for the Bobcat Bay fires. Not so, he said.

These fires, the first of which occurred April 24, have destroyed millions of dollars in property owned by local developer Kingfisher Powell and threatened forests and homeowners in the area surrounding the Bobcat Bay State Forest.

The arsonist wants you and me to know that he, and he alone, is responsible for these fires. The arsonist says the public has been misinformed. He claims this is extremely frustrating as he has worked hard to get his message out. He has left a note at each fire.

When told only one note was found—"Thou shalt not rape God's good earth,"—he becomes agitated. He spews disdain for the media, police, sheriff's office, FBI, "and all the other alphabet soup organizations" who refuse to see his side. Either the Feds are sitting on his notes, he says, or they're too stupid to find them. Neither scenario pleases him. Publicity is crucial to his plan.

The arsonist tosses me a small tape recorder. Never does he get close enough for me to see the color of his eyes.

When I ask what he wants from me, his tone shifts.

From now on, I am to report his activities with the accuracy and respect he deserves; do I understand? He wants his reputation restored.

The arsonist's reputation, as he sees it, is as an "environmental angel."

"I am protecting us all from the evils of sprawl," he says. "That takes objective intelligence and a mindset in touch with reality. I do not set fires for the sake of destruction. I set fires to enact social change."

Lately, he has been enacting a lot of social change. Since April, five houses have burned to blackened skeletons. The arsonist says he is just getting started. "I'm expanding my efforts."

He looks for construction sites along the edge of the 20,000-acre forest, where builders have recently poured concrete onto virgin sand. He chooses homes that are relatively secluded, easy to "compromise," and near completion. He waits for a calm night—no wind—then places a small igniter in a room facing away from the neighboring development. This gives the fire maximum "stew time" before being discovered, often too late.

Is he targeting Kingfisher Powell?

"King has been the worst offender, but no business that profits from destroying the natural beauty of the Bobcat Bay State Forest is safe."

From inside the warehouse, which looks to have been an auto repair shop at one time, I hear the tick of the cassette turning inside the recorder, distant traffic, the occasional crunch of gravel. I conclude we are in the city, maybe in Airport Industrial Park, but I've not heard any airplanes. Doors, windows, vents are closed. I am sweating profusely and know the arsonist must be hotter under that mask. I suggest he remove it, and his anger ignites as would a match scraped across flint.

"You are not here to see me. You are here to tell my story. Florida's natural setting was lost forever the moment the balance between concrete and green tipped in favor of subdivisions. Protected areas like Bobcat Bay are all we have left, and even they are only managed approximations of the real thing."

The arsonist's mission is to influence public opinion through high-publicity actions that will eventually result in strict growth control. When asked how long the campaign will continue, the arsonist gives the vocal equivalent of a sneer.

"As long as it takes the governor to enact some anti-sprawl legislation with teeth. As long as it takes for Kingfisher Powell to go back to the reservation where he came from."

So the fires will never stop?

"I want people to open their eyes, get them talking, and I'm having some success. Not everyone thinks I'm a nutcase."

Why target Kingfisher Powell?

"Powell's developments eat an acre an hour, and are a repulsive reminder the state has no growth plan. The same thing happened to the Everglades in the 50s and 60s."

Fine, but why the terrorist techniques? Why not devote public life to making a difference in a more traditional way, like the Seminoles do, for instance?

"How do you know I'm not?" he says behind clenched teeth. For an instant, I hear the real man beneath the mask, and it disturbs me that I may have heard this voice before. I do not want to believe he walks among us. I would rather he swoop in from this oily place, do his thing, then return, an isolated outsider who has never broken bread with me or anyone I know. He composes himself. Sweat trickles down the nylon jacket. I hear him breathe.

"Do you think this is easy? I anguish over every fire. I do what I can to minimize risk to others, especially the firefighters, who have done their job admirably. And, let me remind you, I burn unoccupied houses. No one has been hurt."

So far.

He is proud of the strikes he has made against urban sprawl but says he is not addicted to setting fires. When his goals are accomplished, he says he can, and will, stop.

The tape recorder clicks off. Our interview is over.

It is time for me to put the blindfold back on. After donning it, I hear him pull off his mask.

I am not tempted to look.

In truth, I don't want to know.

It takes fifteen minutes to reach my drop-off destination. With the cassette, I am shoved from the car and left to lie face down in a ditch. I do not try to capture the license plate number.

I am not afraid.

He is just doing me a public service.

CHAPTER 41

After the police finished with the room where Leigh was attacked, Deputy Salceda had placed Annie's things in Mrs. Voorhis's custody. As she approached the lobby of the Sha-D-Land motel, Annie worked her hair into a low, loose ponytail, secured it with a rubber band found on the sidewalk. Feeling rumpled in yesterday's clothes, she was thankful Pete had had an extra toothbrush in his medicine cabinet. At least she would face Mrs. Voorhis with clean teeth and fresh breath.

What on God's good earth got into me last night?

She had slept with Pete, that was indisputable, but why? Yes, she was distraught over Leigh, and yes, she had a lapse of judgment in a moment of weakness, but holy mackerel, what had she done?

And what of Pete? Annie had been half asleep when, leaving for work, he kissed her on the cheek, said good-bye. He had made coffee, and next to a cup set out for her, had left a note devoid of acknowledgement or emotion—"I thought you'd be disappointed if I didn't leave a note, so here it is." Did Pete regret their night together as well? She would call him later, apologize, assure him she had made a mistake, and ask that he keep their tryst to himself. If Camp learned of her betrayal, he would be devastated. Remorse washed over Annie in cold waves. She worried that she had risked the thing she cared most about—her life with Camp. To preserve that, Pete would have to agree that last night didn't happen, pure and simple.

Yet, it did happen, and it wasn't simple. What started as comfort sex soon evolved into something more complicated. When Annie and Pete moved from couch to bed, they couldn't get clothes off fast enough. They did not devour each other in impersonal, lusty mouthfuls. They made love with eyes open, looked deep into their shared past, their passion and knowledge commingling. Afterward, they lay face to face, quietly touching, in awe of the familiar sense that lingered. What lay unspoken between them was not just comfort.

Annie shook her head.

Focus.

After a perfunctory knock, Annie entered the lobby. Mrs. Voorhis sat behind the counter, TV blaring, and peered at Annie through thick lenses. In the corner of the room, a large shadow moved. Instinctively, Annie jerked around.

Camp lunged, clamped his arms around Annie's shoulders, crushed her to him. "I got here as soon as I heard," he said, voice gritty with sympathy and grief.

Annie had forgotten she had called Camp from the hospital last night. Now, here he was, holding her. A stew of emotions whirled, gained speed, flew from her core, and splattered against the wall that, since their last conversation, had been between them.

"Jesus, Annie, I'm so sorry. My God, how are you? How's Leigh?" Camp buried his face in Annie's neck, rocked her slowly. Little by little, Annie relaxed. He had come because she needed him, and he belonged by her side. She closed her eyes, breathed in smells of leather and sawdust.

"I've been waiting for hours," said Camp, still holding her close. "Where have you been?"

Annie opened her eyes. Camp released her and placed hands protectively on her shoulders. "This nice lady let me use her phone. I called the hospital, but they said you left late last night." He scanned her, concerned. "What did you do, fall asleep in your clothes?"

"Can we talk somewhere else?" Annie asked.

"Sure," said Camp. "Where do you want to go?"

As a child, Weeki Wachee Springs had been Annie's favorite place. After visiting a groggy Leigh in the hospital, Annie and Camp headed to the springs in Camp's rental car, a nondescript white sedan with a spitting air conditioner. From her suitcase, Annie pulled a white cotton shirt and khaki shorts, and while stopped for breakfast at a Wendy's, used the restroom to slip into them. She brushed her hair, put on light make-up. Everything was going to be fine.

The drive to Weeki Wachee took two hours. Mercifully, Camp did not ask again where she had been last night. They talked of Leigh, Della, and the strange reporter who had printed a photo of Eugene Lanier in the newspaper, one her father took before he died. Annie told Camp about the huge Miccosukee land developer, and the serial arsonist still at large. She asked Camp about Kirsten ("She's fine,") barn saving ("I found a beauty in Chelsea,") and how he was getting on without her ("Miserably.") They arrived at Weeki Wachee, and with Annie leading the way, stepped down into a large, dim room, one Annie still visited in her dreams. The air conditioning was cranked to "frigid," a Floridian requirement, it seemed, as if in apology for the very climate that attracted tourists in the first place. A large pane of glass held back the bubbling artesian spring where the mermaids would perform. The rickety benches of her youth had been replaced with upholstered theatre seats, but for Annie, little else had changed. All still evoked great anticipation and mystery.

"Stinks in here," said Camp. A yellow-haired girl turned to look at him, flicked her gaze to Annie, then resumed facing front, one foot swinging.

Annie knew how the girl felt. How dare this grown-up speak heresy in the chamber of the mermaids? It was here, when Annie was nine, that Annie saw her mother. A school friend named Pamela had invited Annie to Weeki Wachee. During an underwater ballet, a lone mermaid broke from performing and approached the glass. Her fingertips touched the glass, like tree frogs suctioned to a sliding glass door. Black hair swirled. Most amazing, Annie noticed, she didn't use an air hose. The mermaid stared at Annie, beckoned with hand gestures and mouth movements. Annie left her seat and moved closer. The mermaid swam back and forth along the glass, much as a tiger at the zoo, trapped in a too-small world. "Get me out of here," she seemed to say. "Help me."

"Momma?" Annie whispered. She lifted her hand to the glass. "Is that you?"

Pamela's mother grabbed Annie's hand and pulled her back to her seat. When she turned back around, the mermaid, of course, was gone.

"Man, this is retro cheese," said Camp, as the mermaids breathed through air hoses and cajoled behind the glass.

"Shhh," warned Annie. Music rasped through cheap speakers. Mermaids lashed their zippered tails, lip-synched to a song about a Buccaneer pirate.

"Disney World is going to drive this place under. I give it another year, tops."

The same yellow-haired girl turned and eyed Camp with adult disdain. "He didn't mean it," said Annie. The girl turned away again.

"Cold in here," said Camp, and rubbed his hands.

"When do you think you'll be coming home?" Camp asked, spooning a dry-ice confection from a paper cup. The bizarre, smoking mound of multicolored dots the size of bb's, once inside the mouth, transmuted into an unsettling texture between liquid and gel. Annie had discarded hers after the first bite. Now she leaned back on the bench, stiff-legged, contemplating Camp's question.

"I'm not sure," she answered.

"It's been four days."

"I know."

"I thought you were coming for a day."

"So did I, but it didn't work out that way. I can't leave with Leigh in the hospital."

"Where will you stay?"

"Maybe Widow Lake. The police are done with the house, and I don't think Della will mind."

Camp spooned the last of the confection into his mouth. "Is there a phone there?"

"Sure. Of course."

Camp crumpled the cup. "I can go the rest of my life without another one of those."

Annie smiled. "Yeah, pretty awful."

He scooted close to Annie. "What about your work?"

"I can work here. I have my camera, and there's a room at the lake house I can convert into a darkroom."

"You're digging in for the long haul, then."

"I told you, Camp. That all depends on Leigh."

"Is that all?"

"What do you mean?"

Camp resettled himself on the bench. "Annie, I realize you're caught up in your father's murder investigation, and if that's what you have to do, then that's what you have to do, but I think I have a right to know how far you intend to take this."

"Take what?"

"Avoiding me," said Camp. A large falcon flew overhead, swooped low over visitors in a nearby grandstand, circled, flapped to a landing on its trainer's gloved arm. An amplified voice crackled over anemic applause. The aviary show had begun.

Camp continued. "I'm so sorry about what I said on the phone the other night, about postponing the wedding. I've been thinking, and I know now that I made a big mistake."

Recalling the conversation, Annie could almost smell the phone booth, see the dog-eared directory dangling from its chain.

"That's not why I need to stay, Camp. I mean, it is, but it's Leigh, too. It's . . . a lot of things."

"Annie, I can feel you withdrawing from me every second we're together. Except for that hug this morning, you've barely touched me all day. Now you tell me you're moving into your father's house indefinitely. I can't tell you how sorry I am that I hurt you so badly."

Annie felt awful. Being with Camp so soon after Pete had thrown her into a multi-textured soup of shame and regret. This was wrong, sitting here, pretending all was well between them, when all was turmoil.

How could she have slept with Pete? True, Camp had hurt her by postponing the wedding, but they were still engaged. And she could talk all day long about how upset she was over Leigh, how she wasn't thinking clearly, but Annie had cheated on her fiancé. Could she keep this terrible mistake to herself, or would it be better to come clean, beg for forgiveness, then work to regain his trust?

"Annie, please look at me." She faced him. "I want to get married. Right away, as soon as you come home. Or now, even. Right here. In that mermaid tank, if you want, I don't care. All I want is you, for the rest of my life." He took her hands. "Say you forgive me. Come home, and be my wife."

A winged shadow moved across Annie's face—another large

bird of prey, circling in an azure sky. That Camp had just asked for forgiveness made her want to skitter like the rodent she was.

"Camp, you don't have to go back on your better judgment just because I got my feelings hurt. I understand your reasons for wanting to postpone. I didn't like hearing them at the time, but hey, this isn't just about us. We have to consider Kirsten."

"Thank you, but—"

"And speaking of Kirsten, what does she think about us getting married right away?"

Before he said it, she saw it in his face. "I haven't . . . really . . . told Kirsten yet."

Annie couldn't hide her disappointment. "So she still thinks the wedding is postponed?"

"Well, yeah. And, technically, it is. That is, until you agree to unpostpone it." Camp smiled at his logic.

"So nothing has changed."

"Oh, come on, Annie. We love each other. That's all that matters."

"What happens when you tell her, and she throws another tantrum?"

"I'll deal with it."

"How? By postponing again?"

"Kirsten will get over it."

"When? After she's devoured all the ice cream in Ann Arbor?"

"That isn't fair."

Annie knew she should shut up, that she was equally to blame for this see-saw, but Kirsten was the fulcrum, and until Camp helped his daughter through her post-divorce trauma, he and Annie would sit opposite each other in an endless up and down.

"Camp, Kirsten is only fourteen. Her understanding of your divorce and remarriage is limited to how they affect her, nobody else. Until she gets counseling, her jealousy, anger and loss will continue to drive her actions. Can't you see that?"

"I'll talk to her."

"No, you can't talk to her. Kirsten doesn't listen. She manipulates, and you give in, usually at my expense."

"If by 'give in,' you mean I give her the emotional support she needs, then yeah, guilty as charged."

"No, that's not what I meant."

"Annie, Kirsten is my daughter. My love for her is unconditional. I will give her whatever she needs, whenever she needs it, because I am her father and always will be."

"I know that, Camp, and I admire your devotion, but without counseling, it will take Kirsten a long time to release you to your own life, if she ever does, and it's unlikely you'll live it without her tacit permission."

"Dee Dee is against counseling," said Camp, and his mouth snapped shut.

What Dee Dee had to do with this conversation was beyond Annie, but if they pursued that path, she and Camp would end up fighting. A great sadness descended. All at once, Annie knew she could not marry Camp. She loved him but did not want to live with him in constant conflict. In time, the dysfunctional quadrangle would turn Annie bitter, fuel Kirsten's jealousy, and force Camp into being a reluctant referee. The movie played out in her head, all jerky angles and sepia shadows. Camp and Annie would grow resentful of one another, and their love, meant to last forever, would sicken and die.

"How about if the three of us went?" Annie tried again. "Or you and Kirsten? I know some very good people who—"

"I told you, Dee Dee is against counseling. I have to keep the peace, Annie."

"What about you and me seeing someone, then?"

Camp turned to her. "You and me get counseling? Why?"

"Something has to change, Camp. Kirsten and Dee Dee have all the power in our relationship. I don't want to be married to you and have to do what they say."

"You're making too big a deal of this. It will all work out. It just takes time."

They went silent. Annie's head boiled with fear. It was clear she had to break off this engagement. The longer she sat without moving, the more terrified she became. The plates of her world shifted, and a cataclysmic tremor squeezed her heart.

"Camp, I never wanted this to happen, but there's something I have to tell you."

Camp dropped his head, sighed. "It's about time."

Annie paused, looked at him, confused. "Excuse me?"

"It's been the elephant in the room since I first saw you this morning."

"What are you talking about?"

Camp sought Annie's eyes. His voice was calm, his face vulnerable as if certain of what he would hear, yet hoping that he was wrong. "Where were you last night, Annie?"

Overhead, an eagle screamed.

CHAPTER 42

Wings, spread wide, cut upward through air. Camp stared into the seat before him, lost in its blue tweed pattern, scarcely aware of being aloft. He felt he was being pulled into hell.

"I was with Pete Duncan."

Sure, he knew what that meant, but maybe things were not as they seemed, like those scenes in bad movies where the busted cheater clutches a sheet against nakedness and declares, "This isn't what you think!" So he kept asking questions, tentative at first, unsure.

"Pete Duncan? Your old boyfriend, Pete Duncan? The one you went to lunch with?"

Annie's stark, monosyllabic answers prodded Camp into unfamiliar terrain. He crouched, wary of the thing around the corner, waiting for him.

"Where did you sleep? Where did Pete sleep?"

She answered simply, looked at her knees.

"Are you telling me you had sex with Pete Duncan?"

In the silence that followed her answer, Camp's bile rose and fell. He twisted on the bench, head swiveling, body temperature soaring. He felt outside himself, in some other reality, a horror movie he'd seen as a child where large, winged creatures cast shadows before striking and screeched at the killing moment. Camp stood, sat, then stood again—anger and pain a kinetic ball in his chest—ready to smash something.

"Do you love me?"

"Yes, but . . ."

He paced before her, trying to listen, wanting to shout—all stuff he'd heard before—Kirsten, Dee Dee, loyalties, uncertainties. He was one man pulled by three women who each wanted all of him, a human version of a frantic ant he had trapped on his school desk in junior high. Each time the ant moved, Camp blocked its path with an index card. The ant stopped, changed direction, and proceeded only to be blocked again. Camp toyed with the ant for an hour, then lifted the index card to free the ant's path, but it had had enough and did not move. At the time, Camp had been surprised that an ant, with a brain smaller than a grain of sand, when confronted with repeated failure, would change its behavior. The ant had, in fact, learned something. It took Camp much longer to learn. It seemed he was the very definition of insanity: doing the same thing over and over, expecting a different result. His pattern: make promises he couldn't keep, avoid conflict, then placate when surrounded. How much longer would he skim the landscape of his own life, change direction each time an obstacle came down, forever chase a destination that would remain blocked for as long as he kept running?

In voices gauged to avoid public scrutiny, Camp and Annie went around and around. At first, Camp blamed himself. He'd been absent when Annie needed him most. What she'd suffered lately would knock anyone senseless, certainly cause behavior outside normal parameters. Had he been here, she would not have turned to someone else for comfort. Instead, with careless promises, his mind had been on coaxing Kirsten from behind her mother's skirt. How stupid he'd been. Well intentioned, but stupid. With the clarity that comes as the shadow descends, the instant before being snatched and carried off, Camp saw himself as Annie did—a spineless puppet in the hands of too many masters. He froze beneath the descending claw but knew it was over.

"I'm sorry, Camp, but I can't marry you. It wouldn't be fair to either of us."

Insult to injury, this. Annie was the one who had cheated on him. What nerve, getting in a second blow even as he bled from the first. Counterattack! his electrified brain demanded. Blame! Name-call!

But Camp could do none of these. He was, after all, a restorer by trade, a "saver" in the poetic sense. Near Ann Arbor, work awaited, an English threshing barn. Its post and beam skeleton misted into his mind's eye. He would lose himself in her oaken fragility, number each peg and post and purlin, place them gently on the ground. The rotten beams he would replace with air-dried lumber milled on site. Like a snap-together puzzle, the bays would come together on the ground, then be coaxed upward. It would take time, but one day it would be whole again, with room for him and all he loved.

Camp wasn't sure who left the bench first, or when. The drive to the airport was devoid of air, sound, or life. Final good-byes were brief, nonphysical circumnavigation.

"Have a safe flight."

"Tell Leigh I hope she gets better soon."

"I guess this is it, then."

"Yes, I guess."

Up, up went the airplane, gray smoke streaming behind. Camp thought about the barn, how he would fill his days with the rhythmic noise of construction, then later, quietly, while breathing the glinting sawdust, let himself fall apart.

CHAPTER 43

Kingfisher Powell smelled smoke. It ribboned through his dreams, curled into the diamond stare of an alligator eye. He looked out a window of the *DeLeon Sun News* building, tapped his thigh with the newspaper. Five times, unseen, unheard, the Bobcat Bay arsonist had filled the sky with *eete yogahe*—fire— then slinked into the night like *kowechobe,* the panther. And with his newspaper interview of the arsonist, this *pootahe,* Jeb Barlow, fanned the flames.

King had gone choleric when he read Barlow's interview. How infuriating, like a common grunt, to read these details in a two-bit newspaper not fit to wrap dead fish. If the sheriff or Fire Marshal had known of this story before it went to press, King would expose the conspiracy, make them pay with their careers.

"Please sit down, King, you're making me nervous," said King's attorney, Jimmy Lee Yancy.

King remained at the window, though there was little to see: grass grew, sidewalks simmered, a dog panted. They were here to subpoena Rip Kirby, editor of the paper, and Jeb Barlow, the reporter. King would force them to turn their records over to a grand jury. The newspaper could squeal about the First Amendment all it wished. That is, if Kirby and his mangy pack ever showed up. The nerve, King thought, keeping me waiting. Then, aloud: "I could buy and sell this paper twice over with one phone call."

Jimmy Lee Yancy cocked his head in King's direction. "How'd you get into real estate in the first place, if you don't mind my asking? I mean, that's rare for an Indian to hold property, isn't it?"

That King and the arsonist had switched ideological roles was not lost on King, an irony worth reflection. In King's world, it was the white man who betrayed, murdered, and land-grabbed, then assiduously labored to cover up such turpitude by falsifying history, ignoring the terms of peace treaties, and donning a sheep's cloak of magnanimity with insulting reciprocity. Such was the legacy of the Miccosukee, and all native people, who had been handed a government that had all but wiped them out. It was incumbent on all Indians to trust no white man and protect their lands and culture from further encroachment and spoil. But King Powell was no ordinary Indian. Born the son of William Powell, direct descendant of the great Seminole warrior, Osceola and Polly Tallassee, of African heritage, Kingfisher Powell came into the world huge, dark, and angry. Back then, much as they had for centuries, the Miccosukee lived in chickee camps along the Everglade's Tamiami Trail, wore traditional garb, and spoke the Miccosukee tongue, a language with no written component. At his mother's insistence, King attended school on the reservation with Muskogee Seminoles, a Tribe nearly indistinguishable from his father's people except for language, which was, for all its differences, comprehensible. With his mother's tutoring, King outpaced his smaller classmates, absorbed the outdated schoolbooks donated by milky-eyed Baptist missionaries, studied the ancient globe that did not turn properly on its stand. King did not mind that he wrote with a pencil nub, which often poked through his government-issued paper. The conditions on the reservation were still better than in his camp by the road. Here on the reservation, the Indians wore shoes with leather soles and lived in stucco huts rather than the wall-less chickee he slept in. He urinated into a porcelain bowl fastened to a cinder brick wall. Children brought lunches to school in small, mulatto-colored bags.

"Why don't we live on the reservation?" King asked his father.

"Because we are Miccosukee," his father replied. "You descended from those brave few who never left the swamps for a miserable reservation of the white man's making."

King thought for a moment. It seemed to him that the "brave few" had it pretty rough. He much preferred the miserable reservation where water ran from a pump.

Against tribal warning, Kingfisher Powell attended Miami Dade High School where he played football and won a trophy, Most Valuable Player. The Miccosukee elders said Kingfisher Powell brought shame to his Tribe with his ability in English and athletics. They could not understand his attraction to the white man's culture, with its insatiable need to conquer, hold title, and amass wealth. So threatened were they by King's assimilation, they turned their backs on him at the Green Corn Dance. Later, when he dated a young black woman, a distant niece of his mother's, the elders threatened violence. King, tired of living among squalor, ignorance, and broken spirits, asked to be heard at a Tribal Council meeting. Out of respect for his father, the elders reluctantly allowed an address.

"Self-reliance," Kingfisher said over and over, "is the only way out of poverty." It was possible, he insisted, to maintain the unique Miccosukee culture while operating in the mainstream economy. "The bullets stopped flying a century ago, but the war is not over. Even on the reservation, the white man throws crumbs, forces our people to stoop without dignity, accept without complaint."

"We have no wish to carry on this war. How would you have us do?" asked the medicine man, Jim Jones.

"We do for ourselves," replied Kingfisher.

"How? You say we have nothing."

"We have our village," said King. "Do you not see the automobiles that slow as they go by on the white man's road?"

"They gawk at our women in the fields," muttered Dan Jumper, a farmer of sugar cane. "They take pictures of our children, offer us dollars for our food gathering baskets."

Kingfisher Powell smiled. "It is exactly so," he said. "Why shouldn't we take the dollars they offer?"

Sam Echohawk, the Tribal Council chairman, stepped forward. "Since our people first met under this tribal oak, we have sworn to uphold our community. We will not exploit it for commercial gain."

"Why not?" King exclaimed. "We have nothing!"

Chief Echohawk chose his words. "The chickees have no walls," he said. "You will stay or you will go."

King left his parents' chickee in the Everglades and labored as a tobacco picker in Homestead until his number came up. He felt at home in Vietnam, bunking on swamp hammocks as his people had done for more than a hundred years. Pleased to discover kin of the Florida swamp cabbage growing in "hell's soup," as the grunts called the terrain they slogged, he squatted over the cook's iron pot and made *taal-holelke,* sweetened it with sugarcane snapped from the roadside. He endeared himself to his unit with hand-threshed tobacco, taught the potheads how to expertly mold their weed inside a cigarette paper, then lick and draw the cylinder through pursed lips. Grunts chided him, sometimes not gently, about his culture, but he had grown used to that in boot camp. There it was widely believed all Indians were named Tonto and said "How." But when the bullets started to fly, those who badgered King admired him for his strength (he humped a wounded man's pack and his own for five miles), his warrior's skill (guerilla tactics born of his namesake, the great Osceola), and his courage. This Indian, ever serene, seemed unafraid of death.

But King was afraid of death. It stalked him as it had stalked Osceola himself, and each day came closer. On the field of combat, cowering from an unseen sniper, King had an epiphany that crystallized his understanding of politics. He was in a trench, shooting at ghosts, because he was poor, disenfranchised, and expendable. He was here because he had nothing.

A bullet thwacked beside him, blew a clod of night soil into his eye. King focused on where the bullet had come from.

War was like politics, he decided—with one exception. In battle, you used bullets. In politics, words. It was all about manipulation, how to outdo the other guy, how to get what you wanted. The only lesson of war was in the winning.

King moved his eyes from tree to tree, listened. To become a medicine man, one must kill a panther. To become a soldier, one must kill a man. Above, a twig snapped. King rolled onto his back and fired. The sniper, no older than thirteen, fell from the branches and landed at his feet. Upon impact, the machine gun, still locked in the dying boy's grip, fired an erratic round before it jumped one last time and came to rest. The "enemy" was shoeless, dressed in rags; another expendable soul, expended.

As King wiped dirt from his eyes, he vowed he would not die in this foreign country. He would learn the lessons of war and politics. He would lead his people out of poverty, and get rich doing it.

When his tour ended, King learned the federal government had finally recognized the Miccosukee as separate from the Seminole tribe and applied for a land grant. He returned to his home on the Tamiami Trail full of capitalistic ideas, but he was not welcomed. He moved onto the Hollywood reservation of the Muskogees and soon opened "Seminole Village" to tourists.

He wrestled alligators and collected money from the white-legged *nognees* who milled among his people, showing skin and teeth. The Seminole Tribal Council, while more open than the Miccosukees, were nonetheless skeptical of King's enterprise. They did not like the tourists touching things that did not belong to them, asking "how much?" King begged patience, and at the next council meeting, presented a cigar box bulging with bills.

"This is what we can do," said Kingfisher, holding the money aloft. "We will take the white man's money and provide for our people, buy food and clothing, enroll our children in schools."

The medicine man's eyes popped like those of a scared fish. King felt let down by the wise man's horror. If he could not win over the medicine man, "Seminole Village" would be short-lived.

Howard Monteau, a childhood schoolmate of King's, spoke up. "It is not our way," he said. Like other young men on the reservation, he wore his hair in the bowl-shaped cut King had left on the concrete floor of Fort Bragg.

"We have to change our ways, bro'," said King, pushing vocally through the ensuing gasp. "We have to do for ourselves."

Howard White raised an eyebrow. "You speak like one of them," he sneered.

"I am not one of them," King replied. "I am Miccosukee. But I know their ways. I see how they get what they want."

"We do not want what they have," said Howard Monteau.

"How do you know?" said King. "Our forefathers would not deny indoor plumbing to every home."

"You do not strike me as an expert on what pleases or insults our forefathers," Howard Monteau replied. "You are Miccosukee, yet here you are, among Muskogee, trying to make us less of who we are."

"No, Howie. I am trying to make us more."

Howard Monteau stood. "I do not wish to be more," he said, and, back rigid, crossed his arms.

Then you will not be, King thought. Dejected, he tossed the cigar box toward the group. "Tourists parked their cars in Mike Billie's vegetable garden," he said. "Make sure he is compensated for the damage."

The medicine man followed King from the meeting, pulled him aside. "They do not want to keep the white man's money," he said, and drew the cigar box from inside his too-large jacket.

"Then throw it away," said King.

"You do not listen. I said they do not want it."

King looked closely at the old man. "And what will you do with it, Jim?"

The medicine man drew a hand before his eyes, gestured, fingers splayed. "Expand," he said.

"Buffalo Smoke Shop" offered discount, tax-free tobacco products to outsiders. With the medicine man's help, Kingfisher created a treasury system whereby distribution of profits benefited all who supported the enterprise. Soon, other Tribes opened their own smoke shops, alligator wrestling shows, air-boat rides, roadside arts and crafts booths, and a flow of money began to lift the cloud of humiliation that had dogged the Indian people since 1837, when the warrior Osceola was tricked and captured under a flag of truce. Osceola's death, one year later, of disease and a broken spirit, foretold a similar fate for the Seminole people.

But it would not be. In 1975, in a close election, King became Tribal Council Chairman and opened a large-stakes bingo hall on the reservation, a national first. He signed a contract with a group of non-Seminoles to run the place for forty-five percent of the profits. A salvo of legal challenges, charging the Indians were offering winnings that exceeded Florida limits, were quashed when the state recognized the Seminoles' rights to conduct gaming operations on their own sovereign land, free of state control. It was the victory King had been waiting for.

His first casino opened when King was thirty-one. Attending the ceremony in tight black jeans, cowboy boots, and traditional patchwork shirt, he was the new, modern Indian leader, a self-taught success living in a two-story house. As the Seminole gambling fortune grew, King ventured into development. On the reservations, hotels sprouted to accommodate gambling guests by the hundreds. As representatives from other Tribes came to him, wanting their own casinos, King struck more deals, employed more lobbyists, and contributed more money to state and national campaigns. By 1980, Tribal Gaming Enterprises, under King's leadership, seeded a Seminole Police Department, a health and human resources program, a school, citrus groves, a swamp safari, a museum, and numerous smoke shops.

Within the Tribe itself, King began the Tribal Loan Program, a one-man operation free of state scrutiny. King gave audience to any Indian in need. King knew that the old father who needed a truck would never pay back the loan, but King did not care. He'd known the man all his life; knew too, he would come back for another loan in a month's time, which King would grant as well. While making a profit was a primary goal, King did not lose sight of the promise he had made to himself that day in Vietnam. He was here to help his people, and the white man's rules didn't apply.

The Tribal Council re-elected King Chairman on the promise of a gambling dividend. Every Seminole would share in the success of the casinos that lured the white man in. The checks would be sent to each Seminole, for a total of one thousand dollars a year. King won easily. The sound of money clinking in Tribal pockets filled the sky.

Then Sada showed up, claiming to be his daughter.

King was used to the Lost and Abandoned washing up on his doorstep. He appointed Alice Doctor, a talkative woman with large hips, to find food and shelter for the Indians who arrived from elsewhere, their pockets empty, hands out. The ones who wanted to work were welcome to stay. Others she encouraged to return to their reservations, seek medical attention, or move on.

Sada told King she was sixteen years old, and that her mother had recently died of a white man's disease. She rode the bus from Tampa as far as her money took her and walked the rest of the way to the Hollywood Reservation where, her mother had said, her father would take her in.

To King's ears, Sada's claim of kinship was the defecation of buffalos. He did not know a Seminole woman named Betty Mae Tiger, of the Wind clan. True, he had been with many nameless women, but he had known of no child. He studied the girl's face, longer than it was round, the protruding ears and black eyes staring back. He saw none of himself in this skinny *phone-she*.

"You must find your mother's mother," King told her. Sada's matriarchal bloodline did not involve him.

"She is dead."

"Her sister, then."

"I tell you, I have no one."

Still, King felt no obligation. He would give the girl a hot meal and have Alice Doctor escort her back to Tampa.

But Sada would not go. "There is nothing there," she said.

"There is your clan," King replied, remembering these same words tossed at him years ago.

The girl craned her head to take in King's face, so high above her own. "I am my own clan, just like you," the girl replied in their native tongue.

"You speak Miccosukee," King said, surprised.

"I am Seminole by birth only," Sada said. "In my heart, I am

Miccosukee. Please, let me stay."

Reluctantly, King granted temporary shelter while his emissaries traveled to the girl's reservation and asked questions. Indeed, her mother had died of gonorrhea. The girl had gone missing shortly after. Whether King was the girl's father, no one could say, but Betty Mae Tiger, the girl's mother, had always claimed this was true.

King's decision came as he listened to Sada read aloud an article about him in *Everglades Magazine*. Her voice was clear and strong. He thought of his mother, who had taught him to read. Smiling, Sada turned the magazine toward King so he could see his picture. "Why didn't you smile?"

"I never smile."

"Then I won't either." Her mouth clamped shut, corners turned down. She lowered her head and looked at him with sinister eyes rolled upward, the look of a feral beast. Then Sada crossed her eyes, and King laughed.

He sought the advice of Jim Jones, the medicine man.

"Is she your daughter, as she claims?"

King took a long draw on his cigar. "I don't know, but I am drawn to her."

"If you allow her to live with you, she must be your daughter, and you must believe she is your daughter. In here." The medicine man tapped King's chest. "Otherwise, you both will suffer."

"I will never allow her to suffer," King said, his voice gritty.

Jim Jones smiled. "Then I think she is your daughter."

King summoned the girl. "You may stay," he said. Sada threw her arms around King's shoulders, which were wider than her reach.

"I am not finished," King said, pulling the girl away. "If you are my daughter, you will honor me as a daughter. You will listen and obey. Everything you say and do is a reflection of me and our Tribe, and you must never forget that. You will go to school, study hard, and work without complaint."

"Of course, father."

The word startled him. Father.

"Earth to King."

He turned toward Jimmy Lee Yancy.

"You still with us?"

King moved his eyes over the men in the editor's office. On one side sat the sheriff, Rip Kirby, and the reporter, Jeb Barlow.

Sheriff Newcomb laced his hands behind his head. "So, King," he said, a smirk forming. "What did you think of Jeb's story?"

King ran each fingertip of his right hand lightly over the tip of his tongue and gripped one corner of the open newspaper. Holding it aloft, pages open and hanging free, he gathered from the bottom, consuming the newspaper as if his left hand were an independent thing, hungrily eating its way upward. When the newspaper was fully scrunched into a dense ball the size of an orange, King chucked it at the sheriff.

Amused, Sheriff Newcomb gave a snort. Kirby threw the wad in a trashcan, folded his hands on his desk. Jeb Barlow lifted himself slightly to release his coattail.

"What King is trying to say—" began Yancy.

"Hell, we know what's eating King," said the sheriff. "He's sore because nobody told him about this article. He's doubly sore because the interview confirms Eugene Lanier is not the arsonist. Isn't that right, King?"

King's gaze fell on Barlow, who looked back with eyes a little too round. "Who is the arsonist?" King growled.

"I—I don't know," said Barlow. "Seriously, I have no idea. He wore a mask, just like I said."

"You also said he walks among us," said Yancy.

"I said, he might. I mean, he could."

"That's enough, Jeb," said Kirby. "It's privileged information, Jimmy Lee. My reporters have a right to protect their sources."

"Not if the source is committing criminal acts," Yancy countered.

"Yes, even then," the editor argued with authority.

"No. Information from a source who is also the perpetrator of a crime cannot be kept secret, and I'm prepared to argue that in front of a grand jury."

"Argue all you want," Kirby said.

"Why do you protect the arsonist?" King asked Kirby. "He's still out there, setting fires, endangering lives—"

"—and property," the sheriff interjected. "Let's not forget property, isn't that right, King?"

King ignored the dig. "He is a felon and remains a threat to the public! And this . . . this . . . *poo-tahe*—" King pointed at Jeb Barlow. "Instead of going to the police, gives him a public platform. This is not justice."

Barlow turned to the sheriff. "What's a *poo-tahe?*" The sheriff shrugged.

"The public has a right to information," Rip Kirby said, visibly restraining himself.

"I agree with you," King said, and nodded at his lawyer. Jimmy Lee Yancy pulled tri-folded papers from his inside pocket. He tossed it onto Kirby's desk.

Kirby snatched his hands from the desk, nodded at the papers. "What's this?"

"It's a subpoena," the lawyer said.

"Get that away from me."

"If you won't disclose what you know about the arsonist voluntarily, you can do it for the grand jury."

Barlow bristled. "How come I don't get one?"

"Oh, don't worry. I have one for you, too," Yancy said and handed it to Jeb Barlow, who looked pleased with himself. "You can testify together."

Without taking his eyes off Yancy, Sheriff Newcomb extended a hand toward Barlow. "Let me see that." Barlow placed the subpoena in his hand. Newcomb scanned the form.

"Boy," he said. "You fellas are thorough, aren't you?"

"We'll see you in court," Yancy said, then stood. "I believe we're done here, Kingfisher."

King's gaze lingered on the sheriff. "You protected the boy, Eugene, and you were right. But it is your duty, Sheriff, to protect everyone."

"I know what my duty is," the sheriff said.

"I am glad to hear it," King said. "The man who hunts on the wrong side of the mountain forever chases his shadow." King rose, then left.

Barlow pulled a pad from his shirt pocket, flipped it open and scribbled.

"Classic," he said.

CHAPTER 44

The lake house smelled of bleach. After seeing Leigh at the hospital, Annie went to work with a mop and bucket. She scrubbed Camp's wounded face from the avocado sink, flushed it from the rust-stained toilet bowl, wiped it from table legs and cabinet shelves. She cut her finger while disposing of glass from a broken window, probably collateral damage from Della's rampage the night Ed died. Finally, exhausted and imagining nothing but an icy beer and one of Leigh's cigarettes, Annie dropped into her father's lumpy recliner and watched the wet spots on her jeans blanch to white.

Growing up, this chair had been proprietary. "No Sitting in Dad's Chair," a stand-alone chapter in the Bartlett Family Story, included incidents of inadvertent occupation by clueless visitors, who, once situated, were bluntly asked to move. The only person Ed had allowed in his chair was Marsha, the Stetson student Helen brought home from the infirmary, and Annie remembered vividly how that had turned out.

I guess I'm my father's daughter, all right, Annie thought. *Why else would I cheat on a man who loves me?*

Annie hit the recliner's armrests with her hands. A cloud of dust, remnants of Ed, rose and dissipated. On impulse, Annie sniffed the armrest as one might the pillow of an absent loved one, straining for that most intimate of scents, a recipe as complex as the cloud itself. She smelled timeworn cotton beneath the arm's thin upholstery, and the vague, sour smell of spilt beer.

Beneath the kitchen sink, she knew, was a lemon scented dusting agent in an aerosol can. With it, she extracted a dingy white rag, once her father's T-shirt, and went to work on the chairs, bookcase, dressers. When she came to her father's desk, she pulled out the drawers. The hodgepodge contents had been rifled by investigators and now resembled the kitchen's junk drawer where, as a child, she went for tape, batteries or trashbag twisties. She scooped the clutter into a box. Wiping the drawer, her mind curled back to the night before.

Pete's arms had felt so right, his body just as she remembered. When he kissed her, Annie believed he was completely present, that nothing else existed for him but her. His eyes had loved her as he arched toward her. It had felt absolutely right.

Yet, it was absolutely wrong. She felt dirty and ashamed. She had ruined two lives, her own and Camp's. The next time she saw Pete, Annie didn't know what she would say. She wanted him, yet felt she should stay away. All this was too raw.

"Is anybody home?" came a voice.

Annie put down the drawer. "Who is it?" she called, and walked toward the door.

"Nosey neighbor. Is that Annie?"

Annie opened the door. Pamela Hooks stood in a purple nylon jogging suit and full makeup.

"Lawdy, lawdy," Pamela drawled. "You haven't changed a bit."

"Wow, Pamela . . . wow," Annie said, with forced enthusiasm.

Pamela held out her arms. "So good to see you." When Pamela moved, her running outfit went shick shick shick. Her hug was warm, and Annie felt bad about her initial reaction.

Pamela Hooks ("Pamela Normand, now,") and Annie had their childhood friendship forced upon them. Pamela's mother had a crush on Ed. Mrs. Hooks contrived play dates for Annie and Pamela and gained access to the house by asking Ed if Pamela could use the bathroom.

"But I don't have to go," Pamela protested, for which she received a thump on the shoulder.

"We'll be out of your hair in a jiffy-jiff," Mrs. Hooks said, pushing Pamela across the threshold.

"No hurry," Ed said, walking into the trap. "Stay for a beer."

The second time Mrs. Hooks came over, she stayed for two beers. The third time, an afternoon. Leigh put an end to the visits by telling Pamela she was fat, after which the injured Pamela refused the Barlett household the pleasure of her company. Mrs. Hooks trickled over a few times alone but seemed to sense Leigh and Annie were impermeable obstacles to the object of her desire. Mrs. Hooks eventually gave up on becoming the next Mrs. Bartlett.

"My God, how do you stay so skinny?" Pamela said. "Me, I have to practically flog myself just to stay under a ton. It's my metabolism. I'm taking a pill that turns fat to water, but it's taking a while to kick in."

"You look good, Pamela," Annie said, meaning it.

Pamela gave an appreciative smile, then took Annie's hand. "Oh Annie, I'm so sorry about your dad. When I heard, I nearly had a coronary. My mother was beside herself."

"Yes, it's been hard. How is your mom?"

"You can't beat her down," Pamela said. "And believe me, I've tried." She laughed and looked past Annie. "What are you doing, moving in?"

"Cleaning, mostly. I don't know what's happening with the house, yet."

"Uh huh. Well, it sure smells clean."

Annie realized Pamela wanted to come in. "Sorry, can I offer you something? I don't know what's around, but there's always water."

"I won't stay long. I just wanted to pay my respects."

Pamela moved directly to the sliding glass door and gazed at the lake. "Still looks the same, doesn't it?"

"Not for long, apparently."

Pamela raised an eyebrow. "Oh? Is something going on?"

"I guess a developer is pressuring people around here to sell."

"Oh yeah? Is that your plan, then? Sell?"

Annie didn't feel like sharing with Pamela Della's claim to ownership. "Like I said, everything's up in the air at the moment." She led Pamela into the living room.

Pamela seated herself in Ed's chair. "It's so hard to believe your father is really gone. The last time I saw him, he was the same old Ed, hale and hearty."

"When was that?"

"Ooh, I'd say a week or so ago, when Leigh was here."

"Leigh?"

"Yeah. Is she okay, by the way? She didn't look very good to me. Definitely an iron deficiency. She should take vitamins."

"Wait a minute, back up. Are you saying you saw Leigh here, in this house?"

"No, I ran into her and Pete Duncan downtown. I assumed she was staying here. Come to think of it, maybe she was staying with him."

Annie's blood went cold. "Pete Duncan?"

"Yeah. What a cutie he turned out to be, huh? Are he and Leigh a thing these days? I thought he used to be your boyfriend."

"A thing?" With great effort, Annie kept her voice casual. "What gave you that idea?"

Pamela straightened, gave a little laugh. "Well, he had his

arm around her and was stroking her hair. I could have sworn I heard wedding bells. Am I right?"

Annie forced herself to return the smile. "I don't know."

"Keeping it a secret, huh? Well, I can't blame them. You sneeze around here, someone on the other side of the lake says gesundheit. Will they live here, do you think?"

"I—Pamela, I'm sorry, but I can't—"

"Sure, I understand. Mum's the word. Tell you what. If Leigh wants to look into a vitamin regimen, I can get her a whole program at wholesale. That's what I do now. It'll be my wedding gift. Have her call me, will you?" Pamela produced a business card. "How about you? You interested in a vitamin program?"

Robbed of her ability to speak, Annie shook her head.

"You sure? Are you getting enough iron and calcium? Most women don't."

Annie stood, agitated.

"Okay, I won't press." Pamela framed her face with L-shaped hands and grinned clownishly. "Don't want to be Mrs. Pushy-Pushy, right?"

Annie didn't answer. The image of Pete stroking Leigh's hair played havoc with her head.

"Well, look, I better go. I'll just leave another card here in case you change your mind." Pamela moved toward the door. "It was great seeing you, Annie. Please tell Leigh I said congratulations."

Finally Annie found her voice. "Pamela, I don't think you saw what you think you saw."

"Right." Pamela pantomimed a lip-zip. "I didn't see a thing." Winking, fluttering her fingers, she closed the door behind her.

Surely, there was an explanation. Pete Duncan did not sleep with her sister last week, then sleep with Annie this week. Whatever Pamela saw, she misinterpreted. Annie reached for the phone, then drew back. If she was wrong, Pete would think her paranoid and needy. But if she was right . . .

Wiping clean the desk drawer, Annie imagined how nice it would be to do the same with this whole week: wipe it clean. She had not looked forward to coming here but had expected to achieve simple goals: hug her sister, put her father to rest. Instead, she had allowed herself to be distracted by Della, Jeb Barlow, Leigh, Pete Duncan and a host of bad memories. Instead of returning to her life, she had destroyed her future with Camp, and why? To punish him for his insecurities? To punish herself for succumbing to her attraction to Pete Duncan, who, it seemed, may have used her as she had used him?

Annie whacked the dust cloth against the drawer, which did not provide the desired release. She beat the drawer with the cloth until she saw herself from a distance and stopped. Before replacing the drawer, she reached inside the desk's cavity to give the runners a once-over, and discovered a paper crushed against the back. She pulled it out, smoothed it, and looked.

It was a copy of the survey done on the lake house ten days earlier. She read the signature and nearly lost the use of her legs.

CHAPTER 45

"Can you meet me at the Orange Belt in fifteen minutes?"

Pete's heart had soared when he heard Annie's voice. He didn't give her the usual third degree, asked only: "Are you all right?" When she said no, he shuffled two appointments, cancelled a meeting, and popped a breath mint. Pete was a white knight, prepared to slay whatever dragon stalked his Lady Love.

The Orange Belt Pharmacy soda fountain stayed busy from three to four, when the school kids from St. Peter's, who didn't tip, ran the waitress into a bad mood. At other times, like now, it was quiet, perfect for an afternoon tryst.

When Annie entered, Pete stood. Judging from the expression on her face, this would not be a social call. She spoke to him in a controlled but fierce whisper. "I can understand Leigh wanting my father's house. She's a screw-up and needs money. Not very admirable, but it beats a conniving bottom feeder like you."

"Annie—my God. What is it?"

Annie held up a crumpled paper. "You ordered a survey on my father's property a month before he died. You were trying to buy his house."

So that was it. Annie'd found the survey, and had put two and two together to make five. "Let me explain."

"I think I have it figured. You and Leigh are plotting to take possession of my father's house. Della is being framed, all right, but I'll bet she never suspected her own lawyer." The truth stung more than Pete's left cheek. "I'm sorry. I tried to tell you last night. You've got this all twisted up, Annie."

"Really? Is Pamela Hooks twisted up, too?"

Pete's head rattled back and forth. "What's she got to do with anything?"

"Pamela Hooks saw you with my sister the day before my father died. You must have looked pretty cozy because Pamela wanted to know when the two of you were getting married."

"I can explain that."

"Can you explain why Leigh's in the hospital, too? What did she do? Decide she didn't want to split the money with you?"

"What?"

"Tell me something. After you murdered my father, did you make love with Leigh?"

Pete grabbed Annie's arm, his face close. "You are treading dangerously close to the edge here, Annie."

Annie jerked free and held him off, her voice shaky. "You don't want to defend Della because, if she's found innocent, she keeps the house."

"That's absurd!"

"Tell it to the sheriff. I'm going to see that you are not only taken off Della's case, but disbarred and arrested."

June, the waitress, broke in tentatively. "Do y'all want coffee or anything?"

"No!" said Pete, and June scurried away. Pete squared his body. "Are you finished? Are you ready to listen to me, now?"

"I thought I still loved you," Annie said. "God, do I feel like an idiot."

It was past time to end this. Pete pulled Annie to the counter. "Sit down."

"No!"

"Sit down, Annie. There are some things you need to know."

He removed his hand from her arm. "Please. Sit with me."

Annie slipped onto a stool, made a pillow of her folded arms, and rested her head.

"I was helping your father get Leigh into a treatment center in Daytona," said Pete. Annie didn't move. "Your father was going to sell the house to pay off Leigh's drug debts and get her into treatment. She's in deep, Annie. Vedra cut her up, not me. I would never hurt Leigh. I couldn't."

Annie turned her face toward him. "Why should I believe you?"

"Because you know me."

Annie scoffed. Pete rested his head on his arms, and put himself in her eyeline. "Look at me, Annie." She did. He locked eyes with her. "You know me."

Annie sighed but did not raise her head. "Why don't I know anything about this?"

"Because Leigh made me swear not to tell anyone, especially you."

"Why?" Pete could hear hurt and confusion.

"She was afraid for her life, Annie. She knew if she didn't stop using, she'd die. She's been in and out of treatment centers for years, you know that."

"I knew she had been to rehab, but I always thought she graduated, or whatever."

"Kicked out, mostly," said Pete. "For using. There was always someone on the outside, keeping her leashed. She's been trying to get away from this Miguel Vedra for awhile, but he's a tough one to shake. The treatment center in Daytona was her last chance. It's a private, lockdown facility; Vedra couldn't get to her there. I was going to buy your father's house so he'd have the money to send her."

Annie raised her head, massaged her eyes with fingertips. "The motel," she said. Pete wouldn't have minded resting on the counter for a while longer. The intimacy went away when Annie broke it. "Leigh was staying at a motel in Daytona and was going to admit herself into treatment the next day. She was scared. Your father met her there to talk her down."

He could see her making sense of his explanation. "As for Pamela Hooks, she saw me put my arm around Leigh for the same reason. That's all I did."

"You should have told me, Pete."

"I couldn't. Annie, if Matt Tatum learns Ed was going to sell the house to me, then Della is toast, and so am I. I should have told you last night, but . . . well, I didn't."

In her eyes, he saw the memory of last night register. He thought for a moment she would acknowledge out loud what they had shared, but her eyes shifted, and he saw she was crying.

"I was trying to help your father, Annie, not hurt him. I swear to you, I had nothing to do with Ed's murder."

Annie nodded. "Okay." She plucked a tissue-weight napkin from a rectangular holder and wiped her nose. Pete wanted to put his arms around her but realized he was sweating dark rings around the armpits of his shirt. He faced the counter and pinned his arms to his sides, then sneaked a look at Annie. "You okay?"

"Not really," she said. "I just found out that my sister is a major junkie, that my father isn't the selfish bastard I was raised to believe he was, and that you're in major violation of the law for defending Della Shiftlet."

"It's a lot to take in, I know."

Annie rolled her eyes at the understatement, then regarded him. "I could have you off this case in two seconds if I went to the Florida Bar," she said.

"I know. I was kind of hoping you wouldn't."

"Why shouldn't I?"

"You tell me."

He wanted to hear that last night meant to her what it had to him, that she cared deeply for him and would not ruin his career. Because she was engaged, however, Annie probably regretted last night and would continue to act as if it never happened.

"Something isn't right," Annie said, turning clear green eyes on him. "You wouldn't get yourself into a potentially serious legal breach unless you were being forced. And no matter how many times you tell me you're doing what's best for Della, I cannot believe you would ignore evidence that might prove her innocent. That is not who you are. So I'm going to ask you one last time, and I want a straight answer. What's going on?"

Pete dug deep, then began. "I saw Leigh in Red's the other morning. It was around nine o'clock. I saw her go in, and I knew she'd drink herself silly unless I intervened. It took a few minutes to work up my nerve, though, because Red's has a certain pull on me, and I was afraid of being swallowed."

Annie frowned. "I'm not following you."

"I'm an alcoholic. Leigh and I, well, we sort of speak each other's language, you know what I mean? So walking into Red's like that? That was huge for me. It's been three years since I've had a drink, but not a day goes by that I don't want one. Even sitting here, at this counter." Pete shook his head. "I get a physical reaction, like I'm sitting at a bar. I'm sweating like a pig." He pinched his shirt at chest level and pulled it from his skin.

"My God," Annie whispered. "I'm sorry. I didn't know."

"Oh, nobody knows. Except Judge Lanier. And here, as they say, the plot thickens. See, the good judge knows all about my past, which is great because I sure don't remember much. She's the keeper of my burnt-out flame, you could say. She covered for me one time when I went on a bender during an important case. If she hadn't, I wouldn't be talking to you now. People around here, they have little appreciation for an alcoholic lawyer, in recovery or not. All they see is the stain."

"What happened?"

"She dismissed the DUI, and swept the Orange County jail of all evidence of my brief, but memorable stay. I was grateful, of course, but I knew I was in her debt. She hasn't made an overt threat, but I have no doubt she'll take her pound of flesh if I ever cross her."

"But Pete, you could survive that. Scandals come and go. People forget."

"Not around here. And I didn't get just one DUI. But here's my point. Before your father was killed, she found out I was going to buy your father's house."

"How?"

"It had to be Ed. I've been over it and over it. No one else knew."

"So, she appointed you to Della's case because she knew you would have no choice but to plead Della out, because if there was a trial, the State's Attorney would discover you were going to buy my father's property. If it came out that you stood to gain by Della's conviction—"

"Or that I had three DUI's—"

"You'd be . . . disbarred."

Pete shot Annie with his finger. "Bull's eye."

"But, why does Judge Lanier want Della to go to jail?"

Pete waited for Annie to figure it out for herself. When it dawned, Annie's eyes went wide. "Because she's protecting the real killer."

Pete nodded. "That's one explanation."

"Eugene," Annie breathed.

"That would be my guess," Pete said.

Annie held her head. "But why would Eugene want to kill my father?"

"Ed caught him setting fires, remember? He took pictures.

That makes for motive."

"No," Annie said. "I've known Eugene since he was six. It doesn't make sense."

"Well, I think he's number one on the judge's list of suspects. And as long as the judge believes her son is guilty, Della is going to jail."

Annie slumped. "Oh, Pete."

"I know. It's a mess."

Annie scanned his face, then brushed his cheek with her fingers. Pete took her hand and kissed her palm, replaced her hand on his face. She smiled; his heart soared.

"My poor Pete," she whispered.

"Nah, I'm okay."

Annie dropped her hand. "Can't you recuse yourself, or whatever they call it? Step down?"

"She'd ruin me, Annie. She'd pull the plug. I'd be disbarred. Through everything—the alcohol, screw ups, recovery—practicing law is all that has mattered to me. I've come too far and gone through too much to lose that."

"So you're willing to let the wrong person go to jail? You call that practicing law?"

"There's no proof she's the wrong person," Pete said.

"My gosh, Pete. What are we talking about?"

"Nothing that anyone can prove! I'll say it again: the physical evidence points to Della. Anything else is conjecture. Tatum will ram that down a jury's throat."

"What about Miguel Vedra? Could he have murdered my father to keep Leigh to himself?"

"Leigh didn't tell Vedra what she was planning. He had no motive to kill Ed."

"But he may have been at the murder scene. That raises reasonable doubt, doesn't it?"

"Has anyone found this drug dealer boyfriend?"

"No, but . . ."

"Then there's no reasonable doubt." Annie closed her eyes and looked at the ceiling. "I'm sorry, Annie. You can see why I didn't want to tell you any of this." Annie did not move. "I was only trying to help Leigh."

Annie sighed. "I know."

"And for what it's worth, I really believe I'm doing the right thing for Della. A guilty plea is her best bet."

"Then there's only one thing left for me to do," Annie said.

"What's that?"

She looked up. "Go fishing."

CHAPTER 46

Shirt sticking to her back, Deputy Salceda squinted at the sun. Hot and humid even in the shade, perfect weather if you're an orchid.

The lake house looked occupied, but no one answered her knock. Annie hadn't mentioned she planned to stay here, but Salceda supposed it made sense. She pulled a card from her wallet, stuck it in the door to let Annie know she'd been by.

Leigh had said something that led the deputy back here. According to Leigh, both she and Vedra had been in DeLeon around the time of Ed's murder. Back in Atlanta, Leigh said Miguel Vedra "guessed" her father was dead before she told him. Vedra followed Leigh back to DeLeon because she stole his money, but what motive would Vedra have to kill Leigh's father? Ed wasn't into drugs; Salceda would know if he was. Did Ed threaten Vedra? Could they have quarreled about Leigh? Or was this a stupid wild goose chase when she could be inside with air conditioning and oversweet lemonade in a can?

The grass was sparse along the side of the house where, if it grew hotter, the sun might melt the sand into glass. Salceda swept the ground with her eyes, looking for whatever the crime unit may have missed: footprints, a cigarette butt, a note that said "For information about Ed Bartlett's murder, call 555-7876." She toed an anthill the size of an orange, watched red ants erupt in chaotic panic. She stepped around the swarm and spotted, half covered in sand, a triangle of broken glass. She squatted for a closer look. The glass had not been rained on, edges still gleaming, a recent break. She looked up, saw a four-light window, with one broken pane.

When she opened the cruiser's door, the radio greeted with a crackle. She took up the receiver. Once acknowledged, Salceda said, "Can I get a fingerprint kit out here at the Bartlett place?" Something stung her ankle. She propped her ankle across her other leg and pulled down her sock. A trail of red ants scurried around her ankle's circumference, angry red bumps already forming.

"And some alcohol."

"Lord have mercy," said the dispatcher. "You booze it up on your own time, honey. The rest of us got work to do."

Waiting for forensics to arrive, Salceda watched a pear-shaped woman emerge from the lake, thirty yards away. She wore a skirted navy swimsuit and an old-fashioned bathing cap, strap hanging at her chin, carefully stepped to the lawn chair where she bent for her towel. Salceda recognized her as the witness for the prosecution, the woman who had seen Della holding the oar. The woman looked at Salceda several times without acknowledgement until Salceda finally waved. The woman stopped drying herself for a moment, lifted a loosely fleshed arm and gave a tentative wave back.

"Hello, Mrs. Vaughn," said Salceda, approaching. "Do you remember me from the Bartlett investigation?"

"Of course I do."

"May I call you Lois?"

"No, but you can call me Lolo." Lolo removed the bathing cap, ran an arthritic hand through short, gray hair. "I was just having a little swim."

"Good afternoon for it."

"I try to swim every day. I usually go in the morning, but there you are."

"Were you swimming the morning you saw Della Shiftlet standing over Ed Bartlett with the oar in her hands?"

Lolo squinted at her. "Is that why you're here, Deputy Salceda? I've already answered lots of questions."

She remembered my name, thought Salceda. She'll be a credible witness.

"Yes, ma'am, and we appreciate your cooperation. I'd just like to go back over some details, if you don't mind."

"Well, I suppose that would be all right."

"Thank you. Were you swimming the morning Ed Bartlett was discovered dead?"

"I was about to, but after seeing the Shiftlet woman, I went back inside and called the police."

"You said that, on the night of the murder, you could hear Ed and Della arguing, is that right?"

"Yes, that's right."

"You must have pretty good hearing."

"Not really. Sound travels clearly across the lake when it's calm. I hear lots of things."

"Like what?"

"Oh, you know. Laughter, a sneeze, silver rattling in a drawer. And not just from the Bartlett place." She nodded at the small gray house in the opposite direction. "When the phone rings over to the White's, I can hear June White answer it. If she's facing the right way, I can even hear what she's saying. It has something to do with the sound waves, I suppose."

"What about breaking glass?"

"Breaking glass?"

"Yes, ma'am. On the night of the murder, do you remember hearing glass break?"

Lolo placed a fingertip in the center of her chin and gazed upward, a gesture that struck Salceda as disarmingly child-like. "No, I don't believe I did. I think I would remember that."

"Okay. I just wondered. I'm sorry if I interrupted your swim."

"Not at all. You know, Deputy, there's no one out here this time of day. If you get an urge to take a dip in the altogether . . ." She swept a hand toward the lake. "Be my guest."

Salceda laughed. "Thank you. Maybe next time." From across the lake, her radio squawked and stuttered.

"Suit yourself."

As Lolo Vaughn toweled her head, Salceda studied the Bartlett house. Draped in Spanish moss, the cinder block looked beyond tired. Ed had let the roof go; that was evident. And if the big oak in the yard ever bent the wrong way in a hurricane, there went the kitchen. Still, the place had an Old Florida charm. Salceda imagined stepping into the rowboat at dawn and pulling her breakfast from the lake with a whirring rod and reel Lolo Vaughn would hear from her bed. Suddenly, Salceda faced Lolo.

"Is there something else?" Lolo said, hand at her chest.

"One more thing. That morning, when you saw Della Shiftlet holding the oar . . ." Salceda rotated slowly and pointed at Ed's boat. "Did you see the other oar?"

Lolo placed hands on hips and appeared to look at her long, white foot. "Now, wait a minute." She gazed at the boat. "No, I don't believe I did. Just the Shiftlet woman, standing there with the one oar. Had blood on it, too. I could see that."

"And the other oar wasn't anywhere around?"

"Not that I remember. I'm not sure I'd notice if it was. Why? Is that important?"

"I don't know. Probably not. Did you see anyone else around?"

"Like I told the sheriff and everybody else who has asked me that, no, I didn't see anyone else."

Salceda heard the weariness in Lolo's voice. "Thanks, Lolo. You've been great. Mind if I look around a bit?"

"They did that, too."

"I know, but I'd like to widen the circle. Routine stuff. But, if you'd rather I didn't . . ."

"No, go ahead, knock yourself out." Lolo took deliberate steps toward her house. "Mind the snakes in the grass."

CHAPTER 47

Summer evenings in Florida, dusk falls slowly. The hours between supper and sundown are well fed, lazy as old dogs, full of shadows too shy for daytime. Fish get predatory when the watery ceiling reflects less light. Gossamer fins fluttering, they ease into shallow places teeming with fat minnows. When under serious pursuit, the minnows skip over the water like tiny rocks side-armed by fairies. Lake dimples give the impression of light rain falling.

Annie held a cane pole, one worm stuck accordion-like on its hook, as she and Judge Lanier's boat drifted. The judge's sleek reel whirred as a shiner looped through the air on the end of a two-foot lead. The bobber slapped down first, then the shiner. Along the riverbank, quiet. The boat drifted past the put-in, past the retaining wall made from sacks of concrete, past the huge cypress, which reached with ropy arms and spindly fingers.

Annie felt at home in this fecund stretch of river, these smells familiar as her own: earth and water reclaiming the life it once nourished, a brackish, liquid melding of birth and death. She had much to discuss with the judge but was reluctant to break the silence. Judge Lanier fished seriously as Ed had, and Ed did not appreciate unnecessary conversation. "Fish have ears," he used to say. "They hear you talking from across the lake." Annie had never seen a fish with ears, had wished desperately to catch one, but they eluded her, perhaps because she was too noisy. Even on evenings when she was quiet as could be, the fish with ears did not take her hook. When Ed didn't come up with one either, Annie suspected a scam. Not since Leigh had set her straight on Santa Claus did a truth come so hard, and fish with ears got tossed into the dusty toy box of childhood, along with tooth fairies, pots of gold, and dream catchers.

A small noise burbled from the judge, then a sharp jerk. "Okay, here we go," she murmured, and positioned herself in the boat for the upcoming challenge. Annie set down her pole and grabbed the scoop net, knelt to assist with the catch. "Okay," the judge said again. The bass jumped, an easy four-pounder, then slapped on its side, oily back swirling serpent-like just beneath the black water. When it broke again, flashing its underbelly, the judge stood. "She's trying to run!"

"Hold on!" Annie yelled, surprised at her excitement.

"Hoooo-ee!"

The smile on the judge's face transformed her. The woman who met Annie at the dock looked as if she hadn't smiled in years. No light winked in her eyes; her shoulders bowed. Annie had wondered if Eugene's media attention was to blame, if it would eventually render the judge indistinguishable from seniors who home-permed and traded taste for comfort. But now, wrestling a fish, it seemed the judge had cast off ten years and a huge weight.

Annie scooped the bass with the net, pulled it, thrashing, into the boat. It beat itself against the bottom until the judge pinned it with her petite foot and, grasping its lower lip, slipped her fingers inside its gaping mouth. With a twist and a yank, the judge freed the hook and hoisted the trophy.

"Nice!" Annie said.

The judge nodded, beaming. "You want it?"

"Oh, no, you keep it."

"I have a freezer full of fish to last me 'til doomsday. I'll clean it for you, if you like."

"I guess I'm a softie. I like to let them go," Annie confessed.

Cradling the fish's belly, the judge admired her catch. Scales glistened in the last of the sun disappearing behind a stand of pines. "This is the best eating size," the judge said, as if to herself, then let the bass roll off her hands. Annie never saw it swim away. By the time the splash settled, it was gone. The judge rubbed her hands on her canvas vest, then peered at Annie from beneath her khaki hat. "Now it's your turn," she said.

"This doesn't seem to be a worm-eating crowd," Annie replied.

"Sure it is. I'll show you."

She plunged two fingers into a round cardboard box and pulled from it several worms, all fat, ribbed and obscenely pink. Annie watched as the judge impaled one, then cast. Bobber and bait flew, plopped down inches from a fringe of waterweed. Annie took up her cane pole and resumed vigil.

"Don't you ever worry about being out here on your own?" Annie asked.

The judge chuckled. "Good heavens, no. You sound like the sheriff."

"How so?"

"Oh, you know how he is. He gets paid to see the cloud behind every silver lining." The judge nudged her fishing basket with a foot. "He doesn't know about Sparky."

"Who's Sparky?"

"Not who. What. Sparky is my protection."

Annie looked at the basket. "A gun?"

"Just a little one."

"That's like saying you just have a little tumor."

The judge laughed. "True. They both get the job done, don't they?"

"Do you really need a gun on the river?"

"No, of course not. Still—" She nodded at the shoreline. Two men in sagging black hats watched from their skiff. "With all the things that have happened lately, one never knows, do one?"

"No, I suppose not," Annie said.

"I'm so glad you called," the judge said. She sat with elbows on knees, fishing pole held loosely. "I thought perhaps you'd already gone back to Michigan."

"No. Leigh's in the hospital."

"Of course." Judge Lanier made a tsking sound. "Poor dear. Have they caught the man who attacked her?"

"Not yet."

"Terrible thing. Is she going to be all right?"

"She's lost sight in one eye, but the doctor says her wounds will heal."

"Yes, well. On the outside, anyway. You plan to leave town together, then?"

Annie nodded, then went quiet. Was it her imagination, or did the judge seem anxious that she leave town?

"So, why are we here?" The judge shot Annie a sideways glance. "I mean, if you're not here for the fish."

Annie thought that the judge's fingers were digging in a lot more than worms. To get to the truth of her father's murder, Annie would have to go through this tiny but powerful woman.

"It's about Pete Duncan," Annie said. She watched for a reaction but saw none.

"What about him?"

"I think he should be removed as Della Shiftlet's defense attorney."

The judge made a face, as if amazed to hear such an opinion. "And why do you think that?"

"Because he's not defending her. He wants her to plead guilty and be done with it."

"It's called a plea bargain, Annie, and I'm sure it's in her best interest to listen to her lawyer."

271

"But he won't even consider the possibility that she may be innocent."

"I'm sorry, but this is out of my hands."

"Are you sure? Because I heard different."

The air between them turned. Whatever good will the bass had brought to the boat disappeared as Judge Lanier drilled Annie with flat eyes the color of steel. "You shouldn't believe everything you hear."

"Then set me straight."

"I don't think so." It was a warning.

"There are circumstances surrounding my father's murder that haven't even been considered, much less investigated, because Pete Duncan's hands seem tied."

"Talk plainly, Miss Bartlett. Tied to what?"

"To you."

An eyebrow lifted. "I must caution you, I don't like where this conversation is going."

"I'm sorry you don't like what you're hearing, Judge, but I don't think Della Shiftlet is responsible for my father's murder, and I believe you think the same."

The judge looked away, her mouth turned down. "I don't know what you're talking about. I came here to fish, even if you didn't, so kindly refrain from talking."

"Did you and my father ever discuss those pictures he took of Eugene?"

The judge pretended she had not heard.

"Take your time," Annie prodded.

Judge Lanier made an impatient sound. "I haven't spoken to your father in years."

"That's strange because the other day, when I was having lunch with Pete, you said that I must get my photography talent from my father. Remember that?"

"It was something to say, wasn't it? Chitchat. Social intercourse."

"Or maybe you had seen the photographs he took of Eugene before they were printed in the paper."

The judge grew more agitated. "That's quite enough."

"Did my father try to bribe you with those pictures?"

The judge summoned her trained voice from the well of her judicial diaphragm. "I said, enough."

"We're not in a courtroom, Judge. I am not Pete Duncan, and you do not have your foot on my neck. My father was murdered, for God's sake. If you know what happened that night, I'd greatly appreciate you sharing it with me because I am not going away until you do."

Judge Lanier pulled a wadded tissue from her sleeve and touched it to her nose, as if the air was sour, and Annie the cause. After a moment, she sighed and shook her head. "My poor little Frankenstein. Not a friend in the world." She scanned the green-black riverbank. When she continued, her voice crackled with age. "I had Eugene late in life, you know. It's not his fault my body didn't nourish him properly, but for that, he has always suffered. I should have sent him away, I suppose, a long time ago, but I was too selfish; I wanted him near me. I regret to say I don't think I did him any favors." She twitched her pole. The bobber danced. "Well, I've had about enough of this, haven't you?" She unlocked the reel and wound in her line. Annie lifted her bobber and bait. Her hook was bare.

The judge sat next to the small outboard and pulled the cord. The engine grumbled and died, as if annoyed at being awakened.

"I heard my father was desperate for money," Annie said. "Did he try to bribe you with those pictures?"

The judge pulled the cord again. "One hears lots of things in a town this small, Annie. You should know that. Especially after

273

what happened to your mother."

On the third pull, the motor caught. Annie knew the remark about her mother was meant to unsettle her, and it worked. Above the motor's putter, she said, "You don't know anything about my mother."

"I know quite a bit, actually. If it weren't for me, she would have gone to prison. You didn't know that, did you? But I felt sorry for her, poor thing. Stealing drugs from the infirmary. Your father begged me to intervene."

"You're lying."

"You would hope so, of course. We don't like hearing truths about our mothers—that they're human and sometimes do horrible things to keep their children close. Very selfish. Such mothers only end up crippling their children in some profound way." The judge steered the boat around a grove of knobby cypress knees. "Your mother died too young, Annie. In a way, I feel responsible. I knew things, you see. I could have destroyed her career, even her family, but I didn't. I understand addiction, unlike most people who think it has something to do with morality. I regret your mother never got the help she needed."

Annie wanted to scream as snapshots of memory flashed: her mother's pockets full of band-aids, medical tape and hard plastic bottles that rattled when she shook them; Helen always groggy, even after sleep; her father's pleas and reprimands, followed by brooding.

"Your father tried to help her, but there were no doctors in town he could trust. Helen was a nurse. Once the truth got around, she'd be untouchable, the madwoman in the attic. She had two small children to care for, and a job that, for the most part, was the family's sole support. Your father hoped Helen would get better on her own. Instead, she got worse." The judge paused, pensive. "So when your father came to me for help when you were a little girl, I felt sorry for him. People blamed your father for Helen's death. I want you to know I never did that. I thought that unfair."

"You helped him?" The judge nodded. "How?"

"I made the infirmary charge go away. Perhaps if I had given him money, she wouldn't have—. Well, I felt terrible when I heard she drowned."

"Not as terrible as me and Leigh."

The judge looked at her. "No, of course not. I didn't mean to suggest . . . And I was sorry to hear Leigh succumbed to addiction as well. Terrible legacy. So, yes. When your father came to me this time with those pictures of Eugene, I felt I owed him one."

So Ed had gone to the judge with the photographs. Annie might have felt buoyed by this admission, but images of her mother overwhelmed the moment. As a child, Annie was used to seeing Helen in a fog, yet she had no reason to suspect her mother's depression was linked to drugs. All these years, wrongly, it seemed, Annie thought Helen's half-a-life due to the strains of a poorly paid night job and a husband who preferred the company of other women.

"How much did you give him?" Annie asked.

"Nothing."

"What?"

"I didn't give him a cent. I told him to print the damn things. I didn't care. I finally realized I couldn't live Eugene's life for him, no matter how much I wanted to, and told your father that he was foolish to try to live Leigh's."

Annie could almost hear it: the judge—authoritative, articulate—berating Ed for his greed and stupidity; and Ed, unused to dominant women, struggling to get a word in. "What did he say?"

"I thought he understood. He told me when Leigh came to

him for help, he felt he'd been handed a second chance to save Helen."

A cold wind from nowhere seized Annie. She hugged herself, feeling her father's guilt and desperation. If only she had known.

"I told Ed it was time he handed Leigh's life back to her and got on with his own. He agreed with me. So, when I saw his pictures of Eugene in the paper, I was surprised, to say the least. I thought we understood each other."

Annie waited until her voice felt under control. "Was that the last time you saw my father?"

"Yes, Annie. That was the last time." As the boat coasted to the dock, Annie slipped a line around a piling, guided them to a stop. The judge cut the motor. "And I'll answer your last question before you ask it because I'm sick and tired. I'm sick of this town and tired of defending my son against every bad thing that happens here. Listen to me, because I will only say this once. I did not kill your father. If I had, I would tell you. That's how sick and tired I am."

"What about Eugene?"

"I'm going to tell you the truth, Annie. I don't know if Eugene killed your father or not. I honestly don't. But I will go my grave before I let anyone lock him up. There is nothing I won't do to protect him from that. Nothing. So, you might as well point your nose in another direction because there's nothing up this tree. Do you understand what I'm saying to you?"

"I think I do."

"Good. Now kindly get out of my boat."

Annie climbed onto the dock and reached for the fishing poles.

"Leave them," the judge said. "I'm going back out."

"You sure? It's getting awful dark."

The judge chuckled. "The dark got awful a long time ago, my

dear." She steered the boat downstream. "Give my regards to your sister."

CHAPTER 48

As Deputy Salceda high-stepped through the tall grass between Lolo Vaughn's place and her cruiser, she regretted the time wasted. After walking through bushes and spider webs, she discovered a few empty bottles of Jim Beam and an abandoned tortoise shell. She followed the edge of the lake where the water was clear. Here, she made out sturdy underwater stalks, gray-brown minnows moving with the stealth of miniature torpedoes, tadpoles in metamorphosis. From a fallen pine branch she cracked off a sappy stick, swept the grass before her for anything that might leap, flush, or slither. Boggy smells rose from her footsteps.

Sure enough, just as Lolo had warned, a muscular black snake, thick as a bicycle tire, serpentined across her path. Salceda froze. This close to the water, the snake could be a moccasin, swift and deadly. Salceda's dog, a black and tan named Tootsie, was bitten by a moccasin, probably as she dipped for a drink. She had swollen grotesquely, died writhing. Now, the sight of a black snake, even a harmless one, paralyzed her.

As the snake, bulging with a recent meal, moved slowly toward the water, Salceda felt her heartbeat return to normal. She watched it, mesmerized. It disappeared into the marsh, and a huge cloud of bloated flies rose as one, dispersed, then regrouped on the ground. Salceda reversed direction, then stopped.

Water seeped around her boots as Salceda made her way to

the lake bank, poking with her stick. Closer now, she heard the flies thrumming. The snake, she hoped, was gone. Just to be sure, she parted the knee-high reeds before her with the stick and nearly passed out. A corpse, covered with black flies, lay face-up in the shallow water, eyes staring, a silver-handled knife protruding from its chest. Salceda yelped and fell back. She lost footing, flailed, sat down hard in the soggy bank. Suddenly inside the cloud of flies, the deputy panicked. She screamed, then struggled up the bank on hands and knees. Her senses returned when the flies left her for their main course. On solid ground, Deputy Salceda lay down, chest rising and falling with each beat of her racing heart.

CHAPTER 49

Jeb Barlow walked into the Back Room and waited for Florida to acknowledge him. Now that a mysterious arsonist had kidnapped him, he was Man of the Hour. Florida waved, and he chose a seat at the bar, assaulted his sobriety two-fisted. Generous with the Wild Turkey, Florida slid dewy glasses toward him without comment or fish eye, even talked to him until business picked up, when she had to spread herself around.

"You working alone tonight, Florida?" Jeb asked as she dunked glasses into a sink of soapy water.

One side of Florida's mouth pulled downward. "Yeah, can you believe it? I swear, these reservation kids aren't worth a lick. No phone call from Sada, no nothing. I got nobody to watch the register when I have to leave the bar."

"I'll watch it for you."

"I'll bet you will. Here, have another one." She toweled her hands then poured. Jeb smiled.

Yes sir, this morning's article was Jeb Barlow's ticket to premium booze and a better place in line. And that was only part of the story, he said, once lubricated, to all who would listen; only he knew the whole truth. He was saving it for a book, Barlow claimed, in which he would tell all. In the meantime, he had an agreement to keep with the arsonist, whom he feared.

Jeb recalled a moment when the arsonist became agitated and dropped his vocal cover-up. Jeb couldn't shake the feeling he knew this guy. One name kept bubbling to the surface, but he wouldn't give it air. As long as the arsonist was at large, he couldn't afford to know anything.

A chinless man in a crisp suit chose a bar stool next to Jeb. Florida slid a beer in front of him before he was fully settled in. Must be a regular, Jeb thought, and said hello, waited for the man to recognize him. When he didn't, Jeb helped him along.

"Did you see the Sun News this morning?"

"I don't read drek," the man said in slow, over-enunciated syllables.

Jeb plowed through the insult. "I guess you heard about the interview with the Bobcat Bay arsonist."

"Yes, I guess I heard something about that."

"That was me."

The man squinted at Jeb. "You're the Bobcat Bay arsonist?"

"No, no. I did the interview. I'm writing a book."

"You don't say."

"Out of all the reporters, he picked me." Jeb jabbed himself in the chest. "What does that tell ya, hah?"

"It tells me he doesn't get around much."

"Hey, that's funny," said Jeb, then shouted, "Florida, give this man another one."

The man shook his head at Florida, moved away with his beer. Florida came over to Jeb and leaned her elbows on the bar. He could tell by the way her shoulders shimmied that her rear end waggled playfully. "Jeb Barlow, are you annoying my customers?"

"Me? Nah. Must be your booze."

Florida smiled good-naturedly, shifted her weight onto the other stiletto. "What's all this talk about a book?"

Slouched over his drink, Barlow lowered his voice for dramatic effect. "Oooh, Florida. The things I've seen, the connections I've made." He touched the back of his head. "The truth is forming at the rear."

"Is that a fact?"

"Bona fide."

Florida smiled, then traced a wet ring on the bar with a fingernail. "Is it true you know who the arsonist is?"

"Ah, ah, ah. Wrong question."

"It's the only question, Jeb. You don't hear what folks are sayin'. If you know something that could stop this guy, you need to tell somebody." Jeb made a dismissive sound, brought glass to lips. "You hear me?" Florida said.

"All in good time," Jeb said; then, because he liked the sound of it, said it again.

"Oh Lord," Florida said. "You're full of yourself today, aren't you?"

"I know something you don't know," he whispered, singsong.

"Oh stop it," Florida said and slapped his hand. "You don't even know what year it is."

"1981," Jeb said, then lifted his glass. "The year of Jeb Barlow. Cheers."

"I'll drink to that," a deep voice added, and Jeb turned. Kingfisher Powell stood holding an unlit cigar. "Set me up, Florida. And give Mr. Barlow one, too."

Jeb did not savor having a drink with a man who, this very morning, had looked ready to break his fingers.

King settled himself next to Jeb. "Tell me about this book you are writing," he said.

"It's nothing."

"No, no, I'm interested. Do you plan to reveal the identity of the arsonist?"

Jeb wanted to leave, but didn't know how without pissing off King, so he told the truth. "There is no book, King. I'm full of shit, as always." He gave a clownish roll of his eyes.

"This is so. Still, I am sorry to hear it because you will need a new occupation soon."

Florida placed two drinks on the bar, took a bill from King. "Keep the change," he said, and Florida retreated, boobs bobbling.

"You don't scare me, King," Jeb said. "And you're not getting anywhere with that subpoena. Haven't you heard of the First Amendment?"

"I am not talking about the subpoena," King said. He lit the cigar—fat, wet lips drawing puffs of gray smoke.

Jeb scanned for an exit. The Back Room was hopping with familiar faces. Carter Whitehall, owner of the J.C. Penney building, sat at a table with Matty "Fatty" Tatum, the prosecutor in the Della Shiftlet case, whose neck flesh hung over his white collar. And Clyde Glenwood, talking to a guy who looked liked Charles Bronson.

"Hey, King, thanks for the drink, but I have to be going. I've got an early deadline."

King folded his hands, cigar protruding from the mesh of fingers. "My people have a riddle. Do you want to hear it?"

"Not really."

"Why is the owl wise?"

Jeb opened his hands. "I give up."

"Because he knows 'who.' "

Jeb suppressed a laugh—another dumb Kingfisher riddle. "Okay," he said.

"It is not finished," said King. "When is the owl unwise?"

"You tell me."

"When he flies too close to the fire."

Jeb shook his head. "That makes no sense, whatsoever."

"Exactly," King said. "So the wise owl should be careful where he flies." He replaced the cigar between his teeth.

Jeb sobered. "Are you threatening me?"

King reached for his drink. "I never threaten, Mr. Barlow."

"You better not be threatening me because I know a little something about 'who' myself, you hear? And believe me, you don't want to know." Jeb was trembling. He closed himself off to King and took a big gulp from his glass. Going down, the whiskey ironed the wrinkles in his chest.

"You would be wise to tell," King said.

Clyde Glenwood approached. "Everything all right here?"

King squinted at Jeb a last time and sauntered to a table. Clyde turned to Jeb. "What was that all about?"

"Nothing. He's just mad because I won't tell him who the arsonist is."

"You know who the arsonist is?"

"No, nothing like that. King just wants me to turn in all my notes so the Fire Marshal's office can try to figure it out."

"Yeah? Are you going to?"

Jeb made a fist and comically pounded the bar. "Hell, no!" he said, cavalier. "A reporter always protects his sources. Always!"

"I'd stay away from King if I were you."

"Roger, ten-four, over and out," Jeb said and added a jaunty salute. Once Clyde moved off, Jeb threw back his drink. Time to get out of here.

"How about another one, Jebby?" Florida said, sugar dripping from her cherry red mouth.

"Nah, that's it for me," Jeb said, still shaky and anxious to take his embarrassment from the Back Room.

"Aw, come on, Jebby Webby. Have another dwinky winky with me." She put her forearms on the bar, leaned over so Jeb could see the white pillows shaking inside their cases. For an instant, he thought he would have a heart attack.

"God help me, you are one beautiful woman."

Florida laughed deep in her throat. "Is that a yes?"

"I guess one more won't hurt."

"That's a good boy," Florida said and removed his empty glass. As she bobbed and bent behind the bar, Jeb watched, pondering the two luscious secrets of her success.

Two hours later, Jeb Barlow stumbled from the Back Room, digging for keys. He berated himself for getting so wasted. Now he had the dubious challenge of finding his way home when he didn't know which direction was up. Seized with an overwhelming urge to pee, he shuffled into the alley beside the building and unzipped, relieved himself against the wall. Gravel crunched behind him, and Jeb, dick in hand, half-turned. The blow caught him across the shoulders. At first he thought it was the arsonist, but the silhouette wasn't right. He fumbled with his pants, and another blow sent him to his knees. He crawled blindly, huffing air. His head was clearing, but the rest of him was well under the influence. Jeb heaved himself to his feet, hugged the wall and crab-walked toward the road. He knocked over a large trashcan, threw another at the darkness pursuing him. Another blow. He fell and gouged the gravel, got up, fell, got up. The last blow, from behind, threw him onto his nose, which cracked like a Christmas walnut. He must have passed out for a moment because the next thing he felt was warm liquid running down his legs. At first Jeb thought he'd pissed himself, but it didn't smell right. When his eyes began to sting, he rolled, and recognizing his attacker, wanted to eat his own heart.

Far away, flaring, a tiny shooting star arched upward before falling. The match landed, and Jeb Barlow lit up the sky.

Chapter 50

Deep inside a disjointed dream, Sheriff Newcomb heard his name. The sound pierced his sleep and rolled him onto his side. The remote radio was at his ear before he was certain which world he inhabited.

"Go 'head," he grunted.

Newcomb recognized the voice, gave full attention. "My God," he said. "I'll be right there." He flung covers and rose naked from the bed.

"Dade?"

Newcomb turned. Marguerite Lanier sat up, eyes questioning.

"Go back to sleep," he said.

"What is it?"

The sheriff fumbled in the dark for his pants, pulled them on. "Salceda found the drug dealer who cut up Leigh Barlett," he said. "He's dead."

CHAPTER 51

Wednesday, July 22, 1981

Stone angels, wing-clipped and sightless, stood among shell-shocked mourners as Jeb Barlow, on the hottest day of the year, descended slowly into the ground. How much more evil brewed beneath this reckless sun, Newcomb wondered as he watched from a distance, multiplied within familiar walls? Solace, for those seeking it, was double edged: the man who attacked Leigh Bartlett was dead. Now, if only Della Shiftlet and the Bobcat Bay arsonist would get themselves gone, DeLeon might stand a chance of returning to normal. In the meantime, this heat was enough to stew a dead man's insides.

From his cruiser, Sheriff Newcomb watched Rip Kirby toss dirt onto his brother-in-law's coffin. He felt for Rip, hidden behind sunglasses, hunched with guilt. Rip had been ready to go after Kingfisher Powell with a bat. One look at Jeb's corpse, and anybody could understand why. Witnesses said Jeb ran half a block before collapsing onto the pavement. Someone put him out with a fire extinguisher, but by then he was nearly gone and likely praying for release, which came soon enough. At the hospital, Rip went from threatening King to talking suicide, and the sheriff called Dr. Neeman, who shot him up with a sedative. When Rip woke, he seemed more himself, save for red rings around his eyes and a tendency to look intently into the distance, as if waiting for a signal from Clara. Sheriff Newcomb had promised to work all the angles. This killer would pay.

287

Florida Sunshine, wearing something low-cut and high-heeled, dabbed her eyes with a white handkerchief. If true that murderers often attend the funeral of their victims, King Powell had one strike in his favor. His bulk was not present among the hundred or so folks now looking down at Jeb's final resting place. It didn't make sense that King would kill Jeb or pay someone to do it. Angry as King was, he still wanted information from the guy.

Then, there was the arsonist: still anonymous, still at large. Had he turned to murder now? The MO certainly fit: a little gasoline, a tossed match, and whoosh. But it was out of character. Unless the arsonist viewed the newspaper interview as a betrayal, it seemed he needed Jeb as his go-between. Maybe Barlow got a glimpse of the man behind the mask and paid with his own cooked goose?

Newcomb was also worried about Marguerite. He knew she was preoccupied with Eugene, especially after those pictures in the paper, but after that fishing trip with Annie Bartlett, there was something else gnawing at her. Picking among the funeral goers, Newcomb zoomed in on Annie. He thought she'd got thinner in the nine days she'd been in DeLeon. She wore a sleeveless, black shift that skimmed her body to just above the knee, her long, dark hair was pinned up somehow, exposing cheekbones he'd never noticed before. Next to her stood her sister Leigh, looking like the invisible man in those bandages, and Pete Duncan. DeLeon had got decidedly more sinister since Annie and her sister swooped into town like they still belonged. Meddling in her father's murder investigation, Annie had turned over rocks better left alone. And look what came slithering after Leigh—murder victim number three. It was time to send these Bartlett sisters packing.

Annie didn't see him until he crossed the street. Once she did, she spoke to Duncan and her sister, and the three came toward him. When Annie removed her sunglasses, Ed Bartlett's eyes took him in.

"Got a minute, Miss Bartlett?" the sheriff asked.

"Is something wrong?"

"Besides three murders in a week and an arsonist on the loose? Naw. Same old, same old." The sheriff looked at Leigh. "And how are you feeling?"

"Like shit on a stick. You?"

Pete Duncan stepped up. "Is there something you need, Sheriff?"

"Can we have a moment alone?" Newcomb nodded at Annie.

Annie squeezed Pete's hand. "Why don't you guys wait for me in the car?" Newcomb saw the hand-squeeze. If these two were getting cozy, Pete Duncan would have some explaining to do to the State's Attorney.

With Leigh and Duncan out of earshot, the sheriff said, "Done any fishing lately?"

"As a matter of fact, I have," Annie said. "Did you know my father tried to bribe Judge Lanier with the photos he took of Eugene?"

He tried not to look shocked. He silently cursed the judge for keeping this from him. What else, bound to bite him in the ass, was Marguerite covering up? He took a wide-legged stance and crossed his arms. "I thought I told you to mind your step," he said to Annie. "Did you think I was talking because I like the sound of my own voice?"

"No, sir," Annie said.

The "sir" reinforced his upper hand; at least Ed had taught his daughter respect. Stepping in to strengthen his height advantage, the sheriff looked down on Annie. "I want you to stay away from Judge Lanier, do you hear me? You stay away from the judge; you stay away from Eugene; you stay away from

Della Shiftlet."

Dade waited for her to acknowledge, and when she didn't, he felt the familiar flash of blood pressure heading north. "I hope I'm getting through, Miss Bartlett, because there are questions I have about Miguel Vedra's whereabouts on the day he died that put you in a bad light." That got her attention; he watched confusion replace stubbornness.

"What are you talking about?"

Annie's intensity again reminded him of Ed. Weird, how much she took after her old man, yet was still all girl. "You and I both know Miguel Vedra was a sack of shit-stained garbage, and the world is better off without him. I would say you had plenty of motive to get rid of this scumbag, wouldn't you?" The sheriff leaned in, conspiratorial. "Now, I'm prepared to look the other way on this thing."

Annie's eyes widened as the sheriff's implication registered. "You don't really think I killed Miguel Vedra?"

"Maybe not, but I got questions that could jam you up for a long time. I'd hate to see you miss your own wedding."

"So you don't care who really killed him?"

Sheriff Newcomb drilled her with his eyes. "I'm giving you an opportunity to get out of here before something else happens, Miss Bartlett. Ever since you and your sister set foot in this town we've seen nothing but trouble." He nodded toward the few people still standing graveside. "Has it occurred to you that if not for you, Jeb Barlow might still be alive?"

"You're crazy."

He heard the tremor in her voice. "Naw, just tired. I don't really want to come after you, Miss Bartlett. That cuts seriously into my fishing time, and that would just tick me off."

A police car pulled up next to the sheriff, stopped abruptly. The window powered down, and a young officer with smooth, tanned skin looked out. "We got another fire, Sheriff," the officer said. "It's the preserve. They're saying it crept over from Seminole Estates."

"That fire got put out thirty-six hours ago."

"I guess not."

Newcomb felt this new burden on the back of his neck. His head dropped forward. "All right," he sighed. "You go on."

"And Deputy Salceda is looking for you. They got the lab reports on the Vedra murder."

"I'm on my way."

The young officer addressed Annie. "How's your sister doing, ma'am?"

Annie managed a smile. "Getting better, thank you for asking."

"Get going, DeStephen," Newcomb said, and the car sped away.

The sheriff shook his head. "One day, I'm going to walk away from all this." He removed his hat and slapped his thigh with it. "Tell that fiancé of yours we're sorry we kept you so long. You do still have a fiancé, don't you?"

Annie didn't reply.

Sheriff Newcomb replaced his hat and deftly rimmed its brim. "All right. Y'all have fun."

CHAPTER 52

Above the roaring fire a helicopter chopped air. Candy pink slurry rained down, smothering flames. On the ground, Clyde drove a Pulaski into the dirt and turned the sandy soil in search of smoldering twigs and pine straw. The fire was creeping beneath the blanket of pine needles faster than he could churn. Without a control line, the creeper would send fingers of fire in erratic directions.

This was the one Clyde had feared, the groundhog fire, burrowing undetected through years of dried downfall. Its heart beat beneath the ground, gathering strength and direction. No amount of surveillance could trump its subterranean path to the woods, which, having suffered from drought and an infestation of pine bark beetles, now crackled with insane life.

Clyde pointed. "Control line! Go!"

The helitacs set to work without further discussion, Pulaskis rising and falling. Clyde itched like hell in Nomex pants, but that was the least of his worries. If they didn't get that hose in the lake fast, they'd have to move the control line further west or set a backfire and hope the wind cooperated.

Clyde signaled his retreat to one of the crew. Here, at the edge of the furnace, the men would stay calm. The fire's center, where temperatures rose in excess of 2,000 degrees Fahrenheit, was a different story. In the center, the balance of energy shifted, laws of physics turned upside-down. Trees flashed, flames skittered up tree trunks, swelled as they fed, then tumbled, literal balls of fire, onto the next tree. A borealis of garish color shot from burning boughs as ash-snow sifted downward; and everywhere, shrouds of smoke made a firefighter lose his way as well as his mind.

Heading toward the source of the fire, Clyde's ire churned. If the fire department set controlled fires, they wouldn't have ground fires like this one. If dead trees were taken out systematically, the downfall would not have a chance to collect and combust. But no, that would never happen. Fire Prevention was big business. The beast stayed caged within a system of fat, defensive spending, but when it did escape, just to clean out a bug infestation or take out an acre of dry grass, it was stamped out, just for doing what it does.

Clyde humped to the edge of a clearing. Sweating and breathing heavily, he took in the sight of Kingfisher's charred building site, where this fire had started. How could he have been so stupid? Had he roiled the ground surrounding the house fire, he would have discovered the hot spot. Instead, he had given the good people of Volusia County another reason to revile his alter ego. He could see the headline now: Bobcat Bay Arsonist Destroys Preserve. Hell, Clyde had tried to protect the preserve, not burn it down. Besides, it wasn't his fault. Those political idiots would rather have him fight a delinquent fire than set a polite one. If they knew jack about Florida's ecosystem, or gave a rat's ass, this fire would not have happened.

Pulaski in hand, Clyde dipped under the yellow tape surrounding the home he had set on fire almost two days before. The area was under surveillance, but even if seen, no one would question his presence. Clyde belonged here, among helicopters rising, park rangers cruising, and cops slurping from supersized cups in unmarked cars. By day, Clyde Glenwood, firefighter, was a hero; by night, an avenging angel.

But Jekyll and Hyde were taking a toll on his psyche. Clyde

could feel seams straining in his warring personas. Soon, someone would hear or read an article about firefighters who set fires, and heads would turn in the direction of the fire department. They would look at the rookies first, the college-aged kids with hero complexes or addictions to high-risk excitement. Eventually, they would look at him.

The police had already questioned Clyde about Miguel Vedra and Jeb Barlow. It was routine; witnesses overheard him at the hospital vowing revenge on Vedra for his attack on Leigh, and well, sorry to bother you, Clyde, old man, but can you account for your whereabouts on the night Vedra was murdered? Ironically, the Bobcat Bay arsonist provided Clyde an airtight alibi. Clyde was putting out a fire he, himself, had set at the time of Vedra's death. As for Jeb Barlow, they just needed information. Clyde told them he had been at the Pier Diner that night, had witnessed King laying hands on Jeb, but he'd diffused the situation, then left. And when police speculated on the arsonist's involvement, Clyde returned his alter ego the favor: "Couldn't have been the arsonist," Clyde said. "Jeb was his mouthpiece, right? Doesn't make sense." The sheriff agreed. Indeed, Clyde had not killed Jeb but knew it was a matter of time before his well-oiled plans rusted. Either Clyde Glenwood or the Bobcat Bay arsonist would have to step down and move on.

But not yet.

Poor Jeb, Clyde thought. He felt bad about kidnapping him that night, but he had had no choice. The media was focused on Eugene Lanier. Eugene Lanier! As if that moron had the wherewithal to pull off what Clyde had done. If the idiots had found his arson notes, he would not have needed to kidnap a reporter. But the public had to know the Bobcat Bay arsonist wasn't just some crazed pyro with a Bible in one hand, torch in the other. He was one man trying to enact positive change with the methods at his disposal, and he needed to explain that to

Jeb Barlow, who had been giving Eugene Lanier the credit Clyde deserved and suggesting the fires were linked to Ed Bartlett's murder. Clyde couldn't let that stand. He was an arsonist, not a murderer. He had nothing to do with Ed's murder. Jeb, he had kidnapped, but murdered? Never.

Clyde was grateful, however, to whoever had taken Miguel Vendra off his plate. Now there was a waste of sperm. Vedra was lucky to have been murdered before Clyde caught up with him: he would have given Vedra a taste of his own medicine. If Clyde had followed through on his threat, though, he would not have the cloak of invisibility he was taking advantage of now.

Still, Clyde knew traps were being set for the Bobcat Bay arsonist and often dreamt he was chewing off a foot as fire licked his heels. On those nights, Clyde woke sweating, the taste of ash in his mouth. The first breath of smokeless air extinguished the nightmares, but the flame of panic burned in his chest for hours. He paced, reminding himself that a trap would work only if he walked into it. He had studied the tightened security measures, noted the changing of the guard. Other than the notes he left behind, there was nothing to connect him to the fires. He had burned evidence, tied loose ends, filled cracks. No one could bring him down.

Except Sada Powell.

Clyde had first seen Sada at the Pier Diner a year ago. Standing behind King, she seemed a twig next to an oak. When she caught Clyde looking at her, she held his eyes without blinking. When Clyde smiled at her, she smiled back. In the weeks that followed, Clyde bumped into Sada every time he turned around. Her schoolgirl crush was flattering, but awkward. She left gifts at his front door: twig people with Spanish moss hair, woven palm fans, an orange. She hung around the fire station like a puppy, waiting for someone to throw her an inviting word. Fellow firefighters called her "little red hen" and "jailbait." They teased Clyde about Kingfisher Powell coming after him with a tomahawk. Then Leigh blew into town.

Poor, fucked-up Leigh. He knew she was a junkie the first time he saw her, and he knew also, if she didn't get treatment, where she'd end up. Clyde had lost an older brother to heroin. Davy's descent had been slow and inevitable, triggered by a dishonorable discharge from the Army, and wracked with further failure, contrition, and self-hate. Before Davy disappeared for the last time, he had a sudden attack of clear-headedness and checked into the VA hospital. Davy vowed he would quit cold turkey; get a job; go to AA, group therapy, church—whatever it took to finally grab this monkey by the balls and snatch it from his back. But Davy had not hit bottom. The bottom was a long way off, in fact—a dark, nasty place that retreated lower each time he got close. Within a week, Davy was thrown out of the VA hospital for using, and the cycle of regress, repent, and rehab repeated. The last Clyde heard, Davy was in the Keys, living on scraps thrown from the back door of Sloppy Joe's. By the time Clyde got there, Davy had moved on to some lesser life.

Clyde knew Leigh was headed in the same direction, but in spite of it, he found himself caring for her, which scared him. Having tried and failed so many times with his brother, he knew he could do nothing for Leigh. She was drowning, and he had to kick away before she pulled him under. She would be out of the hospital soon, and as much as it would hurt, he would not encourage her to stay in DeLeon. He cared for her; he just couldn't get close to anyone for fear of what he might blurt in his sleep, leave in a pocket, or refuse to discuss. Monitoring his behavior at work was hard enough. Add a girlfriend to the mix, and eventually Clyde would slip.

Complicating things further, Sada was now stalking him. On his first date with Leigh, he noticed Sada following. Clyde took the offensive. When Sada took her cigarette break behind the diner, he approached, told Sada he had seen her stalking him and Leigh. Wide-eyed and defiant, Sada told him it wasn't true.

"We both know it is."

Sada's tears flowed as she turned left and right, searching for a comeback, her gestures dramatic and befitting a woman scorned. "Why do you like her?" she cried. "She's not even pretty!"

"I can see you're hurt, Sada, but Leigh is none of your business."

"But I love you!"

"No, you don't. You're sixteen years old."

"Seventeen!"

"Stop following me, Sada."

"I'll tell my father you insulted me!"

It spiraled downward. Clyde finally extricated himself, leaving Sada crying behind the diner.

But sometimes the least expected opportunity presents itself in all its perfection, and this one came in the form of Jeb Barlow, harrumphing through the alley on that tearful morning, summoned to his fate by a damsel in distress. From a distance, in his truck, Clyde saw the moment unreel. He had planned to do this another time, in another way, but it seemed reckless to wait when he didn't have to. Clyde looked at his watch. Sada would have to get back to her shift, and when she did, a moment would crack open. Clyde would be ready, wrench in hand, and the Bobcat Bay arsonist—mute, misunderstood, and reviled—would finally have a voice. Sada went back inside, and Clyde struck. Jeb went down, and Clyde stuffed him inside his truck. The kidnapping had gone well.

Now at the construction site, Clyde crunched over burnt debris. He had three minutes before the next security shift arrived. He would have to put this note under their noses, or the idiots wouldn't find it, just as they hadn't found the others. This was the kind of incompetence Clyde loathed. What did he have to do? Draw a map? Mail them each a copy? As long as his message wasn't getting out, he was forced to strike again. If they'd release the notes to the media, he wouldn't have to keep burning these goddamn houses!

Clyde reached beneath his Kevlar jacket and extracted the note. He impaled it over a charred nail on a black two by four. Devoid of sarcasm, religion, or anger, it entreated simply:

LeT It BUrN

CHAPTER 53

"Oyez, oyez, oyez, this court is now in session."

The judge swept behind a huge desk and sat. Annie had never seen him before. He moved papers with pads of his fingers, then surveyed the court.

"Would somebody shut the door? We don't need to air condition the whole outdoors."

An officer obliged. Della turned around. If she had looked bad before, she looked horrible now. Drained of color, she slouched in her chair, defeated. Miguel Vedra's death had been a final blow. Fingerprints proved he broke the window in Della's house, probably what woke Della the night of Ed's murder. If Vedra saw or did anything else, it went to the morgue with him. Annie tried to convince Della that the prints raised reasonable doubt, but Della had hit bottom and was out of bounce.

"Pete can't prove when the window was broken," Della had said. "The prosecution will say it could have been before the murder or the day after. It's not enough."

"But Leigh says Vedra knew about Dad's murder. He must have been there when it happened."

"Annie, Leigh's not exactly a stellar witness. Matty Tatum will take her apart."

"He had something to do with my father's murder, Della, I know it. Ask for a new attorney and reopen the investigation."

Half of Della's mouth smiled. "No. It's too risky."

"Della, what happened to you? You begged me to help. I'm

telling you this is enough to cast reasonable doubt."

"Thank you for what you've done, Annie, but Pete's right. If I plead guilty, I'm out in fifteen years. If we go to trial and I'm found guilty, I could die. I don't want to die."

"Oh God, Della, don't cry."

"This whole town is against me. I don't have any fight left. You and Leigh take the house—sell it, do something with it. I don't care. I just want to sleep."

"You can't give up."

But Della had given up. Hopelessness curved her spine and twisted her mouth, now carelessly gashed with lipstick.

"Guilty, your honor," she said, and with one smack of a gavel, Della was ordered to the women's facility in Lowell, where she would sleep like a dead woman and dress in a shade of blue that didn't look good on anybody.

CHAPTER 54

When Judge Lanier entered her chambers, Dade Newcomb stood, surprised his legs still worked. He held his hat in calloused hands, turned it gently. Looking at the hand-knotted rug under his feet, his vision blurred, and he swayed.

Marguerite was surprised to see him, as he knew she would be. She closed the door by leaning on it, and after taking him in, walked to her closet while sloughing her robe.

"You smell like smoke," she said.

"Yeah, another fire."

"The arsonist?"

"It looks that way, yes."

Marguerite slipped a mahogany hanger inside her robe and hung it in the closet. Sheriff Newcomb longed to be in there as well, safe from the injustices of the world. He could almost smell the residual perfume that would shroud him in the dark: Marguerite's Chanel No. 5 mixed with expensive wool, and the sea-breeze clean of shampooed hair.

"What is it, Dade?"

"Marguerite—"

The skip in his voice set off her alarm, but she steeled herself. "Eugene?"

"Yes."

"Is he all right?"

"Yes."

Dade waited for this to settle. He saw the fear behind her

301

eyes and almost moved toward her, but she would not allow him to hold her; not yet.

"Where is he?"

"He's in custody. Salceda just picked him up outside the diner. He likes Raina, went with her without a problem."

"Of course he did. He respects authority. I've seen to that."

"I know."

Marguerite paused, eyes shifting. "Is it bad?"

"Yes."

Dade waited. It would not be right to volunteer the information, not this kind. Marguerite had known this moment would come since the day she found matches in Eugene's pocket. She would ask when she was ready.

"I want to see him."

"Of course. First thing in the morning."

"Not first thing in the morning, Dade. Now."

"It's late, Marguerite. They have to process him."

"I don't care what they have to do, Dade. He's my little boy, and I have a right to see him."

The sheriff lowered his eyes. A twenty-four-hour waiting period was imposed on all new prisoner visits, and while the sheriff was comfortable breaching the law by a few hours, a visit tonight would torque jaws. He remained silent, however, and waited for Marguerite to come around.

"Just let me—" Marguerite rummaged in her purse, then opened a round compact, pinky finger in the air. Peering, she touched her hair, and with the pad of one finger, the translucent skin beneath her eyes. Dade had never seen a vain gesture from Marguerite and knew this moment went deeper. She stuffed the compact back in her purse.

"What is he charged with?" she asked, assembling herself. Sheriff Newcomb hesitated. She looked up. "Dade?

"Murder."

She wore the shock like a too-large coat; it swallowed her as she shrank from the news. "No. He sets fires. He would never kill anyone! You know that, Dade. You have to tell them. He sets fires, that's all."

Dade held out a hand. "Marguerite."

"How dare you come and say such a thing?"

He saw now he'd handled this all wrong; he should have told her the second she opened that door. "His fingerprints were all over the knife stuck in Miguel Vedra's chest."

She looked at him as one would a stranger. "Miguel Vedra—?"

"I'm sorry, Marguerite."

"He's been arrested for the murder of Miguel Vedra?"

"Salceda bagged his shoes. There's blood on them."

"This is absurd. I want my son out of that jail right now."

"I can't, Marguerite."

"Dade!"

"I can't."

She lunged, grabbed his shirtfront. His hands automatically encircled her wrists, slender and frail as a bird's, and pulled her to him. He felt her mouth working beneath his heart.

"Oh, Dade. Our poor baby. Our poor, poor boy."

Nineteen years before, when she was forty-five, Marguerite entered the police station and informed a handsome, young officer named Dade Newcomb that she was pregnant. Dade led her to a room where they could talk.

They had slept together twice. Marguerite had not insisted on birth control. At her age, her eggs were numbered. In fact, she thought she might be peri-menopausal.

"Imagine my surprise . . ."

Dade Newcomb listened, stunned. He was married, so their trysts were secret, which suited Marguerite. Neither was in it for the long haul; that was understood from the start. Marguerite was fifteen years older than Dade, and she could not stand the thought that one day he would wake and wonder who the old lady was lying next to him. And a public affair would damage their careers and devastate Dade's wife and daughters, who didn't deserve it. They would get this out of their systems, Marguerite believed, and that would be that. She never thought she could become pregnant.

Marguerite presented legal documents granting her sole custody. In effect, she asked Dade to relinquish all rights as father of her child. When he objected, she urged him to be practical.

"You're a married man with children. You know this would crush them. There's your future to think about: who will vote for a known adulterer as sheriff? Sign this, Dade, and it never happened."

Reluctantly, he signed. Over the years, Newcomb watched from a distance as Eugene's disabilities, evident at birth, stunted his development. He watched Marguerite and admired her devotion. Even if she managed a few things differently than he would have, it was obvious she loved the boy fiercely, and woe to anyone who threatened their bond. He watched Eugene slog through a difficult infancy, childhood, and adolescence and was prepared to step in front of a bus to spare the boy pain. After Dade's wife left him for her therapist, he asked the judge to marry him.

"I don't love you, Dade."

"That's all right. Eugene needs a father."

"I give Eugene all that he needs. Please don't ask again."

But he did ask again, and again after that. Always the answer was no. Even though Marguerite would not let Dade legally into her family, she did let him into her bed. During those fragrant hours, Eugene slept just rooms away, unaware that his mother, looking nothing like an old lady, trembled beneath his father's hands, a sheriff who loved them both.

"Our poor, baby boy," Marguerite cried then as now, and he held her, as helpless as he had ever been.

CHAPTER 55

A lone whippoorwill sounded across the lake. Annie counted the seconds between each forlorn, questioning call. As a child, she had set her heartbeat by these three notes. The first two melded into one; the last note looped upward with desperate hope:

Areyou there?

Areyou there?

Areyou there?

Annie removed her camera's zoom lens and blew sand from its threads. She missed her darkroom. Leigh, having left the hospital but so far refusing the doctor's rest orders, would soon have bandages removed. All that remained to be done in De-Leon was to dispose of her father's ashes. Maybe it was time to give up the ghost, so to speak, and go home.

The sheriff, certainly anxious to see her leave, had threatened to implicate her in Vedra's murder. A charge wouldn't stick—she could account for her whereabouts—but the accusation could complicate her life. Blaming her for Jeb Barlow's murder was a cheap shot, but Annie could not shake the feeling there was truth in it. The sheriff's remarks about her engagement, none of his business, were meant to remind her she had made promises elsewhere and would do damage she if she did not honor them.

Annie felt bad about Pete. He'd called a few times, but she kept the conversation short. "Are we ever going to talk about that night?" he had asked.

"No," Annie said. "It didn't happen, remember?"

"But it did."

"We agreed it didn't."

"Why won't you talk to me? Why can't I see you?"

Even if nothing was technically wrong with being seen together, the appearance of impropriety alone could put Pete's professional reputation at risk. He had been generous and caring since the moment Annie stepped from the plane. At Jeb's funeral, he took her hand as a reminder that he was there for her, and it had been the perfect thing to do. No, Annie couldn't afford to get involved with Pete now. After all his kindnesses, she couldn't stand it if she caused him trouble and convinced Pete they should keep their distance, at least until Della was sentenced.

But when would that be? And was Della eligible for parole? Annie had been too distracted to ask. Maybe she could reach Pete at home. It was a business call, she told herself. She would keep it short. Annie took a deep breath and picked up the phone, but the line was alive.

"Hello?" said the voice.

"Who is this?"

"It's Kirsten."

"Kirsten? How bizarre. I just picked up the phone and there you were."

"Wow, yeah, bizarre."

The boredom in Kirsten's voice sliced through Annie's disorientation. The girl could take the air out of a balloon just by looking at it.

"How did you get this number?" Annie asked.

"I called information. My dad told me you were staying at your old house."

"How . . . resourceful," Annie said, then felt a jolt. "Is

something wrong?"

"No. Well, sort of. I mean, there is to me."

"What is it, Kirsten?"

"You and my dad have to get back together."

Annie hesitated, uncertain she heard right.

"Hello?" Kirsten said.

"Yeah, I'm here, I just—what did you say?"

"You have to get back together with my dad."

Annie fought the urge to be impolite. "That's a pretty interesting statement, coming from you, Kirsten. I thought you didn't like me being your father's girlfriend."

"Yeah, well, that was before. I've changed my mind. When are you coming back?"

"Is this why you called? To ask when I'm coming back?"

"And when you're getting back with my dad."

"Kirsten, whether your dad and I get back together is up to us."

"I know, but when are you?"

"I don't know if we are."

"Whyyyyy?"

Of all she missed, Annie would not have thought Kirsten's nasal, high-pitched whine would make the list, but after months of wanting to throttle the girl, the sound filled Annie with nostalgia. She sat in her father's chair, laughing to herself at the perversity. Ed's smell puffed from the cushions.

"Kirsten, you can't make people love the way you want them to. It's like tipping over a canoe."

"Huh? What's a canoe got to do with anything?"

The memory and metaphor had popped to mind together. "One time I asked my father to take me out in our canoe. I begged and begged for weeks, until I finally wore him down. But when the time came, he invited his girlfriend to come with us."

"Eww. I bet you were mad."

"More like jealous. I wanted him to myself. And I hated his girlfriend. She couldn't fish; she didn't like to hunt; she complained about everything: the heat, the rain. I couldn't understand why he paid more attention to her than me, and I'm afraid I wasn't very nice to her."

"What did you do?" Kirsten asked, almost excited.

"I tipped over the canoe."

"Oh my gosh! Why?" Annie imagined Kirsten's eyes, wide beneath blunt bangs cut too short.

"To see which of us he would save first: me, or his girlfriend."

"Who'd he pick?"

"He threw me a seat cushion and went for her. He knew I could swim."

Annie could almost hear Kirsten processing; this was good. She and Kirsten had never had a talk that wasn't dismissive chitchat.

"Were you mad your Dad didn't swim to you first?" Kirsten asked.

"Yes, at first. Then I figured something out. If you try to make people prove they love you, you're going to get disappointed." Annie waited. As always, Kirsten, when confronted with a difficult truth, fell silent. "The trouble with you and me, Kirsten, is you tip over the canoe all the time. You wanted to sink our wedding plans, and you did. And when your dad let that happen, I saw a whole lot of tipped-over canoes in my future, and I just . . . I don't know. I just don't want to live the rest of my life treading water."

"I didn't do it on purpose."

"Oh, Kirsten, I'm not trying to say this break-up was your fault. It wasn't. You, your dad, and your mom are still adjusting to the divorce, and it's taking longer than anybody thought. And I'm not without blame. In a way, I'm jealous of you, too."

"Me?"

"Sure. I can't remember my father ever considering my feelings when he made a big decision. I'm sure he must have, but I never saw it. Your father shows he loves you every day; you shouldn't make him prove it."

"My mother says he doesn't love me anymore, just his girlfriends."

Annie closed her eyes. She could hear her own mother, long ago, saying the same thing. God, the stupidity.

"Listen to me, Kirsten. Your father would sacrifice his own happiness to spare you the slightest suffering. He is your father, and he will always be there for you. Don't forget that."

"Yeah, I know . . ."

"He has a very big heart, you know. There's room in there for all the people he loves."

"Even Cindy?"

"Who's Cindy?"

"His new girlfriend." Annie sat up. "And she's awful. Worse than you. She tries too hard, and buys me stuff I don't want—personal stuff. She bought me a push-up bra. Like I have anything to push up." Suddenly underwater, Annie struggled against a hold on her ankles. "So I thought if you could come back, then I could tell my dad I like you better, and he'd get rid of Cindy."

"You can't do that, Kirsten."

"Why?"

"Because it's not your choice. If it's meant to be, your dad and I will find our own way."

Kirsten groaned. "Yeah, okay. But just hurry up, okay? Cindy's canoe doesn't tip over as easy as yours."

Annie hung up, unsure of the thing scratching her heart. What had she expected? Not only had Annie broken off the engagement, she'd cheated on Camp as well. Was Camp to declare perpetual mourning, don a black cape and wander the streets muttering her name?

On the other hand, it stung Annie to learn she was so easy to replace. Camp had waited, what—a whole five days before introducing his precious daughter to Miss Push-Up Bra? Well, no matter. It was a textbook rebound. Camp would come to his senses.

And do what? Come back for her? Was that what she wanted?

The doorknob rattled, followed by a sharp rap. Annie glanced at her watch—after nine. When had it got dark?

"Who is it?"

"It's Leigh. Open the door, will ya?"

Surprised that Leigh would return home this early in the evening, Annie wondered if plans with Clyde had fallen through. She fumbled with the deadbolt. "I thought you had a key." She opened the door.

They stood before her, a parody of humanity. Kingfisher Powell, corpulent and dark, towered over the sprat-like Leigh, whose golden hair haloed her bruised and bandaged face. The effect was ominous—clown faces in a window, a crow flying upside down.

Leigh breezed past, smelling of whiskey, and Annie's heart sank. Had their father's willingness to help Leigh recover been another feckless dream?

"King has something to say, and I think you should listen," Leigh said. She riffled through a kitchen drawer. "Does Della keep any cigarettes around here?"

"I thought you were with Clyde."

"I'm seeing him later. Where are the goddamn cigarettes?"

"May I come in?" King asked.

"Oh, sorry. I guess so. I mean, sure." Annie opened the door wide, and King stepped in.

Leigh called from the kitchen. "Annie, have you seen any

311

cigarettes around here?"

"No."

"Shit!" Leigh slammed the drawer.

"Leigh, you're not supposed to drink while you're on medication."

"Who said I've been drinking?"

"I can smell it."

"Look, don't even start with me," Leigh said, hands at halt position. Her bandages covered one eye; the other gazed lazily at Annie. "What about the sofa cushions?" Leigh plunged fingers behind the green and brown plaid cushions, yanked them askew.

"I just vacuumed in there. There's nothing."

"Swell."

"Would you care for a stick of gum?" King said, and Leigh looked startled, as though she had forgotten he was there.

"Sure." Leigh placed the stick between two fingers and brought one end to her lips. "Got a match?"

King stood motionless.

Leigh rolled an eye. "Just kidding, fer christsakes. Jeez, tough house. You guys need to loosen up."

"Can I get you something to drink?" Annie asked King.

"No, thank you," King said.

"I'll have a beer," Leigh said.

Annie's eyes grazed King's. His look conveyed knowledge and understanding, which made Annie feel they were discussing Leigh behind her back. "Excuse me," she said and headed for the kitchen.

"Siddown, King," Leigh said. "Or take a look around, if you want. Your first time inside, isn't it?"

"Yes," King said, and after adjusting a cushion at the end of the sofa, he sat.

"Well, what do you think?" Leigh stood with hip cocked, hands out, game-show style.

A big man on a low sofa, King turned awkwardly. Annie stepped from the kitchen and handed Leigh a beer. "You want to tell me what's going on?"

"King's buying the house. Aren't you King?"

King placed huge hands on huge knees; curiously formal, Annie thought. "I am."

"You hear that, Annie? He am." Leigh grinned and drank from the beer bottle. A trickle escaped her lips. "Damn, I'm such a slob," she said, then sucked her fingers.

"With respect, Mr. Powell," Annie offered, "I don't think this is a good time to discuss this."

"Sure, it is!" Leigh said and worked her long legs past King. She sat, her right knee touching his thick thigh. "Della pleaded guilty, thoughtfully saving the taxpayers the cost and trouble of a trial, so there's no time like the present, right King? King has some amazing news about this land, Annie. You're not going to believe it. Go ahead, tell her." King's eyes moved to Annie, but he did not speak. "Go on," Leigh prodded. "Nobody's going to bite."

To Annie, the moment seemed off-balance. Leigh, drunk and careless, showed no deference to King, who filled the room with his silence. Annie held his gaze. The big man's black eyes took her in without blinking.

"You are a photographer," he said, as if bestowing the title.

"Yes," Annie said. "I haven't done much lately, but . . . yes."

King removed his hat. "I would like you to take my picture."

Had King removed his clothing, Annie could not have been more surprised. The sight of black hair plastered to his skull embarrassed her. She came to her senses, though, and grabbed her camera.

"Whoa, whoa, whoa," said Leigh, placing her beer on the braided rag rug. "Let's not get distracted here."

"Could I get you to sit in this chair?" Annie asked King. "I can move the light around you."

King pushed off the sofa and sat in Ed's chair.

"Oh, for the love of . . ." Leigh began, then laughed loudly. "Hey, Annie, I was about to say 'for the love of Pete!' That's pretty funny, huh?"

Leigh's jab was a sign Annie would have to work fast. No longer the center of attention, Leigh would lob bigger grenades unless Annie pulled her in.

"Hey, Leigh, what do you think? Hat on or off?"

"Like I give a damn." Leigh crossed her legs, upsetting her beer in the process. "Shit! See what you made me do?" Hauling herself up, Leigh left and returned with a paper towel. "Cleaning up the wet spot," she mumbled. "Story of my life."

King sat at rigid attention, tracking Annie's movements without comment. When she finished tweaking, Annie held camera to eye. King lifted his chin.

"No, stay the way you were. Good. Try to relax." In the split second before snapping his picture, King did something so extraordinary, Annie was unsure it had actually happened until, weeks later, she held the developed print before her eyes. Quickly lowering the camera now, what she had seen was there no more. King sat stone-faced, and replaced his hat. Had it happened? Had he really smiled?

"Wait, I only took one," Annie said.

"I would very much appreciate a print," King said. "I will pay, of course."

"But I have a full roll!"

With effort, King lifted himself from Ed's chair and stepped from the lighted perimeter. Clearly, the session had ended. Leigh looked as surprised as Annie, then, with a shake of her bandaged head, said, "Okay!" Leigh clapped her hands. "Can we talk now?"

"Yes," said King, and sat slowly again.

"As I was saying," Leigh began.

King interrupted, his voice smooth and non-threatening. "I wish to buy this house." He looked at Annie. "I will pay you well. I have prepared a contract."

King reached inside his jacket, and Annie caught Leigh's eye, shining with anticipation. King handed the contract to Annie. "You will look it over, of course."

The multi-page contract contained the usual whereases and therefores. Annie skimmed without reading, blindly turning pages as Leigh chattered happily.

"It's a hell of a deal, Annie, you have to admit. You and Camp—or you and Petey, whoever—can start a new life together. Or, you could open a studio, or travel the world taking pictures, if that's what you want. The point is, whatever you want, or whoever you want, there's enough money here to start off right."

Annie, regretting she had confided in Leigh about Pete, cleared her throat. "Why do you want this house so badly, Mr. Powell?"

"Oh, it's not the house—" Leigh began. Annie shot a warning glance, and Leigh shut up.

"I wish to buy it for my people."

"For your—but no Miccosukee people live here."

"No. But they will come. I am building homes for them."

"Well, trying to anyway," Leigh put in, then made her hands leap in imitation of flames. King ignored the mime.

Annie was confused. "I thought Indians lived on reservations."

King's face looked patient, but weary, as if tired of having to explain this yet again. "We can live wherever we wish, just like you. And we wish to live together, just like you. I probably do not have to tell you of the many problems my people face. We have been conditioned to be poor and dependent."

"But you're not going to be poor and dependent any more, are you King?" Leigh said.

"No," he said. "We have been a sovereign nation for twenty years, now. We are free of many government restrictions, which means we can do with our land as we like."

Suddenly, Annie caught his drift. "Like build casinos," she said.

"Yes."

Annie rested the contract on her lap. King's portfolio included a million-dollar casino on the Hollywood Reservation, which had opened the previous year to great controversy and success. "So you wish to buy the Widow Lake properties, declare the area an Indian reserve, and build casinos?"

King held up a finger. "One casino," he said.

"Isn't that exciting?" Leigh chimed in.

"But, can you do that? I mean, just buy up property and turn it into a reservation?"

"If I give the land to the Miccosukee people, it is their land. As a sovereign nation, they can do with it as they wish."

"Don't you see, Annie? The tribe builds the casino, runs it, then takes home the profits, all without the government butting in. King says the tribe could build its own schools, hospitals, stuff like that. And the locals will make money, too. People love to gamble. They'll come like flies on shit."

Annie looked at the last page of the contract, at Leigh's signature. She looked up. "So you like this idea."

"Well, hell yeah! Everybody wins!"

Inside Annie's head, Della's words echoed:

You and Leigh split the money—probably more money than you've ever had. Kingfisher gets his development; Della goes to prison. Happy ending, right?

Leigh leaned in and took her sister's hands. "It's going to happen, Annie. It's going to happen with or without us. King has bought over eighty acres, including the land around Lake Talmadge. In two years, nobody will recognize this place. It's time we move on. We should use this place to change our lives. It's what mom and dad wanted for us." Annie watched a tear work its way down Leigh's cheek. "I need this money, Annie. I have hospital bills, a lot of them. And I could use some therapy, in case you haven't noticed, not to mention a little rehab." Leigh held forefinger and thumb an inch apart. "Just a little bit." Leigh's smile, lanced by Miguel's knife, trembled. She squeezed her sister's hands. "Let's say yes."

The sisters moved into one another and let their foreheads kiss. Leigh sniffled, wiped a hand beneath her nose.

"I hear you," Annie whispered. "But there's just one thing."

"What?"

"What about Della?"

Annie saw wildfire as Leigh leapt to her feet, pressed the heels of her hands into her temples, then erupted.

"Why do you care so much about that woman? She murdered our father!"

"That was never proven."

"Oh, for—" Leigh's hands held her scalp. "What about me, Annie? Don't you care about me?"

King rose. "I will leave you to discuss this."

Leigh switched like a light, grabbed King's arm. "No, no, King, don't go. Please."

"This is your private matter. I will give you privacy."

"Wait! Annie, ask him to stay. Here, take another picture." Leigh shoved Ed's chair forward and knocked over a floor lamp, muttered, "Goddammit."

King moved to the door. His black eyes, opaque as marbles, turned to Annie. "You will not get another offer like this. I will give you twenty-four hours to decide."

Leigh joined King at the door. "For the last time, Annie.

Della has no claim to this house. She pleaded guilty to murder."

"But one day she'll get out, and then where is she supposed to go?"

Leigh tilted her head to the ceiling. After a moment, she said, "I give up," her voice soft. "Sorry to waste your time, King."

King tipped his hat and left, closed the door. Leigh stumbled after him. Annie spoke. "Wait! Where are you going?"

Leigh smiled. "To hell in a hand basket, Annie, just like daddy always said." She spun and walked in King's shadow, bandages luminous in the dark. "Hey, King! Buy a lady a drink?"

Annie stood in the doorway, arms tightly wrapped. Without resources or intervention, Annie saw, Leigh's downward spiral would escalate. Annie doubted her sister had the strength to find her way through the fire of her addictions. She didn't blame Leigh for doubting Annie's love; after all, Leigh had struggled all her life for the attention of her family and came up short. Even after Leigh's attack, Annie's preoccupation with Pete, Della and her father overshadowed her sister's needs. By refusing to sell, was she being selfish? All was done here, after all: her father dead, her mother gone, and Della, guilty as charged.

As King opened the car door for Leigh, Annie felt a great letdown, her body suddenly liquid and flowing into her shoes. Just as suddenly, she felt filled with knowledge of uncertain origin: if she allowed Leigh to disappear inside that black car, she would never see her sister again.

"Leigh, wait."

Leigh stopped, one leg on the ground. About to close the car door, King turned. Annie went inside the house and scrounged for a pen. She picked up the contract and flipped to the last page. A quick scribble, and, when she stepped outside, Leigh stood at the door.

"Here," said Annie. "I signed it."

Leigh saw Annie's signature, then looked up. "Are you sure?"

"Just promise you'll use the money to get well, Leigh."

"I will. I swear."

When they hugged, Annie felt Leigh wince. Her wounds had not healed, and closeness caused pain.

"Come celebrate," Leigh said, tears welling.

Annie shook her head. "That's okay."

Leigh squeezed Annie's hand, then ran toward King's black Cadillac, waving the contract over her head. As Annie watched the black Cadillac pull away, a voice faded up, then out.

. . . your father's girlfriend . . .

Expecting to see her mother, Annie turned, heart leaping. She stood very still, alert to the slightest stir, in silent communion with the whippoorwill still yearning:

Are you there?

CHAPTER 56

At night, the day's heat rose through the floorboards of the Back Room. The ticking fan, paddles coated in gray dust, mixed hot air with cigarette smoke and the bloated stories of people with nowhere better to go. Between the liquor bottles lined along the mirror, a reflection of Clyde Glenwood scowled at a newspaper open before him.

He flipped through a third time—nothing. What did he have to do to get attention? He'd left the note out in the open; why wasn't that in this piss-poor excuse for a paper?

Clyde side-armed the paper into a magazine-strewn corner. Hot rocks pummeled his head from the inside. The Bureau of Fire and Arson Investigations wasn't taking him seriously. Clyde cracked a knuckle. They were laughing at him; worse, ignoring him. Well, that would change. Another knuckle cracked. He had hoped he wouldn't have to resort to more drastic measures, but they were pushing him. With the third knuckle, Mr. Hyde licked at the edges of reason.

Until now, Clyde had burned only unoccupied buildings, and Seminole Estates had been an ideal target. Now, it seemed the media did not find those fires worth mentioning. Time to turn up the heat on a new target, but which one?

"Clyde!"

Leigh came toward him, arms in the air, hands twirling, feet skimming flat across the floor. She crashed into him, almost knocking him from the barstool.

"Whoa, girl! You'll hurt yourself." Clyde smelled alcohol and drew back. "What'd you do? Start without me?"

Leigh gave an exaggerated nod. "Yep. I'm celebrating."

"Celebrating what?"

Leigh presented a folded contract. Clyde glanced down and understood at once. "You sold Ed's house to King." Again the exaggerated nod, now unbearable. "Why?"

"Money! Lots of it! And King is going to give the land to the Miccosukees and build a casino, so we're doing something good for the Indians, too." Lightning bolted through Clyde's brain as Leigh continued, oblivious to his rage. "Do you know what this means, Clyde?"

He knew. Worse than the gated community Sada had spoken of, a casino would destroy DeLeon—increase traffic on roads, bring unbridled development, a great sucking of resources. But the city, with its shrinking tax base, might actually embrace the idea. Clyde could see it now: streams of people dropping Styrofoam cups on the ground, straining the septic system, throwing lit cigarettes from car windows, and City Council bending over and asking for more. Clyde's apocryphal vision went red. Had they learned nothing? They could not rape the earth without consequences. He would not allow it.

"It means I can get well, and we can have a life together, Clyde. After rehab, I'll have enough money to buy a place, nothing fancy, of course, but big enough for the two of us. I'm not asking you to marry me, in case you're wondering; I wouldn't want to scare you off. I'm just saying we can be together. You know, give it a shot, like the rest of the air-breathers?"

Each word, a coal dropping from Leigh's lips, burnt his flesh. A life together! She didn't even know who he was. Leigh had no idea how despicable she was to him now, swooning over a real estate deal with a man steeped in greed. What a mistake Clyde had made in caring for trailer trash who now reached for him with skeletal fingers.

"Don't!" He batted her hand away. How predictable—the look of confusion, the knitted brow, retreating smile. God, he could barely stand the sight of her.

"Clyde? What's wrong?"

Her voice whined in his head. *Clyde? What's wrong? What's wrong, Clyde?* Did Leigh really think he wanted to live with that whine day after day? Her bandaged head was a reminder of the trouble she would bring. Clyde had not planned to kick her away before sleeping with her one last time but found her repulsive now. She was one of them.

"You sell out Nature for a few gold coins, then ask me what's wrong? You come running in here, so goddammed proud of yourself, thinking I'll take you in my arms, like you're not an alcoholic junkie whore?"

Leigh looked slapped. "Clyde!"

"And you smell like a brewery. Get away from me."

She eyed him with that Cyclops eye. "Are you all right?"

"Go take your own temperature, Leigh. I'm fine."

Glenwood pushed away from the bar, hot bile rising from his stomach. Her touch seared his skin, and he tossed her off with one sweep of his Popeye arm. Leigh caromed off a barstool and hit the floor, ass first. King, at her side instantly, pulled her up with a gentle hand. Clyde had never hit a woman and hadn't meant to be so rough. He wanted to go to her, but the sight of King pummeled him into a mix of shame and fury. Everything was upside down.

"You bastard!" Leigh yelled, kicking as Clyde approached. She twisted violently while King struggled to bring her to her feet. "Get him away from me!"

The bar fell quiet as the drama played out, the Back Room becoming quite the source of entertainment these days. For the price of a couple beers, patrons could watch Boy Get Girl, then Boy Lose Girl, and playing the villain, Kingfisher Powell, dressed in black, the mammoth obstacle to Boy Gets Girl Back. You could hear threats, name-calling, the call to action—Come get me, you fat bastard—over the protestations of Florida Sunshine, who swept from behind the bar and stood, referee-style, between Clyde and King. A rhythm section of bystanders chanted Clyde Clyde Clyde as Clyde nudged Florida aside and threw the first punch. King's head barely registered the hit. Then his fist ripped upward and sent Clyde whirling. Florida, wisely, scampered away as the men clashed, mountains ripped from their moorings, until she pulled a ladylike pistol from behind the bar and fired into the ceiling.

"I said, no fighting, and I meant, NO FIGHTING!" Florida's magnificent chest rose and fell beneath a bright pink polyester tank. Clyde and King allowed themselves to be pulled apart. Clyde clutched his throbbing jaw, consoled that King's nose bled profusely. He made his way to Leigh, who watched him approach with feral wariness.

"Let's get out of here," Clyde said, offering a hand.

Leigh spit into the open hand. The foam-edged hock quivered in Clyde's palm, viscous and slightly opaque. Clyde shoved his way out the door to the parking lot, then caught himself mumbling. He shook his head and sent the words flying. All his work, the risks would mean nothing if he didn't get a grip right now.

He walked toward his truck, parked by itself on a shoulder of gravel and folded morning glories. The night was full of the acrid smells of a high summer evening: black pavement cooling, algae growing in stagnant drain water, and the distant perfume of skunk. A lightning image of Leigh in bed with King flashed across Clyde's eyes. He could almost smell the burnt air in his scalded brain.

Clyde stopped walking. What the hell was wrong with him? Since appointing himself Earth's warrior angel, he'd been acting like an assoholic, hell-bent on his own destruction. And he was tired of keeping his warring selves from plunging onto each other's swords. He must be some special kind of stupid, throwing away a woman who loved him to preserve some grandiose ideal. So he couldn't set fires with Leigh around. So what? All he had to do was choose: a life of destruction or a life with Leigh. All he had to do was turn around right now and go get her, beg forgiveness, make promises. Neither of them was perfect, Clyde knew, but that could play to his advantage. We can help each other. We can walk through the fire together.

But what about King and the others who would follow with their subdivisions, strip malls, casinos?

Fuck 'em. It was time for the arsonist to flame out before it all came apart on its own. He'd give Leigh the night to calm down, go see her tomorrow at her father's place. He'd pop for some posies, maybe a box of candy, unless that was too hokey. Ah hell, a man has to be a little hokey once in a while.

Feeling better, Clyde walked toward his truck, keys jingling. He glimpsed movement inside the truck. Great. Probably some kid stealing his eight-track player. Christ, what a night. He broke into a stealthy trot, slipped in close, then yanked the door open, prepared to rip the thief a new one.

The Nixon mask turned toward him, eyes empty and black. He stumbled back. A car screeched, swerved, and missed Clyde, who had scrambled out of its way by inches. On down the road, red taillights like devil's eyes, the horn gave a long, accusing blast.

Clyde turned back to the truck. The intruder was gone.

"What the fuck—" he began, but knew, even before he knew, that the end, not as he planned it, was near.

CHAPTER 57

"Was that Clyde?" Leigh asked, twisting in the front seat.

"Idiot," King said. "I almost hit him!"

"I wish you had," Leigh said and faced front. Something clawed at her stomach, as if trying to escape. She had thrown back a few, but this wasn't nausea. King stared straight ahead, negotiating pavement with minute movements of the steering wheel. What a shit storm this night turned out to be. Leigh had expected to spend the night with Clyde, making love as they mapped out a future together. She had it all figured out. The first thing she would do, she wanted to tell him, was get these bandages off. She was tired of wearing the mark of her errant life like that chick, whatshername, in that book she had to read in high school. Hester Something. *The Scarlet Letter,* that was it. She didn't read all of it, but she got the gist. *Look at me! I'm bad!* the bandages said. *Don't be like me, or you'll end up like this!* Anyway. First, get the bandages off. Second, enroll in drunk classes, or whatever the hell. Not the joke programs she was forced to attend when she got that DUI, but something hard-core, designed for people who wanted to be there. Pay for decent therapy, not the dime store crap the court threw at her, but real, honest-to-God psychoanalysis to jerk her head back around, where you run out of people to blame for your fuck-ups, where you cry into tissues and scream at your dead parents for not loving you enough. She could definitely get into that. And she'd go to AA, take it seriously this time, admit she was powerless over drugs and alcohol, that her life had become unmanageable because she could see now that it was true. Next, put a down payment on a condo, maybe in Ft. Myers or Sanibel Island. And finally, plastic surgery. Maybe that Hester chick didn't know she could rip that scarlet "A" out of her clothes, but Leigh was no fool for punishment. Maybe she'd leave the scar that creased her upper lip and gave her a supermodel pout. Clyde had said it was sexy.

The thought made her eyes sting. After she had spat in Clyde's hand she thought he was going to slug her. Maybe he would have, if not for Florida and King.

King. Jesus, what an unholy alliance this was. Leigh never thought she'd still be sitting next to him at—what time was it?—she squinted at the dashboard clock—midnight-thirty. But she had to get home some way, and after Clyde's freak-out, she wasn't about to get in a truck with him. Christ, what had happened back there?

"Are you doing all right?" King asked.

"Yes. I was just thinking."

"About Glenwood?"

"Yes."

King shook his head. "He is very angry."

"Well, that's not my fault. I have every right to sell my father's house."

"I agree, but that is not what I meant."

Leigh nodded; she knew what King meant. Clyde's anger went deeper than the lake house. Although she had only known him a short time, she knew something strange had got hold of him back there. He had said horrible things, thrown their future in her face, tried to make her small and ashamed. Maybe Annie was right, and Leigh attracted men like her father. She shuddered at the thought, folded her arms across her middle, bent forward.

King turned onto Kepler Road. "You are angry, too."

"Well, of course I am! Look at me. I'm a fuckin' freak show! Who wouldn't be angry with a face like this?"

"I was not criticizing."

"Okay, I know. Leave me alone, will you, King? I'm suddenly very sober and not liking it one bit."

"I'm sorry for what happened."

"Forget it. Clyde started it. I just want to go home and sleep off this nightmare."

"I was not talking about Clyde."

Leigh looked at King. "Oh. Then what do you mean?"

As King's hand came toward her, Leigh cowered. The hand withdrew. "I have no wish to harm you," he said.

"I'm sorry," Leigh said, recovering. "I'm guess I'm a little shell-shocked."

"If it were up to me, I would see that no harm comes to you again."

"Yeah, well. You've been real nice. Turn here."

King braked, triggered the blinker, and turned onto Holly Lane. A "For Sale" sign glowed in the yard of the corner house. The house, a favorite from Leigh's childhood, was now a plucked version of itself, looked scrawny in its newly mowed setting. The past owner had lived among a tangle of palms, elephant ears and morning glories, lush nature grown fat on ample sun and rain. Leigh loved the wild haphazardness, the roof disappearing beneath Spanish moss and spent, brown fronds. Clyde would have loved it, too. "The jungle house," she and Annie called it. All that vegetation was gone now, the house rendered respectable by a knobby-kneed woman who combed the yard daily. Bushes were whacked or yanked, trees pruned. A fuscia bougainvillea dripped from one lone window box. Charming, the real estate ad probably said. Corner lot. Won't last long.

Damn you, Clyde!

Leigh's leg jerked. Her foot smashed upward into the Cadillac's dashboard. The pain was excruciating, yet welcome. She kicked again, then again, each blow fueling her anger and waking the pain asleep in her body. "Damn you!" she screamed and kicked again. With white-knuckled fists she beat the dash as if it were a shark clamped around her middle, pulling her out to sea to spit her bones onto the shifting sand. Thrashing, she howled, spending the pain that had, since she was six, twisted her into this animal. Even with King's restraining hands, she battered the car, breath coming in rasps that shredded her throat, pulled the corners of her mouth into a tragedian grotesque. Leigh's eyes opened, and, through her grief, she saw herself as she believed others did: a pitiful screw-up who got what she deserved. The thought stole her breath, and she struggled for air. A dark force pushed small, hacking bird coughs from her diaphragm. She rocked, trying to dispel it. Finally, the animal broke and skittered into the darkness and she howled, as if her backbone was breaking. Before she fainted, King's voice pushed gently into her consciousness:

"It's gone," he whispered. "It can't hurt you anymore."

Chapter 58

Marguerite Lanier arrived at the jail after midnight, carrying a plate of sausage biscuits. She knew the on-duty corrections officer, Larry Parker, to be a man who enjoyed pig body. Shaped like a pear, jowled like a bulldog, Larry moved slowly, a conciliatory man in bad need of a good dentist. As the judge approached, Parker's eyes, buried beneath a prominent brow, were slow to register recognition. She was nearly upon him before he pulled himself from his chair, tucking in a shirt already tucked. Judge Lanier removed the tin foil from the plate and passed the biscuits beneath the officer's nose. Now, if she could just see her son for a few minutes, that would be grand.

Stomach rumbling, Officer Parker tore his eyes from the sausage biscuits and said in a voice tinged with pain, "I'm sorry, Judge Lanier, but I can't do that."

"Of course you can, Larry. I'm a judge. You'll do what I tell you."

"Yes, ma'am, but the sheriff said you might try something like this."

Marguerite bit her tongue. If she bullied Officer Parker, he'd shut down before she got what she came for. She navigated his lengthy refusal with charm, nodding as he recited the visitation rules, security measures, and his inability to accept even innocent biscuits still warm from the oven, smelling like heaven's own midnight snack.

"I assure you, Larry, Sheriff Newcomb has sanctioned this

visit," the judge said.

"But he told me—"

"Obviously he changed his mind, or I wouldn't be here, would I?"

Dade had told Marguerite to stay away from the jail. He'd pick her up first thing in the morning, and Marguerite agreed, kissed him goodnight, then pre-heated the oven to 350 degrees.

Confused, Officer Parker turned to his radio. "He won't have his radio on," the judge said with friendly authority. "It's past midnight. Why don't you pick up the phone and call the sheriff at home? I'm sure he's asleep by now, but maybe he won't mind you waking him to ask permission for something he's already approved."

Marguerite watched that scene play across Officer Parker's broad face. Still, he would not compromise his duty. "I'm sorry, Judge Lanier. I just can't."

The judge gave an understanding smile. "Of course. I apologize. How's your poker game these days, Larry?"

Parker scratched the back of his neck. "Trying to stay away from all that, Judge. Can't win for losin'."

After a few minutes more, wherein the judge asked Larry about his family and the Key West vacation he had planned, Marguerite sighed her disappointment at having to take the biscuits home, where they would surely go to waste. She put foil back over the plate. "I suppose I could drop these by the sheriff's office in the morning. He'll want to speak with you about refusing me access, I'm sure."

Officer Parker twitched beneath the torture. Not only did he fear the judge's recriminations, but the smell of the biscuits was driving him out of his mind. What harm could there be in letting Judge Lanier see her son? It's not like she was a security risk. And if the sheriff said it was okay, then wouldn't he get in more trouble if he didn't let her in? Besides, she was the judge.

Technically, she could do what she wanted in her own jail.

"I guess if we keep this to ourselves . . ."

"Mum's the word, Larry. Your secret is safe with me."

Officer Parker stuffed the proffered biscuits, three to a pocket, and let Marguerite through the double doors.

"It will be a contact visit, of course," the judge added.

Parker blanched. A contact visit was two feet over the line, but by accepting the biscuits, he was, in poker lingo, pot committed. Marguerite prodded with a no-nonsense stare. "Yes, ma'am," the officer said and led her past steel doors to the visitation room. "I'll go get him."

"He'll be more cooperative if you give him a biscuit."

Officer Parker felt his pockets like a tourist checking his wallet. "He's not allowed unscheduled meals."

"Whatever you say, Larry, but once he smells them, he'll be all over you."

Parker figured if he ditched the biscuits, his clothes still reeked of the grease. Eugene would go apeshit. The officer knew he had no choice. He had to go "all in." He pulled a biscuit from his pocket and continued on his way.

"Of course, if I come with you, you won't have to go through all the trouble of collecting and escorting him out here, where anyone can see us. It would be more private if I visited his cell, don't you agree?"

Officer Parker reversed, shaking his head. "No, now Judge Lanier, with all due respect, I explained all that—"

"I know, Larry, but we won't tell anyone, will we? I'll only be a minute."

"I could lose my job."

"Do you think I would let that happen? I already told you: the sheriff knows all about this visit. In fact, he mentioned your name."

"He did?"

"Of course. 'Just tell Larry I said it's all right.' Those were his exact words."

Judge Lanier knew Officer Parker had lost the hand and was holding cards only to delay the inevitable. She stood still, giving him room to fold. Finally, he caved.

"I hate my life," he muttered, and motioned her to follow.

Eugene sat on an iron bunk in a gray holding cell, hands on his knees. At the sound of Parker's key, he came forward and pressed his face against the small window.

"Step back, Pardna'," said Parker, opening the door.

"Bis!" Eugene said, excited, and Officer Parker handed him a biscuit. Eugene unwrapped it with one swipe, devoured it. Cheeks puffed with food, he reached for Parker's pockets. Parker sidestepped him.

"Stand back for your mama, now."

Eugene obeyed, clapping and chewing, and Parker let Marguerite in. "Ten minutes, Judge. You understand."

"Of course, Larry, but there's one more thing. I'm afraid Eugene is not going to be satisfied with one biscuit. Would you mind terribly leaving a few more?"

Officer Parker mentally counted the biscuits in his pocket. A few more? That would leave only—

"Oh, heavens," the judge asked. "Just give them all to me. I'll make you another batch, I promise."

"All of them?" Parker asked, voice cracking.

"Chop, chop, Larry. I only have ten minutes." Judge Lanier smiled sweetly and held out her hands. As Eugene danced and clapped, Officer Parker relinquished the contents of his pockets.

"Can I have just one?" Officer Parker asked.

"Well, of course you can! Take it back with you."

"Back—? Oh no, your Honor, I can't leave you alone with him."

Judge Lanier stopped smiling. "Larry, I am quite tired of this constant obfuscating. Now, my advice to you is take this biscuit, go back to your desk, and eat it before someone starts asking questions."

With that, Judge Lanier slid into the cell. Eugene was on her at once, fumbling for the biscuits she let tumble onto his cot.

"Shoo!" she said to Parker. "I'll call if I need you."

Larry Parker shook his head, then did as he was told.

Eugene seemed no worse for wear. He was hungry, but he was always hungry. She watched him eat, clucking at him to mind his manners. She found his circumstances ironic; all his life she had fought to keep him from confinement, yet here he was, despite her money and power. That Eugene might be innocent of Vedra's murder was not worth contemplating. Eugene was locked up; that was the problem. She would ride the court, of course, bring new meaning to the term "speedy trial." She would hire Craig Gittleman out of Miami, make it worth his while to leave his very young second wife and whitewashed villa on the beach. Eugene would make bail and come home to her, and the sooner the better.

Marguerite dreaded the lecture she would get from Dade, the I-told-you-so that had not come when he told her that Eugene had used Vedra's own knife and left him to die in the high grass edging Widow Lake. Eugene knew right from wrong, but she would not volunteer that information; the boy must have had a good reason to act so violently. Perhaps Eugene had been threatened by that, that character, who had lighted on their town like some huge, sinister moth. She would never say this out loud, of course, but good riddance to Miguel Vedra. It would not be ridiculous to argue Eugene had done the town a favor.

But that wouldn't exonerate him. Fire-starting was bad enough, but now Marguerite would have to "do" something with Eugene, as Dade often said. Dade would have had Eugene locked up long ago, maybe not in a cell where he was forced to defecate in full view, but something metaphorically equivalent.

"Hooooome," Eugene said.

"Yes, son, we're going home," the judge assured him. "As soon as you finish your biscuits. Chew with your mouth closed, dear."

Dade Newcomb hated waking to a ringing phone. Never good news, and he didn't know how much more bad news he could endure. If this was another fire, he would be sorely tempted to go back to sleep and let the damn thing burn them all to a crisp.

LeT It BUrN. The sheriff had agreed with Bureau Chief Huffman about keeping the contents of this last note out of the press, but that was about the only thing they saw eye-to-eye on, unimpressed as he was with the state's investigation. Surveillance had not worked, and the forensics lab had come up with nothing. The only way they were going to catch this asshole was wait for him to slip up or turn himself in.

Dade rolled onto his back and extended an arm, hand spidering for the phone on the bedside table. He caught a whiff of his breath, strong enough to ignite the sheets, and realized he had not shed his clothes. By the time he got Marguerite settled down, it had been late, and when he arrived home he could think only about a shot of whiskey, neat. In fact, he had thrown back more than one. A pain knifed across the back of his eyes.

"Sorry to call so early, Sheriff," said Larry Parker, "but I think you better get down to the jail."

Dade pinched the crust from the inner corners of his eyes. "What's the problem?"

"It's the judge, sir. She won't leave."

"What?"

"I let her in to see her son—"

"You what?"

"—and now she refuses to leave his cell."

"You let her in Eugene's cell?"

"She told me you said it was all right."

A vise squeezed Dade's brains until they threatened to squirt from his nostrils. Larry Parker had worked for him for fourteen years, and, like most low-level officers, was in awe of Marguerite's authority. Dade could imagine her bullying him into something like this.

"Let me talk to her."

"She won't leave the cell, Sheriff. I tried everything."

"All right. I'll be there first thing in the morning."

"I don't think it can wait, sir."

"Are they locked up?"

"Yessir."

"Then it can wait."

"But, sir—"

"Listen to me, Parker. This is your screw-up. I've had a bad night, and I need a couple hours of sleep before I come down there and beat the crap out of you."

In the middle of Parker's apology, Dade hung up and yanked the phone cord from the wall.

CHAPTER 59

Annie parked the rented mustang in front of The Pier, then saw the "Closed" sign on the door. She checked her watch: six-thirty. She got out of the car and peered at the hours printed on the sign. "Weekdays: 7:00 AM to 7:00 PM." Camera in hand, she pressed nose to glass.

Florida stood behind the counter, back to Annie. She was dressed for work in an off-the-shoulders peasant blouse and short black skirt. Her frothy up-do stood perfectly teased and sprayed, as always. Annie, in khaki shorts, a fitted black T-shirt, and running shoes, wondered at the time Florida must spend on maintenance. Annie knocked on the window, and when Florida looked around, tickled the air with one hand. After a moment, Florida stepped from behind the counter, open-toed heels clicking toward her.

Annie knew Florida would be busy at this time, but she needed to speak to her alone. Leigh had come home the night before looking like death. King helped Annie get her settled, then said something about a bad spirit being broken. After Annie assured King that Leigh would be all right, he left. Leigh slept restlessly. What the hell had happened in that Back Room?

"Honey, we're not open yet," Florida said through the window. The front of her peasant blouse was cut low and gathered with a pull string tied in a loose bow. There were no tan lines on her shoulders, or bra straps, and Annie pondered the miracle of modern science that kept those breasts aloft and secure.

"I was hoping to take your picture before you open. Is that all right?" Annie held up the camera.

It was a cheap hook, but Annie knew gaining access to the diner before it opened would take an appeal to the proprietor's vanity. Sure enough, Florida's face brightened. "Oh!" The door opened. "You want to take my picture?" Florida asked, hand fanned across her chest.

Annie nodded. "It's for this book I'm doing on Mom and Pop establishments." This was true enough, and Annie would use the picture if she liked it.

Florida patted her upswept do. "I wish I coulda known this earlier. I'd have dressed for it."

"You always look great, Florida. What do you say?"

"I say, sure." Florida moved aside to let Annie pass. "How 'bout a cup of coffee? I got a fresh pot just brewed."

"Sounds wonderful. Thanks."

"How's Leigh?"

Annie sat on a counter stool as Florida locked the door, then click-clacked back behind the counter. "Oh, thanks for asking, Florida, but not so good. I was hoping we could talk about what happened last night."

Florida stiffened. "So you're not really here to take my picture?"

"No, no, of course I am. Really." Annie held up the camera again. "All cranked up and ready to go."

Florida smiled big. "Oh, okay." She waved a hand. "Not that it matters. What about last night?" She set two coffee mugs on the counter.

"Leigh said it got rough." Annie said.

"Boy howdy." Florida gave Annie a comic, knowing look.

"What happened?"

"Welllll, Clyde and King got into it, and I had to set 'em straight."

"Leigh told me you pulled an Annie Oakley."

"Yep. Fatally wounded the ceiling with my pistol. Know any good, cheap, fast roofers?"

Annie smiled, shook her head. "My father used to say, 'There's good, there's cheap, and there's fast. Pick two.' "

Florida's eyes drifted downward. "Funny, I don't remember Ed saying that." She pulled the squat glass pot from the burner, poured. "You drink it black if I recollect," she said, then yawned. "Oh, dearie me. I'm really catching flies this morning."

"You must have been up pretty late yourself. Don't you have someone to open for you?"

"I did," Florida said, a scowl wrinkling her brow as she set a mug before Annie. "Before she disappeared."

"Sada?" Annie asked.

"I don't like to be ugly, but that girl is worthless. I only hired her as a favor to King. Leroy will be here in a minute, though, to open the kitchen. He's late, as usual." Florida sipped coffee, eyes fluttering from the rising steam. "So where do you want me?"

Annie held her palm over her mug as she had seen Pete do at the drug store counter, felt the steam warm her skin. "I'm thinking behind the cash register."

"Oh, honey, I don't want to be behind anything." Florida hiked her skirt and struck a bathing-beauty pose, one hand on her hip, the other behind her head. "If you got it, flaunt it, right?"

"Nice," said Annie. "Hold that while I finish my coffee, okay?" In her element, Florida giggled. Annie snapped a picture and advanced the film. "Leigh was pretty whacked out when King brought her home last night."

Florida clicked her tongue. "Poor thing."

"King said Clyde called her names, then picked a fight with him."

"That about sums it up."

"What was Clyde's problem?"

"Oh honey, his tiny little brain is probably roasted from all those fires. They still haven't caught the arsonist, you know. That's gotta be messing with him."

"Yeah," Annie said and sipped her coffee. "Maybe that's it." She looked around. "Let me get a few candids of you opening the diner. Pretend I'm not here."

Florida wiped the counter with a red and white checked towel, mincing like Betty Boop: chest forward, knees bent, free hand aloft, her idea of pretending Annie wasn't there. "So when are you and Leigh leaving?" she asked.

Annie smiled. "You're the third person in so many days to ask me that. I'm going to start taking it personally."

"Oh, no, honey, don't do that. I was just askin'." Florida stacked racks of glasses next to plates. "You must be relieved that Shiftlet woman is going off to Lowell."

Annie rotated her stool, following the strange change of subject. She raised the camera and shot. "Well, no, to tell you the truth. I think the wrong person went to jail."

Florida's eyes went wide. "Really? Who do you think did it?"

"I don't know. Maybe that drug dealer, Miguel Vedra. They have evidence tying him to the scene."

"No kidding?"

"Yeah, but Pete told Della it wasn't enough, so she took the deal rather than risk a trial."

Florida drifted to the far end of the counter. "Well, I think they got the right person, and so do most folks around here. We all feel just terrible about Ed." She pronounced it "turble." "Well. Here's to your old man." Florida lifted her mug; Annie shot the picture, then clicked her mug against Florida's.

"What a pistol he was," Florida added, pensive. She twirled a foot, head tilted, smiling at something private.

"You knew him pretty well, huh?"

"You could say that." Florida chuckled deep in her throat.

A bell went off in Annie's head. "How well?"

"Oh, let's just say we shared a pillow or two."

"Are you saying you and my father were . . . um . . ."

"Lovers?" Florida set down her mug and leaned into Annie. "Yes, we were, honey, but—" She lowered her voice dramatically. "—don't tell Della." She pushed back and laughed, exposing black lines around her teeth.

Annie felt as if Florida had just dropped a burning ember down her back. So Della had been right about Ed having an affair.

"My God, Florida, why didn't you come forward?"

"What for?"

"You could have backed Della's story. They would have looked at everything closer."

"And come to the same conclusion. Besides, she wouldn't have done the same for me."

Dumbfounded, Annie watched as Florida folded and tied the checked towel around her neck like a bandana. "How 'bout takin' one like this?" She put hands on knees and bent forward, all cleavage.

"I think it's been done."

Smiling, Florida pulled the towel from her neck, rolled it like a pastry pinwheel.

"Did anyone else know about you and my father?"

"Not anymore." Florida winked. "Now it's just you and the fly on the wall."

"How'd you manage that?"

"Years of practice, honey. Unlike some people around here, I know how to keep my mouth shut. I hear you're selling the lake house to King."

Speaking of shut mouths, Annie thought. "Wow. News travels fast."

"I overheard Leigh tellin' Clyde. I imagine you'll get a pretty penny, huh?" Florida's eyebrows moved up and down. When Annie didn't respond, Florida sucked her teeth and smiled uneasily. "The incredible thing is how much your father loved you girls, even though you never called, never wrote, never spoke, unless it was to demand money, of course. Even then, he never stopped loving you."

This was a mistake, Annie thought, the conversation heading in a bad direction. Time to disengage, think about what to do next.

"Thanks for the coffee, Florida. What do I owe you?"

"You don't want to take more pictures?"

"I finished out the roll. I can come back when you're not so busy."

"Stay and finish your coffee. On the house."

"I really have to be getting back."

"Oh, sit and talk to me, Annie Bartlett. It's about time we got to know each other. Better late than never."

The words were friendly, but Florida's tone crept like a tarantula up Annie's arms. Florida's eyes flicked to the front door, and Annie recalled it was locked. Sweeping a crumb from the counter, Annie made the decision to stay cool and wait this out, weird as it was, whatever it was. Leroy, the cook, would arrive soon, and she could make her exit then. In the meantime, maybe she could learn more.

"So, how long were you and my father . . . together?"

Florida looked at Annie as if taking her in for the first time. "A while," she said finally. "And it wasn't all roses and sunshine, believe me. Imagine what it was like competing with a dead woman, a live-in girlfriend, and two selfish daughters who came

341

first in his life even though they weren't even there." Florida's eyes flashed.

Annie pushed her coffee. "Florida, what's this about?"

"About? Well, it's about you and Leigh, Annie. It was always about you and Leigh. You have no idea how many times I wanted to call you girls up and give you a piece of my mind. But Ed wouldn't let me. He said you'd come around sooner or later. I guess it was later, huh?"

Just go with it, thought Annie. "Yeah, I guess I sold him short all those years. I see now he was a good man."

Florida, hands on hips, jutted her head forward. "A good man?!" From her throat, one huge "Ha!" shot the ceiling. She looked at Annie, eyes lit with sarcasm and rage. The smile, so out of place, hung pasted on her face. "He was a lying sack of steaming whaleshit, is what he was!"

Slowly, Annie moved her legs around the stool.

"He says he's going to leave Della and marry me, but what does he do? Arranges to sell the house to that weasel, Pete Duncan, for pennies on the dollar, and why? Because that skank sister of yours gets herself mixed up with a Puerto Rican drug freak and can't get clean without taking all daddy's money. That's why!"

"Leigh is sick," Annie said.

"Don't feed me that bleeding heart crap. She's an addict, and no matter what you pour to sweeten it up, an addict is an addict, and always will be. I thought after Ed died Leigh'd stop coming around here with her hand out, but here you two show up, DeLeon's prodigal daughters, and get everyone upset with your prying and your sleeping around. And then!" Florida threw up her arms. "And then, you grab the lake house to boot! Well, you're gonna have to take a number, cupcake, because that house is mine. Ed promised it to me!" She jabbed her chest with a red fingernail. "And if anyone sells it to King, it will be me."

Annie pointed to the front door. "All right, Florida, I don't know what's going on here, but I want you to unlock that door and let me out of here right now."

As Florida came around the counter, Annie tracked with her knees, prepared to move fast.

"Why Annie, you sound like I'm keeping you prisoner here. You're the one who came to see me, remember? You wanted to take my picture, remember?"

Annie scanned for another exit. Leigh had escaped from Miguel Vedra last week by a door near the restrooms. Was that locked, too? Annie's eyes flicked to the phone, then locked onto what hung on the wall above it. Her heart dropped. For a horrible moment, she thought she might vomit. Annie forced her eyes to meet Florida's. She knew now she had stepped on an explosive, and if she moved her foot even an inch, she would be blown to pieces. Attached to the wall was a bit of nautical décor—an oar.

The missing oar.

Annie drew her feet together, slipped one heel off the stool's rung. "Can I ask you a question, Florida?"

"It's a free country."

"Did you kill my father with that oar?" Annie pointed, and Florida followed with her eyes. Annie drew back her knees, then kicked with everything she had. Hairpins flew like lights from a sparkler as Florida hit the floor. Annie ran for the back door, and opened it—a broom closet. Scrambling for another door, she pulled. Locked!

"You didn't give me a chance to answer your question," Florida said from behind, and Annie spun. A side of Florida's architectural hairdo had collapsed; it now covered one ear. She stood in stocking feet, aiming a small .38 at Annie's heart.

"Florida, think. Leroy will be here in a minute."

"I just gave him the day off."

"If you shoot me, they'll hear it outside."

"But you'll still be dead, won't you?" she said, advancing. "If you'da minded your own damn business, none of this would have to happen." Florida motioned with the gun. "Move over there."

Annie obeyed, searching the kitchen for a skillet or knife as she walked.

"Open that door."

Annie stared at a large white door with a chrome latch pull. She placed her hand on the latch, not unlike the handle of the old Westinghouse refrigerator Ed had once dragged home from the side of a road. The memory, a rare happy one, stabbed Annie's heart.

"Why did you kill my father, Florida?"

"Honey, you gotta believe me. I didn't mean to. He just made me so mad! He was going to sell the house to Pete Duncan for next to nothing! Everyone knew King wanted that land. Ed and me could have made a fortune."

"Ed and you—?"

"He was going to marry me, kid, like it or not. But when he told me he planned to sell to Pete Duncan and give the money to Leigh, I—" Florida took a breath. "Let's just say I wasn't very happy about that idea."

"You didn't have to kill him."

"I wasn't trying to. I felt real bad, but after it happened, all I could think of was getting out of there."

"But not before you switched oars."

"Well, I couldn't leave the one I smacked him with, could I?" Florida asked, as if Annie were dumb.

"So you display it like a trophy, like you're proud of what you did?"

"I didn't hang it there until after Jeb—" Florida stopped abruptly. "Enough. Turn around before you make me mad."

Annie screamed as loud as she could, and Florida whipped the pistol around, smashed it into Annie's temple. She slid to the floor, head knifing with pain.

"You do that again, and I'll beat you to death," Florida said. "Now get up and open the door."

Annie pressed a palm to her temple and felt blood. "Florida, you can have the house. We can write something up, right now. I'll sign it, anything you want."

"Do I look stupid to you?"

"I left a note for Leigh. She knows where I am."

"Open it!"

Annie opened the door, then, sensing another advance, turned to take the flat of Florida's gun across the bridge of her nose. Blind with pain, she lashed out, flailing, until another blow smashed her jaw. She fell back and crashed against a steel shelf of boxed, frozen cheesecakes, which, hard as bricks, pummeled her head and shoulders. Nearly unconscious, exhaling small puffs of freezing air, Annie turned to see the last sliver of natural light slammed into darkness.

CHAPTER 60

The phone rang. Leigh sat up, instantly alert. The bedroom, still in shadow, exuded energy. Leigh held her breath. Her eyes tracked the room, lingered on a chair, then the door. Chain secure. The phone rang again; this caller could kiss her ass. After another ring, it stopped.

Relieved, Leigh lay down and pressed heels of hands to forehead. Groping for water, she knocked the glass over, and, rising suddenly, felt knifed in the brain by a hangover. She dropped back onto the pillow. It was just water, not like the time she'd knocked over a lighted candle or kicked over the well-used cat litter box. The worst, however, was the time she'd warmed soup on a gas stove and, suddenly dizzy, grabbed either side of the stove to steady herself. Her hair swung into the gas flame and caught. She managed to douse herself, but not before suffering burns. The haircut afterward, self-administered, made her look worse. Thinking of that, Leigh almost looked forward to rehab. It was definitely time to rediscover the joys of a puke-free lifestyle. Sensing a presence, she rose on an elbow. "Annie?"

No response.

Leigh closed her eyes. Why this churning feeling of dread? Images from the night before shuffled by, bits of conversation, a new car smell. Had she eaten anything? She pawed the floor for cigarettes; time to cut back on the cancer sticks, too, she thought, lighting one. Leigh had gone nuts scrounging for cigarettes last night; she remembered that. Okay, now it was coming back: she and King drew up a contract and—

Annie had signed it.

Leigh threw the covers, a perfect curling wave, high and away from her body. The sudden movement sparked lighting bolts behind her eyes and a searing pain, but she fought through them. In her panties, Leigh rummaged the room for the contract. Finding only a note (Good morning! I'll be back soon to make you breakfast. Love—A.), she mentally retraced. Okay, she had it in her hand when she and King went to the Back Room because she wanted to show it to—

Leigh sat on the bed. Of course. That's why she felt worse than usual. Clyde had publicly nuked her, and she was an idiot not to have seen it coming. Leigh picked clothes from the floor, threw them on the bed. Angry and sad, she tugged on jeans. Clyde was just like the rest. As soon as you fall for them, they turn on you. She picked up a T-shirt, smelled it, pulled it gingerly over her head. After more searching, she found the contract beneath a spindly chair. She smoothed it on her upper thigh, checked the signatures, then put it in her shoulder bag.

In the bathroom, Leigh held a fistful of hair and raked the ends with a plastic brush. She brushed her teeth with a toothbrush she found in the medicine cabinet and dribbled an ice blue blob of toothpaste on her shirt. She recalled her mother telling how to remove such a spot, which she claimed to have learned from a Tennessee Williams play. The trick is never rub. Moisten a hanky and dab, dab, dab. But the toothpaste blob would get no such treatment. Leigh smeared it into a vague cloud on the T-shirt, then rinsed her mouth.

Before the mirror, Leigh unfastened one end of the gauze wrapped around her face and head. As it fell away, growing increasingly discolored, Leigh wondered if her mother had even owned a hanky. Such old-fashioned gentility appealed to Leigh, but her mother was a nurse, germ-conscious and practical, and probably carried packaged tissues in that patent leather purse with the golden clasp. Leigh dropped the dirty gauze in the wastebasket then, leaning on the sink, looked at herself.

God, Mig, why didn't you just kill me?

Her skin, a multihued accident of art, appeared more fascinating than horrible. She thought of a Picasso portrait with its broken and reassembled planes and drew a finger along tiny black stitches running down her cheek, across her chin, over her lips. As the healing progressed the colors had grown garish, removed from the palette of fresh damage, but just as alarming. At other times in her life, Leigh imagined looking like this: the night she passed out on a date, then woke to a man on top of her; the first time she bought pills on the street; the day she left Annie to fend for herself in this house. She touched the swollen flesh beneath her bad eye, admiring Dr. Neeman's fine needlework. He had said her wounds "looked good," which made Leigh laugh. To whom? Quasimodo?

After swabbing with cotton balls, Leigh left the bathroom for a fresh bandage, and again, sensed she was not alone. She stood still, straining to hear, but with no breeze, even the leaves were lifeless. Could paranoia be a new wrinkle to contend with? Leigh unlocked the sliding door and drew it aside. Through the screen she saw the lake, the dark surface dimpled with bream kissing from below. Leigh wasn't often up at this early hour, and its preheated serenity surprised her. The air smelled of freshly turned earth and—something else. She closed her eyes, concentrating. When she opened them, she froze. The thing, crouched in the azaleas and now coming toward her, wore a grotesque Richard Nixon mask—the nose phallic and obscenely pink. She recognized it at once.

Scrambling for the phone, Leigh knocked over a chair. The thing threw aside the screen door.

"Get out of my house!"

From the phone on the kitchen wall, Leigh grabbed the receiver and swung. The figure lunged, grabbed her wrists, yanked. In her peripheral vision, Leigh saw an orange ghost whoosh. One second later, she smelled smoke.

Something broke inside Leigh's head. "You fucker!" she screamed, and pulling free, was on her attacker in an instant, kicking, clawing the mask, hitting with the phone. "You torched my house, you sick fuck!"

The figure wrenched the receiver from Leigh's hand and smacked her on the head. Leigh covered her head with her arms, kicked karate-style in bare feet. "Get out!" she yelled again, but she was crying now and sounded scared even to herself. The intruder knocked her into the wall, then turned aside to dismantle the phone. Surprised to be still on her feet, Leigh looked for the first time at the slender form beneath the flannel shirt, the small hands. This certainly wasn't Clyde, although she had no doubt she had found this same mask in his dresser. Whoever he was, he was not very big, and Leigh grew bold. She grabbed the fallen chair, and, with a surge of adrenaline, swung it high over her head and down. The figure groaned, then collapsed. Behind one hole, Leigh saw a dark brown eye wide with fear, and, all at once, she knew.

"Goddamn you, Sada. What have you done?"

"You can't have him!"

"I can't have who?"

"Clyde! And when he comes, he'll rescue me and I'll tell him you set the fire, and he won't love you. He'll love me!"

"Oh my God. You're a lunatic."

Breathing heavily, Leigh ran outside. Flames licked the side of the house. At the spigot, no hose. "Help me!" Leigh screamed. She ran back inside; Sada was gone. The Nixon mask lay on the floor. Leigh picked up the phone and reconnected it, almost cried when she heard a tone. As the kitchen filled with smoke she dialed 911, dancing with fear. Suddenly, she remembered the contract in her bag, and let the phone drop. At the end of the hall, the bedroom door stood closed. Leigh grabbed the doorknob, yelped, and yanked back a burned hand. Bending, she wrapped the tail of her T-shirt around the knob, turned, and opened onto an inferno.

CHAPTER 61

Dawn broke, and Sheriff Newcomb pulled into his reserved spot. The sky was dirty pink. "Red sky at morning," he mumbled to himself and pushed his door open with more force than it required. Inside the jail, Larry Parker waited, shoulders stooped.

"I'm sorry, Sheriff—"

"I'll settle with you later, Parker. Where is she?"

Mother and son sat on the cot, knees together and hands folded. They looked like schoolchildren awaiting lessons. Dade dropped his gaze from the small window in the door, keyed in. "You stay out here," he said to Parker. "Think you can do that without screwing it up?"

"Yessir."

The sheriff opened the door. "Get out, Marguerite."

"Hello, Dade. About time you got here."

"Get out. Now."

Eugene lunged for Dade's middle. "Dahll," he said, plunging hands into his father's pockets. Dade felt terrible as he pried Eugene's arms from around him.

"Call him off, Marguerite."

Marguerite's face darkened. "He's not a dog."

"I didn't mean that." Dade said. "I only need you to—" Dade huffed, bent to Eugene's level, holding the boy's hands beneath his chin. "Go sit back down, Eugene."

"Dahll."

"I don't have a dollar. Go sit next to your mother."

351

"I'm not leaving without Eugene, Dade," Marguerite said, her voice deep and absolute.

"Look, Marguerite, I'm not fooling around, either you leave, right now, or you're under arrest."

"Oh, for pity's sake, Dade. You can't arrest me."

Furious, the sheriff released Eugene, grabbed Marguerite's arm, and pulled. "Right now. Let's go."

Marguerite came off the cot and wrenched her arm free. "Don't you dare put hands on me!"

"Guard!"

Eugene jumped at the sheriff's sudden command, and Larry Parker came through the doorway with full military intent. He stood legs apart, eyes on the sheriff. In the unfriendly shift of climate, Eugene began to whimper.

"Drag her out of here."

As Officer Parker put on hands, Marguerite let go a scream which ricocheted off the walls of the small cell. Eugene covered his ears and wailed. The noise woke the few prisoners in cells alongside. They shouted curses, adding to the pandemonium. Eugene's chest rose and fell like a bellows, eyes rolling.

"All right, all right," Dade said, urging Parker aside. "Go calm those guys down. We're finished in here. Marguerite, you're only making this worse for Eugene."

"I can see that," said the judge. "I want you to take us out of here. Right now."

The demand, beyond impossible, stirred the sheriff's brain soil, and for the first time, he wondered about Marguerite's sanity.

"Did you hear me?"

"I can't do that, Marguerite. You know that."

The judge stepped forward. "You have to, Dade. We won't get two steps without you."

"That's kind of the whole idea."

"Listen to me. I just want to take him fishing."

Surely she must know how crazy she sounded. Air rushed in and out of the sheriff's nose as adrenaline spiked his blood pressure. He searched for an explanation that would right this very wrong moment and slow his pulse. She was upset, of course. Any mother would be if her son were in jail on suspicion of murder. But Marguerite was not any mother; she was a judge, the mother of a boy they made together, and notoriously intent on getting her way.

"Marguerite, you don't know what you're asking."

"Don't patronize me, Dade. Please take my arm in one hand and Eugene's arm in the other, and take us out of here."

"And then what? Huh? You worry me, Marguerite."

"My car is in the parking lot. I'm going to drive to the lake with Eugene and fish for awhile. Then I'll bring him back."

The absurdity finally got to him. Sheriff Newcomb coughed a laugh and, before he could regain control, was spazzing in the throes of a full-on laugh fit. Marguerite watched without amusement, eyes flat, mouth a thin gash above a raised, defiant chin. The sheriff couldn't help himself; his shoulders jumped as if pulled by strings. Shaking his head at his shoes, he let out a plaintive wail: "Oh, my dear, sweet Jesus."

Smiling, Eugene imitated, his voice a mocking warble: "Oooooh, dahhh."

Marguerite said, "Are you quite finished?"

The sheriff huffed a few more times, wiped his mouth on the back of his hand. "Oh, mercy me."

"Are we ready, then?"

He looked at Marguerite's strong jaw, the angled bone leading to her ear. He looked at her smooth neck with none of the extra fat carried by most women her age. The tanned skin on her chest, freckled and age spotted, vanished inside her denim shirt. He knew exactly what that shirt smelled like. Justinia, the housekeeper, favored a powdered soap that came in a box and filled Marguerite's closet with the vague scent of lemons. With shirttail hanging and khaki pants rolled to ankles, the judge looked every inch a Florida retiree on her way to a fishing hole. Newcomb's radio cackled and brought him back to a world he understood. Another fire.

The judge and sheriff looked at each other as the radio spat static. The sheriff ten-foured his way to closure. "I have to go."

Marguerite reached for Eugene's hand. He gave it and stepped in closer to his mother. "Take your father's arm," she said. Eugene obeyed. "We're coming with you," she said and offered her elbow. The sheriff could only shake his head. "Now," she said, "while the getting's good. And for God's sake, Dade, don't look like a dead man walking. I told you, I'll bring him back." She hooked into him and prodded forward. "Tick-tock, Dade. You're on your way to a fire."

CHAPTER 62

Six cars waited to turn left at the intersection of New York Avenue and the truck route. Florida, number six, honked in frustration, which only served to draw unwanted attention to the purple Pinto headed west. She had forgotten about morning rush hour. Gripping the steering wheel, Florida tried to calm herself, but thinking of Annie put her panties in a twist. How stupid, falling for her flattery like an insecure schoolgirl—*you always look great, Florida, what do you say?* She should have known the real reason the brat showed up, should have been prepared.

After fixing her hair and finding her heels, Florida had managed to placate the few patrons at her front door, Pete Duncan among them, with signature charm. "Sorry folks, but I can't open without a cook. Come back tomorrow, and I'll give you a little extra somethin' special for your trouble." She noticed a question forming on Pete Duncan's face, closed the door fast. Blood sucking leeches, she thought, ignoring taps at the window. The phone rang; Florida pinched the cord from the base. If lucky, she had just bought herself a day and had to act fast.

Florida grabbed her pistol, Annie's camera, the zippered bank bag of cash and receipts, and stuffed all into her pink briefcase. In Orlando, she'd get on the next plane to the Bahamas, then call Emilio, the Cuban punching machine, tell him she couldn't live without him and to pick her up in his sailboat and take her to Cuba, where cooperative extradition policies did not extend

355

to the US of A. After that—well, she'd think about that later.

She dragged a chair beneath the clock and lifted the oar from hooks holding it to the wall. On the way to the airport, Florida would have to get rid of it. Keeping this thing had been a mistake, but the oar reminded her she wasn't an evil person. Sure, she had been mad as hell at Ed, but she hadn't planned to bash his skull in. It was an accident. Even after the fifth or sixth blow, she fully expected him to get up, just as he always had, and shake it off. When she realized he couldn't get up, her overdeveloped sense of survival kicked in. If she bloodied the other oar and left it behind, Florida reasoned, police would think they had the murder weapon, and no one would look for the real one. This oar reminded her of Ed, the man she had loved, except when he was being unreasonable.

Switching oars had been easy: Florida dragged her hands through the sand until they were thickly coated, then shoveled the oar's round end into Ed's wound. She could hear Della calling Ed from the house and had to move fast. After letting the oar drop, Florida kicked off her sandals and tossed them in the grass, grabbed the real murder weapon, and, by starlight, smoothed her tracks. With oar in hand, she jumped from palm frond to driftwood, picked up her shoes and tip-toed to her Pinto, parked behind a curtain of kudzu at the edge of the woods. Florida did not see Della pick up the oar, but by morning the whole town was abuzz: Della Shiftlet had murdered Ed Bartlett. Later, deep in her cups, Florida took the murder weapon from the floor of the Pinto and brought it inside for a bleach bath and polish. She barely noticed the initials carved there, AB + PD, little more than scratches, much like the other blemishes that reminded her of dear, infuriating Ed, who had been about to squander their future on his deadbeat daughter.

With elbows locked, Florida gave three long blasts of the horn, then attempted to rip the steering wheel from its column.

Behind her, a man in a cowboy hat inched up his car and tapped her rear bumper. Florida glared in the mirror. People seemed to like reminding her she drove a death trap. Normally, she would get out of the car and pretend to be a lawyer. Today, Florida shot him a bird, then refocused on her plight.

How many times had she and Ed argued about that house: how much it was worth, who would buy it, how the money would be spent? That he would sell it for the cost of Leigh's drug treatment gave her conniptions. When Ed told Florida how much the twenty-eight-day program cost, she almost dropped her teeth. It was ridiculous, especially for Leigh, who had never committed to anything in her life. A leopard doesn't change its spots, she told Ed. Why do you think this time will be different? Florida presented him with another way to finance Leigh's rehab. She convinced Ed to follow Eugene, take pictures of him setting fires, then sell the photos to the judge. He wouldn't get the full amount he needed, but he'd get something, and Leigh would just have to take it or leave it. But Ed had botched that as well.

What do you mean she wouldn't give you any money?

Florida had been so mad at Ed and Judge Lanier, she stuffed the photos into a brown envelope, wrote Ed's name and address in the upper left corner, and mailed the package to Jeb Barlow. If the judge wouldn't pay with money, she'd pay with her son. And then, finally, Eugene would stop coming into her diner. That was worth a pretty penny right there. The creep deserved to be exposed, and on the front page.

The traffic light, Florida realized, did not signal left turns. She'd been inching forward, cycle after cycle, while oncoming traffic zoomed past. With two cars still in front, she found herself muttering again: Come on, come on, comeon, comeon-COMEON! Every minute meant another mile she could be putting between herself and this puke hole of a town.

A wave of regret washed through her. She wished she could take back that night. Without Ed, she had no lover, no man, no claim on the lake house, and without the lake house, she was doomed to live out the rest of her days with broken fingernails and hair that smelled like grease.

The argument with Ed had started at the Comfy Inn in Daytona. While disrobing, Florida tried to make Ed see he was shortchanging himself by selling to Pete. "After you get through paying off that drug place, not only are you broke, but you're homeless as well! At least if you sell to King you'll have money left over, and you and I can start out together someplace nice."

Ed complained he was being pecked apart like roadkill. He'd had this argument so many times, he was ready to sell the house and keep the money himself, hop in his truck and drive until he'd fled the carrion birds circling overhead. But Florida kept pecking: "I thought you loved me, I thought you wanted a life with me, how can we have a life when you're always rescuing an ungrateful daughter who will relapse the day after spending all your money?" Ed slammed from the hotel, arms waving as if bees bombarded his head. "Where are you going? You come back here right now, Ed Bartlett!" But Ed kept going, and as Florida dressed she stewed herself into a vengeful frenzy. "You wait, Ed Barlett. You will pay for this!"

Revenge compelled Florida to Ed's rowboat. Day was breaking as she made her way with a crowbar to the sandy beach. She found the boat turned over on the sand. What damage she could do would be enough to ruin his next fishing trip.

As she approached the boat, Florida sensed a presence in the thicker darkness beneath it. She picked up an oar, ready for a possum or raccoon to scuttle out. After a moment, she chanced a look and found Ed himself curled up beneath the boat, eyes closed and arms wrapped around his chest. Florida prodded him with the oar, and he came to with a start. He didn't look happy to see her.

"That doesn't look very comfortable," Florida said.

"No, but it's quiet. At least, it was."

"What do you mean by running out on me like that?"

Ed groaned and rubbed the back of his neck. "Christ, don't you ever stop? What do you want from me?"

"I want you to sell the house to King and tell Leigh to go suck a dead tree."

Ed shook his head. "I've had enough, Florida. Don't."

"Or what?"

There was a moment, then the rowboat suddenly rolled off Ed as if made of thatch. Ed leaped to his feet, and even in starlight, looked enraged. Florida stepped back.

"I just spent the last thirty minutes swearing up and down to Della that I'm not cheatin' on her, and if you don't leave here right now, that will no longer be a lie."

"What's that supposed to mean?"

"It means leave, Florida, now, or we're finished."

He was bluffing, but the threat infuriated her nonetheless. A flash of heat sparked adrenaline; a flame flickered. "You're a coward."

Ed's eyes lit up. "I'm a lot of things, Florida: a liar, a cheat, a drunk, bad father, bad husband, bad excuse for a human being, but I am not a coward. A coward would run from a woman trying to turn him against his own blood. It takes a particular kind of bravery to love you in spite of your meanness and greed, but I did it because, unlike most men who hooked themselves to your garters, I saw more than a bottled blonde with her own bank account. I saw a successful, independent businesswoman—full of piss and vinegar—who made me laugh. You made me remember what it was like to wake up and look forward to the day. But I don't feel any love coming back, Florida. You talk about our future, but you're doing everything you can to wipe out my past. You want me to sell my house to a man who will tear it down. You want me to turn my back on one daughter and ignore the other. Here I got a good woman up at the house who knows I'm cheatin' on her. Ever' night this week, I've listened to her cry herself to sleep, just so I can sneak a little slap and tickle after you're done serving overpriced, watered-down hooch to good people who deserve better. It's fucked up, Florida. I gotta ask myself what the hell I'm doin'. I can't turn my life upside-down for a woman who only wants what she wants. I'm too old for that shit. From now on, I don't want to hear another word about my house, my family, or what a coward I am. I'm done talkin' about it." Ed turned toward the house.

"Where do you think you're going?"

"Inside. I owe Della an apology."

"For what?"

"For you, goddammit! I know it don't make up for my cheatin', but I got a chance here to do something good for somebody else and start over. And if Della can find it in her heart to forgive me, I'm gonna ask her to start over with me."

"You can't be serious."

"Go home, Florida."

"We're not through!"

"You haven't been listening. We're through." Ed circled the bow and put out a hand. "Let me have that oar."

How could he stand there looking as if he'd just asked her to dance? Florida clutched the oar and, with a defiant stance, dared him to come get it. Ed dropped his hand.

"Don't give it to me, then. Don't matter. And neither do you."

When he turned his back on her, Florida gave it to him. Over and over, again and again.

Finally, Florida's turn came at the light. As soon as the light turned green, she mashed the accelerator. The Pinto jerked ahead of the white, right-of-way car opposite. Florida steered left as the white car screeched to a halt. As she cleared the intersection, Florida heard the crunch of metal on metal. The rush she felt at having got away with this, too, reminded her of flatulent Jeb Barlow's unfortunate exit from this world. She floored it and sped away from yet another sad circumstance.

At an early age, Florida had learned to work a crush, and Jeb had a big one. She was careful to encourage Jeb's infatuation without inflaming it; she let him look, but not stare; smell, but not taste. As long as she kept possibility alive for Jeb, he would feed her critical information about the Bartlett investigation. The night she allowed him to drink in the Back Room for the first time, he had scared her with his talk of knowing more than he reported, of saving the juicy parts for a book. She could not let Jeb Barlow write a book, even one purportedly about the arsonist. What if he stumbled over an incriminating bit about Ed's murder? Look what he had done with the pictures of Eugene: instead of taking them straight to his editor, he showed them to Annie, then tried to hide them under the table. But Florida had seen, and from that moment, she knew Jeb Barlow could not be trusted. She'd underestimated Annie, but that mistake was cooling its heels in the walk-in refrigerator. Jeb went fairly fast. Recalling the look on his face when he realized who stood over him with a lit match, Florida dabbed a trickling tear. She missed ol' Jebby Webby, almost as much as she missed Ed. Why did the men in her life always have to disappear?

When Jeb finished his last drink, Florida helped him to the door. "I gotta take a piss," he said.

"Then do it over there," said Florida, and pointed him toward the alley. "And not against my building, neither."

Preparation took seconds. Florida tied a chiffon scarf beneath her chin and grabbed the oar, stashed beneath a floorboard in the pantry. Execution took longer. Jeb wouldn't stay down; it seemed he might escape with a mere concussion, and that wouldn't do. Florida fetched a tin of kerosene Leroy kept in the kitchen for his camp stove. Jeb's eyes bore holes as she sloshed. When the match dropped, he was still staring, dead inside.

Now, she was nearly in the clear. Ed's brats would soon leave town, Della would rot in prison, and in time, all would be forgotten. Of course she had lost all claim on the lake house, but you can't have everything. She'd have to settle for starting over in Cuba. She'd have to learn the language; and if Emilio got rough with her, she'd get rough back. There was just one obstacle:

Let me take your picture, Florida, pretty please?

Florida beat the steering wheel with the heel of her hand. Stupid, stupid, stupid! Eventually, someone would find Annie in the walk-in with icicles dripping from her nose, and even Dade Newcomb would figure that one out. She hadn't meant to hit her so hard, but Annie made her so MAD! Oh, well. At least Florida had bought herself time to blow this popsicle stand. That is, if she could get OUT OF HERE! Merging, Florida moved into traffic on I-4, which shone ahead in the morning sun.

Chapter 63

Trembling in blackness, Annie fingered tiny flakes of ice rimming her bloody nose. The compressor blew cold, stale air as pain threatened her sanity. Her jaw throbbed where Florida's pistol had whipped.

Annie slowly moved her knees beneath her. Dizzy, she grasped what felt like a metal shelf leg to steady herself, and, sweaty with shock, her hand stuck. Blind, bleeding and freezing, she felt the first throes of panic rise like bats in a tower. She cried out for Camp, darkness absorbing her cries in its sticky coat. When she calmed, a huge headache clamped her temples. She would not mind drifting to sleep in here were it not so utterly, hopelessly dark. Annie settled on her rump. She was so cold. Where was her mother when she needed her?

Eyes straining to distinguish any lurking shadow, it occurred to Annie she could freeze to death if she stayed like this. Desperate, she concentrated on the hand stuck to the shelf leg.

One-thousand one, one-thousand two, one-thousand three . . . pull!

Skin came away with a sick rip. Annie rocked, holding the raw hand against her body, keening with anger and pain. Blood trickled from her nose. Shaking violently, she forced herself up, and with fists, explored the stocked interior of the freezer until she found the door.

Has to be a switch here, somewhere.

She found it, and giddy with the small victory, toggled the

switch. Fluorescent tubes fluttered, caught.

The freezer was slightly longer than wide, the size of Camp's walk-in closet, with shelves stocked with vacuum-sealed packages covered in frost running the length of the longer wall. She grabbed the tail of her shirt and with it worked the door handle, knowing it would be locked from the outside. Teeth chattering, she turned her attention to the box on the ceiling as it expelled clouds of air. A line ran from the fan and disappeared behind stacks of boxes and shelving. Using her shirt, she grabbed a leg segment from an unassembled shelf unit, a length of gray steel bent into an L, and wedged it under the line. Grunting with effort, she pried it from the wall, worked the line up and down until it snapped. Freon gas escaped in a dramatic hiss. Annie held back tears of joy, knowing they would simply freeze. Now, at least, it would not get colder.

Annie pressed close to the door. Although it hurt like hell, she screamed until her vocal chords were stripped. Then truth hit: No one was coming to rescue her. She kicked the door, a waste of precious energy, then, breathing hard, struggled to stay calm.

She scanned the walls. Between thin layers of metal sheeting was insulation, she guessed. It would make sense that a sandwich wall would join a perpendicular wall in an overlapping joint. Hadn't Annie seen Camp put together something like this? She pictured him holding his hands at chest level, elbows up, curling the fingers of one hand into the fingers of the other, pulling. And where did all these overlapping planes come together?

Annie lowered herself carefully onto her rear end, then skooched within kicking distance of the corner where the floor and two walls met. She pulled back one leg and sent her heel into the corner. The vibration traveled up her leg, turned to pain at her hip, but she ignored it, kicked until she felt something give. After a few more kicks, the corner opened to a pinpoint of daylight. Panting, she wedged the same shelf unit leg into the small hole. Crying out with effort, fear, and pain, she managed only to force one layer of sheet metal an inch to one side. Annie lay back, exhausted.

Her eyes swung to the wall shelves. They sat loose atop metal supports and ran the entire length of the long wall. She stared, trying not to feel the pain in her jaw or the little voice in her head that advised her to make peace with God. She sat up, measured the short distance between walls with her eyes, and allowed herself hope. If she could wedge that long shelf between the walls, climb on top of it somehow, she could maybe force the opening wider. Ideally, she'd create a rent big enough for an escape, but even a small rent would warm the air, prevent her nose from falling off. Her eyes ticked back and forth as she gathered the strength she would need.

CHAPTER 64

On Lake Talmadge, fish weren't biting. The air smelled chemically tainted, as if expelled through PVC. Marguerite pulled the damp shirt from her skin and winged air into her pits. Opposite her in the borrowed boat, Eugene sat slack-jawed and fidgety, his fishing pole rolling from hand to hand. Marguerite reeled in her line and took up oars.

"Let's find a better spot."

Marguerite sensed a large mouth-bass suspended among reeds straight as jailhouse bars, watching with bored disinterest. If she could settle the boat in the alcove and cast into the reeds, she might lure a frisky three or four-pounder from its cell. Eugene, however, threatened to make that prospect difficult.

"Sit down, Eugene. You know better than that."

He pointed. "Feeee."

"Yes, fish, I know. We're going to catch one."

Eugene moved clumsily to the other side of the boat.

"I said, sit down, Eugene. We don't stand in the boat. It might tip."

"Tip!"

"That's right. It might tip."

Eugene sat hard on the seat, and Marguerite realized they would catch no fish today. Well, that was all right. This outing was about freedom, not fish. She regretted she would have to break her promise to Dade about returning Eugene to jail, but there you are.

"If you're still, you might see a mermaid," she said, but Eugene barely glanced her way, as if aware his mother was full of it. She should have coaxed with a dragon instead; dragons enchanted Eugene, perhaps because they breathed fire. But restless as he was, little would rivet Euguene's attention at the moment. Marguerite had always wanted to share her life's joy with her son, but he had never been particularly comfortable in a boat. His disinterest in fishing was her only disappointment in him, except for this murder, of course, but that could hardly be compared. Eugene was not intellectually capable of grasping the complexities of his crime; yet fishing should have been in his blood. Marguerite's father had taught her to fish when she was a young girl, just as his father had taught him. And when she could get him to relax, Dade was known to pull aboard a catfish or two. What aberrant gene conspired to rob her son of this sublime pleasure?

Marguerite leaned forward as the oars winged back and dipped. She pulled, moving the boat through the water; the effort played across her shoulders and back. At Harvard, she had watched men sculling the river, admired their bare arms and backs, the fluid, synchronized motion: knees up, knees down, stroke, pull, faster, faster. She dated the captain of the sculling team, a freckled Democrat with a thick Boston accent, and sat on the bow as he drove them over the lake, riding above the water, until her father made his disapproval known and insisted she break up with the boy. Marguerite did not object strenuously: the captain of the sculling team did not fish. To him, water and sky were elements to be conquered, tranquility usurped by speed. As he rowed his team to the championship, Marguerite let him drift from her shallow pool of suitable beaus. Had she known the pool would dry up, she might have attempted his redemption, but by then the sculling team captain was a Big Man on Campus, and some other petite beauty had replaced her on the bow.

Marguerite blocked the memory. She would think of nothing sad this morning. Her briefcase was full of sad things; her spirit sagged with the weight of this latest catastrophe involving Eugene. Here was where she wanted to be, right here, with her son, gliding atop a lake that reflected them in its black glass.

Eugene stood abruptly, and Marguerite stopped rowing. "Eugene! What did I say about standing in the boat?"

Eugene bounced on the balls of his feet. "Fahhh," he said.

Marguerite scanned the sky. Sure enough, a plume of black smoke rose over the trees in the direction of Widow Lake.

"Sit down, Eugene. Right now."

"Faaaah!"

"Yes, I see the fire. Sit down, or I'll have to take us back, and you won't see it at all."

Eugene sat, body alert and face expectant. Pointing, he whimpered.

"Yes, I see it," Marguerite repeated in a soft, reassuring voice. Eugene twisted his torso to one side, then the other, raking big feet across the bottom of the boat. As another black plume rose, he bounced in his seat; one hand plunged between his legs. "Faaaah!"

Marguerite secured the oars. Using her feet, she pulled her fishing basket and reached inside. The rest of the world lay beyond those trees. Dade would be at that fire, tall with authority, shouting instructions into the radio speaker, sending deputies to block roads. He would have forgotten all about them by now.

Marguerite watched the planes in Eugene's face ripple with ecstasy and felt grateful to the arsonist. Fire took Eugene from a world that held him in contempt, and as his mother, she had been unable to provide such an escape. By keeping him close, she thought she could spare him pain. She was his shield as he toddled to the door, his weapon beyond the perimeters of her protection. How could she have known he would inherit a ferocious sense of justice and punish someone as worthy as Miguel Vedra? Eugene must have seen Vedra attack Leigh Bartlett, she guessed, and Marguerite neither blamed nor accepted. She did believe the groaning wheels of courtroom justice backward in comparison. But compassion for the victim, not her son, would rule the day. Eugene would be locked up, in one form or other, probably for the rest of his life. Perhaps Marguerite had written this ending long ago with a selfishness born of love. Whatever her part in it, the world she had so carefully orchestrated stood on the verge of collapse. Even now, Marguerite could not, would not, allow that to happen.

"Maaaa!" Eugene wailed. A huge erection strained his pants.

"Yes, I know. It's a fire, isn't it?"

"Faaah!"

Such a perfect morning; such a wonderful gift. Eugene stood once again, and this time, Marguerite did not scold. With his back to her, he spread his arms wide and laughed into the hard, smoke-filled sky. She didn't think she had ever seen him this happy. Marguerite quickly drew the pistol from her fishing basket and aimed it at the back of his head. Sure of her target, she closed her eyes and pulled the trigger. Confident the bullet had found its mark, she did not open her eyes again, not even when she pushed the pistol's snout upward into the taut, white flesh beneath her chin and pulled the trigger.

CHAPTER 65

Sheriff Newcomb waved the fire truck onto the lawn, both arms extended and together, one straight and pointing, the other pivoting from the elbow. Firefighters spilled from the truck in slow motion, it seemed to him, took their time with the hose, asked questions instead of moving. Meanwhile, the fire consumed in real time, and Dade knew the Bartlett place was gone. He retreated to his cruiser, sat with the air conditioning on, and watched water arc onto the roof, black smoke undulating as if a living thing. If they didn't stamp this out before a gust of wind took it, the whole county would go up like Marilyn Monroe's skirt. Newcomb looked in the rearview at the figure in the back seat. "You still with us?" When he got no answer, he turned.

Leigh Bartlett stared with dead eyes. Her bandages had come off, exposing Vedra's handiwork, and the doctor's attempt at stitching her face back together. The bum eye was partially concealed by an eyelid at half-mast; the other stared at the house, now dripping charred beams like streams of candle wax.

Dade faced front. Leigh said Sada Powell had done this. He doubted Sada was the Bobcat Bay arsonist, although she'd have a lot of explaining to do—the fire marshal would have her head for breakfast. Why had she burned the Bartlett place? According to Leigh, King had just signed a contract to purchase it. Was Sada's act a vendetta against her father? Christ, who knew? Daughters are a pain in the ass, Newcomb concluded. Boys put their cards on the table, tell you to your face you're an asshole, take their licks, then drop it. Girls pull passive-aggressive shit like this here, drive you crazy with grudges, backstabbing. He'd have to ask King about Sada's state of mind and the nature of their relationship. The sheriff felt a headache come on just thinking about it. He flicked his eyes to the rearview.

"How you feelin'?"

Leigh didn't bother with her usual smart remark; the smoke must have subdued her.

"You get hold of your sister?"

Nothing. Well, he supposed she didn't have to talk if she didn't want to. Hell, if he'd been through what she had in the last two weeks, he'd probably go zomboid, too.

"You ready to go to the hospital, Leigh?" She shook her head slowly, as she had done the last time he asked. "You sure? You might have inhaled more smoke than you think. It'll cook you from the inside out if you're not careful." Leigh stared out the window.

"Okay," he said. "I just don't want you on my conscience if you drop dead."

Newcomb followed her stare to Clyde Glenwood, who trotted toward them in full gear, silhouetted by the orange glow. Newcomb got out of the car, was met with a blast of heat and swirling soot.

"Is she all right?" Glenwood asked.

"Yeah, I reckon. She took some smoke, but she won't go to the hospital."

"Let me talk to her."

Newcomb stepped aside, and Clyde peered at Leigh. "Go to the hospital," he said through the window. "I'll talk to you afterward."

Leigh rolled down the window a few inches. "She might be in there."

"Who? What are you talking about?"

"Sáda. I think she's got some sort of rescue fantasy. She might still be in the house, waiting for you."

Sheriff Newcomb tore open the cruiser door. "What the hell did you just say?"

Leigh said "I never saw her leave."

"Jesus Christ, Leigh! You told me she ran off!"

"I said she was gone; I never said she ran off. She might be under a bed or something."

Newcomb wanted to shake the teeth out of her head. "What the hell are you playing at?"

"I'm not playing at anything, Sheriff. I just think someone should check." She looked at Clyde. "Don't you?"

Head roaring, Sheriff Newcomb snatched the radio and shouted instructions. Glenwood stood gaping at Leigh, and Newcomb dropped the mouthpiece. "Move!" he barked, and Glenwood moved.

As Clyde donned the airpack, long-legged bugs probed the dents in his brain, triggering pulses that singed the hairs on his neck. He couldn't believe what he had just seen. While the sheriff shouted into his radio, Leigh had reached behind and let him glimpse what was tucked into the back of her pants—the Nixon mask. Her good eye locked onto him, and Clyde knew the Bobcat Bay arsonist was toast. He had been stupid to under-estimate the depth of Sada's jealousy and danger to him. When she went missing, he feared something like this. And now Leigh, another woman scorned, was sending him into the fire.

With the airpack's molded mask and mouthpiece over his face, Clyde took a deep breath. He'd have twenty minutes of air if he didn't exert. He looked at his duty partner, a gung ho kid named Isenberg, readied his fire ax and flashlight, and signaled a go.

The fire ran across the ceiling. The dragon snapped and stung and dropped Clyde to his knees to escape the smoke. Hot, black water from the hose soaked his knees in boiling heat. He tried to concentrate on slow, steady breathing. He felt the walls for a window and, finding one, reared up and smashed it with his ax. Smoke escaped in billows as the fire leapt, devouring air, growing hotter. Clyde moved deeper into the bowels of the inferno where visibility neared zero. Through the heat-bent patterns of his flashlight, he slogged in black water, cleared burning rubble from his path. He tossed the burning mattress, booted aside the bed, and finding no one beneath it, signaled Isenberg to move on. A window exploded inward, raining glass. Clyde heard the bell on Isenberg's airpack ring and turned his flashlight on him. Isenberg crawled toward an exit. The bell meant Isenberg still had five minutes of air, but Clyde let him go. Isenberg was young and had not yet learned what a man could do in five minutes when a life was on the line.

Clyde picked his way through the house, more convinced with each step that Sada was not there. Leigh had simply wanted him to risk his own life to settle a score. Even if Sada had stayed behind, the superheated air would have flushed her long before this, unless she had become overcome with smoke. If she was hell-bent on being rescued, though, he supposed she could have crawled into a closet or cabinet. Clyde moved from room to room, checking likely hiding places, until the bell on his air pack rang: five minutes left. The dragon snapped and roared.

As he struggled against the penetrating heat, Clyde felt genuinely sorry for the things he'd said to Leigh the night before, could hardly believe he was capable of such cruelty. He blamed Mr. Hyde but knew Leigh blamed only him. With bandages off, she had looked so vulnerable. She knew he was the Bobcat Bay arsonist, and now she had him on a hook.

Less than a minute left. He raked cabinets, kicked furniture, swept closets of clothes burning on hangers. He checked the garage, alive with flames licking Ed's rickety wood shelving, aware of explosive canisters of paint thinner, gas, herbicides. Across was a closed door, probably a utility room. He heard his brother's voice warn him from the edge of an abyss, then allowed the fire's roar to drown it out. He had to check. Clyde crawled toward the door, breathing the last of his air. Electrical pulses sent up images behind his sizzling eyes: a fire tent surrounded by flames, charred fingers working beneath the tent frame, the lewd, frenetic dance of a man burning.

Through the smoke and heat-bent light, he glimpsed a body behind the hot water tank and knew he had come too late. Another window exploded; a smoke tornado engulfed him. Clyde was out of air. In a gulping rush of black wind, he pulled Sada's body from behind the tank and lifted her. Without air, claustrophobia whipped his psyche. Smoke was everywhere, obscuring his sense of direction. Clyde's knees gave out and he fell forward, dropping Sada to the concrete floor. He needed air. Desperate, he pulled off his mask. Heat reached down his throat with ragged fingernails and raked his vocal package. Clyde coughed, but the intruder would not be expelled. Within seconds, the moist flesh lining Clyde's throat, chest and lungs turned to bubble wrap. He scrambled for control, mind ablaze. Consumed with regret and self-hate, Clyde opened his desiccated lungs to the enveloping smoke, and in one gulping rush of black wind, wheeled himself into the spinning mind of God.

Minutes later, a firefighter emerged from the house, a limp body draped across his arms. Newcomb approached. "Who we got?" he called out, then recognized Clyde's turnouts. Paramedics loaded the body onto a stretcher in quick, efficient movements, strapped an oxygen mask over nose and mouth.

"Is he alive?" the sheriff asked.

"Barely."

"Get him out of here fast."

Newcomb looked to the cruiser. Leigh Bartlett looked back, and he dropped his eyes. He pawed through an inadequate vocabulary for the words to break this gently, not just to Leigh, but to a town that had looked to Clyde Glenwood as a bulwark against the encroaching beast. If he died, it would tear this town apart, and Dade wondered if he could lift himself, much less anyone else, from this sadness.

"Where the hell is Phil Huffman?"

"Here."

Newcomb turned and faced the Chief. "What happened in there?"

"He took off his mask before we could get to him. He took a lot of smoke."

"What about Sada?"

Huffman shook his head. "It looks like she hid in the utility room with the door closed and by the time she realized she was in trouble, it was too late to run for it."

"Jesus. Poor kid."

A reporter scurried toward him, cameraman in tow. Newcomb's radio crackled, and he stepped away, leaving Huffman to absorb a barrage of questions.

"Newcomb, go 'head," the sheriff said into the radio.

"Sorry, Sheriff, but we got a bad situation at Lake Talmadge, over." It was his deputy, Raina Salceda, sounding far away.

"Christ, Salceda. We got a DB over here. How much worse can it get? Over."

The radio went dead for several seconds.

"Salceda?"

Another dead patch, and Newcomb felt a bad wind from Lake Talmadge blow through him. The radio spat.

"It's Judge Lanier, sir. And Eugene." A pause. "Over."

He lowered the radio.

If he walked away right now, he'd never have to hear it, never have to replay the next moment in his head, wonder if, why, how. If he walked away right now, the black stuff of his dreams would not grow claws and tear into his days. His daughters would return to his life. He would have grandchildren, feel the sun on his back, grow old in the stern of a fishing boat. If he walked away right now, his life would not end.

"Tell me. Over," he said, and leaned into the hot wind.

CHAPTER 66

The last time Pete Duncan encountered this smell he had awakened in the street, brains scrambled in vodka, holding a slice of pizza stiff-armed above his head as if offering a sacrifice to Bacchus. How he ended up asleep next to a dumpster with pizza in his hand was a mystery he never solved, but this current situation, which had him inside a dumpster of restaurant waste, was an easy blame: all Annie's fault.

He'd glimpsed Annie at the counter before Florida opened the diner. After Florida told the breakfast folks she had to close for the day, Pete waited for Annie, but she never came out. More strangely, Florida sped from the diner as if her house was on fire. When no one answered the phone at the Bartlett place, Pete followed the purple Pinto.

Guessing Florida was headed for the interstate, he caught up on the truck route, where morning rush hour traffic was worst, and witnessed her near-collision at a stoplight. Once on I-4, Florida drove the speed limit exactly, which watered Pete's suspicion. Thirty minutes down the road, Florida took the Altamonte Springs exit and drove to the back of the mall, where, Pete observed, she stopped behind a seafood restaurant, removed something long, flat, and slim from her trunk, and tossed it—all tip toes and little bounces—into a dumpster. After it, a camera.

With hammering heart and roiling stomach, Pete realized the significance of what he had just seen. Assuming Florida's destination to be the airport, he began to fear for Annie. As soon as the Pinto puttered out of sight, Pete descended on the dumpster. He thought about removing his Tom McCanns, then decided not to risk hepatitis. He found a toehold, grasped the lip of the dumpster, and taking a deep breath, hauled himself inside.

CHAPTER 67

In the hospital room, Leigh sat beside Clyde's bed, gently holding his hand. An oxygen mask covered his nose and mouth. Tubes taped to veins arced toward machines that beeped. Clyde's eyes flickered open, and Leigh smiled.

"Hey."

He stirred, and she moved closer. "Don't try to talk. I had to lie my ass off to get in here. I only have a minute." She lightly stroked his eyebrow. "I have some bad news. Sada didn't make it." He closed his eyes. "You tried, baby. Everybody knows you tried. Nobody blames you for what happened."

He opened his eyes, looked at her gratefully.

"Except me, of course." She smiled.

His eyes changed.

"Remember that story you told me about the fire tent and how you had to decide whether to let in the guy trying to get in with you? No, baby, don't try to talk; you'll hurt yourself. Well, I figured out the ending. The thing is, it didn't end that day. In fact, that was just the beginning, wasn't it? You let that man burn to death, as close to him as I am to you now. No one could blame you, though. It's every man for himself in those conditions. You had to save yourself. Keeping him out was the only thing you could do. And that makes sense to me because I have to do the same thing."

Clyde looked at her, eyes rimmed with dread.

"I've decided I'm not going to mention that Nixon mask to

the police," she whispered. "I didn't want you to wake up not knowing what would happen about all that."

He blinked.

"So don't worry, okay? They don't know a thing about it, and they won't."

He moved his fingers over her hand.

"But I did mention it to someone else."

A shadow moved across the doorway. Clyde's eyes followed and went wide.

"King would like a minute with you, baby. You don't mind, do you?"

His chest rose.

"He promised the nurses he won't stay long."

A leg jerked against its restraints.

"Shhh, baby, take it easy. You're a very sick puppy. Very sick."

He looked at her, eyes pleading.

"I'm going now, Clyde. I just wanted to say good-bye."

Fingers clutched her hand.

"I'm sorry, Clyde, but King paid me a lot of money for that mask. I have to look after myself. You can understand that." She kissed his forehead. "You take care, baby," she whispered, then shook free of his grip.

King moved forward and picked up a pillow. Clyde closed his eyes.

Chapter 68

As she rowed with bandaged hands, the hem of Annie's long, white dress brushed the bottom of the boat. The air smelled burnt, but the sky was the bright blue of Greek pottery, and the high, hot sun beat down on Annie's head. Instead of the baby's breath in her hair, she wished she had worn a hat. Each tug on the oar torqued a muscle in her neck, which triggered a pain in her jaw. Sweat formed beneath the bandage on her nose. Uncomfortable as she was, this was better than air conditioning, which reminded her of being locked in Florida's freezer. After that ordeal she didn't think she'd be able to stand an air-conditioned room again.

Annie had escaped by wedging a long shelf between two walls of a shorter distance, then jumping on it, forcing the shelf to stress the weak corner of the freezer, which buckled, then separated. She tore her hands pulling the thin metal to one side but finally created a hole big enough to crawl through. She was too late to stop Florida, who had apparently boarded a plane to the Bahamas, then a sailboat to Cuba.

Leigh, wearing a long cotton peasant skirt and blouse, sat in the bow facing Annie, holding a marble vase with hunting dogs painted on it. She wore a patch over one eye, and in spite of still healing wounds, looked more beautiful than ever. Her long hair, styled in an elaborate updo, reminded Annie, with its coils and tendrils, of a Roman goddess. Leigh had her feet, in espadrilles, propped on the seat in front of her, skirt tucked behind her knees.

Widow Lake was at its best this time of morning, right after the fog burned off but before shadows shortened. Saw grass, cattails and mud foam floated beside the boat, kicked up by the recent rains. Reflections on the water broke into kaleidoscopic patterns of light, then quickly repaired.

Annie lifted one oar from the water, pulled the other to position the boat. "I guess this is as good a place as any."

Leigh nodded. "God, I'm nervous."

"Why?"

"I don't know. What if something weird happens?"

"Nothing weird will happen."

"Said the sorcerer to the mouse."

Annie smiled. "I think we've both had more than enough weird for a while."

Leigh wrapped her arms around her middle. "King offered me a job."

"King? Seriously?"

"Working in one of his casinos. I'm going to start as a dealer. They make really good money."

"Wow." Annie's enthusiasm was dampened by the thought of Leigh working in a place fueled by alcohol. Nor did an addictive personality like Leigh's need to be around gambling. "Speaking of weird."

"I know what you're thinking," Leigh said. "And King and I already discussed it. I'm going to rehab first, that really good one in Minnesota."

"I can help a little bit, Leigh, but where will you get the money?"

"King is going to pay for it."

Annie suppressed a sigh. "Why? What's in it for him?"

"He says I'm an investment. He wants me to learn the business and manage the casino he's going to build in DeLeon."

"But . . . I thought those jobs went to Indians."

"That's the other thing. He proposed."

"What!"

"Calm down. I didn't say yes."

"Leigh, what the hell is going on?"

"Relax, Annie, nothing is going on. Losing Sada really rocked him, and he's really lonely and sad and vulnerable right now."

"For God's sake, Leigh, that's a terrible reason to marry."

"Don't you think I know that? Give me a little credit."

"I mean, jeez."

"Don't make a big deal of this, Annie. I'm not going to marry him."

"But you're going to let him pay for your rehab and set you up in the casino business?"

"Why not?"

"Why not? It's your same old pattern, Leigh. Making yourself dependent on a man for the things you need."

"It's different this time."

"How?"

"He owes me one."

"What do you mean?"

Leigh faced her. "You're just going to have to trust me on this one, Annie. I earned it. And I don't mean on my back, so save your breath."

"I wasn't going to say that."

"Uh huh."

The sigh escaped. "I don't want to fight, Leigh. I just want you to be happy and well."

"That's what I want, too."

"Then don't marry him."

"I told you, I'm not."

"Okay."

"Okay."

Annie sat and dropped an oar, adjusted the boat's sideways drift with a gentle tug. If King was willing to pay for Leigh's rehab, she supposed she should be happy, but what if King didn't keep his promise or Leigh faltered again? The plan seemed so tenuous, not to mention sudden. She feared Leigh was heading into another rootless venture.

Just like Ed used to do.

And Annie had scolded, just like their mother used to do.

The sun dipped, turning the lake surface black. A high wind traveled through the pine trees one at a time; they rustled and waved, then blew over the burnt lake house and into the darkening sky. A fish jumped, and Annie watched the ripple come toward them, then flatten before reaching the boat. The lake had always looked like this, smelled like this, and Annie had once believed it would never change. The lake had been her playmate, sanctuary, school, and cemetery. It was as much a part of her as the water coursing through her veins, and there was a time when she could not imagine leaving it. But that had changed. And if that could change, anything could.

"What can I do, Leigh? How can I help?"

"Trust me," she said.

"I'll try."

"I know I've messed up too many times to count, but Annie, I'm determined this time. Other people have done it, and if they can, I can. I'm just so sick and tired of being sick and tired. They used to say that in AA, and I get it, now. I didn't get it before, but I get it now. I'm almost thirty-two years old. I want to grow up and have a life."

They watched the water in silence. Behind them, the lake house was rubble. The days following the fire had been mercifully wet, soaking the Bobcat Bay forest in much needed rain. There had been no word or activity from the arsonist in over a week, and many people took this to mean Sada Powell had been guilty all along. Some still believed Eugene Lanier responsible, but they were the minority. The Fire Marshal, conducting a thorough investigation, dedicated all efforts to Clyde Glenwood, who had died in the hospital of sudden suffocation associated with smoke inhalation.

"Are you going to Clyde's funeral?" Annie asked.

Leigh looked away. "I've had about all the death I can stand for a while. I don't think he'll miss me, do you?"

"They say funerals are for the living."

"Amen to that."

"Yeah." Leigh removed the cap from the vase. "Should we say something?"

"Like what?"

"I don't know. Like, a prayer or something?"

Annie blinked. "You want to say a prayer?"

"Work with me here, Annie, I've never done this before."

"Actually, I think a prayer is a good idea. How should we start?"

"Christ, don't look at me."

The boat drifted, slow and peaceful. A thousand watery images whirled in Annie's mind as she searched for words to say aloud. Finally, she cleared her throat. "Dear God," she began. "Please watch over our father because he's not very good at taking care of himself."

"That's lame," Leigh said.

"You want to do this?"

Leigh dropped her eyes. "Sorry. Go ahead."

"Our father wasn't a bad guy. He just wasn't around much. He loved us, though, and that's worth something, even if he didn't know how to show it." Leigh looked up but didn't speak. "I'm sorry he didn't talk more because he was troubled and kept a lot to himself. We might have helped him so he didn't have to find comfort in ways that hurt us. He probably didn't mean to hurt us, but that's what ended up happening.

"I wasted a lot of time blaming my father for things that happened to our family. I blamed him for my mother's death, for my sister's leaving, for not providing for us the way I thought he should. I was just a kid, so I didn't know all that was going on, but I wish I could have found a way to understand my dad while he was still alive. I wish I had known about my mother's drug habit and how my father tried to help her. I wish I had known about how he tried to help my sister. Most of all, I wish I had known about his girlfriend, Florida.

"Tell him we love him, God, because we didn't do that before he was killed. Ask him to forgive us for being blind to all he suffered alone. We can't change the past, so please give us the strength to accept it, learn from our mistakes, and learn to love one another in your name, Amen. Oh! And please ask our mother to be nicer to him, if she's around. And tell my mother I'm not mad, and I miss her." Annie looked at Leigh. "Do you want to say anything?"

Leigh thought for a moment. "Yeah. Um, I'd just like to say that I'm sorry, Daddy, for giving you such a hard time. I feel like a lot of this is my fault, and I'm going to try real hard and get cleaned up so you'll be proud of me. And I hope you find peace." She shifted, searching for more to say, then finally shook her head and gestured with the vase. "I'm going to do this now."

"Leigh?"

Leigh stopped, turned.

"None of this is your fault."

Leigh gave a weary nod, then tipped the vase over the side of the boat. "Ashes to ashes, dust to dust," she said, and slowly poured.

Dade Newcomb opened his tackle box and chose a lure Marguerite gave him a month of birthdays ago, one he'd never tried. He rigged it and cast.

The sisters watched Ed's ashes darken, then become one with the lake that had taken his wife. Annie stared hard into the water, hoping to glimpse her mother in mermaid form, moving beside them, but rainwater had stirred the muddy lake bottom, and she couldn't see beyond the surface. Annie nodded at the shoreline. "You ready to go back?"

"No," Leigh said. "Only forward."

Dade dangled legs over the dock. He saw himself in the brown water and spat on his reflection. His face broke, trembled, and as it reformed, Dade prayed a different man would stare back.

Raina Salceda waited for them on shore, barely recognizable in a yellow sundress, leather sandals and dark hair skimming her shoulders. Salceda was up for a promotion now that Sheriff Newcomb had left his post, and Annie was happy for her. Della, in a print skirt and knit top, approached as the rowboat neared. Leigh tossed a line to King; he caught it and pulled them gently ashore, then helped Leigh from the boat. Annie noticed how King looked at Leigh, tender and protective, like a father, and added a coda to her prayer: *And please show Leigh a love that doesn't hurt.*

"Come here, you," Della said, as Annie stepped onto the lawn, and they embraced. Della's short stay at Lowell had been eventful. Pete presented the murder weapon to Matty Tatum, which reopened the investigation. He then arranged for Della's immediate release. "I'm so sorry for all that's happened. I owe you my life," she whispered, tearful.

Annie breathed in her mother's lemon scent. The smell had always pulled her back to childhood, but now she resisted its grip. "It's okay, Della." They separated. "I'm just glad you're going to be all right, now."

"Yes, I am. Are you?"

"Sure. Don't worry about me."

"Annie, I have a confession to make."

"Oh, God, Della. Don't say that."

"No, no, nothing bad." Della laughed. "I just need you to know I've decided to sell this property to King. I just don't see any reason to hold on to it anymore."

"It's yours to do with what you want, Della."

"Thanks to you."

"Good luck."

"You, too."

Dade felt a tug on his line, then a sharp pull, and got to his feet. His blood pressure spiked, but he didn't give a damn. If he had a heart attack right now, he'd still pull in this fish.

Pete stepped forward and held out a hand to Annie. Annie took it and pulled him to her. "Thank you," she said into his neck.

"Sure."

"No, I mean for everything. My camera, especially. That was above and beyond."

"Tell me about it."

"Leigh's going to need your support."

"And I'm here whenever she needs me."

Annie looked at the big oak carved with the initials AB + PD. She pulled her camera from her bag and snapped the tree trunk, the lake beyond. "I want that oar back when the police are through with it."

"I'll see to it," Pete said.

She looked into his eyes. "I love you, you know."

"I love you, too."

They hugged, and over his shoulder, Annie saw Denise standing patiently nearby, hands folded in front, waiting for Pete. She was dressed simply, in khaki slacks and black sleeveless tank, her long blond hair a perfect column down her back. Annie waved at her, and she waved back.

"Well, I better let you go," Annie said.

"You take care of yourself," Pete said.

Salceda came forward. "We'd best go if you're going to make your plane," she said.

"Okay. I just have to do one last thing."

The bass put up a good fight but lost the battle. Breathing heavily, Dade pulled it onto the dock. His chest tightened, then squeezed him to his knees. The bass flopped into the water, dragging Dade's fishing pole behind. Ah hell, thought Dade. There it goes.

Annie walked to King and handed him a large envelope. Leigh looked at her quizzically. "This is for you." Annie watched King's eyes spark as he pulled the 8 × 10 glossy from its sleeve. He started to smile, then stifled, as if smiling were undignified. "Thank you," he said.

"You're welcome. Thank you for watching out for my sister."

"I have seen bad spirits invade my people for many years. If another comes near Leigh, I will kick its ass."

Leigh's laugh cleared the clouds from the sun.

The sheriff replaced his hat and looked over the water. Marguerite and Eugene waved from a skiff Dade's daddy owned, long ago. With the sun behind, Dade waded toward them, heart brimming. On the far bank, his daddy stood, waiting.

Salceda drove Annie to the airport, chatted pleasantly while Annie thought about Camp. She missed him so much she felt sick.

If she called him from the airport, maybe he would agree to pick her up, and they could go somewhere and talk. It was not too late to mend this rift between them. They were intelligent adults; they could work this out.

Anxious for privacy, Annie insisted Salceda drop her off rather than escort her to the gate. "Thank you for being a friend to me and my sister," she said. "I don't know what we would have done without you."

"Come back and see us."

"I will," Annie said, but they both knew she wouldn't.

Annie went through security to the departure gate and spotted a bank of pay phones. She deposited coins and dialed Camp's number. A woman answered.

"Who's this?" asked Annie.

"This is Cindy."

Miss Push-up Bra!

"Hello?" Cindy said.

"Uh, is Camp there?"

"No, he isn't. May I ask who's calling?"

She paused, swallowed deep in her throat. "Annie."

"Oh, the ex-fiancé! Hi. I'm Cindy."

Somehow, she found her voice. "When do you expect him back, please?"

"Well, I'm not sure. Kirsten was upset about something, so he took her for ice cream. Do you want him to call you?"

"Uh, no. Thanks anyway."

Annie hung up. With Cindy's voice still sticky in her ear, she walked to the seating area, dropped her carry-on and flopped into a seat next to it. Cindy must be a fixture at Camp's house if she was answering the phone, Annie thought. Even after Camp and Annie were engaged, Annie had never felt comfortable enough to do that. And if Kirsten was upset enough to manipulate Camp into ice cream, it sounded like old patterns were still playing out. Annie's heart sank. It seemed Camp had moved on, even if little else had.

As arriving passengers streamed into the gate area, Annie watched faces find loved ones who waited for them. A middle-aged man in shorts and a flower-print shirt came through the doorway carrying a bouquet. He stopped, smiling broadly. His head slowly panned; eyes flicked back and forth. Someone bumped from behind, and he came to, attention now split between getting out of the way and finding whomever those flowers were for. His eyes flicked to Annie, and she looked away, embarrassed for staring.

When she looked back up, Helen stepped through the doorway. Annie lurched and knocked over a soft drink sitting on a low table.

"Oh, for the love of Bob," said a boy. He looked to be about ten and wore a striped baseball cap. "I wasn't done with that."

Helen waved Annie over.

"I'm so sorry," Annie said, sopping the spilled drink with an abandoned newspaper. "I'll get you another one."

The boy's mother intervened. "No, that's all right. Accidents happen, right Jarrod?"

"What did you do, see a ghost?" Jarrod demanded.

"Yeah, I did," said Annie. "She's standing right there—the dark-haired woman in the nurse's uniform."

"You're not supposed to lie to kids," said Jarrod.

"That's enough, Jarrod," said the boy's mother.

Ignoring his mother, the boy asked, "How come you have that bandage on your nose?"

"A lady hit me with a gun."

Jarrod's mouth twisted into a sneer. "Nuh uh!"

"Jarrod. Over here. Now."

Annie finished wiping up the spilled soda and carried the sodden newspaper to the garbage can. Again, Helen waved Annie to her. Annie shook her head and turned away.

Boarding the plane, Annie caught a last glimpse of the man holding the flowers, no longer smiling, light gone from his eyes. Memories of her father squeezed her heart. "I miss you, Dad," she said out loud, and after no response, contented herself with silence and the journey ahead.

ABOUT THE AUTHOR

Irene Ziegler is the author of *Rules of the Lake* (a prequel to *Ashes to Water*), and *Full Plate Collection,* a play. She grew up in Florida and now lives with her family in Virginia. She is also an accomplished actor and voiceover talent. You can contact her at www.IreneZieglerVoiceOvers.com.